Our Hideous Progeny

A Novel

C. E. McGILL

HARPER ◗ PERENNIAL

NEW YORK • LONDON • TORONTO • SYDNEY • NEW DELHI • AUCKLAND

HARPER ● PERENNIAL

Originally published in Great Britain in 2023 by Doubleday,
an imprint of Transworld Publishers.

A hardcover edition of this book was published in 2023 by Harper,
an imprint of HarperCollins Publishers.

HarperCollins books may be purchased for educational, business,
or sales promotional use. For information, please email the Special
Markets Department at SPsales@harpercollins.com.

FIRST HARPER PERENNIAL EDITION PUBLISHED 2024.

Library of Congress Cataloging-in-Publication Data has been
applied for.

ISBN 978-0-06-325680-4 (pbk.)

24 25 26 27 28 LBC 5 4 3 2 1

PRAISE FOR *OUR HIDEOUS PROGENY*

An NPR "Best Book" * A *New Yorker* "Best Book of the Year" *
A Guardian "Best Recent Science Fiction, Fantasy, and Horror" *
CrimeReads "Best Debut Novels Released This Month" * A *Lambda
Literary* "May's Most Anticipated LGBTQIA+ Book" * A Polygon
"Science Fiction and Fantasy Books We're Excited For".

"*Our Hideous Progeny* takes inspiration from Mary Shelley's master-
piece along with the Victorian fascination with scientific innovation
and the prehistoric world. This wonderful debut evolves into a gripping Gothic tale of grief and ambition, passion and intrigue."

—Jess Kidd, author of *The Night Ship*

"A wonderful book; dark, passionate, multilayered, and rich with en-
ticing detail."

—Joanne Harris, author of *Chocolat* and *The Strawberry Thief*

"Compelling and utterly absorbing, *Our Hideous Progeny* is an artfully
crafted debut that echoes the dark essence of Mary Shelley's *Frankenstein* while maintaining a fascinating originality all of its own."

—Susan Stokes-Chapman, author of *Pandora*

"A fantastic read: I felt everything about Mary, her simmering anger
and her intellectual delight, so very clearly."

—Freya Marske, author of the Last Binding trilogy

"Exquisitely written, brimming with imagery both beautiful and shocking, this daring debut makes the rivalries of the Victorian scientific
establishment thrilling and urgent, bringing us a story worthy of Mary
Shelley."

—Sean Lusk, author of *The Second Sight of Zachary Cloudesley*

And now, once again, I bid my hideous progeny go forth and prosper.

— MARY SHELLEY, Introduction to the
1831 edition of *Frankenstein*

PROLOGUE

'COULD YOU,' SAID the inspector, 'run it all by me one more time, Mrs Sutherland?'

I took my time in answering. I paused to smooth out my skirts and steady my breathing, to survey the room – its single grimy window, the awful narrow wood-panelled walls that gave one the impression of being trapped inside a cabinet. I do not consider myself an expert in lying by any means, but if there is one thing I have learned on the subject over the course of my life, it is this: lies cannot be rushed. They must be spun evenly and carefully. Too fast, and you risk tangling up the details; too slow, and it sounds like a stage performance, scripted from the start.

And so, despite my racing heart, I paused.

'I already laid it all out before the magistrate this afternoon,' I said, 'and the constable before that, not to mention Mr Wilkinson and—'

'Yes, well.' The inspector squinted at me rather reproachfully through his pince-nez. 'A man is dead, Mrs Sutherland. We must make sure we record every detail. I'm sure you can spare just a few more moments of your time.'

I looked down at my hands, at the bandages wound around

my palms and up my wrists. Four small red crescents bled through the fabric on each hand where my nails had dug in.

'Of course. Although—'

This part I could not bear to take my time over, though I supposed that was all right, as it was not a lie.

'Would you make a note, sir, that I plan to go by my maiden name in future? In case you need to find me in London?'

The inspector paused, his pen poised above his notebook, and raised an eyebrow. '. . . And what would that be?'

'Frankenstein,' I replied. 'Mary Elizabeth Frankenstein.'

IT WAS A grey and foggy March day when we brought it to life at last.

I had expected there to be thunder, or at the very least some rain; I had expected that, on such a momentous occasion, Nature would have been obliged to provide us with a fitting backdrop. But evidently Nature felt that she owed us no favours, as the morning dawned dull as always, wreathed in a thick mist that dampened clothes and sound alike as it crept over the hills.

I took a measure of grim satisfaction in Clarke's bedraggled appearance as he let us into the boathouse. He had come to us bright-eyed and brimming with confidence; now, in his rumpled shirtsleeves, with grey shadowing his jaw and the skin beneath his eyes, he seemed but a dim reflection of his former self. Henry, meanwhile, outshone us all in his morning coat, the same he had worn on our honeymoon in Lyme, and which had shown the dust of the chalk cliffs so badly. Perhaps he was hoping to make a good first impression.

We examined our instruments one final time: the bellows, to provide the breath of life; the stove in the corner, to drive the spring chill from the room and make its cold flesh warm again; the beakers of elixir upon the worktable, bubbling merrily on their burners. I measured out a vial and handed it to Clarke to administer. Then, having nothing else to do, I leaned in close to the Creature and laid a hand gently upon its neck.

'Is it warm enough, Mary?' Henry asked. I nodded, startled to hear his voice; the room had been so silent before, as still as a church mid-prayer. We had built here, in this half-ruined boat-house on the edge of the Moray Firth, a temple to our own strange gods – to Chemistry and Anatomy and Electricity.

There was an acrid smell in the room as the procedure began. The air felt prickly and sharp, bursting with potential, like the moment before lightning strikes. But there was no bang, no flash, no grand transformation – only something dead one minute, and alive the next. Its flippers twitched; its great curved back began to rise and fall of its own accord. And its *eyes*! I will always hold dear to my heart the fact that I was the first to see those golden eyes open, to see its reptilian pupils narrow and focus on my own – for in those eyes I saw, for the first time, proof that we had created something truly *alive*.

But that isn't right. No; I'm getting ahead of myself. That isn't really how it all began.

PART I

NOVEMBER 1853 – JUNE 1854

I

Our house was the house of mourning . . . she no longer took delight in her ordinary occupations; all pleasure seemed to her sacrilege toward the dead.

— MARY SHELLEY, *Frankenstein*

IT BEGAN, RATHER, with a black-edged envelope.

It must have been late afternoon when it arrived, for I remember the slivers of sunlight that cut the room, casting each mote of dust in gold. Most of the time the study was caught in the looming shadow of the opposing tenements, but for one glorious hour each day the sun shone in and turned the air to honey. It caught upon every gilded title on the bookshelves, lighting up my polished ammonite like a mirror. It was a subject of constant debate between the two of us, whether the curtains ought to be left open or shut to prevent the books from fading. Evidently, however, I had won that day – for it was through a haze of that rare London sunshine that I watched through the doorway as the envelope in question slid from the letterbox and landed, with a gentleness that did not match the gravity of its contents, on the chequered hallway floor.

At first, I simply stared. It was my grandmother, most likely; her nurse had written the previous month to say that she had developed pneumonia and was not faring well. I wondered for a moment whether I could simply pretend I hadn't seen the letter – if I could sit and continue my work in peace for another hour or two, until James brought us the post before supper. But then I remembered (as I had been remembering in jarring stops and starts all week) that we had given James his notice, as we could not afford to pay his wages until Henry found steady work again; and I remembered, too, that Mrs Jamsetjee had been ill earlier that month, with a persistent cold that would not cure. I looked down at the half-finished illustration upon my drawing desk: the stem of a fossil fern, *Equisetum columnare*, the specimen itself resting in my open palm. I had been holding it up to the light, trying to catch every detail of its petrified surface. Now I was gripping it so tightly my knuckles were white.

With a heavy heart, I set it down and rose to my feet.

'Mary? What is it?' Henry called after me as I went to the hall. 'It's not Forsythe again, is it? I swear, if that man writes another word to me about the joys of the Swedish countryside, I shall burn everything he's ever written and send him back the ashes.'

I paid him no mind. The letter's black wax seal glared at me from the floor. Unable to bear the suspense any longer, I snatched it up with trembling fingers and turned it over. There, in a small, neat hand, were the words:

Mr Henry Sutherland
10 Maddox Street
Mayfair
London

After taking a moment to collect myself – it wouldn't do, to let Henry see how relieved I was – I went and laid the envelope gently on the corner of his desk.

'It's for you.'

For barely a second, he blinked down at it, face going pale. But then, as I watched, he drew himself together and picked up the letter, turning it over to stare at the seal.

'Well! I wonder who it is,' he murmured. It was a largely rhetorical question, I knew; the envelope bore an Inverness postmark, and that left only two possibilities.

'Your father?' I asked.

'Possibly. Though he is more likely to *ferment* than die, I think; and my sister's primary ambition seems to be to catch every sickness known to man, so one can never be sure. Care to vote?'

'Don't be horrid,' I replied, returning to my seat and the tray of tea which Agnes had left us, now long since cold.

'Come now, dear. You know you'll be the same when your toad of a grandmother finally expires. Now, who do you vote for?'

I glared at him over the rim of my teacup, but it seemed that he would not open the envelope until I cast my vote. Finally, I relented.

'Your father. I've never met your sister, so I have no reason to dislike her.' Besides the petty tales Henry had told me over the years.

'Oh, you would if you had met her. I, for one, hope it's her. More of the inheritance for me.' With a flourish, he broke the seal.

'"Mr Sutherland,"' he read, getting up to pace about the room. '"We regret to inform you that on this past Saturday, the twenty-sixth of November 1853, your father" – there you go, Mary, it looks as though you will have a chance to meet the dreaded Margaret after all – "Mr John R. Sutherland of Inverness, Scotland, died in the night, due to a sudden bout of palsy which struck him earlier in the day. I am writing on behalf of your sister, as she is altogether too distressed to write. She has assured me, however, that your father did not suffer unduly, and that the very evening before, he was in high spirits and engaged in his usual activities . . ." – oh, he *does* go on.' He put down the first page of the letter and surveyed the second. ' "If at all possible, your presence is requested . . . reading of the last will and testament . . . sort through his affairs, et cetera . . . Arthur S. Whitton, solicitor." '

He set down the letter upon his desk. 'Well, my dear. I hear that Inverness is lovely at this time of year.'

'You do not. You have always said that it is terrible at every time of year.'

He chuckled, though it sounded rather hollow. For a moment, we sat in silent consideration. I cast my eyes back to the fossil fern, and to the draft on Henry's desk, a column on Devonian fossil trees he was writing for *Chambers's*. My illustration was meant to accompany it.

'We shall have to give Mr Roberts the *Equisetum* back before we leave,' I said, for of course the fossil was not ours, but a loan from one of Henry's university acquaintances. We had, to my eternal dismay, no collection to speak of ourselves.

'Yes, yes. I'll write to him this evening,' Henry said absently. He looked down at the solicitor's letter again, staring at the signature at the foot of the page, though his gaze seemed to reach much further than that. 'Will you . . . need new mourning wear before we leave?'

'No.' I found myself looking away as well, watching through

the window as the sun slipped out of view. 'My old things will do. I shouldn't think they'll even have gathered dust.'

OUR TRIP NORTHWARD was long and disagreeable. As no railway had yet ventured as far north as Inverness, we were obliged to go by way of Aberdeen, stopping at an inn overnight so that we might catch a stagecoach the following morning. The stagecoach was a mode of travel new to me, and I found myself instantly prejudiced against it, largely due to the fact that it departed two hideous hours before dawn. For twelve hours we clattered along rutted country roads, stopping only to change horses and to eat a hasty lunch in Fochabers. With every mile, Henry's mood grew worse. For all that he muttered under his breath about the cold or the hard seats or the quality of the food, however – and deserved complaints they were – I suspected that the true source of his foul temper was not the journey itself, but our destination. In the nearly three years we had been married, I had only had the displeasure of meeting Henry's father once, when he had travelled down to London, seemingly for the sole purpose of expressing his thinly veiled disapproval of every aspect of Henry's life – myself included. (I have long suspected, in fact, that this was one of the reasons why Henry had so readily agreed to my proposal that we elope; such a man, whose company left a sour taste in one's mouth long after he was gone, was not the sort of guest one wanted at a wedding.) I could understand, then, Henry's reluctance to return to a house so infused with his father's spirit. Not in a literal sense, of course – I am not one to believe in hauntings – but I do believe that a person's absence in a house can be felt just as strongly as their presence.

It was for that very reason that I had not been into the nursery for over a year.

At last, as evening fell, we arrived in Inverness. The coach deposited us in front of a bustling hotel, where the Sutherlands' footman waited for us with a gig and a rather wretched-looking pony, for the house itself lay some distance from the town proper. It began to drizzle as we set off, rain so fine it was nearly mist – but despite the weather, and Henry's ever-worsening mood, I could not help but admire the view as we trundled out into the countryside. Past the houses, one could see straight down the beach to the Moray Firth. The water was dark, overhung by clouds that cast shadows like bruises upon the sea. Something about the salt-laced air struck a chord of nostalgia within me; evidently, I had missed the seaside more than I had thought.

The house, when it came into view, was a sturdily built thing, all grey stone and slate, the jagged points of Baronial windows jutting up towards the sky. I was taken aback at first by its grandeur; a different beast entirely from our own modest house in London or my childhood home on Wight. Once, in the days of the Tudors and Stuarts, the Sutherlands had been a wealthy landed family – but since then, as Henry often complained, they had frittered away their fortune and connections, their once sizeable estate sold off in pieces to build country homes for bankers and coal men. Now there was barely an acre, and even that apparently could not be kept in good repair. Some way away was a squat brick stable, its roof sagging and mossy; at the edge of the firth sat a boathouse, long since disused.

As we dismounted and stepped out on to the gravel my attention was captured by a noise from the house – a single piercing cry. I looked up just in time to see a shape disappear from the window. Moments later, the front door burst open and out ran a girl, shawl trailing from her shoulders as she flew down the driveway towards us.

'Henry!' she cried, as she threw herself upon him in a flurry of black lace and petticoats. 'Oh, Henry! I'm so glad you're here!'

And with that, she buried her face in his lapels and began to cry.

I stared as the realization dawned on me that this – this slight woman not much younger than myself, who had run heedless across the gravel in her slippers to meet us – was the *dreaded Margaret*. I looked to Henry for some kind of explanation, but he would not meet my eye. Instead, he scowled and prised his sister from his coat.

'Now, that's quite enough. Look at you – no shoes, no coat, outside in the damp! Where's your maid? And where is Mr Whitton?'

'Oh, Mr Whitton is inside,' she replied, wiping her eyes. 'But – Henry, I don't know if I can stand to hear the will just yet. It's his last letter to us, isn't it? I can't stomach the thought that he'll never write to us again . . .'

'He did not write to either of us, Margaret,' Henry said drily. 'You lived with him, and he despised me. Or have you forgotten?'

She did not answer him, for it was then that she seemed to notice me. She turned and clasped my hands in hers, smiling in a tear-stained fashion. 'My goodness! This must be your wife, Henry. Isn't she lovely! It's wonderful to meet you. I . . .' She paused, face falling, and a wave of dread washed over me. 'I am so sorry about . . .'

I knew then what she meant to say next. I could see it in her eyes, the sudden tilt of her brows, the same piteous look Henry and I had weathered countless times this past year. I tried to catch Henry's eye, a silent plea for help, but – as he *always* did – he merely looked to the ground, his jaw tight. His sister was only trying to be kind, I knew, but even so, I could not help but feel how cruel it was that after all this time, I should have to suffer this conversation yet again – for if there exists a way to respond to condolences that does not feel like ripping open the stitches of a wound with one's teeth, I have not yet found it.

'I am terribly sorry about your father, Miss Sutherland,' I blurted, in a desperate and terrible display of hypocrisy. She blinked a moment, clearly taken aback, but to my eternal gratitude she let the change of subject stand.

'Oh, I . . . thank you. *I* am truly sorry that this is our first meeting; I so badly wanted to come and visit along with Father when you first married, but I was terribly ill at the time, as I am sure Henry has told you. It is not often that I'm as lively as this.' She gave another watery smile. 'And I beg of you – we're sisters now, aren't we? Call me Maisie; most everyone does.'

I had never heard Henry call her anything of the sort. I did not have the chance to press, however, for we were interrupted by the arrival of Maisie's maid, trotting out into the drizzle with a pair of her mistress's shoes clutched anxiously in hand.

Before long, we were ushered inside and into the parlour, with a tray of tea upon the table and Maisie installed upon one of the great velvet couches. We met the solicitor, a balding and rather skittish man of middle age, and sat for a while before dinner making conversation of an insubstantial sort. Henry remained silent for the most part; occasionally, he would stand

and examine the framed daguerreotypes upon the wall, or the view outside the windows, or the rather hideous portrait of his father as a young man which hung scowling over the mantle-piece. He seemed to have noticed, as had I, that everything in the house bore a fine layer of dust. The carpets and furniture were faded, which was a puzzle as the meagre amount of light admitted by the heavy curtains was certainly not enough to leach their colour. The whole place had the feel of an aged actress – once grand, but now past her prime, trundling her way to a lonely old age.

I found Maisie to be an odd sort of character, thin and bird-like, her manner both melancholy and cheerful at once. As Henry was clearly still engaged with the wainscoting, she directed most of her conversation towards me, posing questions about London and my childhood on Wight at a frequency that felt almost like an interrogation. I could not complain, however, for it made the conversation blessedly easy to carry on with (and kept us from any more talk of condolences). Before long, the anxious maid called us through to the dining room – and it was there, halfway through a rather watery cream soup, that Maisie made one last valiant attempt to include Henry in the conversation, and in doing so asked him perhaps the worst question possible.

'How is the collection, Henry? You said that you thought Professor Grant might be putting you in charge of fish soon, didn't you?'

I looked from one to the other in astonished silence. It had been five months since Henry was dismissed from his assistant curatorship at the University College collection; five months which we had spent writing furiously for the scientific sections of *Fraser's* and *Chambers's* in order to keep ourselves afloat while he searched for another suitable position. Had it truly been that long since he'd last written to Maisie? Or had he simply never mentioned it in his letters?

'Fishes and Reptilia,' he said coldly as he folded the serviette on his lap into quarters with utmost precision. 'And I'm afraid I would not know how the collection fares – I was let go.'

'Oh!' said Maisie. After a moment of prickly silence, she turned to Mr Whitton and said quite deliberately, 'You mentioned that you were raised in Dundee, didn't you, Mr Whitton? I've heard it's quite the town for boating . . .'

And that was the last we spoke of the matter.

Henry and I retired early after dinner. The upstairs I found to be even more oppressive than the main floor – each step a dull and muffled thing, each lamp a struggling island of light against the dark wallpaper. At the top of the stairs was another daguerreotype, one which made Henry stop dead in his tracks and stare. I peered over his shoulder and saw that it was a portrait of a woman and two children – one a serious-looking young boy standing with his hands behind his back, the other a frail girl whose face was so pale it seemed to shine out from the picture like a moon. Henry and Maisie along with their mother, I presumed. I knew little of Henry's mother, besides that she had died more than a decade before. I was none too surprised to see that she looked like a less gaunt version of Maisie.

'She seems . . .' I began, unsure even as I said it what my next word would be – *lovely? Kind? Younger than I expected?* In any case, it did not matter, for before I could finish, Henry had turned and stalked off down the hallway.

The room we had been given was a small one, the walls lined

with dark wood panelling that served only to make it seem even smaller. I wondered, as we readied for bed, whether it had been Henry's as a boy, or whether his lay elsewhere. It did not seem like a child's bedroom; more like the quarters of a reticent old priest. But then there were no parts of the Sutherland house I had seen thus far that seemed especially fit for children, no lush garden for a boy to explore or corners in which he might curl up and read. It was a relief, in some ways – a guilty one – to know that his home had perhaps been as cheerless as mine.

We were both worn out from travelling, and Henry was clearly no more in the mood for conversation than he had been all evening. But even so, as we settled down against the uncomfortable mattress, there were two questions on my mind which refused to be dismissed.

'Will your sister continue to live here after we return to London?' I asked. 'Or will you sell the house?'

'Well, it would certainly be a waste, keeping up the house and staff for the sake of a single resident.' He blew out the lamps. 'We could persuade her to move to London, perhaps, and live off whatever allowance my father has left her in the will. Though she would have to get rid of that damned pony.'

'The one from this morning?'

'Yes; some doctor or other said the air would be good for her lungs, so of course Father scrambled to get one, no matter the expense.' He frowned. 'Oh, and if she offers to let you ride it, do not under any circumstances say yes. It *bites*.'

We fell into silence then. I lay listening to the grandfather clock in the hall ticking its soft, plodding way through the hours, and wondered whether I ought to ask my next question at all.

'Henry . . . what is it about your sister that you hate so?' I said at last. It had been puzzling me all evening. Henry did not like to speak of his family much – nor did I speak of mine – but the few tales he had told me about Maisie over the years had never seemed particularly heinous. He said that she wasted money, that she had a propensity for lies and exaggeration, that she feigned ill-ness to gain attention. Petty, trifling things; and even these did not seem to match the character of the woman I had met today.

Henry was silent for so long that I began to fear that he had not heard me. But then, quietly, he replied: 'I do not hate her. I simply think she is spoiled and silly and frivolous, and only ever thinks of herself, and—' He heaved a sigh. 'If you had siblings, Mary, you would understand.'

I was not sure that I would.

'COULD YOU,' SAID Henry, in a perilously icy tone, 'possibly say that part again?'

Mr Whitton winced. He looked more apologetic than I had ever seen a person look in my life, including the unfortunate visitor to my grandmother's house years ago who had broken one of a pair of priceless vases – and then, in the process of apologizing, broke the other.

Mr Whitton nervously cleared his throat and began again. '"To my son, Henry John Sutherland, of 10 Maddox Street, Mayfair, London, I give and bequeath: firstly, an amount exactly equal to his current debts accrued through gambling and specu-lation, on the condition that he presents proof, in the presence of an accountant and the executor of this will, that the figure he provides is indeed accurate . . ."' He paused, his eyes darting towards Henry. '". . . And secondly, the sum of one ha'penny."'

A taut muscle in Henry's jaw gave a visible twitch. One could have dropped a pin and heard it clatter.

'"To my daughter, Margaret Sutherland,"' the solicitor continued, '"I give and bequeath the remainder of my estate, to her sole and separate use until that time she may marry, to be sold or managed as she sees fit."'

'Henry!' I cried, for before Mr Whitton had even finished his sentence, he had leaped from his chair and left the room. Maisie, who had remained utterly silent throughout the entire affair, gave a flinch as the front door slammed. From outside came the muffled sound of cursing, and gravel skittering beneath hasty feet; I sprang from my seat and followed after him.

'Henry,' I called again, when I finally caught up with him at the end of the drive. It was a grey sort of morning, the sky threatening rain, but he did not seem to notice as he paced back and forth across the patchy lawn, clutching his fingers to his mouth.

'Trapped my hand in the blasted door,' he muttered, seemingly more to himself than to me. 'Oh, no, I mean I trapped my hand in *Miss Sutherland's* door, didn't I? Forgive me; I should never have stormed out of Miss Sutherland's house in such a hurry.'

'Henry,' I said once more, as if I had no other words. I approached him slowly, and took his hurt hand in mine. 'It is unfair of your father to treat you so, but you must remember that Maisie did not ask for this. I'm sure she feels just as humiliated by this whole affair as you.'

He gave a bark of laughter.

'Ask? My sister never *asked* for anything, Mary. She only whined and wheedled until it was handed to her upon a silver platter. No, I . . .' He shook his head, his gaze distant. 'I should have known he'd do this. He told me, just last month, "You won't get one penny from me, not even when I'm dead!" A man of his word, wasn't he?'

He swiped at his cheek, brushing away a raindrop; or perhaps a tear. Gradually, something he'd said began to gnaw at me. Without quite meaning to, I frowned. 'Last month? You told me your father hadn't written to you in years.'

Very suddenly, he went still. Overhead, the clouds sped by, whipped by some unseen wind.

'I was the one who wrote to him,' he said eventually.

'And why did you do that? Why did he say you wouldn't get a penny from him?'

Henry made no reply. I was struck then by a memory, a moment I had not thought of in years. I had been five years old when I first held a skeleton in my hands – the bones of a mouse I had found in the garden and hidden in the folds of my skirt. I had not known it was a mouse at first. It was not until later that night, when I had laid them out in a patch of moonlight, that I had seen in those disparate bones a shape which I recognized.

Here were the pieces now: the will. The incessant letters from Henry's acquaintances. His dismissal from the collection, and the truly fervent pace at which we had been writing articles in the interim. The year we had just spent in mourning.

'Henry,' I said slowly, my voice cold. 'When the will mentioned gambling, I thought that your father meant while you were at university. You always did say he never forgave you for that. Is he referring to something else?'

'Mary—' he started, but I did not let him finish.

'This past year, while I was trapped in the house in my black lace, mourning the death of *our child*' – he winced as if I'd thrown those last words at him – 'when you were out on Fridays and Saturdays and Wednesdays and, *oh*, just the odd Thursday as well, supposedly at the reading room or staying late at the collection for Professor Grant . . . All those times, you were actually out playing cards?'

One look at his face told me all I needed to know. The world tilted beneath my feet.

'Not every night! It was just a *game*, Mary, a game or two with friends! I needed . . .' He swallowed hard, and went to lay a hand on my arm. 'It was a distraction. I couldn't just stay in the house and weep.'

'And why not! That is what *I* did!' I swiped his hand away. 'How much did you lose?'

'Does it matter? We're not in debt any longer. My father is going to pay it all off. How terribly kind of him.'

'*How much?*'

Henry swore under his breath and stepped away, refusing to meet my eye. I thought of all the nights I had spent alone, curled up in bed or sitting by the fire, staring into the flames; I thought of all the times I had sat nauseous with guilt, wondering how it was that he could muster the strength to work from dawn till dusk while I could barely summon the will to dress; I thought of how, as the months crawled by and I dragged myself towards normalcy, there were days when I had convinced myself that he hated me. That he could not bear to look at me, for I was a reminder of all that we had lost.

'Three hundred pounds,' he said quietly.

I could not speak. Three hundred pounds was a year's

salary – or would have been a year's salary, when Henry was still employed.

'We have no other savings?' I heard myself say, my voice distant. 'Not a penny to our name?'

He gave a harsh laugh. 'Did you not hear Mr Whitton? We have precisely a ha'penny.'

'*Henry.*'

'There will be enough to pay this month's rent. If we put together another article for Mr Chambers, there will be enough for next month's as well.'

I found myself shaking, my entire body trembling with the urge to scream, to rage, to run. It had been years since I had last lived in the shadow of my grandmother, since I had last felt the pinches of my nursemaid or the slap of the schoolmaster's ruler across my palm, but their admonitions still rang in my head whenever such fits of temper arose – *sit still, speak softly, don't ball your fists*. It did not matter if that wretch in the yard had pushed you first, or what horrible things he'd said about your mother. The difference between a proper young lady and a beastly little thing was that ladies were never angry; they took their moods and wove them into lace, stuffed them into pillows. They learned to hold their tongue.

But I have always been a beastly little thing at heart, it seems.

'Finish your damned article on your own,' I snapped. He called after me as I stalked back to the house, but I did not turn around. I was not sure what I would do if I did.

2

But where were my friends and relations? No father had watched my infant days, no mother had blessed me with smiles and caresses; or if they had, all my past life was now a blot, a blind vacancy in which I distinguished nothing.

— MARY SHELLEY, *Frankenstein*

THEY SAY THAT shame can be a living thing. That it gnaws at you, lives in you, lives *with* you; that it makes you hard and withered, wearing you away day by day until nothing remains. I should know, of course. For in my case – in my mother's case, my grandmother's – I myself was the shame. Misbegotten children make the phrase quite literal, after all.

My grandmother did not believe in sugaring the truth. Nor, in fact, in sugaring food, or tea, or medicine, or anything else whose sugaring might have brought some modicum of joy into our lives. As most children are taught to read, to speak, to hold their knife and fork, I was taught of my situation. My mother had been, in order: an orphan, an under-housemaid, a vile seducer, a runaway, and dead. My father had been, in order: a sickly child, a studious young man, a lovesick fool, and subsequently also dead. They were never married, of course. After my mother was banished from the premises and fled to some distant parish, my father had followed her, ranting of love and social conventions. But when he had returned, some weeks later, it was not with a wife but—

'With you,' my grandmother said, always with her mouth a grim line, her eyebrows pinched.

We lived at the time in Norton Green, a rocky little village on the coast of the Isle of Wight where the Solent meets the waters of the Channel. It was a quiet place, the sort of village where one might retire for the sake of one's health; and indeed, that is precisely what had compelled my grandparents to move there, after several decades as an investor in London had left my grandfather with several stress-related ailments. (And little else, given that he was a rather poor investor.) It was in Norton Green that a terrible house fire dented the family fortunes still further; in Norton Green, too, that my grandfather died; in Norton Green that my grandmother remarried and was almost immediately re-widowed; in Norton Green that both men, and my father and a handful of unnamed, miscarried aunts, were buried. We visited them every Sunday, after the morning service at All Saints' Church. My grandmother would stand in stony-faced vigil while I would sit and examine the carvings upon the headstones. I felt sometimes, as my fingers traced the solemn death's head that adorned my father's grave, that I could remember him. Not entirely, but as a fleeting sensation of warmth, of being cradled against a body far larger than my own. I even thought once that I had a memory of my mother, the pale shape of her face floating moon-like above me. But such a thing was impossible; I was only hours old when my mother died, only months old when my father followed her, succumbing in his weak and heartbroken state to the consumption which had plagued him since childhood. And thus I became an orphan, an infant murderer, my existence an equation forever unbalanced – two lives exchanged for one.

There was clearly no question in my grandmother's mind that this exchange had been unequal. Once, after I had begun to learn my letters, I sounded out the syllables of my father's name upon his grave and realized that his surname was not Brown, like my own, nor Whitlock, like that of my grandmother and her short-lived second husband. Instead, it was something long and sharp and foreign; German, as I later learned. I had asked my grandmother:

'Why do I have a different name from Father?'

'Because he isn't your father. Not according to the law, in any case. You have your mother's name,' she replied flatly. And then, as always: 'Stand up, you're dirtying your dress.'

It was moments such as these which stymied any sympathy I might have had for my grandmother's situation. She had suffered so very much, after all – the loss of her children, her husbands, her home; but how much of a comfort might we have been to each other, if only she had allowed it? If she had not so vehemently denied me a part in the family she had lost?

But I wallow. I mean only to explain here that I cannot recall a time before I knew I was a disgrace – though it would be many years before I understood precisely why. An ill-gotten child is a faulty cog; living testament to the fact that rules are not always followed, that sons and daughters cannot always be controlled, that men and women do not always couple as we might think they should. Shame breeds fear, and fear breeds goodness, morality, better behaviour. Such is the hope.

Except that sometimes – as I can attest – shame and fear beget only anger instead.

I can recall with perfect clarity the first time I knew that.

I was five perhaps, or six. Young enough that I had not yet been sent to school, though old enough to be curious about it. I would peer through the gates as my nursemaid and I walked into the village, watching the children laugh and scream and push each other into puddles. It must have been a Saturday that day, however, for the schoolyard was empty as we passed on our way to the shore. It was early spring, far too chilly to paddle, but I still loved playing treasure-hunter, filling my pockets with stones and shells which my humourless nursemaid would inevitably make me empty out before we left. And it was there, in the shadow of the pearl-white cliffs, that I found it.

It was a small thing, dark and lustrous as mahogany, resting atop a pale boulder as if simply begging to be found. I spotted it from a dozen paces away and picked my way closer, rocks slipping and clattering beneath my feet. When I retrieved it and held it up to the light, I saw that it was shaped almost like a piece from a game of draughts – a squat cylinder marked on both sides with subtle rings like the inside of a tree. The top and bottom were not quite flat, but slightly concave, fitting perfectly between my forefinger and thumb. It was lovely; not as beautiful as some of the other stones I had found on the beach, nor as colourful as sea-glass, but fascinating in its singularity.

'What's that?'

I swivelled upon my heel. Somehow, so absorbed was I in my new treasure, I had not heard him approach – a local boy, two years my senior, whose name I could not recall; Tim or Tom or Thomas, perhaps. What I could recall was this: that I had seen him earlier that week in the schoolyard, pushing another boy to the ground. That he had laughed as his schoolmate spat dust, and run away with the boy's hat and his spinning top. That this was a boy who took things.

My gaze darted up the beach to where my nursemaid stood, joined now by another, the two of them absorbed in conversation. They were too far for me to call to, and even if they had not been, I knew my own nursemaid's opinion on trinkets I found on the beach. She would not help me.

'It's mine,' I blurted, my heart a drum. I watched his face sour.

'I only asked what it was.' He stepped closer, eying my closed fist. 'Did you find a penny?'

Of course; I should have realized. His clothes were shabbier than mine. The woman with him was likely not his nursemaid, but his mother. He was the son of a shopkeeper probably, a butcher or a baker. He had little, but (I felt at the time) I had so much less – no mother, no proper place in the world, no means of driving him away. All I had wanted was this, this odd little stone, and yet I would not be allowed it.

I gave him one last warning as I shrank back, legs pressed against the boulder behind me – 'It's only a stone, *go away!*' – but he ignored me and pressed forth, a greedy look in his eyes. He stretched out his hand and that was the final spark that lit the flare.

I bit him.

Hard.

The less said of the hour that followed, the better. I was punished, of course; screamed at by my nursemaid and my grandmother both. The thing I remember most clearly is my nursemaid's hand around my wrist, her fingers pressing hard enough to bruise, the bared-teeth grimace upon her face as she hissed at me: *'What the devil is wrong with you?'* And my unspoken reply: *I do not know.*

Afterwards, I fled to the furthest corner of the garden. I knelt there, my palms smarting from the cane, and fished my seaside treasure – which I had somehow managed to keep in all the commotion – from my pocket, only to discover that it was broken. Cracked in half, along some pre-existing fault.

I cried again, of course. But scarcely had I begun, when there came a voice from the other side of the garden wall.

'Are you all right?'

I paused in my weeping long enough to look up. Poking over the top of the wall was a cloud of red hair; if I stretched my neck, I could just make out a face beneath it, bright eyes and freckles scattered dense as stars.

'Who are you?' I asked, voice wavering but full of intrigue – for as long as I had lived there, there had never been a girl behind that wall.

'Catherine Leveaux,' she replied, which answered next to nothing.

'Why are you in Mr and Mrs Howell's garden?'

'They're my *grand-mère et grand-père*. Papa had to go to sea and Maman was lonely and wanted to see her old friends, and she wanted me to speak more English even though I'm already *very* good at it, I think, so now we're going to live here for a time.' She said all this very quickly and in a practised manner, as if she had given this same explanation to several people already. Suddenly, her eyes brightened. 'What is that? In your hand?'

Hesitantly, I lifted my reddened palm to let her see.

She teetered higher a moment, straining to look. Abruptly, she gasped.

'Oh!' she cried. 'I know what that is!'

Her head vanished. When Catherine returned, it was with a great huffing and puffing and scraping – a sound very much like a small child rearranging wrought-iron garden furniture to make a stepping stool over a wall. The first thing I saw was her hair again, and then a tumble of arms and legs and petticoats as she clambered up and over. When she had landed and smoothed her skirts, she sat down beside me and spread out two books in front of her. One was clearly a book for children, a primer on the *Wonders of the Earth, Sea, and Sky*, but the other was a rather more dense-looking work entitled *Book of the Great Sea-Dragons*.

'We went to Limes Reaches on our way from London,' she said cheerily. (It took me some years to learn that she meant Lyme Regis.) 'And there was a shop with lots of bones from very long ago, fishes and things that got turned to stone – did you know that happens? That's what the lady in the shop said, that there used to be *enormous* fishes and lizards and things in the sea and on the land, and that we only know about them because their bones were turned into rocks and buried very deep in the ground, but on the beach you can find them just sitting on the sand because the waves dig them up. You found that on the beach, didn't you?'

I nodded mutely, trying to absorb a great many things at once: her very presence in my garden, the way she spoke to me as though we were already friends, the knowledge that there had once upon a time existed giant lizards whose bones had turned to rock. As I watched, she opened the great *Sea-Dragons* tome and began rifling through it.

'My uncle – he was the one who took us to Limes Reaches; he lives in London and makes *steam* engines and knows everything – he bought the other book for me, and this one for my *grand-père*, but I do like the pictures. Aha, *voici* !'

She held the book an inch before my face. There, above a careful cursive *Fig. 78*, was a perfect illustration of my little treasure. Several of them, in fact, of all shapes and sizes.

'It's from a fish!' Catherine said rapturously. 'It's a . . . What is the bone in your back, it goes down from your neck?'

'A spine?' I supplied. 'From an ancient fish?'

'*Yes!* Or a lizard, maybe. The lizards are my favourite.' She flipped back to the start of the book and placed it on the ground for both of us to see. My breath stuck in my lungs. On the page, three great reptiles were locked in battle, their hollow-eyed heads rearing against a darkened sky. Beside them, a flock of bird-like creatures feasted upon the corpse of another, their beaks lined with needle-sharp teeth. I could almost hear their triumphant cries, the crash of waves upon that primordial shore. It was one of the famed John Martin's works, I would learn later – wholly inaccurate, as all of his palaeontological scenes tended to be. But looking upon it then, all I could do was marvel.

That was the moment I fell in love with the past, I think. I placed my hand upon the warm grass, thinking of the bones of creatures far below, of spread wings turned to stone. I wondered how deep a hole one would have to dig to find these buried worlds; I pictured myself standing at the precipice of such a pit, calling out a greeting; I heard the echo of dragon-esque cries bouncing back.

'I have this, too,' Catherine said quietly. 'I thought, since yours is broken . . .'

I looked over and saw to my astonishment that she was holding something out to me – another ancient bone. This one was clearly a tooth of some kind, a great fang as long as my thumb. Everything about it was delightfully tactile: its surface smooth and brown, the end tapered to a gentle point. It evidently pained her to give it to me, and I could see why; it was utterly perfect.

'My uncle got it for me at Limes Reaches,' she said. 'But he also said, "One ought not to dig things up from the ground and say they're yours for ever just because you found them," so . . . we can share it, maybe? You can have it for a week, and then I can have it for a week?'

My heart sang as I nodded, taking the tooth gently from her palm. I had never had a fossil before, nor a friend, nor any sort of scheduled social engagement besides visiting my father's grave each Sunday. I looked up at her then, at her kind smile and the freckles upon her nose and that wild red hair which drifted about her face like a flame whipped by the wind – and I fell in love for the second time that afternoon.

3

Death snatches away many blooming children, the only
hopes of their doting parents; how many brides and
youthful lovers have been one day in the bloom of health
and hope, and the next a prey for worms and the decay of
the tomb!

— MARY SHELLEY, *Frankenstein*

THE FUNERAL WAS held that Friday. It was a wholly unpleasant affair. Henry and I had not spoken since our argument, and
I had resolved that this would be the day I would give up my
silence; although I was still furious at him, I reasoned that no
one, no matter how irresponsibly and poorly he had behaved,
deserved to be shunned on the day of his father's funeral. But
when the day itself came, and I was obliged to don my black
taffeta and veil once again, I could not seem to say a word. Even
the sight of the dress in my travelling case had been enough to
put me ill at ease. Now, wearing the damned thing upon my
person, I felt myself sink into the same cold despair that had
plagued me this past year — my heart grew heavy, my breaths
irregular, my throat tight. It was all I could do not to burst into
tears during the ceremony, let alone break the silence between
Henry and me. And so I sat, and let him think that I snubbed

him still, and listened to Maisie's quiet sobs as they echoed through the sparsely populated church.

It had been fourteen months since our daughter had died. Fourteen months, and still the very clothes I wore while mourning her were enough to reduce me to tears. How was it that someone who had spent barely an hour in this world, who had died before we even had a chance to name her, could leave such a hollow in my heart? I knew of women who had lost two children, or four, or ten; I knew of women who were obliged to work throughout their mourning; I knew women who had had another child in the same year the last had died. All these ideas were abhorrent to me. I could not imagine such grief becoming commonplace, routine—

And I certainly could not imagine running off to play cards while my wife sat at home floundering in its depths.

Henry was an impulsive sort. That I had always known; for who else would have agreed to elope with me – with *me*, who had no allowance or family name to speak of – after knowing me less than a year? We had met during the summer of my twentieth year; my grandmother, whose opinion on my marriageability had never been particularly high, had nevertheless spent the previous several months herding me aggressively in the direction of one Mr Thomas Doyle, a widower of forty-seven and a father of three who lived not half a mile distant. This, I knew, would be my lot if I stayed in Norton Green: mothering children not my own and nursing a husband in his old age.

But then along had come an invitation to spend the summer in London, and along had come Henry – Henry, who had sought me out after a meeting of the British Association to say that he wished to hear my thoughts on Agassiz's *Études sur les glaciers*, and who had *meant it*. Henry, who was witty and charming and smart as a whip, who had been not to Cambridge or Oxford but the University College, home to radicals and atheists. Henry, with a fellowship in the Geological Society and a house in London – albeit one, as I discovered when I moved in the following February, that was very poorly kept. I remember sitting in the parlour, head still spinning from the joys of our honeymoon in Lyme Regis, searching rather frantically through a stack of domestic magazines for instructions on how to hire a maid – but even then, I had thought to myself that my decision, while hasty, had been a good one. That this was the life, and the partnership, I had longed for. That the extravagant gifts Henry sometimes bought me, and the late hours he kept, only meant that he was successful and sociable.

And now? Now . . . I was afraid. I had trusted Henry when he had told me months ago that his dismissal from the collection was not a disaster, that between our savings and the bits and pieces we made from articles and newspaper columns we would stay afloat. Even so, we had been living frugally, denying ourselves luxuries; would we now have to deny ourselves necessities, too? Food, coal, winter clothes? At least (though the very thought made me flinch with guilt) we would not have to worry about such things while we remained under Maisie's roof. I could do nothing but wait, and worry, and hope in some sullen childish way that Henry would fix everything.

Ladies are often criticized for being childish, I find – but it is hard not to be, when one's life is so wholly in the hands of another.

HENRY HAD PLANNED for us to stay some weeks in Inverness, settling his father's affairs and – if convincing Maisie to move proved successful – arranging to sell the house. I had wondered, after the debacle with the will, if he might arrange an earlier departure, but he did not seem eager to do so. Perhaps it had occurred to him, too, that every day spent under Maisie's hospitality was another penny saved. I did my best to think of it as a holiday – reading and going for walks, drawing stilted and unsatisfactory sketches of the countryside that·I tore from my sketchbook and fed to the firth as soon as they were done. Eventually, when the sheer pointlessness of it all began to grind away at my very soul, I swallowed my guilt and discomfort and went to find Maisie. She had been sequestered in the library, sorting through her father's extensive collection of books. At first she politely dismissed my offer of help, but I think she must have seen the desperation in my eyes, for she soon relented. I had not realized until then how much I had grown used to working with Henry. As often as I complained about each new bout of illustrations he demanded, each nearly illegible page I was handed to transcribe ('Make this neat for Mr Parker, would you? He does so complain about my handwriting . . .'), I enjoyed having something to show for my efforts at the end of the day. Something I could touch, and see – *there, that pile is gone; there, that shelf is tidied*. (I suppose that is why so many wealthy ladies still work at embroidery or quilled paper, even when they have no need to work at all.) That same evening, as I watched Maisie sew intricate daisies about the edges of a pillow cover, humming under her breath, I wished that needlework brought me the same quiet joy it seemed to bring most everybody else. My life would have been much easier if it had.

I must admit I did not quite know what to make of Maisie in those early days. When not shut up in her room with a headache, or fatigue, or dizziness, or shortness of breath, she flitted about the house from one thing to the next like a bird unsure of where to roost. She talked either incessantly – as often to herself as to anyone else – or not at all, spending long hours staring out through the rain-streaked windows at the firth. Much of what she did say had an oddly rehearsed quality to it, the words dipped in starch, as if she had copied them out before-hand from a book on ladies' etiquette. This had made me uneasy, at first; the bulk of my etiquette I had learned warily and by example, as a new factory girl memorizes the move-ments of the looms so as to avoid being caught by their hungry mechanisms. I still felt oftentimes, as I spoke with the wives of eminent geologists and anatomists and chemists at Society meet-ings, that conversation was a dance to which I had never been properly taught the steps. But the more time I spent with Maisie – the more I watched her chatter through our otherwise silent dinners, stitching together the void between Henry and me with increasingly ridiculous pleasantries – the more I began to suspect that the dance did not come naturally to her either.

My suspicions were confirmed one blustery day in the library, as we sat sorting through a pile of her father's letters. They were a sorry lot, mildewed and cross-written to the point of near-illegibility, and I was forced to stop every minute or two, if not to ask Maisie to identify the persons mentioned (*His aunt? Perhaps we ought to keep this one, then. Oh, they loathed each other? Perhaps not.*), then to unstick pages that time and damp had glued together. It was from inside one such letter, as I carefully pried apart the folds of the envelope, that a small piece of paper fluttered out and slipped away from my grasp.

'Oh! Did it go under my chair?' Maisie asked, looking over.

'I think so. Could you . . . oh, thank you,' I said as she bent to pick it up, fingers scrabbling at the floorboards before she caught hold of it and straightened with a victorious 'A-*ha*!' She made to hand it back to me, but suddenly she froze, eyes going wide.

'Oh dear,' she said, as she always seemed to do whenever other words escaped her. 'It's a ten-pound note.'

'Ten pounds?' I cried. Not a king's ransom, but certainly more than one would expect to find by chance on a Wednesday afternoon.

'Yes. It's made out to my father.' She looked up, a delicate frown creasing her brow. 'Do you know who sent it?'

I surveyed the letter in my hands. 'An R. Thompson, I believe? It sounds as though he had his pocket picked while the two of them were on holiday in Scarborough and had to borrow some money from your father . . . and then they had some dreadful fight, by the looks of it.' I turned over the second page, which was full of pleas and apologies. Only then did I notice that the wax seal was whole and unbroken; it must have simply come unstuck with age. 'I don't think your father ever opened it.'

'Yes, that does sound like him,' Maisie said with a sigh. She looked down at the note, the crease between her brows growing deeper, her foot tapping an anxious staccato on the floor. Then, abruptly, she thrust it towards me.

'Here. I think that . . . Rather, I'd . . . I think you should have it.'

I stared at her, a flush rising to my cheeks. 'What? No, I couldn't possibly!'

'I insist!' she said breezily, leaning forward to press the note into my hands. I startled at how cold her fingers were; there only a moment, but enough to leave a lasting chill.

I shook my head. 'But the will . . .'

'You could redeem it in London, couldn't you? No clerk would suspect Henry isn't his father's heir without having seen the will. And besides, I know that your circumstances are . . . *Henry's* circumstances, rather . . .' She slumped a little in her chair, then flashed me a smile – a weary little thing, wry about its edges. When she spoke next, her words seemed to come easier, albeit with a note of exhaustion that I had not heard before.

'I know that you need it. And I would only waste it, as Henry would say. Better that you have it; you found it, after all.'

And then, straightening in her seat like a wind-up doll coming back to life: 'Would you like some tea? I'll have Flora bring us some more tea. *Flora!*'

I watched in befuddlement as she leaped up and strode to the door (nearly colliding with her maid) and negotiated the delivery of a pot of tea and some apple turnovers. I was taken aback; not only by the suggestion that Henry could be so unfathomably hypocritical in the matter of 'wasting money', but also by that slip of hers. Or rather, the glimpse she had let me see. I felt a stab of sympathy, suddenly – a wish to tell her that she did not need to try so very hard. Not for my sake, at least. But I could not think of a way to say such a thing that would not be terribly embarrassing for the both of us. And besides, who was I to say that she did not find comfort in this cloak of hers? I thought of every uncomfortable silence between Henry and me which she had broken this past week, how it had all seemed – if not graceful or natural – at the very least well practised. How many other fraught dinners in this house had she weathered, I wondered?

'Does Henry often say such things to you?' I asked quietly as

Maisie settled back in her chair. She looked at me with wide and earnest eyes.

'What?'

'That you're wasteful with money. Or . . .' I did not want to continue, did not want to admit all the ungracious things he had said to me of her, and I was grateful when she stopped me with a wave of her hand.

'Oh, no! Of course not. Not . . . recently. It's only . . .' She picked up a stack of letters, busying herself with the prying apart of a particularly decrepit envelope. 'It's the kind of thing he used to say, when we were young.'

I could not help but wonder how on earth a child might be accused of wasting money; or, moreover, what sort of child would be so austere as to accuse another of doing so.

'He's kinder to you now, then?' I asked, aware that the question sounded more like a plea. 'You've . . . made up since?'

There; the cloak slipped once again. Her smile guttered like a candle flame, gasping for air.

'Of course.' Though there was a peculiar kind of sadness to the way she said it; the same tone that I would have used if someone had asked me at that moment if I loved Henry. 'How could we not?'

HENRY FINALLY CAME to reconcile with me later that evening. I had been retiring early, earlier even than Maisie, purely that I might spare myself the agony of readying for bed at the same time as him. It had been almost two weeks since we had last spoken – two weeks of silent meals and uneasy glances, of his slinking about the outskirts of every room I occupied like a kicked dog, shooting me piteous looks as though he could communicate through furrowed eyebrows alone the depths of his remorse. It was at times like this, usually – though we had never before had any quarrels as serious as this – that he would return home with a pear tart or a vial of perfume or a book I had mentioned in passing; some small and pointless gift to appease me. But I suppose, in this case, he had assessed (rightly) that there would be no appeasing me with mere trinkets, and that indeed attempting to do so would only be a waste of money, and thus aggravate me further. And so the affair had dragged on and on, until I was sick to death of it; until, despite all the pains I had taken to avoid him, there was perhaps some part of me that evening which was relieved to hear the creak of his tread on the landing.

I was sitting at the dressing table as he came in, brushing out my hair. I did not pause, but kept my gaze fixed upon my own reflection in the mirror, teasing out each tangle in turn. Out of the corner of my eye, I watched him creep over until he stood by my side. When I continued to pay him no mind, he heaved a sigh and sat down upon one of our travelling trunks, his hands held before his face as if in prayer.

'I finished the article,' he said, 'and I heard from Mr Chambers, who said that his son would like me to write a piece for his new *Westminster Review*. And I have nearly finished with my lecture for the Geological Society in May. It has been quite the strain, transcribing and correcting it all by myself. And,' he added hurriedly, when I shot him a sharp look in the mirror, 'you were right in denying me your help. It has made me realize . . . how very indispensable you are.'

'That I am,' I replied coolly.

When I said no more, he leaned forward and clasped his hands around mine, prying the hairbrush gently from my grip.

'My dear,' he said. 'Please. I cannot tell you how awful I feel. I have been trying to make amends, but I can see that that alone is not enough. So I implore you, what would you have me do, Mary? What do you want of me? I will give you it.'

I sighed and turned to face him at last. He looked so plaintive there, kneeling before me like a boy. I did not have the heart to shun him any longer; but neither did I have the heart to forgive him entirely. A wrong done over the course of months (and which would take many more months, perhaps even years, to fix) could not be forgiven in a fortnight. But I could think of several prerequisites to my forgiveness, at least.

'You must never keep such secrets from me again,' I said.

He nodded, solemn. 'Of course.'

'You must promise never to gamble again. No cards, no dice, no . . . *horses*, or whatever else may tempt you. Nothing.'

He hesitated, and I could see in his eyes the intention to argue, but he relented. 'Done.'

'You must promise . . .' I took a steadying breath. 'You must promise that if we ever lose a child again, you will *stay* with me. Grieve with me.'

He pressed a kiss to my knuckles with a gentleness that, despite myself, tugged at my heart. 'I promise.'

'Good.' I stared at him for a long moment, weighing my dignity against my concern. The latter won out.

'Tell me it will be all right,' I said quietly, 'when we get back to London. Tell me we will not be forced out on to the street, or into debtors' prison, or the workhouse. Tell me you will make it right.'

His mouth was a thin line. 'I will.'

I knew that I ought to ask how. Science was a game of money

and connections, after all; true, one could make a meagre living writing for magazines and penny presses, but work that paid was not the sort that improved one's reputation. One could never compete with those who had the means to fund expeditions, to collect rare specimens and study them at their leisure. And how could we compete at all if we were forced, say, to sell our books? Or to move to cheaper accommodations, and thus announce to all who visited or wrote to us our state of financial woe — a state which most in society seemed to regard as equally distasteful and contagious as leprosy? Perhaps we would have to let Agnes go, or Mrs Hedges, our cook; we only had the two staff now, after giving James his notice, and as it was I knew that they chafed at the breadth of their duties. I helped when I could, in those few areas as I was able, but to dismiss either one of them outright would be the death knell for my scientific pursuits — a solid blow to Henry's, too, if he was forced to work without my help.

It was not as if I had any illusions about how much fame my work garnered me. I illustrated and edited, corrected and organized, wrote and rewrote, and for my troubles I occasionally saw my name in a magazine or the back of a book: *many thanks to M. Sutherland for the illustrations.* (I imagine many assumed the *M.* stood for *Monsieur.*) But it was enough. It was enough to learn, to be in the middle of it, to harbour vague notions of one day having my name in the front of a book as well — perhaps a book of plates, illustrations of the ancient world, like the beautiful volume by Kuwasseg and Unger I had pored over the previous year in a bookshop in London.

Perhaps it was only fate that I, the daughter of a housemaid, should wear out my wrists scrubbing pots instead.

'Is there anything else you want, my dear?' Henry asked, and I realized I had been staring at him for some time.

Oh, so much; so much else, I wanted to say. But I did not.

'Yes.' I frowned. 'You must help me and Maisie sort through the rest of your father's things tomorrow. The letters in particular. For there are so many of them, and they are so long, and so dull, and I don't know any of the people mentioned in them well enough to determine if they're worth keeping—'

'All right, all right!' he chuckled, the relief plain upon his face. He smiled, giving my hand another kiss. 'I will. Though you must know that my verdict will likely be "burn them all".'

'That's precisely why I'm asking you. The job will go quickly.'

He left then, to get a warming pan for the sheets, and I watched him go until I could no longer follow his shadow down the stairs. I wondered whether I should tell him that his place in my good graces was still precarious – but what would that do, besides make things fraught between us once more? There was one other thing I ought to tell Henry about, however, which I had nearly forgotten in all the fuss: the ten-pound note. That would certainly change his mind on the matter of burning his father's letters, though even if we did happen upon any more hidden valuables, I did not think my conscience would let me accept them, no matter how much Maisie insisted.

I paused in the act of blowing out the bedside light, for all this talk of inheritance and of letters had reminded me of something. When I had fled Wight that hopeful winter three years ago, I had taken with me a few sentimental objects. Most of my father's things my grandmother kept locked in a chest at the foot of her bed, and my grandfather's things – what little remained, after that terrible fire – in the similarly inaccessible attic. Still, over the years I had managed to salvage some relics. One in particular, a sleek black fountain pen with the name *Frankenstein* engraved upon the side, I had with me even now, in among my drawing supplies. The others lay in a trunk beneath our bed in London, where I had not thought of them in years.

But perhaps, I mused now as I blew out the lamp, thinking of the letter that afternoon and the ten-pound note hidden behind its crumbling seal, I ought to have another look at them when we returned home. For nostalgia's sake, if nothing else.

And who knew? Perhaps I might find some hidden value there, too.

4

Curiosity, earnest research to learn the hidden laws of
nature, gladness akin to rapture, as they were unfolded to
me, are among the earliest sensations I can remember.

*

I have longed for a friend; I have sought one who would
sympathise with and love me.

— MARY SHELLEY, *Frankenstein*

'AND IT'S YOURS? To *keep*?'

I lay on my stomach on the sun-warmed grass, twirling a buttercup back and forth between my fingers. Before me, Catherine stretched one arm and held the jewelled brooch up to catch the sun. It scattered the light in a thousand coloured darts across her face.

'I know,' she said wonderingly. 'She said it was an heirloom. There's a whole box of jewellery that's going to be mine one day, though "hopefully not for a very long while!" she says.'

Catherine laughed, and I with her – or at the very least, I tried. It seemed so outlandish to me, that one might have a mother to bequeath jewels and trinkets; that one might have a mother at all; that these gifts might be handed out in celebration of something as inconsequential as the impending start of a school year. (Although for me, the start of term bore plenty of consequence, for it meant Catherine would soon be leaving for her boarding school upon the mainland, and I would not see her again until Christmas.) Even when I had turned thirteen that winter, all my grandmother had given me was a bone-handled brush and a bolt of trim so that I might help my maid let down my skirts. The only heirlooms I had were what I had managed to scavenge over time from the dusty ghost of my grandfather's study, namely:

A pen – inscribed with the family name.

A Bible – well worn, with my father's initials (*W. F.*) upon the inside leaf.

A hair ribbon – ivory, grubby, pressed between the Bible's pages; threadbare, as if rubbed to nothing between someone's forefinger and thumb.

And lastly, most recently: a battered leather document case, containing what looked to be several years' worth of receipts and records from my grandfather's business dealings in London and Geneva.

'Have you finished going through those old papers yet?' said Catherine, whose thoughts seemed to have followed the same mental eddies as mine. At once, I groaned, dropping my head to lie upon my folded arms.

'Yes! A hundred times! There's nothing interesting. No awful secrets, no deeds to lost mansions, *nothing*.' I had been terribly excited at first, to go through the contents of the case, as there seemed to be some mystery surrounding it. I had found it swathed in dust at the very top of my grandfather's bookshelf, hidden behind some decorative moulding. When I had shown it to the aged cook, the member of the household most well versed in my family's history – save my grandmother herself – she had grown quite pale.

'That's Mr Frankenstein's.'

'My father's?' I had asked, heart leaping.

'No, miss, Mr Ernest's. Was the only thing besides the clothes on his back he managed to save from the fire; he even ran back in to get it. It made him terribly sick, it did. Your grandmother always said that was what killed him, all the smoke in his lungs.' Her chin jerked sharply towards the case. 'None of the maids would touch it, after that. Said it carried the smell of smoke with it always, no matter how much they shook it out.'

With that, the cook had pointedly resumed her chopping of potatoes, and I had gone immediately to relay this haunted tale to Catherine. But though I spent a solid afternoon leafing through the contents of the case with her – and several more hours in the intervening days, struggling terribly without her help to decipher the Swiss French – I had found nothing. They were empty things, these papers, emptier even than my other sorry treasures, with not a whit of personality or warmth to indicate who my grandfather might once have been.

'Not even any ghosts?' Catherine grinned, rolling her brooch over in her hands. 'No ancient curses? Demons rising out of smoke to murder you?'

'No,' I muttered. 'Well, the case does still smell a bit burnt, but I don't think that counts. I'm starting to think Cook was just telling stories. Do you know, last week, I asked her if she knew why my grandfather had left Geneva—'

'With all the lovely mountains and lakes?' Catherine said dreamily.

'Exactly! And she said that that was before her time, but it had been a great tragedy. I asked her what sort of tragedy, and then she said that one of his brothers was murdered by the nanny, and that his other brother went stark raving mad and disappeared, and then his sister-in-law was murdered, too, only not by the nanny this time—'

'*What?*' she cried, laughing. 'All at once?'

'I know, I know! I'm sure she really doesn't know, and just decided to make something up.' I sighed, then perked up as I was struck with an idea. 'Is Bordeaux close to Geneva?'

Her head shot up suddenly. 'What?'

'Bordeaux. I heard your mother say something about visiting there. That's where your father's from, isn't it?'

'Oh . . . yes.' She looked down at the brooch, studying it again. 'But no, it isn't close. Why?'

Disappointed, I picked another buttercup and began to pluck off its petals. 'I'd hoped maybe you and your mother might visit there, too. You could ask about my grandfather, see if any of it's true.' I shrugged. 'Honestly, though, imagine going back into a blazing fire just to get your accounts . . . his brother can't have been the only madman in the family.'

I paused, waiting for her to laugh, or to reply, *You're terrible, Mary, the poor man is dead!* – but she did not. Instead, she only stared off into the distance, down the bluff to where the outgoing tide lapped at the shore.

'Catherine? Are you listening?' I flicked the remains of the buttercup at her, but even then, she did not look round. I felt a pang, as I always did whenever one of my jokes or stories failed to amuse her, a disappointment that ran to my very bones. It was never like this with my grandmother, or with the other girls at school, all grey and charmless by comparison. Perhaps because, over the years, I had grown immune to their disappointment.

'I must tell you something,' Catherine said softly, finger twining in a blade of grass.

'Catherine! Miss Brown!'

We both jumped at that. Catherine pushed herself up on her knees and peered down the slope, her face brightening with something like relief.

'We're here, Uncle!' she cried – and at that, I sprang to my feet as well.

Mr and Mrs Jamsetjee had only been three weeks on Wight, but already I had decided that I liked them far more than my own singular relative, and had done my utmost to adopt them as my own. Mrs Jamsetjee was a quiet sort of woman, perpetually absorbed in her sketchbook or a novel, but in every other way so identical to her niece, with her freckled nose and shock of red hair, that one might have easily mistaken one for a younger portrait of the other. I had marvelled over her drawings, watching her for hours as she brought the sea to life in soft curves of pastel, occasionally demonstrating with a word or gesture the techniques by which she worked. Mr Jamsetjee, by contrast, had plenty to say, and every bit of it fascinating. He was a man of science, and an important one, as I would later learn; his family had for generations run a shipyard in Bombay, which now – thanks to his talents in business and in naval engineering – built steamships for the East India Company. Dissatisfied with the dry life of a businessman, he had ceded the shipyard to his brother and moved to England to make a study of hydraulics, work which had since earned him a fellowship in the Royal Society. All I knew of him then, though, was that he was the first person I had ever encountered who did not try to direct my curiosities in a direction more suitable for a young lady; who not only did not seem to tire of my questions, but delighted in them.

'The light is fading, and we really ought to take them home,' Mrs Jamsetjee was saying softly as the pair of them mounted the bluff, clutching her sketchbook tightly to her chest.

'But it's such a rare event, Georgianna! We must show them – ah, girls, here you are!' Mr Jamsetjee shot us both a grin, his usually neat salt-and-pepper hair blown hither and thither by the ocean breeze. 'Come quick, the most marvellous thing has washed up near the Needles.'

'Is it a fossil? Another crocodile tooth?' I asked at once – for although Mr Jamsetjee's main business was in engines and hydraulics, he was (like many of his fellows in the Royal Society) a true 'man of science' who, having exhausted all there was to know in his current field, had gone on to exhaust several more for pure amusement. His current favourite pursuit was geology; it was he who had bought Catherine the books and the little fossil tooth in Lyme Regis, the latter apparently from one Miss Mary Anning, a prolific fossil-finder who had unearthed the torso of an ichthyosaur when she was only twelve years old. Hearing this, of course, I had clamoured for the three of us to go fossil-hunting ourselves, and so he and I and Catherine had spent several mornings combing the beachside for treasure. Catherine, reluctant to get herself muddy, had been for the most part a spectator. Mr Jamsetjee and I, however, had turned up three partial ammonites and half a tooth – though still nothing that could hold a candle to the tooth from Lyme. That one

Catherine and I still shared, swapping it back and forth throughout the summer and at the end of each school term.

'Oh, far more terrific than that, Miss Brown!' Mr Jamsetjee said, his eyes alight with excitement.

'If by "terrific" you mean "large and inspiring terror", then I quite agree,' his wife added, looking faintly queasy.

'But shouldn't we be going home soon? Maman did say to be back before dark,' Catherine said anxiously.

I shot her a baffled look. 'It shouldn't take long, though, should it?'

Mr Jamsetjee hesitated, gazing pleadingly in the direction of his wife.

'No, you're right, not long,' she acquiesced, with a good-natured sigh. 'I shouldn't think my sister will mind.'

Beside me, Catherine huffed.

We set off in the direction of the Needles, those great chalk ridges which jutted like teeth from the sea at the island's westward edge. Before long, we spotted it: a crowd of townspeople gathered on the shore, milling like crabs around something huge and black. I thought that the shape must be a ship at first, overturned upon the sand. But it was too misshapen, I thought to myself – too lopsided. Above the crowd, seagulls wheeled and cried in raucous indignation.

It was Catherine who said, with a gasp like she'd been plunged into cold water:

'Oh, it's a *whale*.'

And then I was off, scrambling down the cliff path, heedless of Mr and Mrs Jamsetjee's cries to be careful upon the stairs.

I sprinted across the shore and slipped through the crowd, too quick for anyone to stop me. In a moment I was there in its shadow, close enough to lay a hand upon its dark and slippery skin. The size of the thing, the sheer gargantuan *bulk* of it, drove the breath from my lungs. To think that such a beast had really been alive! To think – judging by the great chunk of flesh missing from its side – it had really been *killed*! Perhaps I ought to have been disgusted, or put off by the terrible smell, which did indeed nearly make me retch even with my nose pinched shut. Instead, I found myself fascinated. Its ribs, which jutted up towards the sky like the Needles themselves, were not unlike those of the mouse whose tiny bones I had put together in the moonlight all those years ago. They were not unlike my own, whose shape I had roughly ascertained by running my fingers over my chest and sides, curious at the corset-like structure which helped my body hold its form. We were all made of the same stuff, it seemed; the most significant difference between myself and the whale was not our species, nor our size, but the fact that I was alive and it was dead.

'Is that Mary Brown?' I heard one of the fishermen mutter behind me, and then a tug on my arm as he pulled me away. 'Get back, girl; if you slip and fall in that muck, your grand-mother will have my head!'

'Yes, please, Miss Brown, don't go so close,' Mr Jamsetjee added, huffing and puffing, for he had caught up by then. The fisherman released me and herded me warily in his direction. The residents of Norton Green were never quite sure what to make of Mr Jamsetjee, I think. In Newport – the closest proper town we could reach from our end of the island, unless you counted the ferry crossing at Yarmouth – one sometimes encountered lascars: Indian seamen, often trapped ashore for months in the winter if there were no returning ships, looking quite miserable in the English weather. Such men were to be viewed with pity, or suspicion, or contempt – but Mr Jamsetjee, who spoke and dressed like a London gentleman, flummoxed them entirely. They were never sure which rank to afford him, which respects he deserved. In that way, I supposed, he and I were alike.

'Do you think there were ever plesiosauri this large? Or ichthyosauri?' I asked him, my voice hushed.

Mr Jamsetjee was straightening his shirtsleeves, still quite out of breath. 'Perhaps, perhaps ... None so big has ever been found, to my knowledge, but that does not mean they did not exist. But a whale is a mammal, in any case, so it does not do to compare the two.'

'I know that,' I said, a tad peevishly. 'I only meant, although they are of different *taxonomic classes*' – he had lent me one of his more advanced books on geology and I was desperate to show I had made good use of it – 'if the sea can support a mammal of such size, surely ancient reptiles could also have been very large.'

'Then, that is what you must say, Miss Brown. A man of science must be precise in his wording.' He smiled. 'Or ... a woman of science, rather.'

It was half a joke, I knew; such a creature, as far as I was aware, did not exist. Still, the words delighted me. I turned to grin at Catherine, expecting to see her close behind me. Instead, she stood some feet away with her aunt, the pair of them pressing handkerchiefs to their noses. Mrs Jamsetjee I would have expected to react so; she was a sensitive soul, nearly brought to tears by the sight of a crushed butterfly or the limp body of a seagull in the surf. But Catherine, with whom I had pored over skeletons both real and illustrated, with whom I had hunted for fossils upon the beach . . .

Catherine, who next to her aunt looked more like a lady than ever, skirts long enough that they would have trailed in the blood had she come as close to the whale as I just had . . .

Her face was twisted in disgust.

'It smells,' I heard her mutter, the sound carried towards me on a gust of wind, and my heart sank in my chest like a stone.

WE TOOK THE longer way back from the shore, a winding path that ran halfway around the village before bringing us home. Besides it being the scenic route, it was the only way which did not lead us past my house before the Howells', and I suspected that was precisely why Mr and Mrs Jamsetjee had picked it. My grandmother, while not an amiable woman, was nevertheless raised in London, and thus – in a cold, instinctual way, like a fish following the currents of migration without quite knowing why – she had invited the visiting couple to dinner the previous week. Alas, Mr Jamsetjee had said, being a Parsee, he could only eat food prepared by those of his own faith; unless my grandmother had a taste for Parsee cuisine or her own staff were willing to section off half the kitchen for his cook, Alma, to use, it would simply not be possible. My grandmother had taken this exceptionally personally, and now made a point of telling him, at length, what we were having for dinner each time she saw him, as if trying to tempt him to Christianity by way of roasted duck.

But it was not of my grandmother or of Mr Jamsetjee's aversion to good Christian poultry that I was thinking as we walked, but of Catherine. While Mr Jamsetjee regaled us with facts on the habits of whales, and Mrs Jamsetjee offered to let me borrow some of her pastels so that I might try my hand at drawing the great beast the following day, Catherine had been utterly silent. She had grown slower and slower, hanging back at every turn, so that by the time we arrived at the back door of the house, she was still coming in through the garden gate. I trotted back to fetch her, meeting her under a swathe of overgrown ivy that dripped its long fingers from the bough of a nearby tree, and hazarded a guess at what was eating her.

'What is it you wanted to tell me earlier?' I asked. 'On the hill?'

'Maman and I are going back to France.'

She said it so abruptly that I hardly understood her at first. It did not seem right to me that something so monumental, so world-shattering as this, could be said so quickly or easily.

'Back to France?' I repeated, like an echo.

She nodded, not looking at me; instead, her gaze was on her feet, her hands clutched in the fabric of her skirt.

'For how long?' I heard myself say.

'Papa's arm isn't healing well, apparently, so the Navy's letting him retire. Maman wants to go back and live in Bordeaux.'

For good, then. She had not said it, but I could feel it, a hollow pit of despair opening up inside my chest. I did not know what I would do without her; we wrote whenever we were apart during the school year, but the only thing that made those small scraps bearable was the knowledge that I would get to see her in person again soon enough.

'Take me with you,' I blurted, knowing even as I said it that it was nonsense. 'Please.'

She met my eye at last, looking at me with some horrid combination of shock and sorrow and pity. It felt as if she had struck me. I watched as she took something from her pocket – the fossil tooth, *our* fossil tooth, which was meant to be hers this term. She pressed it into my palm, folding her fingers closed over mine.

'You should take this,' she said quietly. 'I know you like it, and . . . I've got no use for it, anyway.'

Later, I would think about those words – *I've got no use for it* – over and over, letting them sink like needles into my skin. But in the moment I was too distressed to notice, for all I could think of were the tears pricking at my eyes, the warmth of her hands around mine. She leaned forward to kiss me on the cheek, as friends do. As girls do. As the French very often do.

And then I ruined our friendship entirely.

5

Away, away, from men and towns,
To the wild wood and the downs—
To the silent wilderness
Where the soul need not repress
Its music lest it should not find
An echo in another's mind . . .

— PERCY BYSSHE SHELLEY,
'To Jane: The Invitation'

'POST!' CRIED HENRY, marching into the room with a fistful of envelopes. Triumphant, he dropped them upon the dining table, nearly upsetting a pot of marmalade. 'The post, it's here at last!'

'I didn't quite hear you, Henry. Perhaps you might say it again?' I said drily. Across from me, Maisie made a rather undignified noise into her cup of morning tea.

'Well, forgive me for being overeager. Mr William Chambers said he wants me to write an article for their March issue, and I can't do that until I receive his approval on the proposal I sent him, and I can't do *that*' – he dropped into a chair and began to flick through the stack of letters – 'if all our correspondence is trapped in Aberdeen, can I?'

It was true, we were in an inconvenient position. Henry had announced the morning after our reconciliation his intent to book us passage home before the end of the week, but alas, an ill-timed winter storm had turned the country roads first to slush and then to treacherous ice. Yet more snow had fallen after Christmas – a gloomy affair, consisting largely of Henry drinking too much wine and recounting unpleasant tales of Sutherland Christmases past – and more still, in the new year, had blocked the post entirely for several days. Henry had fretted himself to pieces, but for my part, I had to admit I was enjoying our new routine. I was back at work again, helping Henry with the lecture he was to deliver at the Geological Society in May, an ambitious review of all the marine invertebrate fossils formerly under his care at the University College collection. In the mornings we bickered over the categorization of crinoids; in the afternoons, I went on long and rambling walks with Maisie; in the evenings, the three of us sorted through the last of the old library, Maisie and Henry having come to an unsteady truce.

'No word from Chambers yet, then?' I asked.

'No, blast it, still nothing. Mary, here's one from Mr Jamsetjee. And another from Forsythe – good Lord, it looks as if they're in Sweden again.' At the last letter, he stopped and squinted. 'And one for you, sister dear.'

'Pardon?' Maisie blinked, looking startled. 'For me?'

'Yes, from your solicitor.' He slid it across the table towards her, and she picked it up tentatively, as if it might bite. 'I wonder what that's about; perhaps he's found a new clause in the will stating that any air I breathe upon the estate I must compensate you for at a rate of—'

'Henry,' I cut in, a note of warning in my voice, but Maisie did not even seem to have noticed. She was too busy opening the letter, prying off the seal with an almost reverent care. It occurred to me that this was the first letter she had received in all the time we had stayed in Inverness. Surely she must have friends who wrote to her on occasion, companions from her schooldays? But then, I supposed, I hardly had such things either. Besides the occasional exchange with acquaintances from our scientific circles, my only regular correspondents were Mr and Mrs Jamsetjee and my grandmother's nurse. (A sweet girl, the daughter of the local reverend, who since my grandmother's attack of gout the year before had sent me frequent updates on her health, apparently under the impression that she would have written to me herself if only her joints had permitted it.) I had written to Catherine once, too, of course – more than once. Several times after she had left Wight.

But she had never replied.

My rather gloomy train of thought was interrupted by a cry of outrage. I looked up in time to see Henry push to his feet and stalk around the table, brandishing a sheet of paper.

'Would you look at this clipping Prestwich sent me!' he cried. It was a picture from the *Illustrated London News* showing a sculpture of a gargantuan reptile. With the pointed horn upon the end of its snout, it looked something like a scaled rhinoceros. But this was not the most unusual part of the illustration; no, the strangest part was the fact that inside the beast's hollow back, a number of gentlemen were seated at a table for dinner.

'What on earth is this, Henry?' I asked, peering closer. In sharp woodcut relief, waiters mounted stairs and platforms to bring the diners their meals; candelabras lit the sculpture from within, as strange a sight as it was remarkable.

'*This* is a dinner party Prestwich attended on New Year's Eve. To celebrate Professor Owen and Mr Waterhouse Hawkins's sculptures, which are to be displayed this summer at the Crystal Palace.'

'Oh dear, that can't be – is that really Owen's *Iguanodon*?' I had seen rough sketches of the proposed statues before, presented at the Geological Society, but only the *Plesiosaurus* had been close enough for me to study it in detail. Despite Henry's long-standing vendetta against Owen – a rather one-sided vendetta, it must be said, largely inherited from his mentor, Professor Grant – I had not been able to help the thrill of excitement that had run through me at the prospect. To see such a creature, not as a fleshless skeleton or a picture on a page, but as a *body*, the size it would have been in life! What did it matter, then, if the plesiosaur's neck had been too curved? If Owen planned to show it crawling across the shore in a ridiculous manner its joints would surely not have allowed?

But this creature before me now – well, this was another matter entirely.

'It looks more like an elephant than a lizard,' I muttered.

'Who is Professor—?' Maisie began, before Henry interrupted her.

'It does! Have you ever seen anything more ridiculous? What nerve Owen has, proposing such a model from a mere handful of bones; and what nerve *Prestwich* has, sending me details of an engagement to which we were never invited!'

I paused, having been poised a moment before to join Henry in his mockery of the *Iguanodon*. 'Henry, why would you ever wish to spend an evening in Owen's company? You have always said that he is a malignant fraud, appropriating work not his own.'

'I would not, indeed, wish to spend an evening with him. But I do resent not being invited. Listen here—' He grabbed the paper from me and began to read. '"Mr Hawkins conceived the idea of bringing together those great names whose high position in the science of palaeontology and geology would form the best guarantee for the severe truthfulness of his works." The "severe truthfulness"? Clearly, he only invited those he knew to be supporters of Professor Owen already! And that was intended to verify the work's truthfulness? What a sham. What a sham *indeed*!'

And with that, Henry turned and marched from the room, holding the paper aloft like a flag bearer marching into battle. Maisie caught my eye.

'It is good to see he has mellowed with age,' she murmured, and I could not help but laugh.

'WHAT EXACTLY IS it that has Henry so bothered, anyway?'

It was a grey afternoon, the sky hung heavy with clouds, and Maisie and I were out by the shore. Henry had shut himself in the study since the morning, declining lunch and all attempts at conversation, but even on an ordinary day it was unlikely he would have accompanied us. The firth in winter was 'hopelessly bleak', he said, and although I could not argue otherwise, I was always glad of a chance to breathe fresh air. Maisie knew the country well, but not too well in winter, I think; she was forever ushering me down winding footpaths, saying *there's a wonderful meadow this way, a beautiful little burn!* – only to find the place as grim and barren as everywhere else. She would frown then, and twist her lips in exasperation in the very same way that Henry did whenever something irked him, and I would laugh and promise her that I did not mind.

'You mean about Mr Waterhouse Hawkins's sculptures?' I asked, as we turned on to a little fenced lane we had never taken before, winding up the side of a nearby hill.

'Yes. I've never seen anyone so . . .' She paused, clearly struggling for a diplomatic choice of words.

'So enraged by a lot of statues?' I suggested, and I watched her stifle a laugh. 'Well, it isn't so much about the sculptures themselves as Professor Owen's design for them. His *Plesiosaurus*, for example; Owen has its neck curving like a snake or the neck of a swan, when its vertebrae really don't look as though they could have bent in such a fashion. And the *Iguanodon* Owen has standing like an elephant or some other mammal – with its legs placed squarely underneath its body – while Henry proposes that it would actually have crawled along like a lizard.' I frowned as a suspicion came over me. 'You know, Owen must have modelled it like a mammal on purpose – I'm sure of it. If he had given it a lizard-like stature, that would have fitted with Lamarck's theory that life originated in simple forms which have become more complex over time, but Owen *hates* Lamarck, of course, and so seeks to discredit him by proving that the *Iguanodon* was more advanced than modern lizards and . . . well.'

I made myself stop then, not only because it occurred to me that I was rambling but because we had reached a stile. After we'd clambered carefully over it, Maisie clutching my hand to steady herself as she hopped down off the last step, she swept her hair from her forehead and asked:

'Does it matter?'

I blinked, taken aback. 'What?'

She seemed to realize herself then, grimacing in embarrassment. 'I only meant . . . does it change anything? Whether the creatures moved one way or another? It's not as if . . . *knowing* will bring them back to life.'

I opened my mouth and closed it again, trying to put aside my indignation long enough to formulate an explanation. Of course it *mattered*; perhaps the knowledge would not help to build bridges, or make new medicines, but that was not all that science was about. Science was about the truth, about knowing what was possible and what was not; it was about the fervour I had felt looking upon the beached whale, or the fossil tooth in Catherine's palm. I had spent my whole life since in service to that same longing: the ravenous beast that was *curiosity*.

But how to explain such a thing? Could I explain it to someone who had never known such a feeling themself? Perhaps I could tell her about the whale, or the tooth – but would she be able to look past the bloodiness of it to the wonder within? I cast her a worried glance, imagining her lip curled in disgust. It was unbecoming, this hunger of mine. I knew that all too well.

But when I glanced at Maisie again, I realized that she was clutching a hand to her chest.

'Heavens, are you all right?' I asked, stopping in my tracks.

'Of course!' she cried, though her voice was too high. Her chest rose in short and jagged bursts; now that our footsteps on the gravel path had stopped, I could hear the terrible wheezing that accompanied her every breath. 'It's merely . . . the hill is perhaps a tad too . . . too steep for me.'

'Why didn't you say?' I ushered her over to the side of the path. 'Come now, let's rest a bit. There's an outcropping here, see – we can even see the water through the trees.'

'But what if . . . Henry wants your help this afternoon?' she gasped as we sat down. 'I don't want him . . . to be cross with you.'

'Oh, let him be cross. And besides, you saw the frenzy he was in this morning. He'll hardly have noticed we're gone.'

We sat there for a spell, staring out to sea while Maisie breathed raggedly in and out. After a quarter of an hour, however, I began to worry as her breath simply refused to be caught. I wondered if I ought to get her mare from the house; she had taken it on our walks before, when she was particularly tired, so that she might ride it on the way home. The prospect did not thrill me, for Henry's warning of the creature's temper had proved true, but just as I was about to steel myself and ask, Maisie reached into the pocket of her skirt.

'Speaking of things that will make Henry cross,' she muttered, with a ghost of a smile – and, to my utmost astonishment, she pulled out a packet of cigarettes and a little box of lucifer matches.

'Maisie!' I cried, somehow shocked and delighted and reproachful all at once. She gave a nervous chuckle and showed me the side of the packet.

'They're only for asthma! My doctor recommended them. Father never let me try them before.' She fumbled with her gloved fingers to light the match. 'They're supposed to calm the lungs. Or warm them up, at least.'

'And do they work?' I asked, incredulous. She did not reply at once, for she was busy taking a long breath from the cigarette. I stared at her in fascination. I had never seen a woman smoke before; not in person. Only in cartoons and caricatures, where the woman in question typically wore bloomers and a top hat, ordering her beleaguered husband to feed the baby while she went to the races. But looking at Maisie now, sitting with her elbow propped upon her knee, I forgot all that nonsense. She was a study in contrast: her dark mourning dress against the washed-out sky, the shadow of her bonnet against her pale cheek, the cigarette against the entirety of her personality. She reminded me of something, though I could not say what – a charcoal sketch, perhaps, or an actress resting between performances.

And then the image shattered as she snatched the cigarette out of her mouth and coughed, spluttering, into the crook of her elbow.

'Not . . . very well, evidently,' she croaked.

I nearly laughed at that, which made me feel quite terrible, until I realized that she was laughing, too – albeit in a raspy, watery-eyed sort of way. A moment later, we were lost in a fit of giggles.

'I don't make a very good rogue, do I?' Maisie managed, her hand pressed to her mouth.

'I'm afraid not.' I grinned. 'A shame. I was hoping to see the look on Henry's face when you started carrying around a pipe.'

Abruptly, her smile faltered. I cursed myself, feeling a pang of regret, as I always had in childhood when I managed to coax some small tide-pool creature from its shell only stupidly to scare it back in a moment later. She waved the cigarette back and forth, letting it blow out in the wind.

'Yes . . . I expect he wouldn't like that,' she said carefully, sliding the remainder of the cigarette back inside the pack. 'He never did like smoking. It reminds him too much of Father, I think. And drinking, too. He used to say he'd never touch a drop. But I suppose that must have become quite difficult, at social functions and such.'

'Yes, I suppose so,' I murmured, rather surprised at this; Henry had never expressed to me any great moral hatred of liquor. But he had never seemed overly fond of it, either. 'That explains why that wine at Christmas made him so ill, then. And last year, when we—'

I froze, having sailed myself into dangerous waters. I had been thinking of the previous October, the night before the anniversary – not our anniversary, you understand, but *the* anniversary – when I had come upstairs to find Henry sprawled in an armchair with a bottle of whisky in hand. I ought to have chided him, I supposed; I ought to have pried it from his hand like a good wife and begged him not to start down that road of sin. Instead, I had pried it from his hand and drunk from it myself. I nearly choked in the process, as it was the first (and only) time I had ever had true liquor. Nevertheless, Henry and I nearly finished the bottle, and in the morning I was sicker than I had ever been in my life – sicker, even, than I had been the summer before, when in the throes of morning sickness I had been sure I would die before I saw my daughter born.

And the part that struck me most, even now, was how glad I had been to have him with me. How glad I had been that that night, of all nights, he had chosen not to go out.

Maisie was looking at me, a wary curiosity in her eyes. When had she heard the news, I wondered? When had Henry sat down and put those awful words to paper, as I had done for Mr and Mrs Jamsetjee? Had Maisie mourned, or sent condolences? She must have; I remembered seeing her letters pile up un-answered, along with the rest, on the corner of Henry's desk.

Had she looked forward to being an aunt? Any more than I had looked forward to the slippery, terrifying prospect of becoming a mother?

I wondered, but I did not – could not – ask. It was all I could do to sit and stare out at the grey and anxious waters of the firth, a lump sitting hard in my throat.

'*Oh*,' said Maisie suddenly. I turned to her blearily and found that she was staring at her gloved hand. A moment later, I felt it myself – the pin-prick shock of something cold landing on the tip of my nose.

'It's snowing,' said Maisie wonderingly. I made a soft sound of agreement, watching as she caught another snowflake on her palm. And then, in sudden realization, I leaped to my feet.

'Oh! You shouldn't be outside in weather like this! We really ought to—'

But to my surprise, Maisie reached up and pulled at my arm to stop me.

'Let's stay a little longer,' she said, eyes shining. 'Please? I want to watch it fall.'

And so we did. By the time we walked home, little drifts had gathered at the sides of the road and the bare branches of the trees were dusted white. Maisie took it all in with utter glee, crunching tiny frosted weeds beneath her boot heel and gathering up handfuls of snow to press between her gloved hands. As we made our way down a particularly steep portion of the path, she reached out and took my arm to steady herself – and then, to my surprise, did not let go. I looked down at my feet, pleased to see the way our footsteps began to fall in sync.

'You act as if you've never seen snow before,' I chuckled.

She shot me a slightly conspiratorial smile. 'I haven't.'

I nearly tripped at that. 'What? But surely it snows here every winter?'

'Oh, yes, it does. What I should say is, I've *seen* it snow before, but only from my window. I've never been out in it.' There was a wistful note in her voice. 'In fact . . . before this year, I'd hardly been out in winter at all. Never past the end of the garden.'

'Truly? Not even when you were a girl?'

'Oh, especially not then. Ever since I was small, I've . . .' She seemed to be snatching for words again. 'I had scarlet fever, first. Very badly. And then, after that, the doctors thought I had consumption, but it turned out to be bronchitis, and then troubles with my heart, and asthma, and that's when my headaches started as well . . .'

'Good Lord,' I murmured, before I could stop myself.

'Yes, exactly.' She heaved a sigh. 'It was years ago. I'm better now. Mostly. I'm out of bed more days than not, but . . .'

Her face did not so much fall as drift gently downwards. She seemed too lost in thought to continue. I thought then that we would walk the rest of the way in silence, so that she might rest her lungs, but instead, after a rather shuddering breath, she burst out:

'It's the *sometimes* of it that no one understands. Father and Henry, they always acted as though if I climbed the stairs too quickly, I'd *die*, or else I should be able to do it again the next day or it was proof I'd been pretending, but it's not *like* that, it's not like . . . a missing leg or something of that sort, where I'd need to go about with my wooden one all the time. It's more like . . . the weather. Some days I can go out and walk and ride and sing and kick about in the sea, and other days I'm simply—'

She stopped again, as if she had bitten her tongue. I turned to look at her properly, at her cheeks flushed from the cold and the thin curls of frost-laced hair that had escaped from her bonnet, and I saw in her face something I had not seen before: *anger*. It was there only a moment; as soon as she saw me looking, she hid it away again.

It was as if I was uncovering her, I thought; bit by bit, grain by grain. I was reminded then of my honeymoon in Lyme, when I had watched a girl at a stall chipping out an ammonite from its bed of chalk. I had stood there for an age, entranced by the notion that there, smothered beneath layers of stone, lay whorls and ridges no human eye had ever seen before. Henry had stayed barely five minutes before announcing that he preferred his own fossils clean and tidy and ready to classify – that he would never have the patience for such a task.

But I thought I might.

THE MOMENT WE were back inside, stopping in the hall to shake the snow from our boots, Henry accosted us.

'I'm rewriting my lecture for the Geological Society this May,' he said, holding a stack of papers aloft with a flourish.

'But why? What for?' I cried.

Henry grinned. There was a slightly mad look in his eyes, like a man riding into battle, a general forging on against unwinnable odds. 'The evidence on which Owen based his creation of Dinosauria and their upright stance is pitiful. It's clear to anyone with a brain that he's only doing this out of vanity; the man thinks himself Cuvier, a prophet of science, creating entire orders out of mere handfuls of bones, but I shall expose him! And then we shall see who is one of the "great names" of palaeontology, eh? We shall see!'

'Henry,' I said, resisting the urge to press my fingers to my temples, 'Professor Forbes will never allow it. Owen is one of the Society's vice presidents.'

'And that makes him infallible? Immune to all criticism? Surely that old debacle with the belemnites disproves that. Besides, he is retiring as vice president this year. He is on his way out of the door, and I shall help shove him through it.'

I could see that he was in no mood to be reasoned with. Still, I thought sadly of the diagrams of marine fossils I had worked so hard to produce these past weeks. I heaved an irritated sigh. 'Will it require new illustrations, this lecture of yours?'

At this, at least, he looked a tad apologetic. 'A few, perhaps – but only simple ones, to demonstrate the differences between Owen's mammalian design and the traditional lacertian model. I promise we shall find some use for your other pictures; perhaps that book on introductory geology that Mr Murray proposed I do. I am sure a chapter on ancient sea life would fit quite nicely.' His lip curled. 'We shall just have to hope Owen doesn't turn his attention to ammonites next. He'll have them cartwheeling across the sea floor.'

'Perhaps your ancient reptiles stood up on two legs,' Maisie said absent-mindedly, pulling off her gloves. 'I did see a lizard do that once, at a fair. And a monkey, too. It ran around just like a person would.'

There was a prolonged pause. Henry looked rather startled, as though he had entirely forgotten she was there. I glanced between the two of them, catching Maisie's eye, and nearly laughed.

'Margaret, that is patently ridiculous,' Henry said at last. He turned back to me. 'I propose, my dear, that we leave this week. The annual meeting is on the seventeenth of February, so I shall talk to Professor Forbes about my change of topic then, but there are several books I will need to consult first. And besides,' he said, with a disgusted sweep of his hand towards the out-doors, and the clumps of muddy snow that we had tracked into the hall, 'I am sick to death of the countryside.'

He bustled out of the hall with his papers once more, leaving us in a metaphorical wake of dust. I turned to Maisie, wondering how I might wrangle Henry into giving her a proper goodbye before we left.

'Back to London it is, then, I suppose. I am ... sorry to be leaving you here on your own again.'

'Oh, I shall be all right.' Her tone was perfectly unruffled. I watched as she carefully folded her gloves, carefully laid them on the hall table, carefully straightened the vase Henry had set awry on his way out.

'I shall write.'

The words had spilled out of me with far more force than necessary. Maisie's head snapped up, and she blinked at me, owl-eyed. For a moment I was afraid I had been too bold. Perhaps she preferred her own company; perhaps there was a reason she did not receive letters; perhaps they were only a bother to her.

Perhaps, yet again, I had misread the situation.

But then, to my utmost relief, she broke into a smile.

'Yes,' she said quietly, her face bright as the daisies she had spent all that morning picking out in tiny white stitches. 'Yes, I should like that.'

6

The prospect of such an occupation made every other circumstance of existence pass before me like a dream, and that thought only had to me the reality of life.

*

Shall I not then hate them who abhor me? I will keep no terms with my enemies.

— MARY SHELLEY, *Frankenstein*

THERE IS AN art to socializing, I think; one, like many arts, which must be practised from infancy if one wishes to be any good at it. But then, I suppose, some people will never be masters, no matter how young they start. For I remember that the first time I sat before the pianoforte, watching my teacher's fingers flit across the keys, I thought, *That will never be me. I do not have it in me.*

It was the very same thought I had my first summer in London, while visiting with Mr and Mrs Jamsetjee.

It was my twentieth year then, in life and in Norton Green, and despite all my love for the island's chalk-white cliffs and crashing waves, I felt in that town like a tiger pacing its cage. My schooling was long over; my only occupations were drawing, reading, and agonizing over my prospects. My grandmother had made exceptionally clear to me from the beginning that she had promised my father she would provide for me for the rest of her life – though not, crucially, the rest of *mine*. In fact, the law forbade it, as, being illegitimate, I could not inherit her estate. Two paths stretched ahead of me, then: marriage or destitution. But with neither a dowry nor any of the practical skills required of a working man's wife, my options were few. The most likely candidate seemed to be the widower Thomas Doyle, whose three raucous children I watched slapping each other like feral cats in the backmost pews of All Saints' Church each Sunday, and whom my grandmother was continually inviting over for dinner. For someone who had for the previous nineteen years expressed no interest whatsoever in helping me find a match, this sudden fervour was both confusing and suspicious, founded not at all upon any indication of interest from Mr Doyle that I could see, but rather – I was sure – upon the fact of his recently having purchased a sizeable house overlooking the sea. Our own home was a mediocre affair, its furnishings and decorations hastily redone following the awful fire thirty years before; clearly, after all the years my grandmother had fed and clothed me, she expected repayment in the form of more elegant lodgings in which she might spend her final years. But, to her credit, it was also true that Mr Doyle was likely the only man on the island who would overlook my shortcomings, so long as I could be a mother for his children.

I wondered at times whether spinsterhood was so wretched an option, even if it would mean a life of laundry and piecework, all the toil of servanthood with none of the company. I had even wished occasionally that I could simply *be* a servant – that my ruined housemaid of a mother had lived, and raised me; that I had skills and references and a place among my peers, however lowly. I could be content in such a life, I told myself. It would never even have occurred to me, surely, to want for more.

(It would be some months still before I found the piece of paper hidden between the pages of my father's Bible, covered in words written neatly on the left and messily on the right, as though by two different people – one teaching the other to write. At the bottom, there were names: *Elizabeth Brown, Elizabeth Brown. William Frankenstein, William Frankenstein.* And there, once, in hopeful lopsided letters: *Elizabeth Frankenstein.* It is in all our natures, I suppose, to want for more.)

My saving grace that year had come in the form of a letter. Ever since Catherine had left for France, I had been corresponding with Mr and Mrs Jamsetjee; at first small and stilted letters (*Have you heard from Catherine? Do I have her right address?*) which led to longer ones (*Yes, I have been practising with the charcoals you left me; I like them very much, though I must ask (and I beg your urgent response), how does one remove charcoal stains from a pale dress sleeve . . . ?*) and longer still (*Can you tell me more, sir, of Cuvier? Of the Liassic era, and the Oolitic?*). I kept our correspondence secret, terrified – in the way of all children who are used to being pointlessly denied small joys – that my grandmother would forbid it. And it was no small joy, certainly; each time I collected one of their letters from the post office, answering them while perched on a nearby wall with my pencil stabbing through the paper to my knee below, I felt as though I had entered another world – one in which I was an artist, a naturalist, a woman of letters. Someone *worth* writing to.

I could not fathom at the time why they showed me such kindness. Their motives became clear to me eventually: when Mr Jamsetjee told me of his own mentor, an Englishman who had visited his family's shipyard and invited him to study in London; when I saw in their parlour a daguerreotype of a young girl with dark hair and a garland of flowers about her neck, clutching a book to her chest as if she would not be parted from it even for the time it took to take the picture; when I asked Mrs Jamsetjee why, if she had so enjoyed the year she and her husband had once spent in Bombay, and given how much they both hated the weather in her native England, they had not moved back.

'Our daughter is buried here,' she had said, very quietly. 'We could not leave her.'

I was a replacement, then. But I did not mind; how could I? They were a replacement of sorts for me, as well.

Still, when Mrs Jamsetjee wrote to my grandmother that spring to ask if I might spend the summer with them in London, to accompany Catherine on her 'coming out', I was shocked. Shocked by the generosity of the offer, shocked that Mr and Mrs Jamsetjee clearly did not know that their niece and I were no longer on speaking terms . . . less shocked, however, when my grandmother declared that she forbade it. For a week I stewed in utter dejection, dreading the reply I would have to write to the Jamsetjees refusing their generosity, wondering if it was for the best, after all, that I did not have to face Catherine again – until another letter arrived, one which I was able to snatch directly from the postman under the guise of courteously bringing in the post.

Most unfortunately, it appears that my niece is unable to come, the letter began. *Still, as it is our last summer in London (as I am sure Miss Brown has already relayed to you, we are planning to move to Canterbury in the new year), would she like to come anyway, and see my husband present at the British Association?*

It was not a difficult decision. I sent off my reply before the ink was even dry (feigning my grandmother's approval), poked a hole in the toe of an old pair of shoes which were too small for me anyway, and showed the sorry sight to my grandmother. With the money she gave me for a new pair, I went to town and bought a ferry crossing and a train ticket. If I were to be stuck for the rest of my life on Wight, I reasoned, then at least I would have had one short summer in which to see the world. And I was nigh certain that my grandmother would not chase after me – not least because I had shredded the letter which Mrs Jamsetjee had sent her, so that she would not know at which address to find me.

And so that year I found myself introduced to society, albeit of a very different sort than that to which women of my age usually found themselves being introduced: chemists and geologists, mathematicians and astronomers, men whom I'd known for years as nothing more than names upon a page. Yet here they were now, in the flesh, eating and drinking and talking as though they were ordinary people. And here, too, were their wives, floating about the halls like blooming flowers upon water, with such marvellous tales to tell – particularly the geologists' wives, who spoke quite casually of traipsing alongside their husbands across glaciers and glens, hammering away at cliff-sides in Germany or Spain. Mrs Lyell spoke five languages, all the better to organize Mr Lyell's expeditions; the Lady Trevelyan had met her husband at a meeting of the British Association, and been gifted a box of fossils as a proposal. I remember staring at her over dinner, at the curls in her hair and the rings on her delicate fingers, thinking, *They let you do such things?*

And, *This is precisely what I must be.*

But there were obstacles, of course. My parentage, for one – although I kept that as secret as I could – my dowdy dresses, my provincial manners . . . From the very beginning I stood a step behind, a world apart. I oscillated wildly between speaking too little and too much, scaring away those I was most keen to befriend with the sheer ferocity of my admiration.

I did try, in the beginning, to learn. I threw myself into the study of society as thoroughly as I had thrown myself into natural history; I asked Mrs Jamsetjee to help me put up my hair and alter my dresses, picked apart her every conversation and exchange of pleasantries as if to expose the workings of a complex machine. But I soon found that, despite all her grace and skill as a teacher of art, when it came to the intricacies of socialization, she was little more experienced than myself. She was a quiet soul, with only one or two close friends, and rarely accompanied her husband to social events at the many organizations of which he was a member. I had asked her why, once, during one of our morning sketching sessions upon the banks of the Thames, and she had said with a note of gentle laughter in her voice:

'It simply doesn't interest me very much. Oh, I know, please don't start telling me interesting facts, I have enough of that from Jehangir already. I simply don't like being around all those people. It's always noisy and hot, and sometimes . . .' She grew more serious then, all traces of mirth disappearing from her face. 'Sometimes, they make me very angry.'

As the summer wore on, I came to understand exactly what she meant. Because for all London felt like an ocean into which one might drop like a penny and disappear – for all that scientific society prided itself on being an enlightened crowd, far above gossip or judgement – it was not. I began to notice cold glances, stifled whispers, false smiles. Perhaps my habit of dodging the topic of my parentage had finally led someone to crack the puzzle; perhaps my dresses were simply too awful; or perhaps – and in truth, I suspected it was something of all three . . .

Perhaps it was due to my absolutely wretched temper.

'You must *stop* this,' Mr Jamsetjee said one evening, after he had dragged me from the ruins of yet another conversation and into an adjacent hallway.

'I know, I know it was rude!' I said through clenched teeth, hands balled into fists. 'I am sorry for making a scene. But I simply cannot stand—'

'*You* cannot stand it?' he said, eyebrows arching. I wilted beneath his gaze. The red was fading from my vision now, shame rising in me like bile. It was not the first time I had lost my temper so, after all. Never because of anything said about me – for one can hardly fight whispers outright without seeming like a madwoman, batting at cobwebs – but about *him*. For regarding my mentor, I had learned, most did not even bother to whisper.

I will admit I was ignorant of a great many things before that summer. I knew that India was governed by the East India Company, an administration which I would later see called – in one of the rare dissenting pamphlets – 'an outrage upon all the higher feelings of mankind'. I knew that the residents of

Newport complained about the lascar sailors, their 'uncouth and lazy' ways. But was that not simply the way of the world? Was that not what people said of *all* sailors? Somehow I had thought that whatever prejudice existed against Mr Jamsetjee's countrymen, he himself must be immune, insulated by his position and accomplishments. But minutes earlier, I had listened with astonishment as a young geographer told us both, in the earnest tones of one under the impression he was paying a compliment:

'Each of the races has their own strengths, of course! Negroes have outstanding endurance, for example, which is what makes them so suited to outdoor work. But it is the white race that is naturally the most advanced in terms of culture and intelligence. And of course,' he'd carried on, quite cheerfully, 'there are the differences in facial features – the more rational peoples tend to have thin noses, strong brows, and so on. I can see that you have quite an aquiline nose, Mr Jamsetjee . . . Have you thought you might perhaps have European ancestry? I suspect that many of the individuals who have been able to overcome the natural obstacles of their race and improve themselves to the extent that they rival even the greatest minds of Britain must be—'

At which point I had cut in to ask which natural obstacles had prevented him from being admitted to Cambridge, something I knew from past conversation he had attempted to do upwards of five times – but barely had I begun speaking before Mr Jamsetjee extricated us both neatly from the conversation and pulled me away.

'This is not a stage, my dear,' he said to me now, words clipped. 'There is no audience to applaud you, no line scathing enough that you might change anyone's mind.'

I felt heat rise to my cheeks. 'But that man is misusing science to—'

'That man is the nephew of a Company supervisor. And I think you will find he was using phrenology for precisely the purpose it was designed.' I watched as he heaved a sigh, pinching the bridge of his nose. He looked so very tired all of a sudden, his face thrown into gaunt pools of shadow under the wavering gaslight. 'You may scold all you want when I am not here, but when I am, it shall reflect badly *on me*, do you understand? My family's business partners will think me "uncivilized"; the Company will take their contracts elsewhere. They will construct their own shipyard, staffed by British engineers and British workers. The business my grandfather founded, each one of my countrymen whose wages depend on my dealings in this country – all of that is in jeopardy if I so much as irritate the wrong man. Do you see?'

I stared at him with a miserable sort of indignation. At last, unwinding my fingers from where they were bunched in the fabric of my dress, I managed:

'I am sorry, sir. I promise you, it will not happen again. It is only . . . I didn't . . . I am not used to having the means to make a fool of anyone but myself.'

He gave me a dry look. 'It might benefit you to be more cautious for your own sake, too. A smile and a pleasant manner will open any number of doors.'

'Including the door to the Royal Society, sir?' I retorted, before I could stop myself. At that, he could only grimace.

'I only wish . . .' I murmured, tipping back my head to lean against the florid wallpaper. I wished for so much, and none of it feasible. 'I only wish I could have kicked him. Just once. It's the principle of the thing.'

That drew a chuckle out of Mr Jamsetjee, however brief, before his face grew heavy once more. 'This country ... this *empire* ... is a ship, Miss Brown. It is hard enough to stage a mutiny from the deck, but if one starts in the water, well ... One cannot afford principles, if one is trying not to drown.'

I nodded mutely. A peal of laughter drifted in from the parlour; our heads turned as one to face it. I watched as he visibly steeled himself, jaw growing tight.

'Well, back to the fray,' he muttered.

'Do you want to leave?'

He seemed nearly as shocked by my question as I had been. These past weeks, despite the agony of polite conversation, I had begged to stay at every function till its end, desperate to wring every moment from this summer.

'... Do you?' he asked, brow furrowed in confusion.

'That is not what I asked, sir.'

Once again, he chuckled; but when he met my eyes, he must have seen the seriousness in them, for he grew serious, too. He held my gaze, unblinking, and for one brief moment – one that has stuck in my heart, in all the years since – he was not my untouchable mentor, almost forty years my senior. I was not his daughter's ghost, a flimsy substitute for a girl I had never met. He was simply my friend, and I his.

'I do,' he admitted at last.

I smiled. 'I shall go and hail us a cab, then. If you would pay our respects to Mr and Mrs Brewster ... ?'

He nodded, and returned to the parlour in search of our hosts. Was this one more thing I would have to learn, then, I wondered as I made my way downstairs? Not just the art of conversation, but the art of knowing when *not* to speak? I thought of what Mr Jamsetjee had said, of ships and of drowning – but he held the fate of dozens in his hands. I held only my own. What would I have done, if he had not been with me? Was I drowning enough to merit holding my tongue in the face of malice and stupidity? And what good did they do anyway, these scathing rebukes of mine – what good, *really*?

'Miss Brown, isn't it?'

I stopped at the foot of the stairs and turned to find a man standing in one of the adjacent doorways, drink in hand. We had been introduced before, I knew, although to my mortification I found I had entirely forgotten his name. I had not forgotten his face, however, for it was a singular one: sharp features, a trim moustache, and eyes almost disarming in their intensity. He smiled, adjusting the lapels of his sapphire-blue coat.

'Forgive me, madam. I only wanted to ask . . . it was you with whom I spoke briefly at the British Association last week, was it not?'

'It was, yes. Mr . . .' Something Scottish, I recalled; he did have the accent, though it wasn't very strong, presumably diluted by time spent in London. 'Somerville, was it?'

His lip quirked, and I felt heat rise to my cheeks.

'Sutherland,' he said good-naturedly as he took my proffered hand – for, of course, it was Henry. 'But you were very close. I could not help but overhear, Miss Brown . . . Earlier this evening, you mentioned that you had recently finished reading Agassiz's *Études sur les glaciers* – is that correct? What did you think of it?'

'Why yes, I did. I enjoyed it. I have never seen a glacier myself, and Mr Agassiz's observations on their movements were quite fascinating.' Feeling a need to justify myself then, for the book was not a recent one, I added: 'I have been meaning to read it for some time, of course, but unfortunately my French was . . . wanting.'

He chuckled. 'You are not alone there, Miss Brown! I resolved some time ago that I would read all Cuvier's works in the original French – for the principle of the thing, you see – but it has been the better part of a decade now, and I am still barely halfway through his *Recherches sur les ossemens fossiles*.'

'Oh, but his illustrations for that series are remarkable, aren't they? For the first two volumes, at least; I cannot speak to the others, as I haven't been able to find them yet. Does he include more of his anatomical reconstructions in the rest?'

'He does! They're just marvellous, you must see them. In fact . . .' Over the rim of his wine glass, he gave me a look that was almost appraising, and I could feel a blush creeping up my neck. 'If you would like to read the rest of Cuvier's *Recherches*, Miss Brown, I do have the full set. And not just in French, I must add. I would be happy to lend them to you. It is a rare thing to meet a lady with an interest in such matters, and I would be only too happy to help you foster it further.'

The first part of this offering thrilled me no end; the second part left a bitter taste in my mouth, one that soured further the more I thought on it. For one long moment, I willed myself to dismiss it, to thank him graciously and carry on. But it had been a long and weary evening, and I was already brittle, and so – giving in to the urge with the same sweet relief as finally clawing at an insect bite – I opened my mouth.

'Is it?'

Henry's eyebrows rose. 'Pardon?'

'Is it truly such a rare thing to find ladies who are interested in geology, and the writings of Agassiz and Cuvier? You are standing in a building full of them, as we speak. I heard Mrs Lyell talking of Cuvier not half an hour ago; it is her husband, after all, who is foremost in opposing Cuvier's theory of catastrophism.'

'Yes; yes, of course,' Henry said hastily. 'Forgive me, Miss Brown. I meant it only as a compliment. I—'

'A theory which is, while we are speaking of it, quite ridiculous,' I babbled on. 'And I must say, in truth, although Agassiz's observations on glaciers are fascinating, I find his adherence to such a theory absurd as well. They insist such a model is more consistent with Genesis, and yet, if the eras of geological history were divided by a dozen Great Floods instead of one, would not the Lord have thought to *mention* that, at the very least? And – well. In any case, I see that my companion is ready to leave, so I must go. I hope you have a lovely evening.'

And with that, I turned, face burning, to take up Mr Jamsetjee's arm as he descended the last few steps. I practically dragged him towards the front door, so sure then that I had ruined everything for the second time that evening; so sure that the chuckle which rang out behind me was one of derision or incredulity. And yet, some days later, a package was delivered to the Jamsetjees' house. It was addressed to me, and contained within its brown paper wrapping the third volume of Cuvier's *Recherches sur les ossemens fossiles*, together with a short note.

I am quite sceptical of Monsieur Cuvier's catastrophism, too, as it happens; although his anatomical reconstructions remain sublime. If you wish ever to borrow the rest of the series, I would be delighted to supply it.

Later, in our letters, Henry would admit that his approaching me while my chaperone was elsewhere that evening had been quite deliberate, as he had for some time suspected that Mr Jamsetjee did not very much like him. This suspicion proved to be correct, for on the carriage journey home, when my mentor asked with whom it was that I had shared such a spirited conversation before we left the party, and I mentioned Henry's name, he responded with a carefully measured: 'Ah.' From a diplomatic soul like Mr Jamsetjee, this was such a damning condemnation that I found it almost amusing. My amusement disappeared, however, as the summer wore on, and my correspondence with Henry became – through the sheer force of his wit, and his genuine interest in my scientific opinions – something like a courtship. Mr Jamsetjee's consternation visibly grew, until at last I felt compelled to ask him what on earth was so awful about Henry Sutherland.

'He is not . . . *sensible*, Miss Brown. The very first I heard of the man, it was that he had nearly unsettled a card table arguing with some colleague or other about the classification of fossil cirripedes.' The distaste on his face was plain, more than he ever usually cared to let show. 'And he's one of Professor Grant's disciples, of course.'

'Well, I heard Mr Sutherland's account of the cirripede incident, and he said— Wait a moment, what is the matter with Professor Grant?'

'He is a radical. Which is to say, nothing is the *matter* with him, but you must consider what others will think – which positions your Mr Sutherland will be blackballed for, those who campaign for him to be removed from the Geological Society, just as Grant was ousted from the Zoological . . .' His face twisted in a complicated expression. 'I merely think that . . . you cannot let yourself be blinded by flattery, Miss Brown! You must think of the future, too. You are young yet; you can find someone better, can you not?'

I thought then, as my face fell, that he would realize he had overstepped, but he did not. It wounded me deeply that he thought me so foolish, so vain – that he expected me to articulate why I could not simply 'find someone better'. Were the myriad reasons not obvious? And did he truly believe I was not thinking of the future in all this, that I was just some silly girl in love? Who was he to treat me like a child – like *his* child, who might have lived all her life a spinster if she wanted, secure in her father's affections?

Increasingly, it seemed that Henry was the only one in the world who believed I had a brain.

Despite Mr Jamsetjee's disapproval of my courtship, I still bore a desperate hope that the news might sway my grandmother. After all, had she not been encouraging me to marry? Might the prospect of retiring to a new townhouse in London be even better than a house by the sea? When I eventually returned to Wight in the autumn, however, I knew the cause was lost as soon as I stepped foot in the house. She was in a rage the likes of which I had never quite seen before. I was a wretched child, she said; a liar, a thief, a whore, et cetera. I endured all this with my jaw set and my heart heavy, certain now that not only would she forbid my courtship with Henry – she would never allow me to leave the island again. The mere notion would be a weakness on her part, an admission that I had been right to disobey her. That I was worthy of something better.

I lasted four months. I had to, in any case, for by law I was not allowed to marry without my guardian's permission until my twenty-first birthday. It was the very day after that I sat at my desk, pressed the nib of my pen to the page so hard that it sputtered and bled, and wrote those three words.

Take me away.

There was no guarantee that Henry would agree, of course. To elope against the wishes of one's family was a great stain on one's reputation, a cardinal sin against etiquette. If it became widely known, there was no telling how many of Henry's friends and connections would turn against him. (Nor what my mentor would make of such a decision.) But Henry had told me already of his father, and the 'terrible Margaret'. I could tell that he did not care if he shocked and dismayed his family; in fact, he would probably enjoy it. His letters had by then grown ardent and impassioned, declaring his affection for me with a recklessness I would come to know as quite typical on his part. He was a gambler, after all – to him, risk was hardly a deterrent.

And I suppose, in fairness, there must have been something of the gambler in me, too. For despite how much I longed to think myself a sensible and rational soul, I had sat and penned that letter, wagering all I had left on the chance that he would agree (as he did, without hesitation) to my proposal.

Perhaps I am meant to drown after all, I remember thinking, worrying at my lip until I tasted blood. *But if I do, then at least it will have been by my own hand.*

7

So Cuvier says; – and then shall come again
Unto the new creation, rising out
From our old crash, some mystic, ancient strain
Of things destroy'd and left in airy doubt:
Like to the notions we now entertain
Of Titans, giants, fellows of about
Some hundred feet in height, not to say miles,
And mammoths, and your winged crocodiles.

　　　　　　　　　　　— LORD BYRON, *Don Juan*

The combination of such characters ... will, it is
presumed, be deemed sufficient ground for establishing a
distinct tribe or sub-order of Saurian Reptiles, for which
I would propose the name of Dinosauria.

　　　　　　　　— PROFESSOR RICHARD OWEN,
　　　　　　　　'Report on British Fossil Reptiles'

AS SOON AS we returned home from Inverness, we were
plunged once more into a sea of responsibilities. There were
articles to write, diagrams to be illustrated, budgets to be revised –
for though Henry managed the bulk of our finances, and had
assured me several times now that since his father had paid off

his debts we were close to getting back on our feet, the household allowance was still mine to spend as I saw fit. (And I saw fit to ensure that the household ate as much onion and watercress soup as it could stand.) The social season was not yet in full swing, and would not be until April at least, but as I have said before, science is as much a game of connections as of skill; and so this year, as every year, like a young debutante at court, Henry was desperate to meet every man in London – provided those men were geologists, chemists or anatomists.

By night we attended dinners and lectures and meetings, ears pricked for word of any new position that might suit Henry; by day, we yawned and scrubbed our eyes and set to work. One bright morning, however, as I tried to dash off a letter to Maisie before breakfast, Henry handed me something new – not another article, nor a chapter for the geology primer which Mr Murray had indeed approved, but the latest version of his lecture for the Geological Society. He must have been working on it furtively, so that he might spring it on me now, like a trap, in its finished form. He watched me as I read it, elbows propped expectantly upon his knees. Barely had I reached the last line before he said:

'Well? How is it?'

'Henry,' I said, setting down the papers with a sigh, 'this is the sort of thing I would write.'

His eyes brightened. 'Really? You like it, then?'

'No, I mean it's the sort of thing I would write as a first draft, then have to throw away on account of it being far too scathing to read in public. Did Professor Forbes really agree to this?'

He frowned. 'He . . . agreed to the initial concept. But why shouldn't I be scathing? Owen—'

'I'm not disagreeing with you,' I said. 'We both know that Owen is wrong. I am merely telling you what the rest of the Society will think if you read a lecture as vitriolic as this – that you're picking a fight with a more accomplished geologist out of jealousy.'

'But it is *science*, Mary; the whole point of the thing is that we should argue with each other till we are blue in the face. Why else do we ever meet in person? Rebuking someone via monograph simply doesn't have the same panache,' he said drily. He gave a smile, insouciant, and plucked his papers from the desk. 'Owen has made plenty of enemies over the years; I'm sure I'll find allies among them!'

'Henry—' I began, but he was already gone. Groaning, I slumped back in my chair and returned my attention to the letter I'd been writing. It was a tedious thing, really, meandering on about the weather and the London traffic; but then, that was only because Maisie kept asking me tedious questions. I had been so pleased to receive her first letter – and relieved, too, to find proof in paper and ink that I was capable of companionship after all – but the contents, to my dismay, had been . . . stiff. Polite. Precisely the sort of meaningless pleasantries she would have expressed to me in the first week of our acquaintance. I had lost ground with her somehow, I felt. And with each trite reply I sent, I lost more.

In a fit of frustration, I took up my pen and dashed a line across all that I'd written so far. Before I knew it, I'd continued:

What must it be like, do you think, to run about saying whatever one likes, as so many gentlemen do? To have one's flaws and misdeeds attributed not to one's sex, or the manner of one's birth, but to one's character alone? I should like that, I think; to make an utter fool of myself, and be regarded not as a bad example of womanhood, but merely a bad example.

It was a ridiculous thing to say. Wholly inappropriate. The

sort of thing, once again, I might write as a first draft, before tossing it promptly into the fireplace. But this time, I did not let it burn; instead, I folded it up and sealed the envelope before I could lose my nerve.

It was only later, as I walked back from posting it, that I realized I really ought to have written *Margaret*, not *Maisie*, upon the front.

AS MAY NEARED, the weather grew warm. This was not so welcome a thing in the city as it might have been in the country, where wide-open spaces and breezes might stir the air. In London, the streets were hazy and humid, the stench of the Thames so awful some days that one could not venture out without a perfumed handkerchief through which to breathe. At long last, as the whole of the city seemed to come to a boil – with respect both to temperature and to the growing excitement around the grand reopening of the Crystal Palace – it came time for Henry to give his lecture.

Though we left early enough, the streets of Covent Garden were so congested that we arrived at the meeting almost too late to get in. Fortunately, after some haggling with the doorman, we were admitted, and Henry and I separated to find seating. While there was ostensibly a section for women on the upper floor, clearly signposted in the entryway, there was not a chance I would resign myself to those sweltering heights in such weather, and from the look of the crowd I glimpsed through the doors there were a number of other ladies who had decided likewise. Pretending not to hear the feeble cries of the attendant who called after me, I darted into the main hall and had just found a spot at the edge of the auditorium, pressed against a delightfully cold stone pillar, when I caught sight of someone waving at me from one of the foremost rows of seats. It was Mrs Murchison, an amiable woman of older years and a frequent attendee of such meetings. She and her husband, the esteemed Roderick Murchison, were the regular hosts of magnificent soirées at their house in Belgrave Square, attended by some of the finest scientific and political minds in England. Though I still did not know quite how he managed it, Henry had secured us a rare invitation to one such soirée earlier that year.

'Mrs Sutherland!' Mrs Murchison exclaimed when I drew near. Beside her sat two other ladies, a woman whom I recognized as the wife of Mr Charles Lyell and a pretty young Quakeress I did not know. 'It is Mrs Sutherland, isn't it? I saw your husband's name on the programme today. Might I introduce you to Mrs Mary Lyell and Miss Caroline Fox?'

'Oh – why, yes. It is a pleasure to meet you both. And yes, he is presenting today.' Mrs Lyell (whom I had in fact met before, though she clearly did not remember me) greeted me warmly, and Miss Fox rather more lukewarmly, though I was not sure whether that was due to any prejudice towards me or simply because of the abysmal heat. Fanning herself with a copy of the programme, Mrs Lyell leaned forward and said:

'Well, you'll be wanting a prime seat, then, won't you? *Leonard!*' Abruptly, she reached out and rapped the back of the chair in front of her. The young man currently occupying it, who could not have been older than seventeen, jumped and shot her a reproachful look.

'Nephew, dear, give this young lady your seat, won't you?'

'Thank you, but that isn't—' I protested, but the browbeaten Leonard had already departed. 'Thank you, Mrs Lyell. That is very kind.'

'Don't mention it, my dear. That upper floor is bound to be absolutely dreadful today.'

'And with all that dark wood, and no proper lighting!' Mrs Murchison tutted. 'My eyes aren't what they used to be, you know; those stairs will be the death of me. That's precisely what I said to the dreadful little man guarding the door – are you trying to kill me, sir? Trying to cause the death of a poor old woman?'

'I saw you take three flights at a run last week,' said Mrs Lyell.

'Hush, you.'

'It's a lucky thing we're let in at all,' Miss Fox said gravely. 'Do you remember that British Association meeting, the talk about marsupial reproduction?'

'Oh, yes! Before your time, Mrs Sutherland; they let us in for the geology and natural history lectures, but when it came to zoology, they tried to bar us from the room! "Sensitive topics" to be discussed, they said. Far too inappropriate.'

'For a married woman?' Mrs Lyell asked drily.

'Precisely! Well, Miss Fox, you aren't married yet – what did you think? Were you scandalized?'

Miss Fox raised her eyebrows. 'By the quality of the lecture? Of course. After all that nonsense, and having to elbow our way in, the speaker was simply dreadful.'

'He went so red!' Mrs Lyell cackled. 'Kept mumbling and flipping through his papers; trying to pick out the parts that weren't so "sensitive", I think. We only got about half of it, in the end.'

'What is your husband lecturing on today, Mrs Sutherland?' Mrs Murchison asked.

'Ah – the last, I believe. On Owen's Dinosauria.'

Miss Fox's interest was piqued at that. 'Truly? Have you seen the plans for his statues at—?'

'Oh, it's starting!' Mrs Lyell gasped, waving a hand to quiet us.

The first lecture began, a fascinating presentation on what appeared to be particles of preserved *Ichthyosaurus* skin trapped within scratch marks upon a bone. I was glad for such an intriguing start, for judging by what I could see of the programme over Mrs Lyell's shoulder, the rest of the papers scheduled for the day seemed rather dry. I thought, and not for the first time, what a shame it was that the Palaeontographical Society merely published papers and did not meet in person; it would have been such a joy to hear of the latest palaeontological discoveries without also having to hear about estuarine sediments or coal mining in Somerset. It was not the rocks themselves that interested me, after all, so much as the world they concealed: an entire *sequence* of worlds, pressed flat like the pages of a book, all their snapping and snarling inhabitants reduced to little more than muddles of darkened bone. But palaeontology was a young science yet, geology's eager child, and even if her devotees had never been terribly interested in coal or railways or the digging of canals, we had to admit that such matters were quite inextricable from the study of ancient creatures – a vast number of which, after all, would never have been discovered if not for such excavatory works. And so I listened with as much interest as I could muster to a presentation on the distribution of gold in Wales, and in the meantime let my gaze drift about the crowd, pleased to see that Professor Owen did not seem to be in attendance. (For although the final draft of Henry's speech had turned out – with the liberal aid of my pen – considerably less scornful than the first, it was still not the sort of thing one ought to read to the man's face.)

As the evening went on, however, there was another upon whom my gaze kept snagging. There at the front of the hall, sitting next to Henry with the other lecturers, was a clean-shaven young man in a garish red waistcoat. I could not shake the feeling that I knew him somehow. Henry evidently did, for as the audience applauded he leaned over to mutter something in the man's ear, and the two of them laughed like schoolboys. When the man at last stood up to give his own lecture, Henry clapped him on the back. I found myself taut with anticipation as he mounted the dais and readied his papers, listening carefully for his name.

'Let us welcome to the stage,' the announcer called, 'Mr Finlay Clarke, FRS, presenting his research on the chemistry of the estuarine sediments and their parallels to the putrefaction of organic remains.'

At once, my hands clenched in my lap. *Finlay Clarke!* How could I ever have forgotten his face? He looked markedly different now, I supposed, from the insufferable boy of seventeen I still held in my memory. How dare he be in perfect health, enjoying what appeared to be a thriving career? And how *did* Henry know him?

Clarke's lecture was relatively short, thank God, for if it had gone on any longer I was sure I would have ground my teeth to dust. So intent was I on glaring at him as he exited the stage that I very nearly missed the beginning of Henry's presentation. It should not have mattered in any case, for I had heard him rehearse it so many times that I knew it nearly by heart; I was shocked, then, when I registered that it was taking a different course from the script we had agreed upon that very morning. It was, I realized with alarm, his original draft.

'Professor Owen attempts to follow in the footsteps of Monsieur Cuvier,' he was saying, more impassioned already than any other speaker that day, 'who, it is said, was able to identify the family to which an animal belonged on the basis of a single bone, and who indeed used this technique to successfully categorize numerous fossils. But it must be acknowledged that the sole reason we hold Monsieur Cuvier in such high esteem is that his taxonomical categorizations have since stood the test of time. Ordinarily, one would accuse any man of science who made such bold and untested claims of jumping to conclusions based on scanty evidence! Why, then, do we follow Professor Owen so blindly in his proclamation, nay, speculation, that the entire saurian order – of which there are, as yet, only three known species – adopted such a strange gait? And why, in addition, does he use a crocodile's ratio of vertebrae length to body length in his calculation of the *Iguanodon*'s size, if he is sure that the *Iguanodon* is so very different from the crocodile in its posture?'

There were a fair number in the audience, I noticed, who seemed swayed by Henry's lecture, or at the very least engaged by it; but there were far more who bore disapproving frowns or raised eyebrows, murmuring to their colleagues. Miss Fox, I saw, was especially stony-faced.

'In short,' Henry said at last, and I realized with irritation that he was still using the concluding sentence from the variation of the lecture I had written for him, 'we ought not to let the fact that Professor Owen's creations are now realized in stone . . .' a pause, a rather flippant smile '. . . set his underlying theories in stone as well.'

The hall filled with applause of a decidedly unenthusiastic sort. After a brief closing statement – for Henry's was the last paper of the day – the audience began to rise and exit the hall. Beside me, Mrs Murchison and Mrs Lyell said not a word. Miss

Fox wafted her fan slowly back and forth like the tail of an impatient cat, then snapped it shut and said sharply:

'Congratulations on your husband's research, Mrs Sutherland. Although I suppose it wasn't quite research, was it? More of a paper discrediting another's research. In any case, I must be going. Mrs Murchison, Mrs Lyell – it's been a pleasure.'

And with that, she rose and joined the departing crowd. My other two companions shared a horrified look.

'You must excuse Miss Fox,' said Mrs Murchison hurriedly. 'I believe Professor Owen was her tutor, wasn't he?'

'Yes. They still write, I think.'

Under ordinary circumstances, I might have taken the time to be embarrassed, but at that moment I could think of nothing but finding Henry. I excused myself as diplomatically as I could, and pushed past a sea of skirts and knees into the crowd. It took an age before I was close enough to Henry to grab his arm, and another age still to coax him away from the three elderly fellows with whom he seemed to be starting a very involved conversation.

'Well? How was it?' he asked, ebullient, once I had finally pulled him into relative privacy between two pillars. I was struck dumb for a moment. How could he not have noticed the lecture's poor reception?

'You changed your speech,' I noted, for it was all I trusted myself to say.

'Yes . . . I'd been thinking about it all morning, you see, and I really did like the old version. I brought it with me in case I changed my mind, and I showed it to my dear friend Clarke while we were waiting, and he assured me he liked the earlier version better, too. I think it really shook them, don't you? Given them something to talk about.'

'Your "dear friend Clarke"?' I managed. 'How do you know him?'

'Oh, we met while I was at university . . . about the town, you know.' He looked away for a moment, adjusting the sleeve of his shirt with practised nonchalance. From this, I surmised that the two of them had met in some dim gambling parlour; a rather concerning number of Henry's friendships seemed to have been forged thus.

'Why have you never mentioned him before?'

He blinked, clearly taken aback by my tone. 'Why, my dear, for the same reason I never told you I knew Frederick Field and Edmund Alexander Parkes at university.'

'Who?'

'Precisely! Because I didn't expect you'd have the faintest clue who he was. Clarke is primarily a chemist, though I suppose now he has taken up some work in the geological sciences, too – we don't cross paths often. Why, do *you* know him?'

'We both lived on Wight, when I was young.' I turned, glaring at the corner of the room where I had last seen him, though I had long since lost him among the bonnets and hats. 'He was a scoundrel and an ass.'

'My darling, all young men are scoundrels.' Henry gave a sigh. 'And I am an ass even now, and yet you still love me. You cannot hold a man accountable for every silly thing he did when he was young.'

'I will not have him in the house.'

'What a pity. I was about to ask him to move in,' he said archly. But before I could slap at his arm, Henry stepped aside and craned his neck.

'Ah! Look, there's old Professor Ellis – he taught me

anatomy at the University College. Quite a fine eye for tertiary mammalian anatomy, too, though he claims it's only a hobby. Come, I must talk to him!'

Professor Ellis was a large and ruddy-faced man who walked with the aid of a cane, though that did not seem to slow him in his efforts to push through the other fellows and leave the building; nor indeed did Henry's attempts at conversation, and I soon found myself chasing after the two of them as we descended the grand central staircase into the foyer.

'Ah, Mr Sutherland!' cried the man once Henry had finally caught his attention. 'A very interesting lecture, very interesting. And audacious of you, too; though I do worry you were perhaps too audacious in certain places.'

'What do you mean?' asked Henry, a note of stiffness to his voice. 'My criticisms of Professor Owen are fair. I merely intend to encourage a spirit of healthy scientific debate—'

'No, no. I was referring to what you said about the good *Monsieur Cuvier*. He may be a Frenchman, you know, but he is one of the founding fathers of the discipline.' He sucked air through his teeth. 'And as for Professor Owen — I will admit that I do not think your criticisms unfounded, but at this very moment, with the opening of the new Crystal Palace soon upon us . . . My dear man, I simply do not think that anyone will *care*.'

'Not care? But how could they not?' Henry exclaimed. We were out in the street now, where it had begun to rain quite biblically. The edge of the building was crowded with attendees who were sheltering under the overhanging roof, trying to flag down passing coaches. 'How could we, as honourable men of science, stand idly by while mere conjecture parades itself as fact in front of the public?'

'But the public is exactly the point!' Professor Ellis tilted his head to peer at Henry over his tiny spectacles. 'We are at the dawn of a new age, Mr Sutherland. The Crystal Palace is a celebration of progress, of the work of men of science all over our great empire – and who does not want *that* to be celebrated? Do you think your fellows would rather present themselves as a lot of bickering academics, or as noble detectives uncovering the secrets of the savage antediluvian past? I tell you, my daughter's children never cared one whit before when I tried to tell them about the progression of the geological ages, but ever since they saw that *Iguanodon* in the papers, they've been positively *begging* me to take them to see the exhibit this summer. And who am I to disappoint my grandchildren? Speaking of which, sir, I must get back. I promised them I would visit today.'

The professor tipped his hat in farewell and hailed a carriage. I grabbed at Henry's sleeve to prevent him from running out into the rain after the man, but that did not stop him from calling out: 'So we are politicians now, is that it? Servants of the masses, rather than servants of truth and knowledge?'

Professor Ellis gave Henry a rather pitying look as he opened the carriage door.

'Oh, Mr Sutherland. We have always been politicians.'

And with that, he was gone, leaving me and a scowling Henry in the rain.

WHEN WE GOT back from Covent Garden, sopping wet, I found a letter from Maisie waiting in the hall. I snatched it up at once, ignoring Henry's mutterings as he tore off his jacket and his dripping hat, and went into the study to read it. All the way home I had been in a temper about Finlay Clarke and Henry's bloody lecture and the abysmal weather, so I was quite surprised by the speed with which Maisie's letter pushed these anxieties from my mind – or rather, the speed with which it filled me with a new set of anxieties altogether. I had been wondering for a while now what she would make of my last letter; whether she would be offended by it, its brevity and strangeness, or whether she would indulge me and reply in kind. I had my answer by the first line.

Dear Mary, it began. *Oh dear. You're speaking of Henry, I imagine? What has he done now?*

At that, I had to put a hand to my mouth to stifle a laugh. I could just see Henry through the doorway, wringing out his socks straight on to the wooden floor, and for a moment it was as though she were in the room with me. I missed her, I thought suddenly; I hadn't even realized I did until that moment.

Forgive me, please, if I have guessed incorrectly, and you are speaking of someone else, Maisie continued. *But yes, I believe I know what you mean. When I was young, the neighbour's boy was an absolute horror – pulling my hair, kicking rocks at me when we walked to church, saying whatever horrid things he liked until I burst into tears. And of course, the only time I said something horrible back, my mother happened to hear it. Oh, the trouble I was in! And when I complained and told her why I'd done it, she only said that little boys were always fools – that as long as I set a good example, like a proper young lady, he would grow out of it. But I tell you, Mary, I have been the properest lady I can be all these years, and when I met him again in town last summer, he was quite the horror still!*

Do little boys ever grow out of being fools, I wonder? Or do they simply grow into something worse?

8

*He is eloquent and persuasive; and once his words had
even power over my heart: but trust him not. His soul
is . . . full of treachery and fiendlike malice.*

— MARY SHELLEY, *Frankenstein*

IT WAS IN my fourteenth year that I had the displeasure of
meeting Finlay Clarke. The Clarkes were old acquaintances of
my grandmother, relatives of the Viscount Hardinge of Derby,
though Derby's distance from Wight and the fact that Mr
Clarke had worked all his life as a banker might give a sense of
how distant this aristocratic relation truly was. Still, they were
our betters, and Mr Clarke's bank had earned him quite a fortune before he passed on the management to his younger
brother. Naturally, then, when the Clarkes moved that year to
nearby Yarmouth, my grandmother at once set about obtaining
an invitation to dinner – and to my great surprise, when the
invitation arrived, it was extended to me as well.

Prior to this, whenever my grandmother hosted or attended
a dinner, I was always hidden upstairs or left at home – though
whether this was due to my illegitimacy or simply my age, I
could not tell. I did not mind; I had never been a particularly
sociable creature, and ever since Catherine's departure for

France I had become even less so. Every hour I was not obliged to sleep or eat or learn my lessons, I would curl myself into the uncomfortable armchair in my grandfather's old study and read. The selection of books was not large, nor particularly to my taste – mainly novels and histories, essays upon business or theology. Still, I read it all. I read as a drowning man gasps for air, as if by filling my head with words I might also fill the hole Catherine's absence had left in me – as if I might make myself un-notice the fact that, though I had written to her twice already, she had sent no reply.

I knew why, of course. Or rather, I knew what I had done. But I did not know why it meant we could no longer be friends.

I wouldn't have needed much coaxing, then, to stay behind and spend the evening as I usually did – perfecting the art of self-pitying despair – had my grandmother not made one crucial mistake. For as she lectured me that afternoon on manner and dress (the possibility that I might not *want* to endure an evening of such scrutiny clearly never having crossed her mind), she added:

'. . . And you will by no means trifle with any of Mr Clarke's books, do you understand?'

At that, of course, I knew I must.

It was clear from the moment we entered Mr and Mrs Clarke's home which of the two had chosen to include me in the invitation. While the latter welcomed me quite amiably, Mr Clarke paid me little attention – even less when it became clear that my grandmother would not be offended by his doing so. My introduction went unacknowledged, my attempts at conversation ignored. I made my way through dinner in silence, eyes downcast, milling my hurt into anger. As a further

injustice, the moment dinner was over I was exiled to the garden along with the other five Clarke children. The eldest,
Finlay, was sent out as well, which mystified me and clearly
infuriated him; at seventeen, even a rather gangling and
smooth-jawed seventeen, he ought to have been included in the
realm of adults. Furious at the indignity of our respective situ-
ations, we sat on a bench under the eaves making sullen
conversation while the younger Clarklings frolicked under the
watch of a weary-looking nanny.

'He loves to make a point, my father,' he told me, leaning
back and placing his hands behind his head. He had a peculiar,
leisurely way of moving; it came through in his voice, too, a lazy
self-satisfaction that reminded me of a cat lying in the sun. 'The
last time we had company – the Harrisons, you must have met
them – Wilfred Junior and I managed to spill wine on some
awful old French dictionary of his, and I swear he's going to
hold it over me until the day I die. He nearly tore up my ticket
to London, all over a damned book.'

My ears pricked up at that. 'You're going to London?'

'Yes, I've got an apprenticeship with Smith & Bentley's, managing the books. I'll be leaving next week.'

If he had been seventeen before in my eyes, he was now
squarely thirty-five. I could not imagine – for so many reasons –
what it would be like to have such a future arranged, to be old
enough and trusted enough and man enough simply to hop off
to London on one's own. And yet he sounded so utterly unen-
thused, as though the prospect were no more exciting than
going into town to buy a pair of shoes.

'One would think,' he said, a touch of bitterness cutting
through the apathy, 'that I would be sent to apprentice at my

father's old bank, but *no* – my cousin has already nabbed the spot, apparently, even though he's a year my junior. And thick as paste to boot. Never mind; if Smith & Bentley's disappoints, I think I shall go to university. Father's against it, but then he's against absolutely everything. Wilfred Junior has an uncle who used to teach at Cambridge; he can put in a good word for me.'

Finlay sat forward and flicked away a fly that had perched on his knee. There was something else about his manner that annoyed me, I realized; he spoke as if he were talking to himself. As if the conversation were not a conversation at all, merely an entry in his diary. Feeling increasingly put out, I cast aside politeness for a moment and steered the conversation sharply in the only direction that interested me.

'I do wish I could see your father's books,' I said wistfully. 'Is there no way he'd let us in?'

'Never. But don't worry yourself; they're all rather dull anyway. Not many novels – it's Greek and Roman classics, mostly.'

'No books on science?'

He raised an eyebrow. 'Actually, yes, a few. I wouldn't have thought you'd be interested in that sort of thing.'

I huffed a little at that. 'Then you would have thought wrong, sir!'

He chuckled, low and quiet. When I looked over, I found that he was staring at me, unblinking. It was not often that I was paid such undivided attention; not since Catherine had left. The thought of her prickled me, like a burr in my shoe, but just as I opened my mouth to ask him what on earth he was looking at, he suddenly pushed himself to his feet.

'All right, then. Why don't we go now?'

'What – to the library?'

'Of course.'

'But you said—' I began to protest, before I saw that he was pointing to the end of the garden. There, under the shade of an old oak, the nanny was fast asleep, her chin against her chest.

'But what if your father finds out?' I asked, horrified.

'Oh, don't worry about that. We can be quiet. Let's go now, before she wakes up.'

I hesitated a moment longer. But then, in my mind's eye, Mr Clarke's sullen, drooping face swam into view; the temptation to spite him, even if he would never know it – and moreover, the temptation of the books themselves – was too much. I rose, and together we crept across the garden and into the house.

The library was in all likelihood no bigger than a parlour, but to me then it was the grandest thing I'd ever seen. I gasped as I entered, heart sparking with the sort of untroubled joy I hadn't felt in months. I scampered about the room, running my fingers over gilded spines and polished oak shelves, while Finlay made himself at home on the velvet settee.

'You have so many maps!' I exclaimed, pulling out a book which seemed entirely focused on the currents of the Channel. 'Do you have books on other geological topics?'

'What sort?'

I clutched the book to my chest and sat down on the settee. 'Well, I am very interested in natural history. Ancient creatures, the formation of the Earth . . .'

'Like that *Vestiges* book?'

'Pardon? Oh! *Vestiges of the Natural History of Creation*, you mean?' I asked eagerly. I knew of it only what I had happened to read in a review column the previous week (when I had tired of my grandfather's endless Roman histories, and in desperation turned to the footman's discarded newspaper). It was the talk of London, the reviewer said; a sign of the times, surely, that a scientific text was enjoying such popularity in high and low society alike. The summary alone painted such a glorious picture in my head – the Earth's formation from floating dust, the transmutation of species across the centuries, an unbroken dynasty of razor-toothed monsters and peculiar mammals . . . I had never heard anything like it. I had begun, in tentative steps, to write about it to Mr Jamsetjee, for he was the only person I knew who might have read such a thing; or at least, he had been until this afternoon.

'Do you have a copy?' I pressed. 'Have you read it? Do you think that I might—?'

'Oh, I wouldn't bother,' Finlay drawled. 'I *tried* to read it, certainly; quite the load of nonsense. Everyone's saying it was probably written by a woman, in any case. Geology is barely a science to begin with, if you ask me – there's no rigour to it, no *laws*, just a lot of digging up fish bones and collecting rocks. Now, physics – there's a science. Every man ought to know something of how the world works, I say.'

I blinked. I had once seen a moth in our back garden, so young that it was only just dry enough to fly, take wing from a blade of grass – only to be pounced upon immediately by the kitchen cat. In that moment, I felt a good deal like that moth.

'Is that what you want to study at university?' I managed at last.

'What, physics? Yes, I think so. Or chemistry, perhaps. I'm hoping I'll have time to attend some lectures in London. I hear Mr Faraday gives a fascinating series each winter.'

'Mr Faraday?'

He gave me an odd look. 'Michael Faraday – one of the foremost physicists and electrochemists of our time. You really haven't heard of him? I thought you were a connoisseur of science, Miss Brown.'

'I never said anything like that,' I protested.

'Next you'll be telling me you haven't heard of electricity – or gravity!'

'I have, of course I have!'

'Well, go on, then.' He crossed his arms. 'What is electricity?'

I hesitated. I had indeed heard the word, and seen it discussed in several books, but everything I had read seemed to assume that the reader was already familiar with the concept. I fumbled ahead.

'It is . . . a sort of fluid, I think.' I could feel the heat rising to my cheeks. 'It exists in the blood. Or the muscles? And it gathers in the air—'

'Whatever are you talking about?' Finlay laughed, a short, sharp noise that stung like a slap. 'You have no idea, have you? Does this island have no schools?'

I was just about to make some smart retort – perhaps I would ask him what *he* knew of plesiosauri – when, without warning, he leaned towards me and tucked an errant strand of hair behind my ear.

'It is a good thing you have someone to teach you about these sorts of things, then, isn't it?' he said quietly, fingertips lingering on the curve of my jaw.

I froze, still as a rabbit. His fingers were gentle, the barest glance of a touch – gentler than anything I had ever known. My maid had dressed me that morning, of course; when I was younger she had brushed my hair and scrubbed me clean. My tutor had guided my hands over the piano. And Catherine . . . Catherine had held my hand more times than I could count. She had pulled burrs from my sleeves and tied ribbons in my hair and kissed me upon the cheek, just that once – but all those touches seemed businesslike now, compared to the brush of Clarke's fingers against my cheek. There had never been any intent there, never anything beyond childish affection.

At least, on her part.

I stood up.

'We ought to go back to the garden,' I said stiffly, 'before we're missed.'

'Come now, there's no one to see.' He stood up as well, and I realized for the first time how very tall he was. How very alone we were.

'I should like to *go*,' I insisted, my heart rattling against my ribcage. I put the book of maps on the side table and made to leave – but he wrapped his long, cold fingers around my wrist and pulled me back to face him.

'Lord, you're a tease, aren't you? You lure me in here, and now you won't even give me a kiss for my troubles?'

There was that tenderness again as his arm snaked slowly around my waist, drawing me closer. I could feel his hand on the small of my back, the fabric of my dress crumpling between us like the petals of a flower in the crush of a palm, and—

And for the barest second, I stilled. For the barest second, I was . . . *relieved*. For ever since Catherine had kissed me on the cheek that day – ever since she had begun to step away, and I had instead cupped her face and pressed her startled lips to mine – I had told myself that I had not meant it. Not in such a way. I had merely been lonely, craving the affection that I had heard about from books and servants' talk, that I had seen in young couples walking arm in arm by the shore. And here, now, was my chance to prove it. *All you have to do is kiss him*, I thought, my pulse pounding so hard in my throat that I thought I might be sick. *Kiss him, and prove you did not mean it. Prove that you are not broken.*

But then my legs hit the table behind me and I felt his breath, soft and warm, upon my cheek, and I was struck with a wave of panic so acute it made my entire chest ache. Once, twice, I tried to jerk my arm free, but met only his tightening grip. He made a noise, half a chuckle, half a 'shh', as one might try to calm a frightened animal. I flinched like I'd been struck.

At a loss for what else to do, I swung my foot back and, with a force I did not know I had in me, drove the pointed tip of my shoe into his shin. He cried out, losing his hold on my wrist, and I wriggled free; though not before I'd landed another kick, and one more for good measure as I backed away.

'Goddamn – you *bitch*!' he hissed, clutching at his leg. 'Father was right about you, wretched little bastard! I do you a damned favour, and you go and . . . Go, then! Run off, like your whore of a mother did!'

I wish to this day that I had said more to him. I wish I had gone back and spat in his face, called him names – though I do not know what I might have said that would have cut as deeply as what he had said to me. Instead, I turned and ran to the garden (where, blessedly, the nanny was still sleeping) and sat among the children until it was time to leave. Only when I was home and readied for bed, the house dark and quiet about me, did I finally let myself fall apart.

The skin of my wrist crawled where he had grabbed me. I

ran my fingertips across it, and then my nails, as if it might be better if I had real bruises to match those he'd left on my pride. Would it have been different, I wondered, if I'd been able to explain to him what electricity was? If I had tried harder to refuse him? If I *hadn't*? Was there ever a world in which I might have made him respect me? Or would I simply have ended up like my mother, ruined and despised, all because she had wanted what she could not have?

It was no wonder I had driven Catherine away, clinging desperate thing that I was; it was no wonder Finlay Clarke could not see me as his peer. In a fit of pique, I marched to my writing desk, where there lay two half-written letters – one to Catherine and another for Mr Jamsetjee, about that damned book *Vestiges* – and tore them to pieces. For a moment, I considered burning them, too; I considered giving up my studies entirely, and devoting my young life to art instead; I considered bursting into tears.

After a few introductory sniffles, however, I decided against it. I would go to bed, I resolved, and in the morning I would begin my letter to Mr Jamsetjee again. I would ask him if *Vestiges* was really so awful, as Clarke had said, and if he really thought it might have been written by a woman.

And perhaps I would ask him if he could explain the workings of electricity to me, too.

9

There were iguanodons walking on the land, pterodactyls winging their way through the air, monitors and crocodiles in the rivers, and ichthyosaurs and plesiosaurs in the ocean.

— CHARLES LYELL, *Principles of Geology*

Theirs was the pre-Adamite, the just emerged from chaos-planet, through periods known only to God-Almighty; theirs an eldritch-world uninhabitate, sunless and moon-less, and seared in the angry light of supernal fire; theirs a fierce anark thing scorched to a horrible shadow; and they were the horrible chimeras — inexplicable and wonderful incarnations of the myriad generations of the after-times which denned that dreadful earth alone.

— THOMAS HAWKINS,
Memoirs of Ichthyosauri and Plesiosauri

ON THE TENTH of June, in the presence of Queen Victoria and — if the papers were to be believed — half the population of Britain, the Crystal Palace opened its doors. It had been open before, of course, only three years prior in Hyde Park, but that did not matter; enough time had passed, and so many new exhibitions had been added, that all the world was clamouring to see it once more – all the world, of course, save Henry.

As I'd feared, Henry's lecture was not well received. Which was not to say it was *universally* despised; he received a few admiring comments, and a few rather more cold ones. For the most part, however, it seemed that the Society had simply shared a collective grimace and resolved to ignore it. I, for one, was glad, though Henry seemed almost offended that Owen had not yet shown up on our doorstep to challenge him to a duel.

For more than a fortnight, Henry moped about the house like a jilted lover, remarking frequently that he was tired to death of hearing about Owen's reptiles – though that did not stop *him* talking about them, and tiring me half to death as well. Finally, one bright morning, as Henry was complaining that a Canadian geologist friend of his had had the nerve to ask him to send over some clippings about the Palace's exhibits, I set down the chapter of our geology primer I'd been trying to edit for nearly an hour and said:

'We ought to go.'

'What? You don't mean . . . to the Palace?'

When I nodded, he looked at me as if I had just declared myself a spy.

'Are you mad? And patronize those wretched sculptures?'

'To patronize them is exactly the point.' I walked over to where he sat, taking the letter from his hands and setting it gently on the desk. 'Do you not think that it would make you feel better to go and stare daggers at them, to be able to say that you have seen with your own eyes the work you so roundly condemn?'

He glared at me for a very long while.

'I suppose . . .' he said at last, begrudgingly, 'we never did get to go together that first time, did we?'

It was true; Henry had made a brief visit to the exhibition in Hyde Park to meet with a colleague, and I with Mr and Mrs Jamsetjee on their visit back to London that summer. (Henry had been supposed to accompany us on that occasion, but had come down with a nasty cough; although now, knowing him better, I wondered if that had been an excuse to avoid Mr Jamsetjee's stern looks all afternoon.)

'No, you were far too ill,' I said, smiling, and at the rather guilty look that flashed across his face, I knew that I had won.

'All right, all right,' he sighed. 'But only if you join me in loudly disparaging the statues in front of the other visitors.'

'I would not have it any other way.'

ONE DOES NOT truly appreciate the size of London until one sees all its peoples amassed in one place – and that one place, it seemed, was the park in front of the Palace that summer afternoon. Bright-skirted ladies and their lace parasols covered the green, looking from a distance like a carpet of flowers; small children darted through the crowds, mindless of whose shoes or hems they stepped upon; and there at the head of it all, just visible above the trees, stood the Palace itself. The name was apt, for it looked like a palace – or a temple perhaps, devoted to the modern world. Each floor was packed with exhibits and displays, machinery and artisanal goods, artefacts from all corners of the world. Even the building itself was a marvel; until only a few years ago, the machines to make such a thing simply had not existed. And now it stood, a towering castle of steel and glass, testament to the accomplishments of British science.

'British science, indeed!' Mr Jamsetjee had muttered to me as the pair of us had toured the first exhibition three years prior.

'West Indian cotton in the looms, Amazonian rubber in the hydraulics . . . and all bought with sapphires from Ceylon and diamonds from Kollur. My, what wonders the British have made, with their own wit and gumption.'

'There is no end to the arrogance of these men,' I had replied sourly. I was in a surly mood then; earlier that week, I had tailed Henry to my first annual meeting of the Geological Society, at which I had attempted to propose to one of the vice presidents that it might one day admit female fellows. (After all, women had been permitted in the Zoological and Royal Entomological societies since their inception.) But the man had merely shot me a look as though I had told a bawdy joke and said, 'We do not need dilettantes, madam.'

'Men alone?' Mr Jamsetjee had retorted then, casting me a sharp look. We'd been passing between the North and South transepts, the floor made nearly impassable by the vast and stationary crowd that had formed around the famed Koh-i-noor diamond. It sat within a marquee of sorts, the walls draped in lurid silk and tiger skins, an immense gilded cage shielding it from theft. A small sign read: *A GIFT from THE HONOURABLE EIC for HER MAJESTY THE QUEEN OF ENGLAND – won in the annexation of the Kingdom of Punjab.*

'No,' I had admitted quietly. 'Not only men, I suppose.'

I could not help but recall this exchange now, as Henry and I crossed the green, the crowds gathered about the newly cut and polished diamond just visible through the nearest windows of the Palace. Henry had been quite outraged to hear Professor Ellis's words – that science was a matter of politics and spectacle, rather than truth – but I could not find it in myself to feign surprise. The truth was unappealing, after all; ugly and complex and inconvenient. Truth had never opened anyone's heart – or purse strings – to a cause. It was no wonder that most preferred a spectacle.

'Can you believe,' Henry was saying as we turned down a tree-lined path, the Palace sliding slowly out of view, 'that I've been denied another curatorial position? I already inquired at the British Museum and the Linnean Society and the Zoological Society – though I didn't expect them to take me, not with Owen on their board – but just this morning I heard back from the director of the Derby Museum in Liverpool, who said—'

'*Liverpool?*' I exclaimed. 'Henry, they say the factory smoke is so thick in the air there that when one blows one's nose it turns the handkerchief black.'

'Well, you needn't worry your handkerchiefs now, as I was turned down!' He waved a hand exasperatedly, as if swatting a fly. 'I am confounded, Mary. Just last week the director wrote me to say that he'd received my recommendation from Professor Grant and was quite impressed, prior experience perfect for the job, et cetera, then this morning I hear they've chosen Louis Fraser instead. The man's an ornithologist, and they have him managing reptiles and molluscs!'

I mused on this for a moment. The name sounded awfully familiar.

'This Mr Fraser,' I said. 'Is he not a former colleague of Owen's?'

Henry's brows furrowed. 'Come to think of it, he is indeed . . . I believe they worked together on that giant ostrich fossil Owen never ceases talking about.'

'Not an ostrich, dear, the *moa*. I wonder . . .' I gave him a sidelong look. 'Do you think, perhaps, Owen had a word with Lord Derby himself? You know how well acquainted he is with the aristocratic collectors. It would be quite easy, for a man with his finger in so many pies, to put in a word here and there.'

'Oh, that *swine*,' muttered Henry. 'He's too cowardly to challenge me in the open, so means to quietly sabotage my career instead, is that it? He thinks he can blackball me . . . simply squash me and never hear from me again?' His expression was so fierce that a pair of passing ladies gave us a berth of several feet. 'We shall see about that. I shall give another lecture – I shall write a *book*—'

'Please don't, Henry.'

'You'd have me give up, then? As easily as that?'

'I *would*!' I cried, far too loudly, as I swivelled to face him. I made myself take a measured breath. 'For now, at least. Owen may be a liar and a manipulator, but he still commands respect. When we were still infants, he was already publishing research and gaining the favour of important men. He knows George Hamilton-Gordon, for goodness' sake! For my part, Henry, I believe the way to beat him is not to keep denouncing him like a street-side prophet declaring the end of times, but to build a *reputation*. Show everyone that you are as skilled a comparative anatomist as he. Finish that book for Murray. Present that lecture on marine fossils at the British Association next month—'

'I cannot,' Henry replied sullenly, and for a moment I simply despaired.

'And why is that?'

He looked surreptitiously about him, as though Owen might be listening from the shrubbery. Finally, he muttered:

'I did not pay the dues this year.'

Well. That did explain why he had mysteriously declined all invitations to attend the last general meeting. I pinched my nose, a wave of exasperation and worry threatening to overwhelm me.

'Is there anything else you wish to tell me, Henry?' I found myself saying.

'No, there is not.'

I tried again. 'Is there anything else you *ought* to tell—'

He came to a stop, gravel skittering under his shoes.

'Mary. I have told you that I would manage it, and I will. I had nothing good to present at the BA this year anyway, so why not let my membership lapse? It will save us money. Would you rather I had done differently?'

'No, but I would have preferred that *you tell me*—' I began, but stumbled to a halt when I saw Henry's expression. He had spotted something over my shoulder, it seemed, and his face had gone slack with surprise. I turned to follow his gaze, down the gently sloping path, to where our destination had just become visible through the trees: the Geological Islands. In a breath, all my exasperation seemed to melt away.

'Oh,' he murmured. 'There they are.'

And there, indeed, they were.

As we drew closer, I realized that what had been called a lake was more of a sliver, offset from a larger body of water by means of a small island planted with lush grasses and ferns. In the shallower waters sat the earliest reptiles, the squat *Labyrinthodon* and sabre-tusked *Dicynodon*; to their left, in what was evidently a recreation of the Liassic era, a long-snouted *Taleosaurus* and an *Ichthyosaurus*, its eyes strange and angular like cut jewels. Around them, the water lapped, wavering grasses nearly obscuring the pair of pterosaurs which sat bickering on an outcrop. Lastly came the Oolitic and the Wealden reptiles, these the most gigantic of all, lounging amid the island's foliage while a pair of Owen's stocky-legged *Iguanodon* watched lazily over it all.

They were so finely wrought, those sculptures, that even at a distance one could see every scale upon their backs. But the one which had drawn my gaze first, I found, was not the stout *Iguanodon*, nor *Megalosaurus* with its great hunched back, nor *Hylaeosaurus* with its fearsome ridge of spines, but one of the plesiosaurs. *Plesiosaurus dolichodeirus*, to be precise. It seemed to sit alone from its Liassic cousins, snake-like neck curling above the water, one single piercing eye turned towards its audience. As with all the statues, there was some inscrutably alien quality to it; something that made it seem to *loom*, even from across the water. In flashes I was there, aeons ago, watching as that narrow head turned towards me and fixed me in its hungry stare.

'They're quite good, aren't they?' I said at last, rather solemnly, as we reached the water's edge.

'*Hmm*,' was Henry's response.

'Though that *Plesiosaurus* seems rather ill proportioned.'

'It is! That neck is far too long for its body – it looks as if someone has sewn a snake on to a dolphin.' Henry scowled and leaned forward to prop his elbows upon one of the wooden posts which held up the rustic fence surrounding the lake. For a moment we were silent again, listening to the awed exclamations of passers-by.

'Owen is wrong,' Henry said quietly. 'He is. I'm sure of it. It is only because he's been given a sculptor to work with – someone to bring forth his ideas – that his models seem almost plausible. Ah, if we but had a *sculptor*, Mary; if we had money, if I had a position, if I were admitted to the Royal Society . . .' He gave the bitter shadow of a laugh. 'Even Clarke's a fellow now, and he's almost three years my junior. As you say, my dear, we need *something*. A discovery. An idea.'

There was a keen edge to his voice, a hungriness in his eyes. At the mere mention of Clarke's name, I'd felt it, too – a stab of longing. Electric, knife-sharp. It is a ravenous thing, ambition; even more so than curiosity. For some, I have heard, it is a fair-weather companion, evaporating at the first sign of hardship and leaving its bearer behind with only modest dreams. For others, however, it is merciless – a burning, aching, gnawing thing that refuses to abandon its host no matter how long or hard they work, until either they succeed or are left hollowed out, prideful to the last.

I knew without a doubt that Henry and I were of the second kind.

THAT EVENING, AFTER dinner, I found myself at a loose end. I tried for a spell to read, and then to draw, and finally to go to bed, but alas, it seemed to be one of those restless nights when sleep escaped me entirely. At last, I rose and went down to the study, thumbing through the papers on my desk by the dim glow of lamplight. Here was a letter from Mrs Jamsetjee, thanking me for the pastels I'd sent for her birthday; there, an idle sketch of Owen's plesiosaur which I had scratched on the back of an envelope; there again, the latest letter from Maisie.

This last I had read perhaps three times already, but I sat now and read it again. I had tried several times to reply, but each time I found myself at a loss for what to say. Maisie had written of her mother; this past week, she said, was the anniversary of her death. The letter was an offering, I felt, an invitation to talk of my own grief if I so wished – but I did not. I did not want to pick at those memories, to make myself bleed once again. I shook my head, hard, and skipped towards the end.

. . . said she would die a happy woman, knowing that Henry and I

would carry on without her. We were her legacy. But – it pains me to admit that I do not think I am a very good legacy, Mary. Long after you and Henry are gone, someone, I am sure, will look upon your drawings and your writings and know that you were here; but what will they know of me? Or of my mother, for that matter? It hurts me to remember her, even now – but then, it hurts me far more to think of forgetting her.

I suppose that is why it often makes me sad to read about history, or even natural history, as you do; I cannot help but think of everyone whose tale cannot fit in one book, those poor creatures who remain lost or forgotten. Do you think that one day, some Mary of the future will sketch our bones and wonder what we might have been in life?

My bleary eyes shifted across the paper, words jumping out at me one after the other – *legacy . . . forgotten . . . lost.* I pressed my palms to my eyes, but that did not stop the disjointed images flitting through my weary mind: the nursery upstairs, bare and dusty; Maisie's smile as she sorted Mr Sutherland's letters by my side; Henry's weary face that afternoon at the lake, murmuring, *we need something.*

A legacy – that was what he meant, was it not? Our contribution to the future, some discovery or theory so brilliant that it would outlive us. Was not such a thing more stable than any legacy of blood? And less risky? My own mother had died bringing me into the world; now all that remained of her line, and my father's, were a handful of trinkets. A Bible, a hair ribbon, a battered leather document case . . .

A document case which, I remembered, I had promised myself weeks ago I would take another look at.

I sat up then, blinking, and set down my pen. If I could not bring myself to write a reply to Maisie this evening, then I might as well make use of the hours in a different fashion. Careful not to wake Henry, I crept back to our room and knelt by the side of the bed. Underneath a mess of hatboxes and luggage I found the trunk I had brought with me from Wight, and pulled out the case in question. Perhaps, I mused – if there was any justice in the world, for bastards and orphans – my grandfather's documents contained some small secret I had missed in all my poring over them as a child. Perhaps the directions to a lost Swiss bank account, which I had been unable to read with my abysmal French. Perhaps something in German, or in code. Or perhaps I was going mad, and ought to go back to bed.

But I did not. For whatever reason, madness or fate or misguided hope, I carried on.

Back in the study, I emptied the contents of the old letter case on to the desk. The papers looked just as I remembered them, albeit slightly yellower with age, and smudged here and there with . . . What was that dark substance? I tried to pick up a flake of it which had skittered across the desk, but it disintegrated at once, smearing my fingertips black. Was it charcoal? Ash?

With a slight shiver down my spine, I recalled what our old cook had once said – *it carried the smell of smoke with it always, no matter how much they shook it out.*

Shaking myself, I sifted through the pages again, but none of them appeared burnt. Could ash have somehow got inside the case, as my grandfather carried it from the fire? I lifted it up, turning it this way and that, and then, frowning, turned it again. It seemed ever so slightly heavier than it ought to have been when empty, weighted in an oddly lopsided fashion. I shook it, and felt something shift.

A weight inside the lining.

No, I thought, incredulous, resisting the urge to laugh. *No, I must truly be going mad.* But when I brought the lamp closer, it was unmistakable. There, tucked almost invisibly into the corner, was a seam where the fabric had been cut away and stitched carefully back into place. I ran my finger along the seam's edge and saw it come away black with soot. How fine it was; how many years must it have taken, a few more grains slipping free with every subtle shift, to have made such smudges upon the letters within? How many more years might have passed without my noticing it?

And what on earth had my grandfather gone to such trouble to hide?

Heart in my throat, I ran for my sewing scissors. Once the stitches were snipped and the lining pulled free, I reached within and found . . . another stack of letters. I will admit to being disappointed; I had been hoping for something of concrete value. But here, at least, was the source of the ash. The first few pages were thoroughly charred, eaten through with dark-edged holes. At first I thought this must have been the fault of the house fire, but if that were the case, then why were the rest of the pages undamaged?

No, I thought, chewing my thumbnail anxiously, as I had not done since I was a child. No, it looked more as if someone had tossed them on to banked coals, and then thought better of it.

I turned the pages carefully one by one, trying to piece together the contents, but all that remained of the first ones was a sort of nonsense poetry – *The apparition . . . a blessing . . . my pride . . . mine – mine . . . till death.* The first readable page I found, I lifted up to the lamplight:

. . . I know it was your brother's last wish that his work not be known, but I cannot help but think that it is no coincidence I happened upon him during my expedition. Perhaps the Lord only meant to give

him some company during his final days, or perhaps He meant for this tale to be known, that all those who read it might know the evils ahead of them should they follow such a path; but I will leave the matter in your hands, sir. My only hope is that you find solace in this account, and in knowing that your brother did not leave you out of madness or self-ishness, but a desire to protect you from that which he had made. However badly his experiments went astray, and whatever misery they wrought, I am confident at least that his intentions were always noble.

With deepest sympathies,

Captain R. Walton

The following letters – of which there were many – were all in the same hand, albeit messier, the lines meandering up and down each page as if they had been written hurriedly on some-one's lap. It seemed to be a biography of sorts, though apparently not of Captain Walton himself; the letters spoke of Geneva, of the family Frankenstein, and there – *there!* – a first name.

Victor.

I thought again of Cook's stories, of the tragedy that had driven my grandfather from Geneva: one brother murdered, the other mad and missing. But it was not madness after all, it seemed, that had driven this Victor – my great-uncle, I supposed – to flee Geneva. My eye went again to the mention of *experiments*, and my curiosity burned.

Unable to resist, I turned to the first page once more and began to read.

HOURS LATER, I shook Henry awake.

'I have it,' I said, shivering with excitement. 'Our *something*.'

PART II

JUNE 1854 – MAY 1855

10

I paused, examining and analysing all the minutiae of causation, as exemplified in the change from life to death, and death to life, until from the midst of this darkness a sudden light broke in upon me — a light so brilliant and wondrous, yet so simple, that while I became dizzy with the immensity of the prospect which it illustrated, I was surprised that among so many men of genius who had directed their inquiries towards the same science, that I alone should be reserved to discover so astonishing a secret.

— MARY SHELLEY, *Frankenstein*

'IT ISN'T POSSIBLE,' said Henry.

Outside, beyond the curtains, I knew the sun must be rising. I had not slept a wink, but that did not matter — I was consumed with a rattling, ceaseless energy that did not allow for rest. I had spent the previous hour, perhaps more, telling Henry about the letters, reading passages aloud where my memory failed or some turn of phrase delighted me. An idea had struck me as I read, this long and sleepless night. It was an extraordinary idea, an outlandish and impossible idea, an obscene and unnatural and *nigh-heretical* idea — and it had seized me heart and soul.

'Why not?' I replied. Now, as I had since the moment I first shook him awake, I paced. Henry sat in bed still, his features thrown into sharp relief by the flickering candlelight.

'Why not? Mary, where to start!' He waved a hand, frustrated. 'The man is clearly mad!'

'Which one, Captain Walton or Victor?'

'Both! You mean to tell me that your mysteriously vanished great-uncle turned up in the middle of the Arctic tundra, raving about being pursued by a monster of his own creation, and this Walton fellow who fished him from the ice simply took him at his word?'

'Ah, but the captain claims he saw the creature, too!' With trembling hands, I snatched up the letters again and spread the final pages out on the bed. I could see it in my mind's eye, clear as day: the enormous misshapen figure which Victor Frankenstein had brought to life hunched beneath the cabin ceiling, the withered body of his creator splayed on the berth before him. The shock upon Captain Walton's face as the creature spoke, voice heavy with regret, vowing to lay himself upon a pyre and follow his creator into death before the day was done. I wondered what it had been like for my grandfather to read all this; to have a letter from a perfect stranger half a continent away lance the pain of his brother's disappearance like a boil, revealing an even greater sorrow beneath. Had he been horrified to hear of his brother's gruesome experiments? Or simply glad to have an explanation at last? Perhaps both, I thought; perhaps that was why he had tossed these pages into the fire, only to snatch them out again. Why he had taken such pains to ensure no one would ever find them, yet had risked his very life to prevent them from being destroyed entirely?

'Then the captain was certainly mad as well,' Henry said

flatly. 'How on earth did he manage to send this account to your grandfather anyway, if he'd never met the man? Are you sure this wasn't all a grand ruse designed to . . . ?'

'To what, Henry?' I asked, half laughing, when he trailed off. Evidently, he hadn't been able to think of an explanation either. 'Extract money from him? Walton never asked for a penny. I truly think all he wanted was for Victor's brother to know what had become of him. And as for how – well, Victor told him the name of the very lake where his family home was situated. I shouldn't think it would have been hard to have these letters directed there, even without a precise address.'

Henry was frowning still, shaking his head, and I knew that we were coming to the meat of the thing. The most unbelievable part, after all, was not that this sea captain might have stumbled across my great-uncle in his flight across the Arctic, or that he might have been able to track down my grandfather to deliver these letters; no, it was what my great-uncle claimed to have done.

He had created life.

'It cannot possibly be true, Mary,' Henry murmured. 'I do not care if Walton claims to have seen this . . . *creation*, too; long expeditions can do things to a man's mind.'

'And yet, do you not see . . . ?' I sat on the edge of the bed and took one of his hands in mine. 'I am as much of a sceptic as you are, Henry. Perhaps it was all a hallucination, a fit of madness. But on the merest chance that it *wasn't* . . . would it not answer one of the greatest mysteries of our age? That great puzzle of natural history – the origin of life? Have you not said yourself what a frustration it is to find fossils of species that seem to have no ancestor, that seem to have sprung forth from nothing? Who is to say that whatever mechanism brought them to life could not be replicated by man? And if it could – on the barest sliver of a chance that it could – would that not be a worthy subject of investigation? And . . .'

I found, suddenly, that I could not voice my idea. I could see it clearly enough, memories knitting themselves together in my mind's eye: the jutting ribs of the whale beached upon the shores of Wight, the staring stone eyes of Owen's plesiosaur, the fossil tooth of Catherine's I kept still among my drawing pens. Had I not thought, standing at the edge of the Geological Islands the previous day, how very close to life those statues had seemed? And had Henry not said that we needed a sculptor for our ideas? Was this not the age of science and reason, of miracles wrought in electricity and steam, of the mysteries of the body unveiled to us through the wonders of chemistry and microscopy? There would be obstacles, true; the biology and anatomy of living things was not at all my strong suit, nor Henry's. But when one was offered a miracle just out of reach, was it not worth stretching to grasp it?

Still, despite all my reasoning, I found I could not bring myself to voice my idea just yet. In the light of dawn, with Henry's gaze upon me, it seemed altogether too ambitious and strange. I was just wondering what I ought to tell him instead when I looked up and was struck by the intensity of his expression. He did not *look* like a man unconvinced – no; rather, he looked like a man stuck with a difficult puzzle. An engineer gazing into the depths of a broken machine, endeavouring to make it work. That was when I realized: this was not an argument in the typical sense, wherein each party struggles to bring the other around to their point of view. Instead, it was the sort of argument shared for millennia by priests and philosophers and scientists alike, wherein each party is trying to convince themselves of a miraculous truth.

'You believe it, don't you?' I said softly, a smile in my voice. 'You play the part, Henry, but you cannot fool me. You think that it might be possible – to create *life*. To restore it to that which is dead.'

He looked at me, eyes glinting, and I knew that I was right.

'Perhaps,' he said. 'But it does not matter, in any case, whether I believe it or not.'

'Oh?'

'Because the only thing that matters,' he said, leaning in to whisper to me, as if we were conspirators in some grand plot, 'is *if it is true*.'

WE DID NOT leave the study all that morning. Agnes must have thought us up to something truly sinister, for every time she entered the room – first to bring us breakfast, and then later to clear away the plates we'd hardly touched – we stopped mid-sentence, following her every movement in perfect silence until she was gone. Then we would resume our whisperings, debating in circles upon circles.

New species do seem to have arisen spontaneously in the past, as you say; but is that new life entirely? Or a transmutation of some existing life form?

It does not matter. Whatever the case, life must have begun at some point, arising from nothing or from non-living matter. Why couldn't it happen again? And not necessarily in the form of Cuvier's 'multiple creations' – but uniform over time?

Ah, Mr Lyell's approach! For every species which falls to

extinction, some new form appears. And does God have any hand in these creations, or are you finally revealing yourself a heathen?

He may do. Perhaps He fashioned the world like a well-wound watch, so that every hour, as it were, it strikes life into inanimate matter.

But why wouldn't we have noticed this clock striking before? Ah . . . well, perhaps Lamarck is correct: any new forms originating today are too small and too simple for us to notice, and will only rise to complexity later . . .

Perhaps. But in any case, that is life generated from nothing; we are concerned with life restored. Surely that must be an easier task; the pieces are already in place.

And so on, and so on.

Eventually, tiredness overcame us, and we were forced to leave our books and stacks of hasty, half-formed notes to rest. When I woke some hours later, I found I was alone; Henry, having snatched a good four hours of sleep the previous night to my none, must have woken already. All was hazy and muffled as I made my way downstairs, soft about the edges in that peculiar way of early evening.

'Ah, there you are!' Henry exclaimed when I came into the study. He was sitting by the window in his dressing gown, a translation of Liebig's *Animal Chemistry* on his lap. 'I've been making a list of the books we'll need. There are some I can find in the Society reading room, and some I can borrow from friends, but the rest—'

'We'll simply have to go shopping for,' I cut in, and he gave me a knowing smile. We rarely ever purchased books on these shopping trips – our budget simply would not allow for it. But many was the time I had hidden in the back corner of O. E.

Janson's or Percy Young's on Gower Street, copying out figures from an expensive reference text while Henry sent the owner chasing after a first edition of a book that did not exist.

'I've been meaning to ask you, Mary,' Henry said as I settled into my usual chair, 'if you had any thoughts on the matter of what, exactly . . . we should bring to life?'

There was a peculiar tone to his voice, caution verging on worry – or perhaps on *fear*. It was a question I had been avoiding ever since the previous night, urging our conversations in the direction of theory rather than practice, as I feared the absurdity of my answer. But meeting Henry's eyes now, I realized that he, too, had been avoiding it, although for an entirely different reason. I thought of the marshy hilltop to which I still had not returned, the marble headstone crowned with cherubs which had cost two weeks of Henry's pay – the only luxury we could ever give her. I imagined those rows of graves lit by moonlight, the weight of a shovel in my hand—

'No!' I cried at once. 'Good God, no! How could you think such a thing?'

'You hadn't?'

I stopped, a hitch in my breath; for of course I had. More than once. Each time the thought came to me, it drove the breath from my lungs, filling me with terror and longing in equal, painful measure.

It was such a tempting abomination.

'We couldn't. We can't.' My throat was tight. I shook my head, hard, as if to shake the vision away. 'Besides, do you not remember what happened to Victor? Perhaps if he hadn't abandoned his . . . *man*; if he had raised him as he should . . . Perhaps things might have ended differently. But we cannot be sure, I think. Far better to make something that does not know enough of the world to resent its place in it.' I chuckled, bleakly. 'Something that cannot hold a knife.'

'All right,' said Henry, and I was glad to see his face soften with relief. 'I concur. I was just afraid that you were hoping ...' He waved a hand. 'In any case. It is settled, then – an animal of some sort. But what kind? Something small and easily obtained to start with, I think, at least until we have identified the correct method. But we'll need something more impressive than that in the end. At least a man can speak, and attest that he has been brought to life; how can we prove that we have done the same with an animal, short of performing the act live, in front of the Royal Society? But even then, it could be viewed as a stage trick ...' His eyes brightened suddenly. 'Your Victor stitched together parts of multiple men, did he not? Perhaps we can do the same. With parts of different animals, like those awful mermaids you see at circuses – or parts of the same animal? That may be easier. But then, we can't have the Royal Society think we've simply embroidered a rat ...'

As he went on, I pulled from the clutter of my desk the lovely leather-bound journal Mrs Jamsetjee had sent me for my last birthday. I opened it to the first page and took up a piece of charcoal, laying down rough shapes and sweeping curves – a hasty thing, work I would have been ashamed of under normal circumstances. But the artistry needed not be impeccable here. It needed only to communicate to Henry the image which had seized me the night before, the idea that would put Richard Owen's statues to shame, which would bring his stony-eyed creations to life in a way no one had ever attempted before ...

... the image of an antediluvian monster. A fossil, rendered flesh.

A *Plesiosaurus*.

When I turned the book around, Henry stopped and stared at it agog. And then – though not in an unkind way, not in the way I had feared – he began to laugh.

'*Mary*,' he cried, eyes alight. 'What a remarkable creature you are.'

II

To the head of a Lizard, it united the teeth of a Croco-
dile; a neck of enormous length, resembling the body of a
Serpent; . . . the ribs of a Camelion, and the paddles of
a Whale. Such are the strange combinations of form and
structure in the Plesiosaurus . . .

— WILLIAM BUCKLAND,
Geology and Mineralogy

AT FIRST, AFTER his initial enthusiasm had worn off, he
argued. If we were to create a living rebuttal to Owen's theories,
why not an *Iguanodon*, the most outrageous of all his designs?
But such a thing would be too impractical, I reasoned; it was too
large, too difficult to engineer – for, after all, being a land animal, it had to support its own weight as it moved. Not to
mention that there were scarcely any existing fossils, so any
attempt we made would be even more of a leap than Owen's
model.

'If we had a complete skeleton, perhaps,' I mused, teetering
on a stool as I searched our bookshelves for Cuvier's *Lessons on
Comparative Anatomy*. 'Then we could simply extrapolate the
musculature, and let whatever natural gait it takes be our proof.
But there are no such fossils; we would have to base our

construction so heavily on modern reptiles that we may as well present the Society with an iguana.'

'True . . .' By the pensive look on Henry's face, one crooked finger pressed to his chin, I knew he was coming round to my proposal. 'We would have more claim to accuracy, with your idea. And we do want something distinctive; so different from any existing creature that it could not possibly be taken for a hoax, or some naturally born mutant.'

My trailing finger found the book's spine at last, and I drew it out. 'We could make ours with a proper neck.'

'*Yes* – chip away at Owen's reputation inch by inch! Once that particular theory is undermined, his peers may be more willing to disbelieve his other models, too.'

'And, if it is aquatic, we need not worry about whether it is strong enough to lift its own weight. If it breathes, it will float. All we must do' – I hopped down off the stool, gripping Henry's proffered hand for balance – 'is get it to breathe.'

Henry did not release my hand then, but held it tighter, his smile a sharp and hungry thing. I found I liked it quite a bit.

'You make it sound so easy, my dear.'

BY THE END of the week, the house was full of lists. Lists of supplies, of methods of preserving flesh, of books and bones and ligaments, covering every surface like some morbid découpage. Longest of all, it seemed, was the list of things we did not know; for although we were both well informed in natural history and geological formations, in the comparative anatomy of reptiles both ancient and modern, we knew staggeringly little of physiology or chemistry. But somehow, strangely, this did not dampen my enthusiasm in the slightest. I had never paid much attention before to the workings of nerves and organs and circulation, as the subjects of my interest generally possessed none of the above; now, however, I found myself poised before a great unexplored wealth of knowledge, as ravenous as I had been as a child when I first began my studies of natural history. Henry, I could tell, was experiencing much the same, poring over bibliographies and catalogues of texts with the lustful gaze of a glutton surveying a trolley of desserts. We were giddy, two explorers embarking upon a nigh-impossible quest, all the more tempting for its impossibility.

Before long, we had put together a recipe of sorts, a rough estimation of the essential components of that nebulous thing we call life. This list hung in pride of place above my desk, and it read:

Vital force (action of the brain and nervous system)
Respiration
Circulation
Taking in sustenance
Movement (animals)
Senses (animals)
Growth/self-reparation (to an extent)

'We will need a laboratory,' Henry said as I tacked it up, the pins between my teeth. 'Somewhere private. By the water, eventually, though for the moment we can make do without, if we wish to refine our methods on rats and such first.'

'Could we rent somewhere by the docks?'

'Too expensive. And impractical, too. We can't be travelling down to the docks every day, lugging all our supplies and notes – and dockhands gossip just as much as fishwives. But we could start here for now, in the house. Perhaps . . .'

He paused, shooting me a wary look. I knew already what he meant to propose; worst of all, I agreed with him, even if the very thought filled me with dread. It was our only spare room – well lit, and scantily furnished. We couldn't afford anywhere else. So why not use it, I asked myself? Was I to spend the rest of my days tiptoeing about my own home, forgoing this or that room because it was where she ought to have slept, ought to have eaten, ought to have played?

No. Far better to wash away such memories. Open the windows and air them out.

'We could use the nursery,' I heard him say.

I closed my eyes, and when they were open again I was resolved. A paper-thin resolve, perhaps – but a resolve nonetheless.

'Yes,' I said. 'We could indeed.'

ONCE, WHEN I was very young, I'd run sobbing to the kitchen with a dying rabbit in my arms. I'd found it in the garden, bloodied and shaking as the neighbour's cat loomed over it. I'd known even then, I think, that nothing could be done for it; but I'd brought it in regardless and laid it in the lap of our old cook.

She'd taken one look at the thing and snapped its neck. I remember my breath catching at the sound, that awful, fleshy *snap*. Bones, I knew; dead things, I knew. There was a certain sadness in them, true, but also an emptiness, like the site of an ancient battlefield, its bloody past too distant to grieve. But this, watching life crumble to nothing before my very eyes – this was another matter entirely.

'It was a mercy, Miss Mary,' the cook said, clearly exasperated. 'The world won't miss one little rabbit. They have scores of babies, you know. They have to, to account for all them that gets eaten.'

At that, I'd only cried harder. How awful, how unthinkable it was, that a mother might look upon her babies and think, *Only one of you shall live. The rest of you are fodder.*

I remembered the rabbit later that year, when the butcher's boy caught his hand upon a nail and died within the week. When the Reverend Walker's niece fell down the stairs and snapped her neck. When scarlet fever swept through my school, missing me only because I was already at home with a cold, and cut the class in half. The church that winter was full of mothers and fathers wearing black, crowding the aisles like blackbirds gone to roost. I took to opening my eyes during the prayers, staring out across the rows of bowed heads and thinking, *Why would you make a world such as this?*

I prayed, when Henry and I first married, that ours would be one of those marriages barren of children. It happened, I knew; the Jamsetjees had nearly been one such case, as I had learned from a particularly heartfelt missive Mrs Jamsetjee sent me when she heard of my elopement with Henry. They had gone nearly ten years of marriage with no children until the birth of their daughter in the cold winter of 1830 – the same year in which I had been born – only to be rendered childless again before the decade was out. My heart ached to read that letter, not only out of sympathy but also a wretched, guilty hope. Henry had never seemed eager for children; he had mentioned the idea, in the distant way one might speak of retiring to the country in one's old age, as the inevitable consequence of a life well lived. But whenever a tottering infant bumped into his leg on the street, or a host brought out their talented young daughter to play a sonata after dinner, he responded with a sort of wary confusion. I had once found this hilarious, teasing him mercilessly when he went so far as to give one such pianist a pat on the head, as if she were a stray dog.

And yet – despite my prayers, despite our obvious unsuitability for the task – we were to be given a child. I recall still the wave of panic that gripped me when the doctor delivered us this news, as well as the equally panicked expression that passed across Henry's face – soon replaced, to his credit, by something in the broad vicinity of joy. But I was angry with him in that moment, quite hypocritically; furious that, as I was being wrung out by sickness and fatigue, subsisting on sips of water and crusts of toast and whatever foul tinctures my doctor recommended, he should be worried at the mere *notion* of fatherhood. My reaction was unfair, and I knew it. Henry had plenty to worry about. Week after week, as he flitted about answering congratulatory messages and arranging nursery furnishings and buying flowers for my bedside which would inevitably have to be discarded as their smell made me ill, I could see it in his eyes: the knowledge that, just as surely as my own birth had killed my mother, this could be his widowing.

That is when I began to pray – though I knew this wasn't the sort of thing one ought to pray for, not at all – that I would lose it. Or at the very least, if I was to be denied even that, that it all be over quickly; that I be delivered of it swiftly and painlessly; that I might hand it over to a nursemaid and forget the whole affair.

What a silly hope that was.

Cruellest of all, I think, is that even after everything, I did not want to hand my baby to the nursemaid. I forgot all the promises I had made to myself the day before – that I would not love her, not until she was five or ten or twenty; that I would not stake my heart upon such a fragile thing. But I discovered then that it was not a matter of choice. No matter how much I fought, my foolish heart went against me. The moment I first held her in my arms, too small and too light and too perfect to be true, I loved her. And the moment I caught sight of the doctor's face, heard him mutter, 'She really ought to be crying by now' – I knew I had been right. She was too good to be true after all.

Within the hour, she was gone. Barely had they let Henry in, pale-faced and full of questions, when she slipped away in my arms. I must have asked the doctor one hundred times, clinging at his sleeve: 'Why? What was it? What did I do wrong?' But he only looked at me sadly and told me not to worry; these things happened on occasion. I was young. I would have another.

I tried not to think of all this, as I stood at the threshold of the nursery. I tried not to think of the cot she had never used; the last prayer I had ever made, a single voiceless *please*; the chair in the corner where I had found Henry slumped the year before, murmuring over a bottle of whisky: 'What would we have done with a child, anyway?' All that was gone now, stripped away. The dusty furniture had been taken out, the floor covered in wax paper to protect it from spills. I walked to one of the dormer windows and ran my hand across the glass, cold and whorled with age. Beyond stretched the roofs of London, an undulating sea of grey tile and red, plumes of black smoke drifting up towards the heavens.

'Did you see?' Henry said, and I turned. He was gesturing

rather sheepishly towards the workstation he'd put together: a pair of second-hand tables, rickety but sizeable, and a set of shelves on the wall for our notes and books. Pinned to the middle shelf, like a poet might hang up his favourite verse for inspiration, was our list – *Vital force, Respiration, Circulation.*

'I saw,' I said. I drew myself together, grabbed hold of the strings, pulled them tight – and managed, at last, to muster a smile.

'It's perfect.'

12

Sometimes I endeavoured to gain from Frankenstein the particulars of his creature's formation, but on this point he was impenetrable.

*

She was no longer that happy creature who in earlier youth wandered with me on the banks of the lake and talked with ecstasy of our future prospects.

— MARY SHELLEY, *Frankenstein*

THE FOLLOWING WEEK, we begrudgingly returned to work on Henry's geology book and the series of articles he had promised to Mr Chambers. But every moment that he could spare, Henry spent at various reading rooms – at the old University College collection, the Geological Society, the Zoological and the Linnean. Although ladies were not officially debarred from the reading rooms, my presence there never failed to elicit unwanted attention, so I spent my time at home instead, scouring what texts we already owned for useful information.

Every evening, we compared our findings. Henry, it was decided, would concentrate on anatomy, and I on physiology and chemistry – though there was also, of course, the matter of *electricity* to be considered. Victor had been quite careful not to reveal his method outright, precisely so that no one might attempt to do what we were doing now – but there was one solitary phrase, one slip of the tongue, which I felt may be the key to it all: the 'spark of being'. I still remembered the first time I had read of the experiments of Aldini and Galvani in the little book on electricity Mr Jamsetjee had sent me years ago; there had been only one illustration, a woodcut of a splayed frog, but I could see the entire scene in my head nevertheless. First, the careful touch of the wire to either side of the chest, followed by the spasmodic jerking of limbs, the clench of its tiny heart – the slick opening of an eye. Remarkable, true, but still nothing more than a haunting imitation of life. What on earth had my great-uncle done differently, then, to make that imitation *true*?

I could not say yet. But if the answer lay anywhere in our borrowed library of Liebig and Lavoisier and Dalton, or my well-thumbed copy of Faraday's *Experimental Researches in Electricity*, I would find it.

I felt quite rotten, after our laboratory was put together, that Henry had had to do it all himself – though at least he'd had some help with the lifting and carrying from a pair of Agnes's strapping brothers. Consequently, when it came to finding specimens for our experiments, I promised I would handle the matter myself. At first, I feared I would have to find a rat catcher to bribe, or, failing that, go out into the streets myself and scour the gutters for corpses; but as it happened, I was spared the indignity of such a thing. One wet afternoon, I glanced out of the rear window on the third floor to see Mrs Hedges in the alley, surrounded by a handful of children. I crept down the stairs and peered out of the kitchen window for a closer look.

She was handing out bits and pieces from a basket – a crust of bread, a shrivelled parsnip, the bronze flash of a ha'penny – all of which were snatched up at once, tucked away in pockets and sleeves. One by one, the children thanked her and scampered off.

When Mrs Hedges came back in and spotted me, her face grew pale.

'Mrs Sutherland! Ma'am, I—'

'Who are those children?' I asked.

'Only my cousin's girls! Well, it were only them at first, come round here asking for a penny for their lunch, so I gave them some peelings as well to take back to their mother – I would have only thrown 'em out anyway, ma'am; I know how Mr Sutherland feels about peel soup – only then they went and brought their blasted friends, all clamouring to help sweep the stoop for a penny, and Lord knows, I've a soft heart, Mrs Sutherland, but everything I gave 'em was out my own pocket, I swear—'

I held up a hand to stop her, and she stuttered to a halt. I should have been cross, I supposed; it was quite unprofessional, and we ought to be saving every scrap we had at a time like this, even if Henry did turn up his nose at peel soup. But I could hardly complain, when she had just dropped such a perfect solution into my lap.

'They're wanting for money, are they?'

Something like pride crossed her face. 'They ain't beggars, ma'am. My cousin, he's no country lord, but he works hard—'

'Oh, I'm sure he does; I meant no offence, Mrs Hedges,' I said hurriedly. 'Only, if the children are at a loose end, and looking for something to do . . . well, perhaps I can help.'

She frowned. 'Help? Ma'am?'

'Yes. Or rather, I suppose, they might help me.' I was already making a mental tally of the contents of my money box, wondering how many rats I'd get for a shilling. 'The next time your cousin's children come round, ask them to bring more of their friends, would you?'

'HALF EATEN? *Again?*' Henry exclaimed. 'Dear Lord. Did they even listen to your instructions?'

'Well, it was better than the eel one of them brought me last week,' I said, reaching forward to smack away an ember that had landed on the sleeve of his coat. Henry swore and batted wildly at the smoking mark it had left, earning him stern looks from several of the passengers aboard the train. Second class certainly bore its risks, particularly on days such as this, when the crowds were so thick one was forced to sit pressed up against the unglazed windows.

'Was the eel fresh at least?' Henry asked. That was the chief condition we had set our little band of hunters: mice or rats, it did not matter, as long as they were recently dead. For just as a rusted clock cannot be coaxed back to life no matter how much one winds it up, we reasoned, one could not restore vital force to a rotting vessel. But such a thing was hard to find in London, it seemed, a city rife with rot and hungry street dogs. I hadn't denied any of the children their pennies so far, but had promised a whole fruitcake to the first who brought me a proper specimen.

'It was fresh from the fryer, certainly,' I replied drily.

'He brought you a *fried eel*? Good Lord, the youth grow more audacious every day.' Henry rolled his eyes heavenward, before settling into a look of concern. 'I do wish we didn't have to involve Mrs Hedges in all this. Will she not wonder what we're up to?'

'I've told her that we're practising dissection.' At the shocked look he gave me, I very nearly rolled my own eyes. 'Henry, it's no worse than what she does every day in the kitchen to chickens and fish.'

'I suppose,' Henry muttered. 'It would be quite a leap to guess that we are dabbling in *dark alchemical arts*. Oh – here we are; I can see the station coming up.'

The train soon juddered to a halt, and we were poured from the carriage into a crowd that moved with all the speed and stickiness of a pool of molasses. I had not expected to be in Canterbury that day, visiting Mr and Mrs Jamsetjee for – what was, to my shame – the first time since they had moved away from London, and yet here we were. It had begun the week before, when in the course of my research I had happened upon a book called *An Essay on the Recovery of the Apparently Dead*. One suggested method was by means of an electric shock to the heart, using a Leyden jar to store and subsequently deliver the charge. The device sounded possible (if fiddly) to construct ourselves, so I had written for advice to Mr Jamsetjee, who had begun to research the use of electrical engines aboard his family's ships earlier that year. To my surprise, he had replied that not only did he have a Leyden jar in his possession, but that Henry and I might have it outright if we were willing to come to Canterbury to collect it.

This had seemed like a fine proposition to me, if rather odd. Mr Jamsetjee had always been generous with his time and advice, but this – giving away his tools at the drop of a hat – was something else altogether. Had he changed the subject of his research already? And something else puzzled me, too; for while the words in the letter were certainly his, the penmanship most definitely belonged to Mrs Jamsetjee. They often wrote jointly, of course, but now that I thought of it, I realized I had not received a letter from him alone in some time. I could not help but worry.

And when we finally spotted him on the platform and pushed our way over to meet him, I saw that I had been right to.

'Oh, my dear! What a pleasure to see you!' he cried, reaching out with one visibly trembling arm to grasp my hand; his other hand, I saw, rested heavily on a cane. Turning then to Henry, he gave him a rather wan smile. 'And Mr Sutherland, of course. How fares the collection?'

'Oh – well. It is . . . well,' Henry said, fumbling. I could see him trying to catch my eye, silently asking if I had neglected to mention to my mentor that he had been let go the previous year. The answer to which was *yes, of course* – I did not need to give Mr Jamsetjee another reason to have doubts about Henry. And had not Henry neglected to mention his dismissal to his own sister?

'And how are you, sir? Are you well?' I blurted.

He must have caught the worry in my voice, for he gave a sigh, a rueful look crossing his face.

'Ah, the tremors.' Even his speech was different, I noticed; soft and slightly slurred, such that I strained to catch his words amid the clamour of the station. 'Yes, they've been getting rather worse of late. Shaking palsy, the doctor says. Nothing to be done.' And then, before I could so much as draw breath to utter my condolences, 'But in any case, I have a carriage waiting. Shall we?'

The journey was a short one; I had barely enough time to ask after Mrs Jamsetjee (who had a cold once again, according to her last letter, and whom I now worried I would find half dead) before we arrived. The house was different from what I had expected, too – well built, but undeniably in need of dusting and a good coat of paint. Henry and I shared a look as Mr Jamsetjee let us in the front door himself, clearly without any expectation of a footman; it appeared we weren't the only ones who'd had to tighten their belts of late.

'Oh! Here they are!' cried Mrs Jamsetjee as we were led into the parlour – or, at least, a room which looked like a parlour in the process of being eaten by a library, which was in turn being gradually subsumed by a naval museum. I was pleased to see that although she looked tired, Mrs Jamsetjee seemed to be in good spirits as she rose from her armchair to greet us. Alma, the solemn widow who had been the Jamsetjees' maid and cook ever since I'd first known the family on Wight, stood and offered us a bow.

'It is so good to see you again, Mary,' Mrs Jamsetjee said. 'I saw those illustrations of yours in *Chambers's*, of those fossil trees – they were just marvellous. And, Mr Sutherland, I was so sorry to hear about your father; what a terrible shame.'

Henry thanked her politely and reached out to shake her hand. Mrs Jamsetjee had always been more friendly towards Henry than her husband had, as – given her deliberate ignorance of the pettier dramas of scientific society – she had never had any reason to be predisposed against him.

As we settled down on the parlour's faded couches, Alma laid out a tray of the wonderfully spiced and milky tea which I had quite fallen in love with during my stay with the family. Mr Jamsetjee thanked her and bid her take the rest of the afternoon to do as she wished until dinner. As she nodded and turned to go, I saw her pick up from the side table a copy of the *Bombay Samachar*, the newspaper Mr Jamsetjee's family sent him in great crates several times a year. (And which had taken up several cupboards in their former home, much to Mrs Jamsetjee's despair.) Instead of looking as though she meant to put it away, however, I watched as Alma carefully unfolded it, already beginning to read the front page as she climbed the stairs. Mr Jamsetjee must have caught the surprise on my face, for he said:

'Ah, yes. I was in need of someone to help me write my letters home, and it was high time Alma learned to read, in any case. She seems to quite enjoy it; I thought it only fair that she have the run of the library in return. Though I will admit,' he added with a dry chuckle, 'Canterbury is not overflowing with books in Gujarati . . .'

'But I thought you'd found an assistant who knew Gujarati as well as English?' I said, confused. 'Just last year – Mr Townsend, was it?'

Suddenly, it seemed he could not meet my eye. I watched Mrs Jamsetjee, too, grow curiously still.

'Yes, Mr Townsend; we had to let him go, unfortunately,' she said quietly. And then, without pause: 'Jehangir, would you like my cup instead? It is less full; otherwise I worry it might spill . . .'

Once we had finished our refreshments, we were treated to a tour of the library proper, and all the various curios within: working model engines and steamships in bottles and voltaic cells, all sitting under a velvety layer of dust. Along with the Leyden jar, Mr Jamsetjee pressed upon us an entire set of flasks and a bizarre device that looked something like a wax sealing stamp, albeit one the size of a dinner plate. ('An *electrophorus*!' he had proclaimed, hefting the thing suddenly into Henry's arms. 'It generates the static electricity necessary to charge the jar; one simply takes the handle, spins it against the accompanying disc of resin like so . . . Oh, I ought to have asked, how much charge do you need? For . . . what was it? Testing the cardiopulmonary responses of reptiles?' 'Something like that,' Henry had muttered in reply.) I waited until Henry was thoroughly occupied, he and Mrs Jamsetjee puzzling over how to pack everything into the trunk we had brought without the glassware shattering, before I pulled Mr Jamsetjee aside and asked:

'Are you quite sure you're well, sir? It is only that – grateful as I am, do not mistake me – I cannot help but notice that you are shedding possessions as if you were on your deathbed.'

He paused in the act of polishing his glasses. 'Oh, I'm not as bad as all that.'

I watched as he held the glasses up to the light, inspecting their sheen – only they wobbled so badly one could hardly tell if they were smudged or not. He heaved a sigh and set them unsteadily on his face once again.

'I believe my days as a worker of science are over, Mrs Sutherland,' he said quietly.

'They need not be,' I insisted. 'Was your last assistant so unsuitable? Surely you could hire another; you still have your knowledge and your wits, all you need is a steady hand to—'

'The Royal Society did not renew my grant this year.'

I stopped short at that, momentarily too taken aback to speak. Science, as I have said, favours those with the means to fund their own work, but there were always a scant few – those with the talent and the need and, of course, friends in the right positions to petition on their behalf – who were issued a grant or civil pension. It was a distant dream of mine that Henry (or even *myself*; the great astronomer Caroline Herschel had once been gifted a royal stipend, after all) might be awarded such a thing.

'But I thought you were to be given funds for two years at least, you said? For your electric engines?' I pressed.

'Yes, yes, I was under that impression, too – but they have changed everything. The old fund is to be replaced, headed by a new committee or some such . . . I am not entirely sure. The letter I received merely stated that they had reassessed my application and found it "unlikely to yield any scientific usefulness".' His voice grew bitterer with every word. 'I am sure it had nothing at all to do with the utter disdain the man in charge of the committee showed me when we met at the last general meeting.'

'But that's – that is – *atrocious*!' I managed, aghast. 'Is there no one you might speak to? Who might speak for you, and the value of your work? Surely there are rules—?'

'My dear, who do you think sets the rules?' he said, his voice so low and tired that it was nearly beyond recognition. 'And I have spoken. To my friends and acquaintances, the former committee . . . They are all sympathetic, of course, but there is little any of them can do. The funds have already been reassigned and the committee is, at least for this year, wholly in the hands of its elected panel.'

'The panel which *they* elected, did they not?' I asked hotly. He gave a shrug, his gaze trained on the floor, and I realized then – with a deep pang of sorrow – that he was embarrassed to speak to me of this. As embarrassed, perhaps, as I would have been to admit to him Henry's dismissal from the collection, or his gambling away our savings. Mr Jamsetjee's posture bore the mark of a man who believed he had failed; and that, perhaps, was what made me angriest of all, the thing which made my chest hot and my knuckles clench white. But what could we do, in the end? Neither Henry nor I bore any sway within the Royal Society. My rage was as useless as my sympathy.

'But . . . what will you do?' I asked at last. 'You've already purchased the voltaic cells.'

'Yes – the most expensive part,' he said, wincing. 'Sell them, I suppose, if I can find a buyer. My brother wishes us to return to Bombay, but . . . it is such an arduous trip. I am not sure I am up for it at present. And what with the warehouses he lost last month in the floods . . . things aren't what they were. No, I will not burden him further. We will go back to London, I think.'

'But—' I stopped myself short of saying, *But you love it here*, for he and Mrs Jamsetjee had written many times of how they adored Canterbury, its peace and quiet and quaint Tudor architecture. If they had to leave, I would not salt the wound. 'Is it not more expensive in London?'

'Yes, but there are more of my countrymen, too. My two cousins arrived earlier this year to study engineering; perhaps they might be willing to share accommodation. Georgianna and I moved here to retire, to escape the bustle, but . . . well, I am sure we will readjust.' He raised an eyebrow, his gaze at last growing hopeful. 'And there is a lovely new Parsee cemetery in Woking, I have heard.'

'A *cemetery*?'

'Not that I plan to make use of it soon!' he amended, hands flying up in hasty protestation.

'Good, good.' I clutched at my chest. 'I meant to say, when you said you were thinking of returning to London, I had hoped you meant *alive* . . .'

He gave a laugh, which pleased me. 'No, no! It is only – I had thought that perhaps poor Georgianna would have to ship me back to India, when the time comes.'

And with that, the mood was grim once again. There was a *clunk* from the adjacent room, and a chorus of gasps, as if some bit of glassware had very nearly met its end.

'Is there no way at all you might continue with your studies?' I asked. 'What of your wife? Or Alma? They already help with your correspondence; could they not assist you in your work as well?'

He was already shaking his head, which vexed me at first – was it such a ridiculous prospect? – but with a rueful smile, he explained:

'My dear . . . they do not *want* to. Alma nearly fell asleep last week when I tried to translate some Faraday for her; and Georgianna tolerates my rambling well, but she has no true interest in science. It is kindness enough, and imposition enough, that they write my letters for me. I will not force them to do more.'

I will do it. I bit my tongue then to stop myself saying it – though I could not stop myself *thinking* it. It would never work, I knew. Between helping Henry with his regular work and researching our own project, my days were already full to bursting. And even if I gave up the latter, there was still the matter of us living – at least for the moment – in different cities. The most Mr Jamsetjee would be able to do with my meagre weekend help was tinker, not any kind of useful research. And even then, he would not have the money to purchase more voltaic cells when his current supply ran dry.

But with the research that Henry and I were working on . . .

I met my mentor's eye then, for a moment lost in a far-flung fantasy: Henry and I with all the scientific renown we could ever hope for, with the sway to petition the Society on Mr Jamsetjee's behalf, with money from the crown and Royal Society to spend as we wished. A grand house somewhere, with a magnificent modern library; quarters for Mr and Mrs Jamsetjee, and for any other guests or collaborators or student cousins who might have need of them. The start of a scientific circle all our own.

I cringed at first, at the childishness of this dream. But then again, why should it be considered childish? There were already plenty of men, American inventors and English lords, who lived such lives. Why should it be ridiculous, to imagine such a thing for ourselves?

I was about to say as much – though perhaps not in so grandiose a manner, merely to express that I *would* help him – when Mr Jamsetjee's eyes shifted to the window behind me. I watched as his face registered first surprise, then delight. From the adjacent room, I heard Mrs Jamsetjee call out:

'Oh – Jehangir, they're here!'

'Wonderful!' Mr Jamsetjee cried, scrambling to pick up his cane. 'Oh, Mrs Sutherland, have I got a surprise. I wasn't sure if they would arrive in time; they did say they might be delayed . . .'

'They?' I began, bemused. 'Sir, who—?'

But before I could finish my question, it was answered. Upon the drive was a young woman, the same age as myself, with a child in her arms and two more – barely old enough to walk – tottering about her feet. She was exceptionally well dressed, her face obscured at first by the curve of her bonnet and the angle of her body as she turned to pass the infant to a harassed-looking nurse, though I hardly needed to see her face to recognize her. My breath caught in my throat.

She lifted her head at last, a twist of red hair slipping free from the lace and ribbons, and I saw the moment she recognized me through the window as well.

It was Catherine Leveaux.

MR AND MRS Jamsetjee took the children (and a rather disorientated Henry) into the garden, leaving Catherine and me to 'reacquaint ourselves'. What that meant precisely, I had no idea – and neither, it seemed, did Catherine. We sat across from each other in a pair of faded armchairs, offering each other tea and sweets from the tray Alma had brought in; both trying to pretend, I think, that we were not avoiding the other's eye.

'I should say . . .' she began at last. She did not have an accent as such – English and French were equally her mother tongue – but there was nevertheless something slightly strange about her speech. Stiff from disuse, like a gown put away for too long. 'It's Mrs Carré now.'

For the first time I could read something in her expression – a slight mischief about the eyes – though it took me a moment to catch her meaning. When I did, I flinched, remembering how I had bumblingly introduced her as 'Miss Catherine Leveaux' to Henry. Of course the children were hers; of course she was married; of course we ought to address each other properly now, as grown women.

'Oh, how wonderful! Congratulations!' I managed. 'I should say, too – it's Mrs Sutherland now, for me. As you know, of course. You just met him. My husband.'

She cut short my rambling with a glowing smile. 'Yes, well met! He looks like a very fine gentleman. Sugar? Milk?'

'Yes, please. And thank you.' I poured rather more milk than I had meant to into my tea, then offered the jug back to her, but she shook her head.

'Oh, no, I have to take it entirely black these days. Sweet things tend to make me ill.'

With a laugh, she laid a hand upon her stomach – and that was when, with a dizzy feeling like I had been sliding further and further down a rain-slicked slope, I bore yet another realization. The wide waistline of her gown, the way it sat slightly high upon her belly – it was not just that she had grown broader with age.

'You're expecting,' I said quietly.

'Yes!' She beamed. 'Our fourth. You met the others. Claude is the youngest, named after his father; Clémentine and Justine are our twins, quite unexpected . . .'

'You must be very busy,' I heard myself say.

'Oh my, yes! That's why we're passing through at the moment, in fact; we were touring England, but this one came as a surprise, so we're going back to Calais so that my mother can help when the baby arrives. She's even found another nanny for us.' She smiled again, in that glowing way that women who are with child are always said to do, although I could not recall ever having done so myself. 'Truly, I'm surprised Uncle never said anything . . . I didn't even know you were still in correspondence. Whatever do you two write about, if not news?'

I was surprised, too, though I supposed Mr Jamsetjee had always assumed that Catherine and I must keep in touch of our own accord. And he was, like Henry, always far more eager to talk of 'concrete things' than of matters so inconsequential as health and family.

'Scientific news, mostly,' I said. 'I keep him abreast of all the happenings in the Geological Society and such – Henry is a fellow, you see, so I quite often go with him to meetings.'

I was not sure, as I was saying it, why I was playing down my own scientific interests. It was a thoughtless instinct, like a turtle curling up inside its shell. And then Catherine's face crumpled, and I remembered precisely when this instinct had been forged.

'Oh dear, he drags you along, does he? My condolences! Does that mean you get to travel often, at the very least? Claude met a pair of geologists visiting Paris last month, said they'd travelled all over Europe, what fun – even if their wives were forced to play secretary.'

She laughed again, freckles creasing beneath her eyes. I laughed along with her, and conjured up some highly edited tale of my honeymoon in Lyme Regis, for anything was better than saying what I truly wanted to say – than revealing to her yet again what a freakish specimen I was.

You have changed, and not for the better.

'My condolences'? You ought to have mine, madam.

I loved you once, when you were not so dull.

But I was being unfair. She had not changed, not truly; she had only grown up. It was I who had refused to let go of childhood – believing in magic and miracles, digging about in the mud for interesting stones. She had done all that she was meant to do, and seemed all the happier for it.

'I'm glad that you are happy,' she said as I came to the end of my story, as if reading my mind – or as if she, too, had been thinking of other things. Her smile was a complicated one; fond, guilty, with a note of pity. I felt a flash of anger, but tamped it down – bit down, too, my jealousy and bitterness and lingering sorrow – long enough to speak the truth.

'I'm glad that you are, too.'

Dear Maisie,

I know precisely what you mean, when you speak of legacy. Death is one thing, but death in the minds of everyone you once knew – the death of your name, your reputation – is another matter entirely. I do think you overestimate my and Henry's importance, however; I hardly think that our smattering of articles, or our single (rather derivative! Don't tell Henry) geology primer will live on in the minds of men. They barely live in the minds of men now (and not only because the latter is not yet published). But perhaps, someday soon, if our latest avenue of research goes well—

A pause; a sigh; a nervous tap of the pen. I leaned forward and scratched that last sentence from the page. It was entirely too soon to get into all of that.

But I would say, Maisie, that even by holding your mother in your memory, you are a better legacy than most. Perhaps it is only because I never knew my own parents—

Another pause, another feverish scratching-out. Another sigh as I regained my courage and wrote it all back in again.

Perhaps it is only because I never knew my own parents, but it seems to me that one of the worst tragedies of all is to have a child who does not think fondly of you after you are gone – either because you died too soon for them to know you, or you were obliged to leave them in the care of another, or you made yourself so perfectly hateable that you do not deserve such fondness. I resolved long ago that if I should ever have children of my own, I would keep them by me. I would give them reason to love me.

I sat back and grimaced at the page before me. I looked at that *if* before *children*, and I hated it; it seemed to me that I was dancing about the issue at hand, too cowardly to mention it outright. But how could I? How could I commiserate with her on what a wretched legacy *I* was, having married against my grandmother's wishes and tried and failed at motherhood, without rendering her an even worse legacy, for never having tried at all?

'Mary!' Henry called out from the floor below, and I jumped, the tip of my pen smearing ink across the page.

'Yes?' I called back, trying feverishly to wipe up the mess. Maisie and I had been writing for half a year now, though our letters had become gradually less frequent of late – on my part as well as hers. Was she growing tired of me, I wondered? Was I growing tired of her? Did we truly have anything in common, *truly* – or were we simply both pleased that we had proved ourselves capable of friendship?

Henry's voice came again, drifting up the stairs. 'Mary, you must see this!'

'In a moment!' I saw, with a cry of exasperation, that I had dripped ink on to my letter to Mr Jamsetjee, too – another painful, half-written thing, beginning with a polite *Thank you for hosting us*, et cetera, and veering off almost immediately into a maze of crossings-out, a chronicle of my many attempts to express what I had been unable to put into words that afternoon: my vow to help him. To repay him, both literally and figuratively. To claw out a place in the world for us both, in which we might finally be allowed the respect we deserved.

I heard the creak of Henry's tread on the stairs and marvelled anew at the man's impatience. I turned, ready to snap at him that nothing could be so important—

When I saw the bundle he was carrying.

'Is that—?' I asked, breathless.

'It is.' He was grinning at me, a manic energy in his eyes. 'Our first usable specimen. It's perfect, as far as I can see.'

I bit my lip, casting one last look at my writing desk – before I pushed to my feet and followed him upstairs.

WE LAID OUR instruments upon the table: Mr Jamsetjee's Leyden jar, to provide the spark, and the electric-shock device copied from Mr Kite's book on resuscitation, with which to administer it. In the middle, we tacked down a square of wax paper and tipped the rat out of its bag. I have never been one for squeamishness, but somehow that very first rat, stiff and slightly warm, turned my stomach just a bit. Nevertheless, we both leaned in to examine it. It was still dirty, its fur uneven and its paws grey with grime from the street. Its mouth lay open, tongue lolling out on to the table.

When I looked up at Henry, I saw that his excitement seemed to have faded somewhat. He had done a thousand dissections during his time at the collection, I knew; he had spent whole weeks putting small dead things in jars. I, meanwhile, had only ever seen such things in books. For him, this might be the tiresome part, the long stretch of hard work between the project's conception and its completion, but for me – for me, it was all brand new.

From this point, there would be no more dreaming. It was time to turn our theories to flesh and blood.

13

But these philosophers, whose hands seem only made to dabble in dirt, and their eyes to pore over the microscope or crucible, have indeed performed miracles . . .

*

With an anxiety that almost amounted to agony, I collected the instruments of life around me, that I might infuse a spark of being into the lifeless thing that lay at my feet.

— MARY SHELLEY, *Frankenstein*

'DO YOU THINK we ought to try a higher voltage?'

'Higher? Dear Lord, Henry, we nearly *cooked* the last one. Perhaps it is more a matter of applying a subtle current to multiple locations at once.'

'But did we not already try that with specimens nineteen and twenty? I still think the freshness must—'

'But the one we used last week was practically still twitching. And besides, Victor took his fragments from a graveyard; that's hardly fresh.'

'I suppose not. Damn it all.' Henry sighed, turning to glare out of the window. It was a dismal afternoon; we had already exhausted that day's rat, and by lunchtime it had begun to rain, big fat drops leaking through the roof and pooling upon the wax paper. We had retreated to the study to sulk and ponder, searching through books we had already read ten times over while outside the storm clouds boiled.

It had been such a thrill to see our electrical devices working those first few times – the buzz of the wires, the arcing *snap* of sparks in the air. But now, each specimen only one more wasted body left in our gruesome, rodenticidal wake, that excitement was waning. No matter how many attempts we made, no matter what other techniques we used concurrently – heating the body, applying intestinal stimulants, simulating respiration through use of bellows – our rats remained stubbornly dead.

I had always thought myself a patient woman, but in these past weeks I'd felt that patience begin to fray. I'd taken to pacing, to long walks through Hyde Park along the banks of the Serpentine. I let my correspondence pile up, answering in great guilty batches of ten at a time. *Once we are done*, I promised myself; once we had something to show for our efforts, and I could be truthful, I would be a more faithful correspondent.

I tried not to think, as the weeks ticked by into months, how long that might be.

With a sigh, I shut my sketchbook. Somewhere, distantly, a church bell rang the hour.

'Suppose it is all divine intervention?' I said suddenly.

'Hmm?' Henry, apparently bored of the silence, had turned back to his book – a hefty Bridgewater treatise with the rather eclectic title of *Chemistry, Meteorology, and the Function of*

Digestion. I recalled quite clearly having written its name on a list I had composed the previous week, entitled *Last Resorts*.

'Suppose there is no such thing as spontaneous generation,' I said. 'What if, every time some small thing comes to life, it does so by the hand of God, and we are running a fool's errand?'

Henry snorted. 'Surely God doesn't have time for all that. Every weed, each blade of grass? Every inconsequential beetle?'

'He is infinite and all-knowing, Henry,' I replied, equally derisive. 'Time means nothing to Him, I'm sure.'

Henry grew quiet for a moment. A great gust blew by, lashing rain against the windows in diaphanous sheets. Finally, he said softly:

'I find it rather difficult to believe in an infinite, all-knowing God since our dear—'

Our dear—. There it was, the space in which a name ought to have been. But of course, she'd never lived long enough to have been given one.

I watched as he slowly closed the book upon his thumb.

'Do you believe there is a God at all?' he asked, not meeting my eyes.

It was a dangerous question. One which might ruin one's prospects and connections if answered incorrectly, or in the wrong company. Even Mr Jamsetjee's Parsee faith seemed to draw less scorn than atheism or deism – though I supposed that was because most viewed it as nothing more than an exotic party trick, powerless to affect England's own good and moral citizens. There were some, to be sure, who proudly wore their disbelief on their sleeve – and an unknowable number more, like Henry and me, who kept our doubts behind closed doors.

'I believe there is,' I said at length, 'but . . . I don't believe He is omniscient. There are some events too miraculous or coincidental, I think, to have occurred by chance . . . and some too terrible to occur by intention.'

'Many would say such things are meant to teach us a lesson,' he said wryly. That wrung a laugh out of me.

'What sort of lesson? That the world is cruel and aimless? I knew that already.'

He ran a thumb along the edge of his book, worrying at the corner. 'Perhaps, then, God is not benevolent and inattentive but all-knowing and cruel.'

'Which would you prefer?'

He thought awhile. 'The first, I think. It would make for a kinder world. And you?'

'The second,' I answered at once.

He blinked, clearly taken aback. 'Why?'

'Because it means that we are justified in exacting our revenge.' It was a foolish, grandiose thing to say – but it was a foolish, grandiose thing we were doing, and I could not help but love the look on Henry's face when I said it. 'We shall steal fire from the heavens, and I shall not repent, even for one minute – for what sort of god would condemn us to such a cold world without it? We're merely taking what should have been ours from the beginning.'

It still felt perilously unreal, this whole affair. A story to tell children to make them behave. And yet, in that storm-dark room, as Henry gave a slow and mischievous smile and leaned forward to press a kiss to my knuckles, I could almost believe it true.

'Look at you,' he said, a savage glitter in his eyes. 'This – *this* is why I married you, my dear. That fire of yours. You look as though you are about to storm the gates of Heaven.'

AUGUST SLID ERRATICALLY into September, then October, then November. At length, we finished the geology primer for Mr Murray, its sale a balm to my nerves that was almost immediately negated by an outbreak of cholera on Broad Street. This being not ten minutes from our front door, we became veritable hermits – each door and window plugged with rags to keep the miasma out, each day running into the next as we pored over the same notes again, and again, and again.

We had long since exhausted our reputable sources and now resorted to the disreputable, books that spoke of quintessences and panaceas and *aquae vitae*. Victor had, after all, mentioned the teachings of Agrippa and Paracelsus, no matter how little stock Henry and I put in such archaic nonsense. But still, even when we attempted to stimulate the archeus of each organ, even with the application of distillations of blood or mercury, we had no success.

Until, very suddenly, we did.

By now it was mid-December, and our workroom's lone window rattled as the wind threw sleet listlessly against the glass. We were both wrapped in scarves and gloves, the little brick-heater which was meant to provide our specimen with the 'warmth of vitality' doing a poor job of heating the room at large. Perhaps, I thought afterwards, it was our growing exhaustion that made the difference between this trial and all the others; perhaps, like every pot which doesn't boil until you look away, it was our utter despondency that caused our experiments to yield a result at last.

The noise was the most remarkable thing. The rat was eight hours dead by my count, and stiff as a board. We had decided, this time, to do without any elaborate alchemical processes or tricks; this trial would be a standard, one to which we could compare others in future. Henry held the wires in place, and I discharged the Leyden jar, and it seemed for a moment that we had failed once more, as we always did . . .

. . . until I noticed that there, in the dark, its eyes were glinting. Nigh imperceptibly, its small chest rose and fell.

My heart skipped.

And before I could say a word, before I had even time to realize what this meant, it opened its mouth and *squealed*. I reeled back, shivers running down my spine. And then, just as it had been moments before, it was still. Henry and I met each other's eyes, and I was gratified to see that he looked as shaken as I was – that it had not all been a hallucination, brought on by troubled sleep and desperation.

With unsteady hands, I reached out to touch it, feeling for movement – a breath, a heartbeat, anything at all.

Nothing. It was as still as before.

'That was it, wasn't it?' I whispered, startled at how loud my own voice seemed in the silence. I had never expected the aftermath of a miracle to be so ordinary.

'That was it,' Henry echoed. A breath, a pause. 'We did it.'

14

Nothing is more painful to the human mind than, after the feelings have been worked up by a quick succession of events, the dead calmness of inaction and certainty which follows . . .

*

My abhorrence of this fiend cannot be conceived. When I thought of him I gnashed my teeth, my eyes became inflamed . . . my hatred and revenge burst all bounds of moderation.

— MARY SHELLEY, *Frankenstein*

OF COURSE, WE could not reproduce it.

That would have been too much to ask, I mused the following day as I stirred sugar sullenly into my tea. We'd risen that morning feeling like gods, glowing with our success; at the faint sound of the kitchen door opening, I had sprung from bed and snatched the latest rat from the boy's hands as he blushed to see the mistress of the house still in her nightclothes. We had rushed upstairs and tried again, setting up the experiment exactly as we had before—

And it had not worked.

'Perhaps it was simply a very special rat,' said Henry as I passed him the sugar, and I shot him an exasperated look.

The rest of the day was spent examining our workspace and our notes, searching for anything that might have set this experiment apart from all the others. In a flash of inspiration, I ran down to ask Mrs Hedges who had brought in the previous day's specimen, and when the child arrived later that evening I bombarded him with questions – where did he get it? How did it die? Had it seemed to him more resilient somehow than the others? But no, he told me with some confusion, it had been perfectly ordinary. And so we were left at loose ends again, no closer to understanding the secrets of life than we had been before.

'We've been invited to a New Year's dinner next week,' said Henry later that day, as we sat in the study going over our notes for the hundredth, thousandth time.

'By whom?' I asked. It did not matter much, for I was sure we would not go. We had declined nearly all invitations since embarking on our great project. Which was a foolish luxury – foolish in that, in the wake of Henry's blundering lecture, we really ought to have been doing all we could to appear respectable and personable, to smooth the feathers he had ruffled.

'Mr and Mrs Murchison,' Henry said. 'One of their grand parties.'

I tapped my pen upon the page ruminatively, suddenly conflicted. Among all the Society wives, Mrs Murchison had been one of the friendliest towards me, despite the social gulf between us. It had been such a kind and surprising gesture at the Geological Society, for her to wrangle me a seat, and I had not yet had a chance to thank her for it. Besides, there would surely be a great many important people at such an event – the sort that it would be very beneficial to have as a patron or a reference to one's character, if one were planning in the near future to unveil a discovery so miraculous it was nearly beyond belief.

'We should go, I think,' Henry said, though his tone was grim. I suspected he had followed the same train of thought as I.

'I think so as well,' I said with a sigh. Perhaps it would be pleasant, after all, to spend one evening away from the company of rats.

BELGRAVE SQUARE WAS an imposing place. In the centre lay the square itself, a thicket of bare trees whose jagged shadows reached like fingers past the surrounding fence; about each side was a wall of gleaming white terraced houses, their facades positively brimming with balconies and pillars and faux Greek finery. The first time we had come to the Murchisons' house, I'd baulked as our carriage pulled up to the kerb. It was all too bright, too fanciful, a candle too close to the eyes – too different from our own narrow little townhouse on Maddox Street.

This evening we were shown directly into the parlour, where we were greeted by Mr and Mrs Murchison and introduced to a flurry of politicians and Oxbridge fellows whose company made me immediately ill at ease. I had been concerned that the embarrassment of Henry's lecture would have spread beyond the Geological Society, to Owen's more influential contacts, but to my surprise even men who I had heard were personal friends of the professor did not seem to react to Henry's name. Either they had already forgotten about the spat, or it had been so inconsequential a thing that Owen had not even bothered to speak of it – to do anything, it seemed, beyond crush Henry's attempts to secure a curatorship, and promptly move on.

It was a generous fate, all things considered. True, Henry's audacity had convinced half the Geological Society that he was an impertinent twit, and cost him at least one position – but then, Owen himself had once been expelled from the Royal Society council for stealing another's research, only to rise again to the peak of his career. Yes, that was what galled me the most about this whole affair, I think; that Henry could err and argue and throw a fit, and have the slate wiped clean. I could not imagine the same generosity being extended to me, if things were reversed. (Perhaps, I thought later, this was why he felt so drawn to games of chance. They must seem a wonderful pastime, if all the world had conspired to convince you that there was no loss from which you could not recover.)

Among the Murchisons' various connections were some we already knew from various scientific circles – and it was here that we found our truancy had not gone as unnoticed as we'd hoped. Again and again we were asked what on earth had kept us holed up for so many months, each time wheeling forth our alibi: a book on the hypothetical biology of the *Plesiosaurus dolichodeirus*, based upon that of modern reptiles. But the mention of a book in progress only drew more questions.

'Which modern reptiles do you plan to use for this comparison?' asked Professor Ellis, who thankfully seemed to bear no hard feelings since Henry had chased him down at the Geological Society. 'I do hope you're not still railing against Professor Owen's model—'

'Have you thought about a publisher yet?' asked Mr Charles Darwin, illustrious biologist of HMS *Beagle*. 'You might try John Murray, or perhaps the Ray Society; they're the ones putting out my barnacle books at present . . .'

And so on, and so on. At long last, to my relief, we were called to dinner. The dining room was long and narrow, rather cramped for the number of people in it, but decorated beautifully in wine-coloured velvet and gold. Henry and I would be seated apart – it was the customary thing, at these sorts of events, to arrange the seating so as to encourage conversation between those who might not have previously met. Of course, this could not always be expected to work, and our table that evening was testament to the fact. Even before I sat down, it was clear that the men opposite and adjacent to me were already well acquainted. They were perhaps the oldest and baldest trio of men I had ever seen in my life, and were already so deep in conversation that they did not so much as glance up at my arrival. And so it was that I turned instead to the guest to my left and realized, with slowly dawning horror, that we were acquainted as well.

It was Finlay Clarke.

For a moment, I simply stared. He was too absorbed in conversation with the young brunette to his left to notice me at first, and so I waited for the inevitable. When he finally turned around, it was all I could do not to break into a scowl; the very sight of him was enough to make my blood boil.

'And you must be Mrs Sutherland!' he cried in a disgustingly jovial fashion. 'I saw you and your husband earlier, but couldn't quite make it across to speak to you both. He and I have known each other for quite some years, you know. Finlay Clarke, by the way – lovely to meet you.'

He did not remember me. For a moment, I was speechless.

'We have met,' I managed at last.

He faltered, smile still wide. 'Pardon?'

'We've met before. Some years ago.' I tilted my head ever so slightly and smiled – sweet, sharp, unaffected. 'On the Isle of Wight?'

Ah, there it was – a flash of recognition.

'Forgive me! How embarrassing. You must excuse me. It's been so long. How have you been, Mrs Sutherland?'

How have I been? How have I been? I hadn't the words to reply, and took an unsteady sip of my aperitif instead. Was it possible he'd forgotten what he'd said to me the last time we'd met? Had it really troubled him so little? How utterly, reprehensibly unfair it was that after all this time I still bore the marks, his fingerprints pressed into me like candle wax, while he went on unburnt.

'I have been well.' I forced myself to meet his eyes. 'And you? You're a chemist now, I hear? I saw your presentation at the Geological Society. I thought you were set to go into banking, like your father. What made you change your mind? The spirit of Christmas Yet to Come, perhaps?'

The corners of his smile tightened. Behind him, the brunette made an odd noise which might have been a laugh, though she swiftly turned it into a cough.

'I'm afraid not,' he said. 'Actually, during my apprentice-ship, I happened to become acquainted with one Professor Cumming – the chair of chemistry at Cambridge, you know – who found that I had a natural talent for his subject, and convinced me to apply. Balancing accounts and balancing equations are not so terribly different, I suppose. I'm a consultant for the EIC at present, mostly in the business of fertilizers and soil chemistry; that is how I came to be interested in organic sedi-ments. And you, Mrs Sutherland . . .' He lifted his drink to his lips, his smile slow and unctuous. 'Where did you . . . study?'

That pause spoke volumes. So did the one after it – the brief but all-too-long silence wherein I seethed, and stared, and searched in desperation for something to say. I *could* have studied – that, I think, was what infuriated me the most about his assumption. The same summer I met Henry, I had heard of a new institution recently opened in Bedford; not another governess school, but a proper ladies' college. Perhaps in a different world – one in which I had my grandmother's support, and funds set aside for my education – I might have gone. But in this world, I had married instead. Was that truly all I could say of my life so far? Marriage, my sole accomplishment? I had done more, I felt, so much more; but all of it was in Henry's name.

'Why, if it isn't Finlay Clarke!' boomed a voice, and I was spared the agony of responding by the arrival of a large man of middle age who, between his sideburns and tremendous moustache, seemed to be made mostly of hair. He lowered himself into the seat directly opposite Clarke, small eyes gleaming. 'How've you been, old boy? Coach driver got lost; took me half-way across the city before I noticed where we were going.'

Clarke's demeanour changed at once. 'Captain Strachey! How good it is to see you. I didn't know you were in London. Visiting the family?'

'Yes, that's it. And the Crystal Palace, of course – I was in Nepal for the first grand opening, couldn't miss it a second time. Back off again on Wednesday morning, though. But where are my manners! Who's this young lady you were talking to? I don't believe we've been introduced.'

I realized with a start that he was referring to me, the brunette being already engaged in another conversation. Clarke glanced my way and said, a tad begrudgingly:

'Yes – Captain Strachey, this is Mrs Sutherland. You know

Henry Sutherland, don't you? He's a fossil man, used to work in the University College collection. Mrs Sutherland, this is Captain Strachey of the Bengal Engineers. I worked under him in the Punjab two years ago, on some irrigation works.'

'You sell yourself short, Mr Clarke,' boomed Strachey, and I wondered how it was that every noise he made seemed to come out of him twice as loudly as it needed to. 'That project was all but yours! I was still occupied with those awful roadworks, if you recall . . .'

And on they went, talking about bridges and roads and the difficulties of working around the monsoon – speaking always as if *they themselves* had been the ones digging the ditches and laying the pipes. As if it were a crying shame that the Punjabi locals spoke so little English – as if, in the five years that had elapsed since the territory's annexation, it ought to have been their foremost priority. Beside me, the older men were still discussing the intricacies of taxation. Further down the table, I could just make out Henry deep in conversation with Professor Ellis. I watched him then, as Captain Strachey boomed and the old men slurped their way through their gravy soup, and resolved to ask him later how on earth he could stand to be friends with such a man as Finlay Clarke. I could only assume – only *hope* – that Henry would cast him aside, once he knew the truth of his character.

And then, like a fish upon a hook, my attention caught on a word – for Clarke and Captain Strachey were talking about chemistry.

'Ferments?' Strachey was saying, clearly confused. 'Such as wine? Bread?'

'No, not the wine itself, but that which *makes* the wine,'

Clarke explained. 'Or which raises the bread, or brews the beer, and so on. There is currently quite a debate as to whether organisms such as yeast cause fermentation, or are caused *by it* – that is to say, whether they are somehow seeded in the liquid from the air, after which they cause the liquid to ferment, or whether the organisms are in fact a by-product of the fermentation process, initiated by some nitrogenous reaction. I, for one, adhere to the latter theory. There have been a number of experiments in which liquid exposed to finely filtered air has fermented on its own, and only afterwards developed yeast. It's terribly unreliable, though; and thus very hard to prove. But wouldn't it be remarkable, if it were true? It would confirm once and for all that abiogenesis is—'

'Abiogenesis?'

'Forgive me, Captain. Abiogenesis is—'

'The spontaneous generation of life from non-living matter,' I cut in.

I had not even meant to say the words; they had simply spilled out. The two men turned to me in utmost astonishment, as if the roast duck on the table had begun to talk.

'You are speaking,' I continued quietly, 'of life induced by chemical reaction.'

Clarke cleared his throat. 'Well ... I would not say it was *spontaneous generation of life*, as such. It is only after the reaction occurs that the yeast is created. But, in essence, yes.'

'My, my,' said Captain Strachey. 'Fascinating stuff, I must say. Did you say you put out a paper on this?'

'Yes, back in May. It is indeed fascinating, as you say, but largely outside my purview ... too close to *philosophy* for my liking. The one I read out at the Geological Society was focused specifically on the action of ferments in estuarine sediments, in the decomposition of organic matter and the like. Fermentation and decomposition are far closer than most would like to admit.' He gave a significant nod towards the wine, smirking as he swilled the dregs up the sides of the glass. 'But yes, it really is quite amazing how much the composition of soil is affected by the reproduction of the fungi within. Do you remember, on that one farm just outside Jullundur—'

And with that, I was once again an island, quite cut off. But it was a satisfied sort of isolation in which I now sat, for deep within the recesses of my mind, an ember was stirring – the beginnings of an *idea*. I thought of Clarke's nitrogenous reactions, and of their terrible unreliability, and of a piece I had read on catalysts some time past, and I schemed.

In time, the third course was cleared away and replaced by a series of immense fruit tarts. It would not be long now, I assured myself. I had only to last until after dinner, when the men would retire to the smoking room and the women to the parlour, and I would be done with this odious affair. But then, as Captain Strachey dwelled terribly over his last few bites of lemon tart, he said:

'Oh, Mr Clarke! I cannot believe it nearly slipped my mind – I must thank you for putting me on to this parliamentary grant business. It looks as though we'll be able to double the size of our next expedition – quite wonderful! I wasn't even aware the Society did such a thing.'

I stilled in my seat, trying to be sure I had not misheard. Beside me, Clarke grinned and crowed:

'Yes, not many people are! And all the better for it, I say; fewer competitors for the pot. Good Lord, but if you'd seen some of the applications this year ... I was talking with the committee head—'

'Who is it now – Melville?'

'The colonel, yes, brilliant man. In any case, he was telling me that Mr ... oh, what's his name? Jamboree? I always forget. The Indian fellow. In any case, he wanted some ridiculous sum to investigate battery-operated engines. For ships, of all things! Do you have any idea how many Galvanic cells that would require?' He tutted. 'This is precisely why we need men of *robust* education; anyone with even a passing knowledge of chemistry would have known that to be a hopeless cause. We cannot simply let any bumbling fool who can slap together a ship—'

'And what would you know of it?' I spat.

The pair of them blinked at me. Slowly, Clarke's eyes narrowed.

'I'm sorry, Mrs Sutherland; I forget, of course, that you are a veritable *expert* on electricity. Pray tell, how would you account for the impracticality of powering an electric ship with Galvanic cells?'

Before I could reply that that was, of course, the very line of inquiry Mr Jamsetjee had been endeavouring to research, Captain Strachey cut in:

'Now, now, I'm sure Mrs Sutherland did not mean to be rude. Perhaps the rich food has upset her constitution. You must learn to be gentler with the ladies, Mr Clarke, if you ever hope to find yourself a wife!'

He gave me a sort of mischievous squint, almost a wink. I smiled back, and in the theatre of my mind's eye I shoved him off his chair.

'I don't have the time to find myself a wife, Captain Strachey,' Clarke said drily. 'I am far too busy. And besides' – he cast a glance in my direction that was so pointed I could almost feel it beneath my skin – 'it is so hard to find women of good breeding nowadays.'

'Is it truly?' Strachey chuckled. 'I confess, I've been in Nepal for so long that all the English ladies seem well bred to me!'

'Oh, I imagine,' Clarke drawled. 'Tell me, sir ... do you know of Monsieur de Gobineau? He's an old friend of my father's, and he has this most fascinating theory about why the lower classes everywhere seem so inclined to laziness and vice. He maintains that in the days of all the great ancient civilizations, the races remained separated by geography; but in the centuries since, the common people of nearly every region have become terribly mixed, muddying the barriers originally set by Nature. Only the most careful noble houses of Europe have avoided doing so, thereby retaining the traits of our distinguished ancestors.'

I could not restrain myself any longer from saying, 'That is patently absurd.'

'And what would you know of it?' he retorted at once, a perfectly infuriating echo. 'Ah, but I forget. You are uniquely qualified in this field also, are you not?'

I glowered at him, my fingers clenched so tightly around the stem of my wine glass that they ached. 'I have seen with my own eyes, sir, men who think themselves noble and yet who exhibit the most wretched behaviour, and men gifted no such advantages by birth who are infinitely more noble of character.'

'I am with you there, Mrs Sutherland,' Strachey cut in

blithely, still savouring the last few bites of his dessert. 'But I do think, perhaps, that this is not a matter concerning individuals, but groups.'

'Precisely!' Clarke nodded in Strachey's direction. 'It is the same with chemicals. Some mixtures thrown together may turn out quite well, whereas—'

'People are not chemicals, Mr Clarke!'

'. . . Far more turn out quite foul,' he carried on, giving no indication at all that he had heard me besides a slight raising of his voice. 'It is our punishment, I suppose, for meddling with Nature's order. Hence why so many of the lower peoples of Europe – the Irish, for example, the Gauls and Iberians – have ended up with the worst traits of several races combined—'

'You, sir, are—'

'. . . Such as the inability to carry on a civilized conversation,' Clarke said, each word knife-sharp. 'Typically, Mrs Sutherland, one waits for one's conversational partner to finish speaking.'

'Typically, one gives one's conversational partner the opportunity to speak at all,' I snapped.

'Yes, well.' He plucked his glass of wine from the table with an air of finality and turned back to Strachey, casting him a smugly exasperated look. 'Such rules only apply when one's conversational partner has anything of use to say.'

For a moment, I could hardly think. I felt my nostrils flare, my jaw creak; it was as though I were teetering on a precipice, my entire body poised to leap. Words spilled out of me before I could stop them.

'If you possess any of the admirable qualities of your

distinguished ancestors, Mr Clarke, they must be entirely of the superficial sort; for while you may style yourself the gentleman, it does not change the fact that you are a vile and hateful character!'

I was aware, dimly, that this last outburst had gained some attention – the brunette was blinking at me in astonishment, and the old men had ceased their conversation at last to turn and stare. I saw something flash in Clarke's eyes. He leaned towards me and said in a low and venomous voice:

'And while you might style yourself the lady, Mrs Sutherland, it does not change the fact that *you* are descended from a common tart who couldn't—'

But I never found out what it was that my mother could not do, for I had just tossed my glass of wine in his face.

To my dying day, I think, I will treasure the look he bore then. Wine dribbled from his nose and his chin; it dripped from the pointed collars of his shirt on to the tablecloth. The rim of the glass must have cracked him on the nose, for there was a line across the bridge of it. As I watched, he raised a finger to it and winced.

Silence spread through the room like a ripple through a pond. I placed my empty glass back on the table. At the other end of the room, a fork clattered against a plate, the noise as clear as the chiming of a bell.

'Terribly sorry,' I said. My own words sounded far away, my voice belonging to someone else. 'I must have slipped.'

I stood and nodded at my shocked hostess. 'Thank you for having us, Mrs Murchison.'

And then I took my leave.

Outside, I stalked to the kerb and waited while the footman

fetched me a coach. I had put Henry in an awful fix, I knew, but I could not bring myself at that point to care. It was all I could do, in fact, to keep myself from screaming.

Moments later, I heard heavy footsteps down the stairs. Henry joined me, still shouldering on his coat, looking positively murderous.

'What in *God's name* was that?' he hissed through his teeth. 'Mr Clarke was mortified, *I* was mortified – in front of the best scientific minds in the country! What will they think of us now? We'll be exiled. We'll be a laughing stock. We'll be—'

'Is that the first thing you think to ask me?' I said flatly. 'Not what he did, to deserve such behaviour?'

Henry threw an arm in the air. '*What*, Mary? What did he do?'

I wanted to recount the entire affair, quote every vile and preposterous word Clarke had said, but my mind was a useless, jumbled thing. 'He . . . insulted my mother, for one. He claimed that—'

'Lord, Mary, of all things,' Henry muttered, pinching his nose. 'I should have thought you would be used to that by now.'

At this, my mouth fell open. '*Used to it?*'

'Yes, Mary! I am sorry, but surely after all these years – why choose to make such a scene over it *now*? Clarke says the stupidest things sometimes, it is true, but I am sure he did not mean it. All night I had people making thinly veiled remarks about my lecture, about Professor Owen's brilliance and those damned statues, and did I throw my drink in anyone's face? No, I did not. I expected—'

The footman, who had been about to help me into the hansom which had just drawn up to the kerb, stared directly ahead with practised indifference as I wheeled on Henry, one forefinger raised.

'*Don't! You! Dare!*' I hissed. 'You chose to deliver that awful lecture and disgrace yourself in front of the entire Geological Society. How could I have chosen to be born as I was? Year after year, I have watched you, Henry – I grin and bear it and bite my tongue, all for the privilege of watching you ruin chances I would die for, throwing away more than I've ever had – you have no idea, *no idea*, how easy you have it!'

To my shame, my voice broke on those last words. I turned to grab the stony-faced footman's hand and stepped up into the cab, letting my head fall against the worn leather backing. My eyes – my treacherous, cowardly eyes – brimmed with tears. I swiped them away, willing myself to push it all down, as I had always done.

I would not break.

I would not crumble.

I would not cry.

I heard Henry's footsteps then, and at first I thought that he was rounding the cab to enter on the other side, but it sounded rather as if he was walking back to the house. Wiping my face one last time, I leaned forward and saw him mount the Murchisons' front steps, at the top of which stood none other than Finlay Clarke. The two exchanged some words that were too low and terse for me to hear – although 'exchange' was perhaps the wrong word, for it was Clarke doing all the talking, gesticulating like a shadow puppet in the light of the Murchisons' doorway while Henry simply grimaced and nodded. One might expect, perhaps, after being harassed and insulted by another man, that it would be the duty of one's husband to step in and defend one's honour; to put aside any friendship the two might have had, in the name of loyalty to his wife.

One might have expected that, I thought as I shut my eyes and leaned back once more. But I supposed I ought to have learned by now, in Henry's case, not to expect much at all.

15

I packed up my chemical instruments and the materials I had collected, resolving to finish my labours in some obscure nook in the northern highlands of Scotland.
— MARY SHELLEY, *Frankenstein*

IT WAS NEARLY a fortnight before we spoke again. It was not as one-sided as our falling-out in Inverness, nor as easily resolved, neither side willing to relent before the other. I passed most of my time in the study, searching for mentions of ferments, while Henry passed most of his out at the reading rooms. At least, that is where I suspected he was, for he came and went each day with a satchelful of papers and a haggard expression. Not the look, I think, of a man who had spent the day gambling – or, at the very least, a man who had spent the day gambling and *won*.

Perhaps, instead, he was looking for work. A not-insignificant part of me hoped that he was. I hadn't forgotten that we were living on borrowed time; every day we devoted to this damnable project, supported only by a few illustrations and newspaper articles for the *Illustrated London News*, was another day without a steady income. One afternoon, in a fit of worry, I rifled through Henry's bureau for his accounting book, and spent a handful of hours laboriously checking the figures – but the thing was so riddled with errors and crossings-out as to be nearly illegible, and only ran to June besides. Of our accounts from the past six months I could find no trace.

The storm finally broke that Monday morning, when Henry presented me at breakfast with a small flat box. It was dropped before me with all the elegance of a cat dropping a mouse upon his master's pillow, and when I looked up at him in confusion, I found Henry's face impossible to read.

'What is this?' I asked at last.

'A gift,' he said flatly. 'To make up for Mr Clarke's poor manners towards you at the dinner.'

'From Mr Clarke?'

His face twisted in some expression of displeasure I could not quite place. 'No, from me.'

Of course. I would never have expected Clarke to repent for his actions; and yet, it seemed by his manner, nor did Henry. My first thought when I opened the box and saw its contents – a bracelet upon a bed of velvet, made of several strands of seed pearls connected by a golden clasp – was that it was beautiful. My second thought was that it was expensive; not the best jewellery money could buy, by any means, but still more expensive than anything I might have chosen for myself, for it would make any of the dresses I owned look cheap by comparison. I could hardly wear it at home, either, where I spent most days writing or drawing or handling dead rats in elbow-length gloves – it wouldn't last a day, I thought, before I ended up catching it on something or ripping it off in irritation as it dug pearl-shaped welts into my skin. It was clear that Henry had done this at the recommendation of some friend or eager jeweller, someone who did not know me at all – *My wife will not speak to me, what shall I do? Oh, buy her a bracelet; that will cheer her up.*

I did not want a gift. What I had wanted was for him to understand me; and if he did not understand, then to *ask*, and to listen, as I explained why Mr Clarke had upset me so badly, and what an awful specimen of humanity he was. But I could see, clear as day in Henry's face as he watched me open the box, that he did not wish to understand. He wanted only to move on, to sweep everything under the rug with a gift so generous that I could not deny it without seeming an unreasonable shrew. Because—

Because, much as I was loath to admit it – much as Clarke had *deserved it* – I knew in the guilty depths of my heart that I had misstepped also. My moment of rashness would cost us. It would be far worse for my own reputation than Henry's, of course (for who could not have sympathy for a man saddled with a mad wife?), but he had the right to be angry. If not the right to say what he had said.

It was with that thought that my anger finally drained away. I was instead exhausted, nearly wishing that I could crawl back up to bed and spend the rest of the day in silent, empty solitude. Instead, I closed the box and set it back on the table, saying in a tone as flat as Henry's:

'Thank you.'

He nodded then – solemnly, as if in conclusion of some dry business dealing – and rounded the table to sit. Carefully removing the top of the soft-boiled egg Mrs Hedges had brought him, he said:

'I think we ought to go to Inverness.'

I puzzled a moment, trying to think if I had missed some news or a letter from Maisie. But I had written to her only the evening before the party – a letter I felt was wasted now, full of inconsequential news and a long, faintly amusing anecdote about a pair of ice skaters I'd seen on the Thames – and although I had watched like a hawk for her reply, none had come.

'I never thought I'd hear you say such a thing,' I answered at last, drily. 'Why?'

'Well, we did say we'd need access to water eventually, and after investigating several locations along the Thames, I really don't think London will do.'

Was that where he'd been, all this time – surveying the docks? I'd thought we had already ruled out such a possibility.

'Isn't it still too soon for that?' I said. 'We haven't even managed to keep our rats alive.'

'Perhaps, but we shall need to move at some point. Might as well do so sooner rather than later.'

'But why your sister's house? Surely any other seaside town would do.'

'Yes,' Henry said hesitantly. 'But, if we take advantage of her hospitality, it would mean . . . a significant reduction in our living expenses.'

Ah, I thought. So that was it. I tried to catch his eye, but he made it impossible, deeply absorbed in the task of stirring sugar into his tea. I thought of the missing accounts, the expensive bracelet, and my stomach twisted with apprehension.

'Henry,' I said. 'I don't have reason to worry, do I?'

'You do not, as I have told you many times before,' he replied, voice only slightly clipped. 'My only thought was that if we stretch our savings by staying with my sister for a spell, we may devote as much time and attention as possible to our *creature*, and less to' – he waved a hand – 'articles on the Lesser Antillean iguana, or whatever else it is Chambers would have me write next.'

I nodded. This mention of 'savings' was news to me, but I supposed Henry's father had indeed paid off his debts, enabling us to start anew. And Henry must have managed, somehow, to find the money for the bracelet. Perhaps the royalties from the geology primer were larger than I had thought. 'For how long would we be away, do you think?'

'Some months. Long enough to merit the effort of moving there, at least. We can go as soon as the snow clears in the north. I wrote to Margaret about it last week, and she said she'd be delighted to have us. Well – to have you, at any rate. "Mary was telling me this, is it true what Mary said about that, please give Mary my warmest regards", et cetera . . . she's quite attached to you, it seems. I don't suppose she gets much female company in Inverness, besides the staff.'

Despite the lingering chill of the conversation, that thought – of Maisie wishing for my company – warmed me like a coal fire. I had been quite taken aback, this past fortnight that Henry and I had been at odds, by how badly I had longed to write to her about it. She was my sole close confidante, I had realized – besides Mr and Mrs Jamsetjee, whom I hardly wished to consult about my marital woes. But if this was rather an embarrassing realization, then at least it was made less so by the knowledge that she seemed to miss me as much as I missed her.

I raised my teacup to my mouth so Henry could not see my smile; it was not for him, after all. 'What are we going to tell her about our experiments?'

'Oh, I'm sure she won't be that inquisitive. I thought we could use the old boathouse as our laboratory; once the cobwebs and dust and . . . general *slime* are gone, I think it should be quite suitable. Cold, so our rats will last, and far away from the house, so we needn't worry about my sister poking about. But if she does ask, we can simply tell her we're trying to make a new kind of rat poison – one that is less harmful to humans than arsenic. She'll be sure to keep out of our way then, if she thinks our lab is full of rats.'

'Will it not be harder to find them in the countryside?'

'Perhaps, but the old stable has quite a population. We could ask the kitchen boy to catch us some. Oliver – you remember him? Always running about underfoot. I'm sure he'd like nothing better.'

It certainly sounded manageable. And perhaps it would be good to get out of the city – to breathe the fresh air that blew in from the firth, to separate Henry from potential temptations, to see Maisie once again. I took a long and steadying sip of my tea.

'All right. There are a few new sources I would like to investigate before we leave, however.'

Henry's brow furrowed. 'New sources?'

'Yes. One book and several essays. I should be able to find most of them at Percy Young's – they have quite a few older issues of the Royal Society transactions. There's one by a Professor Allman, "On the Development of Ferment Cells", or something along those lines, and another from . . . Robert Rigg, I believe? I have a list.'

'Ferment cells? Are you planning to start making beer?'

'I simply want to look further into organic chemistry. Perhaps it will aid us in the construction of the creature's digestive system.'

I knew from a glance that he could tell there was more to be said. I met his eye, daring him to press me further. It was a pointless thing to keep to myself, really; it would be better to have two pairs of eyes for the research. But so much else was his, and this, *this*, no matter how silly or improbable, would be mine — at least, until it became clear whether the idea would bear fruit or not.

'All right,' he said, pushing himself to his feet. 'I'd better go and pack up some of our instruments. Maisie did say that this last bout of snow was a light one; it ought to be gone by the end of January. We can leave then.'

'But what of the annual Geological Society meeting?' I asked, and he turned on his heel in the doorway to face me.

'Why ever would we go there? So I can deliver another "awful lecture" and disgrace myself further? So you can throw something else at Finlay Clarke?' He seemed to rein himself in then, one hand braced upon the doorframe and the other pressed to the bridge of his nose. When he spoke again, his voice was not cold but carefully neutral. 'I think it is best, Mary, if we avoid the societies for a short while.'

I watched as he turned and shut himself in the study, my resentment simmering, but I found that I could not even summon the will to be properly indignant. After a long while, I stood. At first I left the small jewellery box, and then — worried what would happen if Agnes or Mrs Hedges found it; what a wasteful and ungrateful woman they would think me, leaving such a gift discarded on the dining-room table — I brought it with me. In the parlour, I took up my portable drawing desk, shoving the little box for the moment in among my pencils and pens, and drew out a fresh sheet of paper.

Maisie, I wrote — for even though she still had not replied to my last letter, and I would see her again in person soon enough, I simply could not wait; the words rose in me, irrepressible – *I have a question to ask you. Perhaps it is foolish, but I beg of you, tell me honestly nonetheless. You said to me once that you and Henry had reconciled; that you forgave him the cruel things he said when you were young. I ask:*

  How did you do it? How did you forgive him?

  I don't think I've ever forgiven anyone in my life.

BY THE END of that week, we were ready to leave for Inverness. This was altogether sooner than I had expected; it had taken Henry nearly as long to arrange our travels the previous year, and that had been without having to transport the contents of a makeshift laboratory. But this time, Henry was all efficiency. While he booked tickets and porters and wrote furious stacks of letters, I helped Agnes to wash and pack our clothes and lay sheets across the furniture in preparation for our absence. As for Agnes and Mrs Hedges themselves, I was at first not sure what to do; the previous year, we'd kept them on for reduced pay while we were away, but I suspected that if I did the same again, and possibly over a longer period, it might incite a mutiny. Instead, I arranged work for them in the interim with Mrs Prewitt, our neighbour, who had just been delivered of twin girls and was in dire need of help. When I mentioned this to Henry, expecting him to be pleased – for it would save us a great deal of money – I was surprised to hear him groan:

  'Oh Lord, did you really tell her everything? Mrs Prewitt's cousin is in the British Association, you know. If it gets out that we're leaving for Scotland for the next however many months, we'll be completely inundated – people insisting on meeting us for dinner or tea, colleagues demanding I return their books . . . Before we know it, our departure will be delayed a month and it shall snow again and we'll have to put it off till March.'

Which seemed a tad dramatic, in my opinion – and unrealistic, considering we had not received a single invitation since the Murchisons'. But I did not press. In truth, I was glad to slip away unnoticed. I would not have to think, then, about whatever whispers must be circulating about me – whatever apologies I must eventually give, swallowing down my dignity like bile.

Despite my queasiness reading while travelling, I brought my new research material with me on the train: Allman and Rigg, and a series of essays upon ferment cells and catalysts. It was hardly light reading; but then, of course, the problem I was attempting to solve was hardly a light matter. I read in snatches, whenever we were stopped at stations, and spent the remaining hours staring into the distance, gnawing at the problem like a dog on a bone. By the time we finally pulled into view of the Sutherland estate in Maisie's little gig, the sight nearly obscured by the pouring rain, I had arrived at . . . well, I hadn't arrived at anything yet. But I felt that I understood the path better, at least. I saw, perhaps, the direction in which I ought to go.

'I'm terribly sorry, sir,' said the footman, as he helped lug our crates and trunks inside – which were, like ourselves, quite soaked from the ride. 'But I'm afraid Miss Sutherland won't be coming downstairs to receive you. She's quite ill today.'

'Really?' Henry set down another dripping box upon the hall carpet – I dearly hoped that he had packed our books in oilcloth, as I had asked him to – and shot me an exasperated look. 'Today, of all days. She chooses her moments, doesn't she?'

I said nothing. I had pointed out to Henry the previous

winter that he was not, despite his many studies in reptilian anatomy, a practising physician, and thus could not possibly be qualified to determine whether Maisie 'chose' to be ill or not, but that had merely prompted an argument. I did not truly know her, he had said; I did not know the extent to which she would go to garner attention and sympathy. But even if that were true, I did not think it a crime to wish for sympathy.

'She has asked if you might like to come up and see her though, ma'am,' said the footman. 'Once you are settled in.'

'Really?' I exclaimed, startled. I had never bothered her before during one of her spells. It seemed rude somehow, an intrusion. But if she had asked for me . . .

'And not me?' Henry laughed, though there was an indignant edge to it. 'She doesn't want to see her own brother, after a year apart?'

The footman looked very much like he wanted to grimace. 'She really isn't too well, sir. I believe one visitor at most is—'

'Never mind, Ramsay.' He picked up the box again. 'I'll see her later, if she deigns to come down for dinner. Help me get these upstairs, will you?'

We were served a rather sombre lunch, silent but for the drum of rain against the windows. I had hoped to find the house less dreary than I remembered – my recollection tarnished, perhaps, by the miserable circumstances of our last visit – but alas, it seemed to suffer from a kind of permanent greyness. Later that day, I would watch Maisie's maid clean the mantlepiece, only for the dust to settle back down upon it within the hour; it was no wonder, really, that Maisie suffered from disorders of the lung among all this damp and dust.

The maid had told me after lunch that Maisie was awake,

though I was not sure I believed her, for my initial knock went unanswered; when I gathered my nerve and cracked open the door, the room was entirely dark. But sure enough, when the light from my lamp fell upon the bed, I saw the covers shift.

'Come in,' said a faint voice. 'Close the door, please . . . It lets in such a draught.'

I will admit to no small amount of anxiety as I crept inside. After all our letters, I felt that I knew Maisie better than ever before; and yet, somehow, that made it harder. I was not sure how to talk to her now, outside the confines of a page. Skittish as I was, I nearly jumped when I neared the bed and Maisie let out a gasp.

'Oh, Mary, is that really you? Forgive me, Flora did say you were here, but . . . I thought that might have been a dream. I thought you were Miss Macmillan, from next door. She comes to see me sometimes, though only because her mother makes her. She sits and reads to me as if I were an old woman – the most *terrible* books, too, you wouldn't believe.'

I let out a breath of laughter, and some of the tension in me eased. I set the lamp on her bedside table and pulled up a chair. 'A dream? You must be out of sorts. Or do you often dream of— Goodness, you're freezing!'

That last was because I had reached out to lay a hand upon her arm and found her skin as cold as ice. Damp as well, though that I did not say. As my eyes grew accustomed to the light, I saw too that her hair was plastered to her forehead. Her pupils were so dilated they looked almost black.

'Good Lord.' I took up her hand, squeezing it between my own as if I could somehow press some of my own warmth and vitality into her. 'Is it always like this?'

She hesitated, an odd look coming across her face. 'No. No, it isn't. My doctor . . .'

She trailed off. I gripped her hand again, overcome with a sudden, ferocious fondness.

'What is it? What's the matter?'

'It's . . . His name is Dr Gallacher,' she murmured. The words were quick and quiet, bubbling out of her as if she wished to get them over with as quickly as possible. 'I've been seeing him for years now, ever since he moved up from Kent – that's where we met him, in one of the convalescent homes where I was staying. It's his specialty, complications due to childhood illnesses; disorders of the heart and lung and such . . .'

I was a tad shocked by this; not by Dr Gallacher's list of qualifications, of course, but by her mention of a stay in a convalescent home. In England, no less – and more than once. Would that not have been prohibitively expensive, for a family such as the Sutherlands? Or perhaps—

Or perhaps, I thought, remembering Henry's comments about Maisie 'wasting money', the family fortunes had not always been so dire.

'He always wanted to have me try laudanum,' Maisie was saying, oblivious of my revelation. 'Only a few drops, he said, just as a headache or a spell of asthma is coming on, can work wonders. But Father never . . . he said it was too habit-forming. A weakness of character. I ought simply to . . .' she squeezed her eyes shut, her breathing shallow and quick '. . . offer my pain to God. But after he passed, after those awful cigarettes didn't work either, I . . .'

'A *weakness of character*?' I found myself saying, horrified anew. The doctor who had been with me during my delivery had said something similar. When I had begged for morphine or chloroform, he had only laughed – pain brought moral fortitude, he had told me. *Moral fortitude*; if sinking a knife into the doctor's chest then would have ensured my own child's life, I would have done it. If it would have brought me but five minutes' relief, I would have done it. It hadn't made me stronger or brought me closer to God, my brief experience of motherhood. It had made me sour and hateful, a bone that had not healed right. One has a choice in such circumstances, I have found: one can hate oneself – believe that the pain is weakness, punishment for Eve's sin – or one can hate God.

And it did not seem to me that Maisie hated God.

I pushed the hair back from her forehead, my heart aching. If only there was something I could do; more, at least, than holding her hand or lending her my ear or venting my spleen at Henry later on her behalf. But I had already declared war on the heavens, on a different front. There was little more blasphemy I could do.

'Does it help?' I asked. 'The laudanum?'

'It did. Not with the frequency of anything, but with the discomfort. All the headaches, the attacks of asthma, the pains in my chest – it made them more tolerable. But I—' She swallowed hard. 'I stopped. I've stopped taking it.'

'What? Why?'

'Dr Gallacher . . .' She pushed herself up from the bed suddenly, her eyes wide with urgency. 'He *proposed to me*, Mary!'

I felt my heart tumble from my chest. 'He did *what*?'

'Three weeks ago. The last time he came. He started talking about his fondness for me, and how long we had known each other, and . . . oh Lord, Mary, I—' She clutched at my hand, turning my knuckles the same pale shade as her stricken face. 'I didn't know what to say! It was all so sudden!'

'Well, what happened?'

'I told him I needed time to think it over. He didn't look terribly happy . . .'

'He didn't make a scene, did he?'

'No, but I could tell it wasn't what he expected. And I could tell he knew what I would have said, had I the courage. You don't think—?' She stopped, looking pained, and continued, almost in a whisper: 'You don't think I ought to have accepted him, do you?'

'Of course not!' The forcefulness of my own answer seemed to surprise us both.

'Why not?'

'Because the very idea of it seems to terrify you! And it isn't as if you need him. You have a perfectly decent fortune of your own – you could live quite happily by yourself for ever, if you pleased.' I tried hard not to think of my own long-ago dreams of spinsterhood. I was not mistaken, was I? Not simply trying to convince her to accept the future I had wished for in my youth?

No; I shook my head. I could not be misreading her – the relief that was settling upon her features now was unmistakable.

'But . . . how does your medicine fit into all of this, Maisie?' I pressed, and the relief at once disappeared.

'That's what Dr Gallacher was coming to bring, three weeks ago. But he forgot to give it to me in all the fuss, and I couldn't bear to call him back, so I eked out my very last bit . . .'

'Why didn't you get some at the pharmacy?'

'I tried! His brother owns the nearest one. I went with Ramsay and Flora and had them ask for it, but as soon as the pharmacist saw me, he gave me a horrible look and said that they didn't have any. The same thing happened at the other two. How can every pharmacy in Inverness be out of laudanum? He's said something to them, I'm sure of it. That I was planning to drain the lot and put myself to sleep or some such. That's what they all think, anyway. No husband, no children, no father – I *must* want to die.'

'Stop that,' I said, as gently as I could. She was shivering now, sweat beading her forehead. I tugged at the blankets, trying to encourage her to lie down once more. 'It's going to be all right, I promise. They don't know me in Inverness. I shall go this very afternoon and get you some more. How much do you take?'

She tried to rise again. 'Oh – no, no! I'm all right, Mary, truly!'

'You're not all right – look at you!'

'But I wasn't taking much. I can wean myself off it—'

'Why would you, when it's done you good? It helped you, didn't it?'

Her face was a grimace. 'Yes.'

'And nothing else ever has.'

'Not . . . as such, no.'

'Then we'll simply have to make do until we find something better, won't we? And speaking of which – we ought to find you a new doctor. And write to Dr Gallacher, to tell him his services are no longer needed.'

'Oh, I couldn't possibly—'

'Then I will, if you'll allow it. You can read it over and tell me if it's Mary enough.'

Her thin brows creased with confusion. 'Don't you mean Maisie enough?'

'No. I'm afraid this is a letter that will require substantial amounts of Mary.'

She laughed then, a soft sound like the letting out of a long-held breath.

'Thank you, Mary.'

I looked down, at our hands intertwined upon the bedspread, and my anxiety of earlier crept back. *Letters* – that had reminded me. I frowned, searching for the right words.

'I . . . ought to apologize,' I said haltingly. 'For being such a poor correspondent of late – writing so scarcely for so long and then bothering you with two in a row before you even had a chance to respond to the first.'

'Oh, nonsense! I've been terribly slow to respond to you, as well.' She hesitated. 'And your last letter, I haven't . . .'

'You needn't worry about that!' I cut in hurriedly, suddenly embarrassed by the mere mention of it. It had been an ugly thing, that letter, written in anger, far more about Henry than about her. 'You've been ill; I'd hardly expect you to be keeping up with correspondence at a time like this. You can throw that one away. I am here now, to speak with you.'

'I suppose.' She looked down, tracing the flowers embroidered upon her bedspread with a fingertip. *She must be tired*, I thought; with one last squeeze of her hand, I rose to leave, promising to get her medicine as soon as I could. She nodded silently, and I was nearly at the door before I heard her call out after me.

'Mary!'

I turned to see her sitting up again, brows knitted together. 'Yes?'

'I did read your last letter,' she said slowly, as if she was

forcing the words out through a fine sieve. 'Your question –
how did I do it?'

She paused for breath. I found myself clutching the doorway
by my side.

'I never did tell you how my mother died, did I?' she asked.

I shook my head, puzzled. 'Not precisely. It was a fever,
wasn't it?'

'Yes. Only it was . . . It was at a convalescent home. Henry
was away at school; it was just Mother and Father and me.
It was very . . . very sudden. Father always said she must have
hidden it from us at first. We tried to send word to Henry, but
he couldn't get there in time. It was—' Her voice broke, ever so
slightly. 'Scarlet fever.'

The very illness which Maisie had had.

I closed my eyes, overwhelmed. What was it like to watch
your mother die of a fever she had caught at your bedside – to
think that you had killed her yourself? I did not think Maisie
was to blame, of course; I hoped she did not think so, either. But
I thought she might.

And I suspected I knew who else might, too.

'Oh, *Henry*,' I murmured. A number of mysteries unravelled
before me: the accusations of wasted money, of Maisie feigning
illness, of only ever thinking of herself . . . I could see precisely
how all the pieces of this tragic affair might come together in
one lonely boy's mind. And I could attest to how, in the confused aftermath of grief, the mind longed for something,
someone, to blame. Terrible and unreasonable and undeserved
as it was, I understood.

What I did not understand was how a grown man could still
hold such a grudge against his own sister ten years later.

'Don't,' blurted Maisie, perhaps seeing the spark of anger in my expression. 'Please, don't say anything to him. I know he thinks terribly of me, I know it, but . . . He never got to say goodbye. And Father was always so strict with him, far more than he ever was with me. And after all that, too, there wasn't any money to send him to university as he wanted, so he took a pair of Father's cufflinks in the end and went off to London on his own, and of course he and Father hardly spoke again after that . . . He only began writing to us again when the two of you were married. To show you off, I think.'

I could not help but let loose a small huff of air at that, half in laughter and half in exasperation. I had done the very same with my grandmother, writing to her of my marriage to prove, somehow, that I was not a failure; that I was worthy, and wanted, and grown. Only in retrospect could I see how very childish an act it had been.

'So, then . . . will you tell me? How you forgave him?' I asked, wondering still how *I* might forgive him for this cruel, unfounded grudge of his.

She met my eye at last, the dim light of the hallway illuminating the look of quiet despair upon her face – and that was when I knew.

It had been a lie, of course.

She did not even know how to forgive herself.

16

The most beautiful and elevated problem for the human intellect, the discovery of the laws of vitality, cannot be resolved, nay, cannot even be imagined, without an accurate knowledge of chemical forces.

— JUSTUS LIEBIG, *Animal Chemistry*

THE MOMENT WE were unpacked, I began my research on ferments in earnest. 'Unpacked' was a generous word, perhaps; although Maisie had happily lent us a shelf in the library for our books, as well as the under-stairs cupboard, Henry insisted on keeping the more 'sensitive' materials (pertaining to dissection and resurrection and such) in our room, and so I picked my way to bed each night between open trunks and teetering piles of books and notes. Our experimental equipment we put in the boathouse, which — with the addition of a small worktable and the subtraction of several years' worth of grime — was slowly turning into a proper laboratory. I had not been overjoyed by the boathouse when Henry first showed it to me; besides the dark and the damp, there was hardly any floor space to be had, merely a horseshoe-shaped rim of stone around the central pool. But the pool, as he pointed out, was the most crucial part. It was quite deep, and open to the firth at one end, so that one might steer a rowing boat straight inside and then haul it up into the rafters; or, for our purposes, dive down and secure a net across the open end of the pool, closing the large wooden doors to block the view of any passing ships on the firth. It would make the perfect enclosure.

All that remained now was to make something to put *in it*; to find out why that one rat had come back to life, when the others had not; to unravel the mysteries of life and death, and weave them back together in a shape of our own choosing. Put that way, it almost sounded simple.

'Do we have any more lime?' I asked one day, rifling through our chemistry set. I winced as I leaned too close to one of my bubbling vials, overwhelmed by the powerful smell of yeast. It had, indeed, begun to feel like a brewery here of late, the air pungent and humid.

'Pardon?' Henry looked up from his own contraption – a pulley system formerly used to lift boats from the water, which he thought might be used to construct an elevated worktable. He squinted at the bottle in my hand. 'Is that from the little cabinet? Mary, that's not ours!'

He was right, of course – for this, along with several other chemical texts, Henry had borrowed from his friend Mr Forsythe before we left London. (I was sure that, had we gone to Mr Jamsetjee again, he would happily have given us all we needed, with no expectation of return – but I refused to entertain any more of his pessimistic declarations that *his days of science were over*.)

'Good grief, Henry. It's only lime, not powdered gold.' I placed the bottle back in its small velvet-lined drawer and drew out the brass scales instead. 'I'll just buy some more in Inverness.'

He heaved a sigh. 'I simply wish you'd be more conservative with our supplies. I can't believe you've used all of it already.'

'And I shall replace it. Presumably Mr Forsythe knew that we intended to *use* the set. He can't possibly mind if I top up the bottle.'

'Forsythe?'

'Yes.' I turned just in time to catch a confused furrow between Henry's brows. 'You haven't forgotten him already, have you? We've hardly been away a month.'

'Ah – of course. I misheard.' He scrubbed his face with his hands and then, realizing he was covered in oil from the pulley, gave a dismayed cry and reached for his handkerchief. After a few moments of watching him wipe ineffectually at his face, I sighed.

'Give it here.'

He sat obligingly while I wet the handkerchief in the pool and began to scrub at the greasy marks across his face. I watched his gaze slide over to the table, eying the myriad beakers and vials. There were some fizzing and some not, some stoppered with cork and some with cotton. In the corner sat a beautiful swan-necked beaker connected first to a reservoir of sulphuric acid and then to one of potash – to rid the air of any pre-existing animalcules which might taint the sugar solution inside.

'What is it you're cooking over there?' Henry asked, barely moving his lips as I wiped a smudge from his chin.

'I'll tell you when I'm done, won't I?'

'Such a tease,' he murmured.

For a moment, my hand stilled. I thought of another place, another time – *Lord, you're a tease, aren't you?* Sometimes, it felt as if every year that passed brought only another painful recollection, another bruise of a memory. Soon enough there would be not a single word which did not dredge up something I wished to forget, not a single part of me that did not cringe to the touch.

'There; you look less like a chimney sweep now.' I straightened. 'We should put a stove in here, I think.'

He raised his eyebrows. 'For your cooking?'

I tossed the now grey handkerchief at his face, and he recoiled. '*No*, for my fingers. And my toes, and my nose, and everything else that will fall off me if I continue to work in the freezing cold.'

'Ah, but it's—'

'If you say "It is spring", I shall kick you.'

He chuckled and heaved himself to his feet. 'You could move your experiments inside, if you like. The room under the stairs could be your winter laboratory.'

'The cupboard, you mean?'

'It's a *large* cupboard.'

I rolled my eyes towards the heavens. 'Perhaps. But even so, we'll have to put the plesiosaur together in here, when it comes to it. It'll be winter again by that time, no doubt, and how do you expect to bestow the "warmth of vitality" upon our creation with frost upon the walls?'

'It's cold-blooded, isn't it?' he muttered. 'All right, I'll go into town tomorrow and see what I can do.'

'You may have to wait to use the gig; Maisie was going in with Ramsay to pick up some books.'

'Well, by all means, if she has *important business* to attend to—'

'Stop that.'

He turned to blink at me, clearly startled by my snappishness. I turned back to my worktable, my temper now simmering along with my vials.

'It is her gig,' I said quietly. 'And her house. And her boathouse in which we are currently working.'

From the corner of my eye, I saw his face twist in a complicated sort of hurt. He had always thought that the house ought to have been his by rights. In nearly any other case, it would have been. But that did not make it any less hers; and I would not, I had vowed, let him vent any more of his frustration at that fact upon his blameless sister.

I expected him to argue, to vent some of said frustration at me instead. But perhaps, for once, he realized that he was in the wrong; or perhaps he was simply tired of going over the same old ground. Whatever the case, he muttered at last:

'In which *you* are currently working, you mean. Seeing as you refuse to let me assist you in . . . whatever it is that you are doing, I may as well go to bed.' He heaved a sigh. 'Are you coming?'

I cast a glance at my vials once more; the one on the left was not doing particularly well. I really ought to clean it out and set up another trial before the day was done.

'No, not yet,' I said. 'I shall be a while, I think.'

'THERE,' I SAID. 'That should last you through to April, at least.'

'Thank you so very much, Mary,' Maisie said, tucking the two tiny bottles under her shawl. It was not good weather to be out as we were, sat overlooking the banks of the firth. The air was sharp, the wind lively, promising rain. But Maisie always insisted we do this exchange outside in case Henry might see. I had told her before that she need not be so secretive, and that I would happily tell him off if he gave her any trouble – but, of course, she had refused.

'*Oh* – look!' she cried suddenly, interrupting my thoughts. She was pointing out across the firth.

'What? What am I looking for?'

'There! A dolphin!'

A moment later, I spotted it: a slender fin sliding through the water. But that was not what made me laugh – rather, it was Maisie, turning to me with her eyes alight with joy. It struck me then how alike she and her brother were, in this respect if not in any other. That enthusiasm, the same that gripped Henry whenever he told me about a new species unearthed in Germany, or an interesting specimen that had come into the University College collection – it seized Maisie so often for the smallest of reasons. A blooming poppy by the wayside might do it, or a teacake studded with raisins in perfect symmetry. It might appear childish at a glance, and at first, of course, I had thought it so – but it was not. In that dark bedroom of hers, in this lonely corner of the country, she salvaged small scraps of joy wherever she could. It was a learned thing, I think, learned for the same reason that every rabbit can run and every mouse can hide – if she had not done so, she would not have survived.

She blew out a long breath and huddled tighter into her shawl, rubbing her hands together in her lap. Without thinking, I took them up and held them between my own, squeezing warmth into her fingers. Her skin always looked so pale against mine, as if she'd been fashioned out of rice paper. When my head rose again, I found her watching me, a curious smile plucking at the corners of her mouth.

'You are always doing that,' she said. 'Like a nursemaid, making sure I'm not too cold.'

'Am I?' Suddenly self-conscious, my heart in my throat, I took my hands away. 'I'm sorry; I didn't mean to—'

'No, it's quite funny!' she laughed. 'I'm surprised you haven't knitted me gloves yet.'

I did my best to laugh with her, though I knew it must have sounded thin. It was good, that she found it funny. And why shouldn't she? What else was I so very anxious about?

But I knew precisely what had me on edge, of course.

The first time Henry had kissed me, I had frozen. I had not been able to help thinking of Clarke, of *Catherine* – of his hands on my waist and her lips upon mine, his hand around my wrist and my hand around hers as I begged her not to go. It had taken me the better part of a decade to understand truly what I had done wrong. She had kissed me first, it was true, but as girls do; as friends do. I was not supposed to kiss her in return, nor to feel in my heart the same lovely ache I felt, years later, as Henry drew back and asked with worry in his eyes: 'What's wrong?' What was wrong was that I had wanted it. That must have been what she had seen in me that day as she pulled away, shock and revulsion on her face; it was the intent of it.

But there was no intent here, was there? There shouldn't be; there *couldn't* be. I was only worrying, set apart from any female companionship for so long that I did not know how to behave. It was only right, that I cared for her health, as friends did.

'You wouldn't say so if you'd seen my knitting,' I replied at last, in as cheery a tone as I could muster. 'Good Lord, but I hope this weather improves soon. I miss the sun.'

'Tell me, where does one typically find this "sun"?'

My laugh now was genuine. 'Oh, I don't know – the south of Spain? Henry's friend went there last summer and said there was a grove of oranges right next door to the house, and fresh marmalade for breakfast every morning!'

'Oh, that sounds divine!'

'You needn't go as far as that, though. Even Wight gets warm in summer; or London. You could come and stay with us.'

Her smile faltered. 'Oh, I don't know . . .'

'I could sedate Henry before you arrived,' I said, earning me a roll of her eyes.

'You're very kind. But I'm not a very good traveller, truth be told.' She chewed upon her lip. 'Even when I was in England, touring every single doctor in Kent, I saw more of the inside of a carriage than the countryside. I was always too tired, or too sick . . .' She gave a bitter laugh. 'We drove right through London once, and I couldn't even look out of the window, my head hurt so badly.'

Ah – of course, she knew only too well what England was like. I felt horrid now for bringing it up. I followed her gaze out across the choppy grey waters; the rocks about the edge of the shore were so dark against the waters that they looked almost black, outlined in ink.

'I have always wanted to see Paris,' Maisie said, the words so quiet that it was as if she meant to sneak them by without my notice.

'Is that so? I've heard it's a beautiful city.' I hesitated. 'I bet there is plenty of it that can be seen from the inside of a carriage, if one is too tired to disembark.'

'Perhaps.' Carefully, her smile returned. 'Do you know where else we should go?'

'Where?'

'*Inside!* If we stay here any longer, I shall freeze to these rocks and you will have to pry me off with a knife.'

'Oh dear! Well, we can't have that.'

We picked our way back to the path across a carpet of early-blooming daisies. Maisie hooked her arm through mine as we went, and I consoled the nervous flutter of my heart with the fact that it was she who had chosen to do so – that I had seen a pair of women in Inverness doing the same, just last week.

'Do you fancy a game of draughts when we get in?' she asked.

'Alas, no; I have work to do, I'm afraid.'

She made a 'hmm' of disappointment, and we continued on. Just as my thoughts began to drift, returning to my experiments, and whether I ought to bring my yeasts inside if it was going to rain, Maisie asked:

'What is it exactly that you two do all day in that boathouse?'

I nearly tripped, at that.

'Didn't Henry tell you?' I said carefully, casually. 'We are trying to make a new sort of rat poison.'

She sighed, and for a moment I caught a glimpse of Henry again – it was that same exasperated look they shared, like a schoolmaster telling off a student for getting chalk on his sleeves.

'No,' she said. 'I mean, what is it you *really* do?'

I should have known that she would see through our ruse. Nonetheless, it was a shock to hear her express it so frankly. I could feel her gaze on me as I scrabbled for an answer – and then, unexpectedly, she chuckled and bumped her shoulder against mine.

'Good grief, it must be something quite important for you to be so secretive about it! It's all right. You don't have to tell me this second. But' – she shot me a grin, ever so slightly sharp about the edges, and there was Henry, too – 'I am curious. Promise you'll show me eventually, won't you?'

And, despite my better judgement, I did.

IT IS A difficult thing, keeping secrets. Or rather – for I had kept secrets before, plenty of them, but none that I had actually wished to tell – it is difficult keeping an *interesting* secret. I could sense Maisie's curiosity, her eyes upon me every time I set off for the boathouse or came back smelling of ozone and yeast, but she was a patient soul. She had seen that I did not wish to speak about it yet, and so she had not asked again, a display of trust that made me feel both deeply touched and deeply guilty. I made a vow, then, which I ought to have made much sooner: that I would never lie to her again. I might delay the truth, in cases such as this wherein any reasonable soul would think me quite mad without any proof to support my claims, but I would never again deny her it.

Nor was Maisie the only one with whom I had not been entirely forthcoming. I still had not told Henry the precise nature of my studies with ferments, no longer out of sheer pettiness but for more practical reasons. It was only sensible for Henry to continue researching other explanations for our temporary miracle of life, I reasoned, in case my ferments proved useless. By the time that March slipped into April, however, it became clear that he was at a loose end. He had finished installing his suspended worktable in the boathouse, and finished rereading all of our notes, and re-enacted our one temporarily successful experiment dozens of times, to no avail. He had even written a short paper on the speculative biology of *Plesiosaurus dolichodeirus* – precisely the topic we had told everyone we were researching, at the disastrous New Year's party – which was scheduled to be published as a monograph by the Palaeontographical Society. Having accomplished all of this, he fell into a brief and rather performative fit of despair which abated only when I asked if he would like to help me clean out my latest batch of yeasts. Even so, I still had not fully explained to him what I was *doing*, the intricacies of abiogenesis and nitrogenous reactions. But he helped nonetheless, happily tweaking burners and measuring out solutions.

It was neither Henry nor Maisie, however, who proved the most challenging of all to keep in the dark, but Mr Jamsetjee. My letters to Canterbury of late had been largely absent of details of my own life: *How are you both? How is your health? Have you decided whether you will move back to London?* The letters I received in return, written in Mrs Jamsetjee's careful hand, were similarly evasive, littered instead with questions about Inverness and the progress of our research. I found it ever more difficult to avoid the latter. It had been Mr Jamsetjee who had sent me my first book on the science of electricity; he who had explained to me engines and motors, who had enthused with me about the fascinating interconnectivity of magnetism and current. Every time I used his Leyden jar, every time I attempted to revive another vial of dead yeast, I yearned to tell him every detail. But I could not.

Somehow, when I had first learned of my great-uncle's experiments, when I had come up with this ludicrous idea, I had hardly hesitated a moment before telling Henry; I suppose I imagined that if he did not believe it possible, I would simply argue with him until he was convinced. But he and I had devoted so much to this project now that it was not just Victor's, but *ours*; if Maisie or Mr Jamsetjee pronounced it mad, they would be pronouncing us mad along with it. And how could it possibly not seem mad, to anyone who had not read those half-burnt letters? Who had not seen the miraculous rise and fall of our lone successful rat's chest?

How could even *I* – who had witnessed this miracle with my own eyes – continue to believe such a thing, when our countless attempts to reproduce it over these past months had yielded nothing but dead rats and vials of yeasty sludge?

It was, then, with an exhaustion that verged on hopelessness that I trudged to the boathouse that one grey morning in May to begin my daily murdering of yeasts. As per usual, I boiled each vial over the little stove that Henry had installed until I could be sure that it was thoroughly dead, then decanted it into a container with some sugar water and my latest variation of nitrogenous solution (all of which had been thoroughly cleansed of existing animalcules). I discharged the Leyden jar to run a current through the solution, let each batch rest near the warmth of the stove while I went in for morning tea with Maisie, and came back – inevitably – to find my yeasts still resolutely dead.

Except that this time, that was not what happened. This time, I came back instead to find each container bubbling with brownish foam.

I stood in front of my workstation and blinked. I removed the stoppers of cork and cotton, and inspected each container thoroughly. I emptied them outside, trying very hard to calm my racing heart, and began the trial again.

And again.

And again.

After lunch – or rather, after lunchtime, for I had skipped the meal entirely – I strode to the house in a daze. I stood in the doorway of the parlour, where Henry sat reading, and announced:

'I think it's ready.'

'What's ready?' Henry murmured, looking up, his mind still clearly between the pages of his book. As I watched, his gaze focused, sharpening as he took in my oilcloth apron and my wild expression.

'Oh,' he said. '*Oh.*'

And then, with a grin: 'I'll get my coat.'

THERE WERE TWO sparks necessary to the process, in essence. The first was literal: a small current, as we had used before on our briefly successful rat. The second was more metaphorical: a chemical spark. A collection of compounds which were, perhaps, naturally occurring in small amounts, and which we had activated purely by accident on that first occasion. All this I explained at last to Henry as I drew up a syringe of the solution with shaking hands. He made a cheery noise of disgust as I held it up to the light – yellowish brown, like bile, and floating with strings of albuminous matter. It was not nearly so glamorous as electricity, the arcing flash of lightning tamed and bound; but hopefully, if life was indeed but a reaction, the result of electrical and chemical processes within the cells of the body, then our two 'sparks' in conjunction would be enough to spur those processes into action once again.

The mouse was so small that Henry and I kept bumping heads in the process of preparing it, but it had been all little Oliver had been able to find at such short notice. The storm that had been brewing all morning broke just as we finished, the rain beating an insistent tattoo upon the roof. The air felt charged, wound tight as a spring. Henry and I met each other's eyes. The applicators were poised in his hands, ready to touch to each side of the mouse's tiny chest.

'To stealing from God,' he said, grinning, and brought them down.

It was just as miraculous, just as swift, as the first time – except that this time, our subject *stayed* alive. Its tiny chest expanded, heaving in thimblefuls of air. I watched, hardly daring to breathe myself, as its beady little eyes, black as polished jet, slid open.

It was Henry who first dared to touch it. '*Oh* – Mary, oh, Mary, it's warm!'

I swept all our tools aside and scooped up the mouse in my cupped palms. The thing weighed hardly more than air, but still – *yes*, I could feel it! – the faint heat from its feather-light feet. It trembled upon my hand, blinking and twitching, but did not run.

'It worked,' I whispered. I could not stop looking at its nose, its slender fingers, its velvet-brown ears. I had done my best to ignore such things with all our previous specimens, insensitive as I must be, but with this one I could not help myself; it was beautiful in our success.

'We've done it, my dear!' Henry exclaimed then, springing to his feet. He jumped about the room, performing some sort of wild improvisatory dance that ended with a kiss pressed to my cheek. A laugh spilled out of me, soft and giddy with relief.

'Do you hear me?' he cried, flinging one arm around my

shoulder and the other up towards the heavens. 'We've done it, we have it! Nothing can stop us now!'

Then, as loud as the proverbial crack of thunder, there was a knock on the door.

Without hesitation, Henry yelled, 'Go away! We're busy!'

'Oh, stop it!' I chuckled, slapping at his arm. 'Don't be rude! It's probably just Flora, calling us in for tea.'

'We don't need tea; we are *gods*.' He leaned in to kiss me again but I laughed and ducked under his arm, laying the mouse gently on the table.

'You keep an eye on this little darling, and I'll see what she wants.'

The knock came again, insistent and sharp.

'I thought I was your little darling,' Henry called, and I took the time to kick his foot before I turned and opened the door.

And that was how I froze – flushed with pride and joy, a laugh caught upon my lips. For a moment, I was a statue, turned to stone.

For there under the eaves, with rain spattered across his shoulders and his hat held neatly against his chest, stood Finlay Clarke.

'Good afternoon, Mrs Sutherland,' he said, white teeth flashing in something like a smile. 'I hope I'm not interrupting anything.'

PART III

MAY 1855 – MAY 1856

17

The Devil, I safely can aver,
Has neither hoof, nor tail, nor sting;
Nor is he, as some sages swear,
A spirit, neither here nor there,
In nothing – yet in everything.

He is – what we are; for sometimes
The Devil is a gentleman . . .

— PERCY BYSSHE SHELLEY,
Peter Bell the Third

MAISIE WAS A darling, as always. Though she was clearly shocked to see our awful trio enter the house – Henry looking like a kicked dog, I the one who'd kicked him, and Clarke the cat who'd watched the whole affair – she collected herself marvellously. Within minutes we were arranged stiffly in the parlour, the uncomfortably starched manner which Maisie presented to those who did not know her for once a relief, for it tempered the air of hostility within the room. With relentless civility, she fluttered here and there, promising the imminent arrival of sandwiches and tea and filling the conversational void with pleasantries.

Once Flora had brought in the sandwiches, Clarke set upon

them with a ferocity that made further attempts at conversation rather difficult. Desperation in her eyes, Maisie looked from Clarke to Henry to me and seized, unfortunately, upon the one question I had been fervently hoping she would not ask.

'So how did you and Mr Clarke become acquainted?'

'Oh, the same circles, you know. We met during my university days,' Henry supplied hurriedly.

'And Mrs Sutherland and I were childhood friends,' Clarke added with a cloying smile. I smiled back, and in my mind's eye, tossed my saucer as one might throw a discus and cracked his waxy forehead like an egg.

'So you're Henry's sister, Miss Sutherland?' Clarke continued, leaning back. 'He's certainly kept you quiet, I must say. I didn't think there were any more Sutherlands left – besides the two, of course. For which I offer my deepest sympathies, Miss Sutherland; it must be difficult, losing one's parents so young.'

Maisie blinked, poise momentarily shattered. 'Oh, I . . . thank you.'

'What's the occasion for this fine family reunion, then? Not another funeral, I hope?'

'Oh no, thank goodness,' said Maisie, and I felt suddenly as though I were watching something very heavy topple from a high shelf before I could reach it. 'My brother and his wife are working on—'

'A book!' Henry cut in, with a most unnatural laugh. 'About . . . rats. Rat poison. It is a wonderful place for writing, you know. None of the distractions of London. Sister, dear, would you . . . ?'

He waved a hand in mid-air, clearly trying to produce some errand that would keep her occupied for a suitable length of time, but unable to think of one. The sentence dangled.

'Of course!' Maisie said, with evident relief. 'I ought to leave you to catch up. Mary, would you like to join me in the library?'

Clearly, she thought she was rescuing me, but I shook my head. There was not a chance I would leave Henry and Clarke to their own devices.

It had caused quite the change of mood, the sight of Finlay Clarke standing upon the doorstep of the old boathouse. I had taken one look at him and slammed the door in his face, turning on my heel to hiss at Henry:

'What in God's name is he doing here?'

'I have no idea,' he muttered back, but there was something distinctly peculiar about the way he said it. It was in his eyes, *too* wide, and in his shoulders, too tight. He put me in mind of a hermit crab, curling up into its shell.

My own eyes narrowed. 'You are worried.'

'What?' Hunched there with the mouse cradled in his hands, he looked suddenly ridiculous. 'No, why would I be worried?'

'Did you invite him?'

'I most certainly did not.'

There was ice upon my words. 'But you do know why he's here?'

He went very, very still.

'Henry,' I said, and, good God, I was so *sick* of this, of having to pry the truth from him at every occasion, of doubting him and doubting myself and always, always, being proved *right*. 'What have you done?'

He turned to put the mouse in the little cage we used for live specimens. It was unthinkable that only minutes ago we had been laughing.

'Mary, just . . . let him in, and we'll see what he wants. We can't leave him out there in the rain; he'll catch his death.'

'I will not. Not until you explain to me why he's here.'

'Mary—'

'*Tell me.*'

He slammed the cage shut and wheeled round to face me. 'Money, Mary. Obviously, he wants money. I thought— Oh, for God's sake, don't give me that look. I *wasn't gambling*. I haven't even laid eyes upon a pack of cards since my father died. I promised you I wouldn't, and I haven't. I simply asked Clarke, after that debacle with the will, if we might borrow a small sum to help us find our footing once more. Gentlemen borrow from each other all the time, Mary – it's just what's done! I never truly expected that he'd want me to pay him back; the Clarkes have more than enough to spare.' He ran a hand through his hair, grimacing. 'How was I supposed to know he'd go and get himself *disowned*?'

At any other time, the news of Clarke's apparent disgrace would have made my day. Now, all I could think of were the letters I'd seen Henry writing, the furious clip at which we had left London. *Gentlemen borrow from each other all the time* – was that what he'd been doing? Begging his acquaintances for money? Trying to pay off Clarke's loan with another? I pressed my palms to my forehead.

'It was just something to sustain us until I found another position, Mary.' There was a pause, and I could almost hear him weighing his words. 'You knew we were short of money when—'

'Oh, I *knew*?' I cried. 'I knew, did I? You told me I had no reason to worry, you told me you would take care of it! If I'd known we were in such dire straits as to have to beg from the likes of Finlay Clarke, I would never have suggested we play this stupid game – I would have suggested that you ignore Owen, that you write another book, while I took in laundry and piecework!'

He snorted. 'You wouldn't have—'

'I would!' I could not help but think then of Mr and Mrs Jamsetjee, of my mentor's abandoned tools; I had thought his fate grim enough, never knowing that we ourselves were but one loan away from the poorhouse. 'To *hell* with our research, Henry, if it would drive us to bankruptcy!'

Another tart knock sounded on the door. What would happen, I wondered, if I simply did not open it? My head swam with thoughts of the police, litigation, debtors' prison – no, this was not a trouble that could be ignored until it went away.

'You never cease to enrage me, Henry Sutherland,' I hissed, and opened the door.

Clarke stood, his fist poised for another knock, and said, as if there had been no break in the conversation at all, 'It is so good to see you, Mrs Sutherland. And Henry, too, of course.' He waved over my shoulder, flashing Henry a hollow smile that did not reach his eyes. 'I hope you don't mind. I asked at the house and the footman said you were here.'

'I do, in fact, mind,' I said coolly, before Henry pushed past me and put out his arm to shake Clarke's hand.

'Clarke, old boy, it's good to see you. Come, let me show you to the house.'

And so, here we were. I had been so happy, not even an hour before – over a mouse, of all things! How small it seemed now; such a delicate, tenuous thing. Yes, we had brought it back from the dead, done what no one (save my great-uncle) had ever done before, but what proof had we? What sway, what influence? What would become of our careful research, if Finlay Clarke decided it would suit him better to see us in prison?

I eyed him as he lounged on the faded velveteen sofa, leaning back to cross one leg over the other. He always *lounged*; even when he was sitting bolt upright, his posture impeccable, he was lounging in spirit. He filled up every chair as if he were not simply a mediocre chemist with too much wax in his hair, but the Sun King upon his throne. *God*, how I longed to kick him. I longed to kick them both, in fact.

'So then, old friend,' Henry said with false cheer. 'To what do we owe the pleasure of your company?'

Clarke levelled his cool gaze on Henry. 'Well, if you recall, I lent you a number of important papers last year. Along with a chemistry set and some books of mine, but don't worry about those. You can keep them for now.'

Across the room, Henry studiously avoided looking at me. I thought of how concerned he had been about my using up all the lime in the chemistry set weeks ago; he had lied then, to my face, as he must have been doing for months. As for *papers*, I could imagine just the sort Clarke was referring to – small ones, bearing the Bank of England's name in curlicued script.

'The papers, however, I did say I needed back by February, but when I came to call on you then ...' He raised an eyebrow. 'I found your house quite empty, and your staff completely unable to tell me your forwarding address. Imagine my dismay. Fortunately, I'm good friends with one Mr James Gallacher – old Company friend of mine, you know, a remarkable geographer ...'

I felt a pang of dread.

'. . . Who happened to mention that his brother, who prac-
tises medicine in Inverness-shire, had recently made a fine
young lady a proposal of marriage, and had been rudely
rejected.'

He paused, clearly waiting for some sort of dramatic reaction. Henry merely blinked, visibly confused. Clarke looked
from me to Henry as realization dawned.

'Oh *dear*. Your sister didn't tell you her doctor proposed to
her? How terrible. I'm sorry if I've overstepped,' he said, though
he did not sound sorry in the least. He relished Henry's shock
for a moment more; then, with a businesslike finality, he
straightened and placed his teacup back on its saucer. 'All this is
beside the point, however. I think we've exchanged enough
pleasantries, don't you? Do you have my papers, Henry?'

I watched as Henry's mouth opened and closed, as the gears
of his mind ground together. My own were ticking along at
double speed. What were we to do? The only one with any
money here was Maisie, and she certainly couldn't lend it to us;
aside from the fact that I was loath to ask her such a thing, the
terms of her inheritance were very strict. She received a yearly
allowance, she'd told me, which she might spend as she saw fit,
but any additional funds could only be withdrawn with the permission of her husband or her lawyer – who would certainly
baulk at sending large sums of money to Henry or his creditors.

Abruptly, Henry arrived at a solution. I watched it happen –
I saw the moment the gears clicked into place, his eyes darting
to the door through which Maisie had just left. I saw him hesitate. And all at once, I knew precisely what he was thinking.

'I have,' he said slowly, 'an . . . alternative proposition.'

No. Not this. Anything but this.

I stood. The two of them looked at me, startled, as if they'd entirely forgotten I was there. I met Henry's eye and shot him daggers.

'So do I,' I said.

IN THE DOORWAY, Henry grabbed my sleeve so tightly it nearly tore.

'What are you doing?' he hissed in my ear, teeth clenched.

'What were *you* about to do? I'm making a necessary sacrifice, Henry. You ought to try it.'

I wrenched my arm free and marched out into the rain. The two of them followed, cursing and holding their arms above their heads, and by the time they reached the boathouse, I already had the mouse out of its cage. I worried at how sluggish it seemed – a far cry from the unnaturally strong creature my great-uncle had created. Still, it was, undeniably, alive.

'Here.' I thrust it out towards Clarke, who received it with open palms and an expression of utter bewilderment.

'You are offering me . . . a mouse?'

'I'm offering you,' I said, 'a part in our research.'

Ah – that had him intrigued. 'And what would that be?'

I tossed him a thick cloth and, ignoring Henry's cry of protest, said:

'Smother it and I'll show you.'

'*REMARKABLE*,' CLARKE BREATHED.

Though the sight of his long fingers leafing through my journal made me twitch, I will admit that some small part of me felt a savage pride in having impressed him. Such was my consolation as I watched his eyes slide from page to page, drinking in all my months of careful research – the fact that *I* knew something Finlay Clarke did not.

'You said all this was based upon the work of your uncle?' he murmured.

'Great-uncle,' I replied. In the corner, Henry sulked against the wall; the mouse sat still and docile upon the table. Every so often, Clarke would look across at it, as if to prove to himself that it was still there. I found myself doing the same. I had been immensely glad to see it come to life again, not entirely sure the process would work a second time – and not at all sure what I would do if it didn't. 'He claimed to have made an artificial man out of parts of corpses. But he made it too intelligent, too strong; he died hunting it down.'

'Good Lord. Is it still out there?'

'No. It was driven to madness as much as Victor was, it seemed. The pair of them died in the Arctic.'

'Pity. It would have been a wonderful example to study.' Clarke made to turn another page – and then froze. My heart sank as I realized what he'd spotted: a passage on the stages of fermentation that I had copied out from his paper into my notes.

'And,' he said slowly, 'based upon my work on ferments, too. I'm flattered, Mrs Sutherland.'

'The *fundamentals* are based upon your paper, yes,' I said icily.

'Hmm.' I despised that 'hmm'; an arrogant little noise, rife with doubt. He straightened. 'But how did your great-uncle's experiment succeed, then, with nothing but an electric current?'

'Well, we do not know his method, exactly. My suspicion is that the ingredients necessary for the reaction must be naturally occurring, though usually in such small amounts that the application of an electric current will do nothing at all. If one is very lucky, however, and one's subject begins to decay in precisely the right way, then the current alone may be enough to spur them into activation. We had such a result several months ago, though it was a partial success. The subject remained alive only for a moment.'

'Your great-uncle must have been exceedingly lucky, then. Or perhaps it has something to do with the soil in which the corpse was buried . . . It may be worth going to the original site of his experiments and taking some measurements.'

'So you'll accept the offer?' said Henry, somehow managing to sound both cross and relieved at once.

'Yes, yes. It's an unconventional method of payment, I'll grant you that, but certainly an intriguing one. I must say, I would have thought it a trick at first, but . . .' He bent down to examine the mouse again, running a finger along its curved spine. 'I *felt* it die. I felt it come back. And the method is just plausible enough.'

He turned to Henry. 'But how on earth do you plan to convince anyone else? Even if you cut the thing into pieces and resurrect it again in front of the entire Royal Society, most will assume you've just switched one mouse for another. Simple street magic. I wouldn't have believed it myself if I hadn't seen it so close at hand. Goodness, you really are fortunate to have me to vouch for you – I daresay they wouldn't even let you in with such a ridiculous proposition otherwise, especially after that debacle with Professor Owen and the Murchisons' party.'

'We're not just presenting a mouse,' I cut in, and finally he turned back to face me.

'Oh?' he said, one eyebrow arched. His eyes were eager, hungry. 'Pray tell.'

CLARKE DEPARTED THAT evening, intending to return the next morning with his belongings from the room he'd taken in Inverness. It was too far to travel each day, he said; and besides, the inn was draughty and the food poor. The ease with which he had invited himself to stay at once amazed and infuriated me. He did not even stop to ask Maisie if there was a suitable room to spare – he simply assumed it would be so. As it happened, there was, although it was the master bedroom, left largely untouched since Mr Sutherland Sr's death. I could see how it unnerved Maisie and Henry to have the room cleaned and made ready for guests, as if their father's ghost might be shaken loose from the curtains. Part of me hoped it would; the thought of him haunting Clarke brought a smile to my lips.

For the entire evening, through Clarke's breezy departure and a nearly silent supper with Maisie, Henry avoided my eye. He knew an argument was brewing, I think, and hoped that if he pretended otherwise, I might forget my grievances and let it pass – but I would not. I could not. And so, when we were finally alone, readying for bed, I paused in letting down my hair and said:

'You would truly sell your own sister?'

He had been in the middle of tugging off his socks, but at that he stopped and threw his hands into the air instead. 'Sell? *Sell?* Good Lord, Mary, what dramatics; it's marriage! Were you *sold* to me when we were married? It would be good for Margaret to have a husband – children, even. Would it not? She spends so much time in her own head. I would have thought you'd wish her to be happy.'

I'm glad that you are happy. I shook away Catherine's words, shaking my head along with them. 'With him? You don't know his true character, Henry. He is a foul man, hateful and prejudiced.'

'I don't know . . . ? Dear God, Mary, is this still about some petty childhood grudge? You must let it go! I've spent far more time with him than you, and he's a good fellow. And far more respected in his field than I am, I might add.'

I wondered then if I should tell him everything that Clarke had said to me at the Murchisons' dinner, what had really happened to form my 'petty childhood grudge'. But I could not think of any way to phrase it that did not sound trivial. *He thinks the poor are of mixed blood, and lazy; he insulted my mentor's knowledge of chemistry; he almost kissed me; he almost – maybe – did worse.* It was nothing.

'You speak so kindly,' I said coldly, 'of the man who could take us to court and ruin us.'

'He would never do that,' Henry replied, but I heard the slight note of uncertainty in his voice. He truly did not know how far Clarke would go. 'He's a friend. The only one of my friends, in fact, who was willing to help tide us over when we had nothing.'

'Only until it inconvenienced him!' I remembered, suddenly, what Henry had said earlier. 'And is he really so respected, Henry? Now that he is in disgrace?'

'What? *Oh* – Lord, Mary, it's nothing so serious as all that. It never sat well with him, I think, that his cousin was named successor to his father's business; and it never sat well with his father that he chose to go off to university and gallivant around India rather than take second place at the bank. There was some sort of row at his uncle's funeral, in the middle of the service – an utter mess. But no one will hold that against him, I'm sure. Everyone knows his family is quite unreasonable.'

'Well, good for him,' I muttered sourly. It only made me angrier to learn that the reason for his disownment was so trivial; I'd been hoping for a far greater sin, something that would expose him for all the world to see. Henry came up beside me and took my hand.

'Mary, it's not too late. We could tell him it was all a ruse, a stupid game – something to delay him until we had the opportunity to ask my sister about the proposal. I'm sure she'd be amenable; how many more wealthy young chemists do you think will turn up on her doorstep? It's the perfect solution, Mary. A boon for everyone involved.'

I snatched my hand away and stood up. I wanted to say something as I left, something cold and cutting – but there were angry tears welling in my eyes, and I refused to let them fall in front of him. Out in the hallway, I went to the window and pressed my forehead to the glass. It was icy, the sort of cold that saps the heat from your skin in a moment, leaving numbness in its place. At last, when I began to fear that I would fall asleep standing up and wake with my forehead frozen to the glass, I peeled myself away.

I found, however, that I could not make myself go back to my and Henry's room. My feet led me on to the end of the hall, where Maisie's door lay. I rapped gently, afraid to wake her; relief swept through me when I heard her voice call out:

'Come in!'

Inside, a single candle burned. Maisie sat propped up in bed, reading a book by its dim and wavering light. She smiled as I entered, and closed the book upon her thumb – *Gentleman Jack*, I saw by the cover. I had been surprised at first to learn of her fondness for penny dreadfuls, those scandalous little tales of horror and romance that poured from the presses a penny a piece. It had seemed to go entirely against her character. But that, I think, was what made it so charming; I never felt more fond of her than when she was curled in her favourite chair by the fire, a glitter in her eyes and an elegant needlepoint upon her knee, telling me about *Varney the Vampire* or the bloody barber of Fleet Street who turned his customers into pies.

'You ought to keep this locked,' I said as I shut the door behind me.

'Why is that?' She frowned. 'You don't mean . . . ?'

I could not bring myself to elaborate. Instead, I simply deposited myself on the edge of the bed, staring through the window at the cloudy night beyond.

Maisie poked at my arm. 'Come, Mary, you can't say something like that and not explain what you mean! Who is he, really? This Mr Clarke? Tell me I haven't let a murderer into my house.'

'No, he isn't that.'

'A scoundrel of a different sort, then? A criminal? A thief?' Her eyes grew wide with a strange kind of relish. 'A poisoner, upset that your research into rat poison will disrupt his business?'

I could tell that she was trying to make me laugh, but I could not. I scrubbed at my eyes. 'No, no – I will tell you, Maisie. I will, I promise. Just . . . not now. I'm so very tired.'

To my mortification, my voice broke. Gently, she pried my hands from my face and held them between her own.

'All right,' she whispered. 'It's all right.'

'Just promise me you'll be careful. Don't let him catch you alone.'

'I promise.'

I closed my eyes, shutting out the stars and the candlelight and the look on Maisie's face, the one so full of worry that it made my heart ache. 'I'm so tired.'

'You said.' She chuckled and shifted aside, drawing back the duvet. 'Come on, then.'

I froze for a moment – unable to think, unable to move. Then, at her insisting pat upon the bed, I dragged myself forward and curled up against her side. I only meant to stay a moment; that, at least, is the lie I told myself as I let my head fall against her shoulder. And more lies, too: that I did not treasure the way her finger plucked at the corner of each page as she turned it, that I was asleep by the time she finally blew out the candle, that I did not notice when she swept the hair from my forehead and sighed.

I lay awake for hours more after that, picking that sigh apart, turning it this way and that, telling myself the biggest lie of all – *it is nothing, it means nothing, nothing at all.*

18

Invention, it must be humbly admitted, does not consist in creating out of void, but out of chaos; the materials must, in the first place, be afforded: it can give form to dark, shapeless substances, but cannot bring into being the substance itself.

*

I required kindness and sympathy; but I did not believe myself utterly unworthy of it.

— MARY SHELLEY, *Frankenstein*

'I TOOK THE liberty of purchasing a turtle,' Clarke said to us over breakfast.

Across the table, Henry nearly choked on his tea. Once sufficiently recovered, he threw a significant look in Maisie's direction, but Clark ignored him; as did Maisie, so it seemed, though I could tell somehow that she was listening. For my part, I merely sat back and resigned myself to another of Clark's audacious pronouncements. It was not the first time, after all, that he had taken liberties in the fortnight he had stayed with us.

At first, it had been his taking my notes up to bed with him to read; then, rearranging the boathouse to make room for the new equipment he had ordered, and hiring a pair of local men to start building an icehouse against one wall for the preservation of specimens; most recently, he had taken it upon himself to plan out a series of gruesome trials we might perform to test our ability to resurrect creatures formed of disparate parts. It made sense, to test such things – our plesiosaur was in many ways an even riskier project than my great-uncle's constructed man, for it would necessitate piecing together the limbs and organs of multiple species, not just the one. But I wished that Clarke had not rushed ahead to construct such plans without consulting me or Henry. I wished he would not discuss the necessary deaths of our rodentine subjects with such apparent glee. I wished, ultimately, that he were not involved at all. It did not matter that it was I who had suggested this arrangement, for, after all, I had only done so to repay Henry's debts – debts that I had not even had a chance to be properly furious about.

'I heard talk of it in the pharmacy yesterday afternoon,' Clarke continued, ignoring Henry's grimaces. 'It was . . . oh, who's that old spinster who cooks for The Elephant? Never mind. She was complaining that she saw a turtle for sale at the harbour and had her heart set on making turtle soup, but it was much too expensive, et cetera, et cetera. I managed to find the crew involved and paid them to deliver it directly to us today, off the firth. Truly, I don't know why you haven't tested any reptiles thus far; their anatomy is entirely different.'

Clearly, we hadn't used any reptiles for the same reason that we had not previously constructed an icehouse – because such ventures were costly and tricky to arrange, as Clarke's current venture demonstrated. But the look upon his face showed that he already knew this. *You see?* it said. *You need me. You owe me.*

Even in his exile, cut off from his family's fortune, it seemed his pockets were still far deeper than ours. Which made me wonder on occasion, in a sort of wild panic – exactly how much *had* Henry borrowed from him? How much would it take to coax Finlay Clarke out of London, all the way to Inverness? I tried not to worry; our debt was paid now, after all, by his part in the project. But still, the question gnawed at me.

Later that afternoon, we waited on the banks of the firth, the brisk wind whipping away the early warmth of summer. It was easy to forget that the firth was connected at one end to the sea; it saw plenty of traffic, of course – narrow canal boats and sharp little sailing ships, barges laid low with cargo – but those passed us by for the most part, headed for the harbour or the Caledonian Canal. As we watched, a small fishing boat broke from the main thoroughfare and skimmed across the waves in our direction.

Henry made a brief effort to convince me to stay ashore, but I refused, and rode out with the two of them in a little rowing boat to meet the ship. I would never have admitted it, but I regretted my decision almost instantly. Henry and Clarke had hefted the thing down only that morning from its place among the boathouse rafters, where it had sat mouldering for more than a decade, and I was not entirely sure of its seaworthiness. But there was no quantity of spiders prodigious enough to dissuade me entirely, for this was an important occasion.

'Do you catch turtles often, sir?' I called out to the captain as Henry and Clarke struggled to lift the creature, swaddled thickly in sailcloth, into the boat.

'Aye, from time to time,' he said. 'No too common, though. It's more dolphins you find in the firth. The odd whale, sometimes.'

I asked the man to send word if he captured any such

creatures again – the skin of a dolphin, I thought, was likely close to that of a plesiosaur – and we rowed the boat back to shore. The turtle was a beast of a thing, quite easily two hundred pounds, and nearly too heavy for the pulleyed platform Henry had put together. It creaked and swayed alarmingly as they dropped the turtle on to it, but it seemed to hold. When we finally untied the rope and folded back the sailcloth, Henry drew in a breath through his teeth. Clarke let loose a curse.

The turtle bore welts and gashes from its time trapped in the net, and there was a deep scratch across the back of its shell; the remnant of some past altercation, perhaps. But that was not the worst of it – all of that could be fixed. No, the worst part was the immense chunk missing from the side of its head, exposing a mess of brain and bone beneath.

'Swindlers,' Clarke growled. 'I should call them right back here and demand they return my money.'

'To be fair, they probably assumed we wanted it to eat, not to bring it back from the dead,' I said drily. 'Is it even worth trying? It can't possibly survive, with only half a brain.'

'I beg to differ, my dear; a great percentage of the population survives perfectly well with less,' Henry muttered. 'We could use it as practice, I suppose? For our stitching?'

'Or for the preservation of flesh,' Clarke replied, his nose an inch from the turtle's scaly skin. 'Even when the icehouse is complete, cold alone will not keep our specimens fresh for ever. And for the construction of a creature so large, even scaled down as you propose, we shall have to find some way of preventing the pieces from rotting while we connect them all together.'

'Arsenic is standard for the preservation of specimens,' Henry cut in.

Clarke scoffed. 'In Professor Grant's collection, perhaps. For something we plan to bring back to life, injecting poison into its veins seems rather counter-intuitive.'

For once, he and I were in agreement. 'Cuvier used alcohol, did he not? And I remember reading somewhere that arterial injections of turpentine have been used to preserve bodies before dissection; though that may be just as harmful . . .'

'Yes, we shall have to see. I believe Monsieur Gannal conducted a study on embalming procedures some years ago. He used an acetate solution, if I recall correctly. Acetate of alum— or was it mercury? No . . .'

As Clarke muttered on about dichlorides and alcoholic solutions, I bent down to examine the turtle's remaining eye. It was a noble creature, really; larger than I had thought it would be, with a kind of grace that even death could not strip away. Even though most every scholar in the field of natural history dismissed the theory of transmutation, I had to admit that, ever since I first read of it in *Vestiges* and in the writings of Lamarck, it had held a special place within my heart. It was a miraculous notion, that we all perhaps originated from the same simple seed, shifting and changing over countless millennia. I could not help thinking of it then, as I examined the delicate scales about the turtle's eyelids.

What were you, once? I wondered. *Was it your forefathers and foremothers who slithered, long-necked, through the Liassic seas? Do you remember what it was like to have teeth that rent and tore?*

I shall give them back to you.

ON THE ROUGH stone wall of the boathouse, I fastened a sheet of fabric upon which I drew in charcoal the skeleton of the *Plesiosaurus dolichodeirus*. It was a sleek and beautiful beast, the first of its genus, christened as such by Conybeare and de la Beche. This particular specimen, unearthed by the same Miss Mary Anning whose exploits had sent me running off fossil-hunting along the shores of Wight, was the length of two men laid end to end. Such a monster would be far too big for our little boathouse, however, so we had decided to shorten ours to about seven feet. It was from Mr Conybeare's own litho-graphs that I copied my diagram, writing the name of each bone in minute script – and, under each label, possibilities for substitutions.

These were a matter of near-constant debate. Ought the pad-dles to be those of a dolphin, or a turtle? Ought the skull be a turtle's or a crocodile's? How would we obtain a suitable tail, when nothing with such a magnificent appendage existed in the present day? And these were only the bones; the creature's innards and skin would be another matter entirely, for we had no fossils with which to compare them. The easiest path, of course, would have been to sew a snake on to the headless corpse of a seal and be done with it, but that would not give us the correct skeletal or muscular structure – and it was this, after all, that we wanted to depict most accurately, in the hope that the creature's natural posture would match Henry's theories. It could not be denied, either, that the overall silhouette and texture of the skin mattered too; it would never gain popularity with the masses if it did not *look* right.

Summer came and went before I realized the season had even begun. There were many reasons I enjoyed Inverness – the peace and fresh air, the blooming yellow gorse across the hills – but I will admit to a twinge of despair when I asked Maisie when the warm weather would come and she replied, quite earnestly: 'What do you mean? We had those three lovely days in June.' I worried about what would become of her in this grim and lonely house, after we returned to London.

Yet another source of anxiety was the mouse; or, to be more specific, the first mouse. In between our debates over the construction of the plesiosaur, we conducted as planned a series of tests on the substitution of the organs and limbs of one being for another. None of us had any practical instruction in surgery, and though I had pored over every book on the subject I could find in preparation for this very venture, it revealed itself to be an even trickier and grislier business than I had expected. Moreover, with our unfortunate subjects being so small, it was nearly impossible for more than one person to work on them at once; thus, it was I who found myself doing the bulk of the stitching, while Clarke disappeared most days into his new icehouse to experiment with preservatives, and Henry took care of a variety of auxiliary tasks. In addition to readying each new subject and taking care of the old ones, he was kept busy brewing flask upon flask of nitrogenous solution, which had likewise proved to be an infuriatingly difficult task. The amount required to revive a rodent was far greater than that required to revive yeasts, and the solution was prone to curdling if not held in every stage at precisely the right temperature. As a result, we managed only a fraction of the dozens of tests we had initially hoped to perform.

Still, it was not long before Henry baulked at his relegation to 'nursery maid for misfit mice', and demanded that we dispose of our half-dozen former subjects. Most of these did, indeed, seem to be in good health, and I had to admit that there was little benefit to observing them longer – but the same could not be said, sadly, of our first mouse. From the start, it had been so docile as to seem almost unresponsive; it ate little and drank less, and was clumsy and uncoordinated. I had thought that it would liven up as time passed – perhaps, for some, it took more time to get used to operating a body again – but it had not. It was because of this, perhaps, some twisted sense of pity, that I argued we should keep it. There should be at least one subject, after all, which we kept on hand to observe the long-term effects of resurrection. Thus – in the hope that it simply needed more care and attention than Henry's apathetic ministrations – I had given it to Maisie, telling her it was a leftover specimen we no longer needed. Though she had loved it at first, wondering aloud at its calm temperament and its habit of falling asleep in her lap, I think she began to suspect that something was wrong with it . . . particularly when it began to smell.

'It's decomposing, I think,' said Clarke after Maisie had brought it down one evening, to sit next to her while she crocheted. The smell had lingered even after she had left the room, damp and rotten, like something dredged from the bottom of a lake. 'It *did* die twice. There must be some part of the decomposition process that was set in motion at the moment of its death, and continues on even now.'

'But it's alive,' Henry protested.

'Living things can still rot. Take gangrene, for instance. And it is rotting more slowly than it would have done had it remained dead, I'll grant you that.' Clarke tapped a thoughtful finger on his chin. 'It must be a matter of stopping the decomposition *before* it happens. Infusing the flesh with a long-lasting preservative that will stop the rot from taking hold. We should inject our next few subjects with the oil of turpentine and acetate of alumina I have been studying, and see how it affects them.'

I was grateful – begrudgingly so – that Clarke had taken such a particular interest in this aspect of the project. For one thing, every hour he spent shut up in the icehouse testing draughts of chloride of zinc or nitrate of potassa was another hour I did not have to see him – an hour I might spend instead in Henry's marginally less infuriating company. And while the two of us had greatly increased our knowledge of chemistry since we had started this grand affair, there was still only so much one could learn in a year. Clarke's expertise was . . . *helpful*.

These alone were the thoughts that soothed me in moments such as this, while Clarke chattered on about precisely which trials we should try next, and when. *I am not following his orders*, I reminded myself; *he is not our master, merely our patron. Our consultant. However much he might think he owns this project – owns us – it will never truly be his.*

'DO YOU KNOW,' Maisie said to me one day as she lay abed, in that strained voice of hers which I had learned meant she was only talking to distract herself from the pain of her head, 'that I . . .'

'That you what?' I said, looking up from the book I'd been trying unsuccessfully to read for the past half-hour. It was a Saturday afternoon, and a listless one. For days now, the clever little traps that Oliver had set up in the old stable and the nearby meadow had come up empty. Forced into an unwilling holiday, I had occupied myself at first with research and then correspondence, copying out for Mr Jamsetjee a passage I had happened across about the actions of nerves (and a possible aid for palsy), but as the day wore on I found it progressively harder to concentrate. It was not just the waiting – though that was bad enough, my entire being consumed with the restless urge to continue the work to which I had devoted more than a year of my life. It was also ... an anniversary. One that had largely passed us by the previous year, so lost had we been in our experiments. But now, with October looming just around the bend, I found myself increasingly drawn into the past.

As was Henry, apparently. For, only hours earlier, I had discovered him and Clarke in the under-stairs storeroom, each with a fan of cards in hand.

'It's only rummy!' Henry had protested, as if I hadn't seen the pile of coins he'd hastily slid under some papers a moment before. As if they weren't playing in a cupboard. As if I were entirely without a brain.

Which was why I had retreated here, to Maisie's room. Not only was she in sore need of company on days such as this, but it was one of the few places in the house where I could be assured of privacy. I was tired of arguing, even more so of arguing in front of Clarke. The way he'd simply raised an eyebrow as I raged, squashing me down to nothing – the way he'd turned to Henry and muttered quite audibly: 'Good Lord, is she your wife or your mother?'

I closed my eyes for a moment, shaking such thoughts from my head. 'What were you saying, Maisie?'

'Never mind.'

'Go on.'

'No, I shouldn't. It's terrible.'

'Ah, but I love it when you're terrible!' I got to my feet, picking my way around her scant furniture – a little desk, an end table, the old canary cage which housed the poor, sickly mouse – and perched on the side of her bed. 'What is it?'

She was silent for a long moment, chewing her lip as she always did when she was thinking intently. 'Do you know ...

that I think sometimes, whenever I hear you and Henry quarrel, how glad I am not to be married?'

It was a hard blow, though not necessarily a sharp one. Not an entirely surprising one, either. Like those great gusts of wind that blew up sometimes from the firth, strong enough to throw one off one's feet. I always found myself thinking in the moment, as I teetered on my heels, *Well, I ought to have seen that one coming.*

'Yes,' I said quietly. 'I suppose that's fair.'

She gave a grim, humourless laugh and tugged at a loose thread on the sleeve of her nightgown. 'No, that's all wrong – you're supposed to tell me it's worth it. That you wouldn't trade it for the world.'

'Maisie . . .' I sighed. Some weeks ago, unable to keep yet another secret from her, I had told her the truth of why Clarke had come to Inverness: that Henry owed him money, and that Henry had briefly intended to settle this debt with her marriage. I had expected her to be angry, but . . . no, that was not true. I had *wanted* her to be angry, longed for someone else to share my outrage, for her to cry: *He would do such a thing? Play me like a chess piece?* But instead, she had simply grown small and sad, and murmured: 'Well, I might as well. It isn't as if I have anything more worthwhile to do.'

'Do you think one has to be able to spin properly in order to be called a "spinster"?' she muttered now, her head falling back against her pillow.

'Maisie, you wouldn't have been happy with Dr Gallacher. And you *certainly* wouldn't be happy with Mr Clarke.'

She gave another sharp tug on her sleeve. It dawned on me that I had seen her mend that same sleeve only the week before, and the week before that. I thought of the battered copy of *The*

Odyssey I had once read in my grandfather's study – of Penel-
ope, weaving by day, unravelling by night.

'I know, I know. But how will I know when I *should* say yes?
Providing I ever get another offer, that is.' There was a bitterness in her words which I had rarely heard before. She looked
up at me suddenly, a rather desperate look in her eyes. 'Why did
you marry Henry?'

The first and most cynical answer that came to mind – *because
he was there* – was far too harsh to utter aloud; and besides, it was
not the whole truth. Even if things had soured since then, even if
he had been my only real option to escape from Wight, things had
once been good between us. It made my heart sink now to
remember how I had once thrilled to receive his letters; how we
had scrambled, laughing, up rocky bluffs on our fossil-hunting
honeymoon in Lyme; how I had loved his snide wit, the way his
tongue seemed to lash out at everyone but me. In that way we
were alike, united in our anger at the world. I only wished I had
seen it then for what it was: spite. Jealousy. The lingering effects
of a childhood spent unloved.

'He was interesting,' I said now, quietly. 'And I enjoyed his
company. We could talk for hours, about all sorts of things. And
he listened to me, when no one else would.'

'And?' Maisie pressed, looking as if she was waiting for me to
reveal some grand secret, a universal test of men. *Dip him in
litmus; if he turns blue, let him go.*

'Well,' I said drily, 'it certainly didn't hurt that he was handsome. One can overlook any number of flaws for a pretty face.'

'*Pretty?*' she cried, derisive, then slapped a hand over her
mouth. I laughed, quite delighted.

'So cruel! You don't think so? Well, I suppose he is your

brother.' I leaned over to prop my chin upon my hand, peering at her sideways as I grinned. 'Go on, then. What sort of fellow catches your eye?'

She blushed bright red, and I loved the sight more than I could stand. 'Oh, I don't know. I've ... never really thought about it.'

'You don't know? Come, now. The handsome young postman, let's say – you've never seen him come by, and thought, *My, I wouldn't mind if he stayed for dinner*?'

'Stayed for—? Of course not!'

'I don't mean you'd actually ask him! Only that you'd think it.'

'No. I don't think I'm very good at that sort of thing. At telling handsome men from not-so-handsome ones.'

I shook my head, bemused. 'It's not the sort of thing one can be *good* at – it's a feeling. You can tell at a glance.'

'At a glance?' Her hands fell away from her face. In both of her eyes there shone a spark of gold, a reflection of the afternoon light that slid through the gap in the curtains. There was an odd weight to her words, somehow; something that teased. Something with ... intent.

The breath caught in my throat. I turned away.

It would not do, to imagine things.

'You would do it all again, then?' I heard her say.

'What, marriage?' I stared sightlessly around the room, as memory after memory rose to the surface of my mind. The cliffs of Lyme Regis. Parlours and lecture halls. The study at our house in London, the quiet flip of a page or scratch of a pen as we worked side by side. Such a life was better than anything I might have had as a spinster on Wight, surely.

But, of course, thinking of the past in any form was

treacherous at this time of year. In my mind's eye, the blood of rats and mice and turtles became my own; the study became the nursery, its florid wallpaper the bedspread which I had spent so long contemplating in the awful weeks that followed, the months stretching out like a stain upon my memory—

'Yes,' I blurted out. Then again, like a spell to dismiss the spectre of the past: 'Yes. I think so.'

When I met Maisie's eye again, she looked taken aback. Shocked, even. Suddenly, I felt exposed; had she seen the wave of grief that had washed over my face? Had she remembered which month it was? Which month it *nearly* was?

'Even with . . .' she said, painfully hesitant. 'Even after . . . ?'

Ah. So, indeed she had.

I looked once more at the opposite side of the room, where I could just make out the shape of the poor mouse, climbing up to drink from its saucer of water. I listened to the faint lapping sounds it made, the soft rasp of Maisie's breathing, in and out.

'Yes,' I said at last, aware even as I said it that I condemned my daughter to death. For if I had not married – if I had stayed on Wight and denied Mr Doyle and lived the rest of my life alone – she would never have died. But then she would also, undeniably, never have been born. Which was worse, I wondered? To deny her existence to begin with, or to give her life, however briefly, only for it to be snatched away? The latter seemed the crueller by far. And yet, selfish as it was – shocking as it was, for I was sure that not so long ago I would have done quite the opposite – it was this option I chose. For it was this option that led me here: to this house, this grand project, this endeavour which was the closest thing to a *purpose* that I had ever known.

And to Maisie, who was looking at me now with a sympathy so acute that it was almost painful.

'I am terribly sorry,' Maisie said suddenly. 'I didn't mean to remind you. I should never have mentioned it.'

'No, no,' I said, closing my eyes. 'It is quite all right. I would only have been reminded of her later, anyway.'

'Her?'

She sounded surprised then, as if she were hearing this information for the first time. I turned to Maisie, confusion briefly eclipsing my grief. Had Henry merely referred to the baby as 'it' in his letters?

'Yes. Did Henry not say?'

'Well, no. He . . .' Maisie stared down at her hands, squirming, as if there were something she very much did not wish to tell me. 'He wrote to say you were expecting. And I wrote back with my congratulations, and then again hoping that you were well, and then again asking if you were not past due, and if anything had happened. I begged Father to send someone down to London, or to let me go myself, merely to check that you hadn't taken ill with cholera or something . . .' I could see tears welling in her eyes. 'But then I came down with a cold anyway, and couldn't argue, and when Henry finally wrote back, there was no mention of a baby, just the two of you, so I had to guess – had to assume – that you didn't want to talk about it, and—'

Her voice grew too muffled then to hear the rest of what she said, for I had pushed myself from the end of the bed and wrapped my arms about her shoulders. She felt so much more solid in my arms than I might have thought from just looking at her, though she was still far thinner than she ought to have been. I felt the tickle of her hair against my cheek, the surprised intake of breath she made when I murmured:

'I'm sorry.'

'But I . . . She was *your* baby!' she spluttered.

'And he was your brother.' I thought of all the letters from Maisie I had seen arrive during those bleak months, piled on the corner of Henry's desk. I thought of all the nights I had spent alone, waiting for him to come home. He had been in mourning, yes, but – did he truly know how to mourn? Or did he only know how to run, leaving all those who knew and loved him behind? Such an instinct had been born from pain, I knew. I could no more truly blame him for it than I could blame a whipped horse for shying. But every time he did it, it would be Maisie or me who suffered.

Maisie had lifted her own arms to wrap them around me, her chin pressing into my shoulder. For a long moment, we simply sat in silence.

'I had thought, when you came to stay, that at least he and I would talk. Not even about Father, or . . . or the baby, but *something*,' Maisie murmured at last. She began to pull away, and I let her go at once, wary of holding her even a moment longer than she did me. 'What did you call her? Your daughter?'

The question hit me once more like a gale, blunt and forceful. But at least, I mused, it was not the agony it might have been three years ago.

'She did not live long enough for us to discuss it,' I said quietly. 'But . . . Elizabeth, I think, is what her name would have been. After my mother. She named me after her mother, I'm told, so it seemed . . .'

'That is a good name,' Maisie replied gently, after it became clear I did not plan to finish my sentence, although I hardly heard her – for my wandering gaze had spotted something across the room. Every other thought in my mind sputtered and died. I pushed off the bed, my feet carrying me there before I truly realized what I was doing.

'Mary?' Maisie said, clearly concerned. 'What— *Oh*.'

That must have been when she spotted it, too, as I stopped before the unfortunate mouse's cage and fumbled open the door. I peered closer, reaching inside as if to help, but I could already see that it was too late; that the little mouse lay still and open-mouthed in its saucer of water, dead.

19

So much has been done, exclaimed the soul of Frankenstein – more, far more, will I achieve; treading in the steps already marked, I will pioneer a new way, explore unknown powers, and unfold to the world the deepest mysteries of creation.

— MARY SHELLEY, *Frankenstein*

ONE BY ONE, parcels began to arrive at the house. Some of these were small, objects brined in jars; some were larger, packed in ice and intercepted by Clarke at the foot of the drive so that Maisie and the servants would not see; some came directly off the firth, from various fishermen or traders on their way to the canal.

The process of arranging all this had been, and continued to be, quite maddening. It was one thing, after all, to say 'the skull ought to be a crocodile's' or 'the spine should be an alligator's', and another matter entirely to get one's hands on such a specimen. The fishermen kept us stocked with as many dolphin carcasses as we could reasonably store, and once or twice a seal – which, although mammalian, offered the closest approximation we could manage to the bulk and skin of a plesiosaur. For the more exotic bits and pieces, we had to think creatively. After several pleading letters and a sizeable bribe, one of Henry's old friends at the University College collection sent up the skull of a recently deceased juvenile crocodile. After only one letter – God knows what it must have contained – a colleague of Clarke's on expedition in the East Indies was persuaded to send us several brined monitor lizards. I had asked Clarke once how it was that every man in England (and without) seemed to owe him a favour. He had apparently taken it as a compliment, chortling away for quite some time before he finally met my eye and said:

'Just because I was deemed unfit to take over my father's business doesn't mean I didn't learn anything from it. For what else is banking, Mrs Sutherland, but the strategic management of debt?'

That had made me think, of course, of what Henry had said to me months ago: 'I never truly expected that he'd want me to pay him back.' Perhaps Clarke had never intended to be repaid, either – not in money, at least. Not until he found himself cut off. Perhaps he had simply been investing in Henry, waiting for him to become successful. To accrue interest, as it were.

It was good that Clarke was useful in this way, for now that the matter of preservatives was settled he was quite useless in every other. While Henry and I continued to refine our grisly shopping list, bickering incessantly over the layout of muscles and bones and organs, Clarke hovered over our shoulders, offering inane comments that betrayed his utter ignorance of palaeontology. Once, memorably, he said:

'But shouldn't its flippers be bigger? They don't even reach the ground. How is it supposed to drag itself around the beach?'

At which Henry had exclaimed '*Good grief!*' and marched out of the door, leaving me to explain that this was precisely one of the theories we were hoping to disprove.

As our strange library of skin and muscle and bone and viscera grew, filling the shelves of the icehouse up to the rafters, I found myself positively itching to put it all together. But we couldn't, not yet; Clarke was 'still waiting on some eyeballs from a colleague at the Reptile House in London Zoo', and we had all agreed in any case that it would be best to wait until the first frosts struck, and the truly cold weather began. Even with the aid of Clarke's turpentine and acetate of alumina, we would need every advantage we could get to stop the creature from rotting before we could fully assemble it.

'So it doesn't end up like that mouse,' as Clarke had said with a flippant smile, and I had felt my stomach turn.

I found myself upset by the little mouse's death. Upset in a way I would never admit to Henry and Clarke; upset in a way that was quite hypocritical, really, considering how many others of its kind we'd sacrificed to our cause. But the others, at least, had had lives – small, brutal, mouse-ish lives – before they had died their small, brutal, mouse-ish deaths. This one had been different. It had died three times, but I was not sure it had truly *lived* three times. It had eaten and slept and breathed, to be sure. But it had not seemed particularly to enjoy any of it. And in the end, it had died – by drowning? By suicide? By chance, as it stood above its water bowl? I did not know.

Even so, it seemed silly to grieve. There were countless mice in the world which died futile deaths, not nearly worth the lives which preceded them. But it is one thing to acknowledge the existence of the glue factory, and quite another to watch a horse die oneself, slowly and painfully. One is felt by the brain, the other by the heart. I consoled myself with the knowledge that at least our trials were done now; no more creatures need meet such a grisly end. And once we brought our own creature to life, it would stay that way.

'TODAY, THEN, YOU think?'

It was November, the trees now bare and spindly, their reaching branches black against the clouds above. The three of us hovered about the front door, wrapped up tight against the wind.

In answer, Clarke stepped over the threshold on to the steps and cast his eyes about. For a moment I expected him to sniff the air like a dog, or raise a finger to test the wind, but he did not. He merely stared. I do not know what it was, exactly, that he saw – the sky was as grey as it ever was, dark with unrained rain and unsleeted sleet. It looked to me like any other day of the past week. But perhaps it was, and this was simply Clarke putting on a show.

'Yes,' he murmured. 'I think so. Time for the main event.'

'The main event, indeed,' Henry echoed, in a reverent fashion. They exhausted me, the both of them.

'Well? What are we waiting for, then?' I pushed past Clarke, nearly shoving him off the steps. My boots landed, crunching, in the frost-sharp grass. 'We have work to do.'

IT WAS AN unremarkable thing, at first. Henry and I had planned the creature's construction so intricately over the past months – so intricately, indeed, that I dreamed of it at night, stitching muscles to tendons as I slept – that the process seemed almost familiar. From the beginning I had noted how strange it was, that surgery and sewing should be so similar, yet the former should be restricted to those who had never held a needle in their lives before their first days at university. The unpleasant difference here, of course, was that unlike sewing, our fabric was cold and wet and bloody, slipperier than even the worst of silks. (Not to mention the stench of turpentine.) Clarke claimed to have some experience 'stitching wounds in the field' – although if I had sewn stitches as uneven as his in my embroidery lessons, I would have been given a ruler across the back of my hand – but Henry, as we had discovered during our initial experiments with mice, was quite incapable. Instead, he acted as a sort of director, readying each piece of flesh for us to work on and consulting our notes with unsullied hands so that he could instruct us as to what ought to be sewn to where, and in what order. As the one of us least covered in gore, he also took up the task of answering the door whenever Flora brought us refreshments. It was best that no one saw us, we thought, in our oilcloth aprons and elbow-length gloves, with scarves across our mouths to keep out the cold and the stench.

'You look like surgical bandits,' Henry said one afternoon as he carried in our cups of hot water (there was no sense in wasting tea, with our senses already shot from the smell). Clarke snorted at that, and I laughed, too; a brief moment of good humour that was spoiled almost immediately when Clarke added:

'Ah – careful!' He gestured to the cup which Henry had set down on my left. The previous afternoon, he had set it to my right, precisely in the middle of a loop of catgut, so that it had almost spilled when I pulled the loop taut. 'She's clumsy with drinks, that one.'

He and Henry laughed heartily. How wonderful it was that they could find it all so funny now, I fumed. It had never been a joke to me. It had been a concession, in fact – had I not tossed my wine in Clarke's face that evening, I might have wrapped my hands around his chicken-thin neck instead.

But that was all over now, wasn't it? Water under the bridge. Henry had never used to be a water-under-the-bridge sort, at least not when we first met. While others pled civility, he would stand his ground. 'I cannot abide people who persist in holding idiotic opinions,' he'd said to me once, and I'd taken comfort in that. But somewhere along the line, he'd changed. Or maybe I had simply never realized that by 'idiotic' he meant 'those who believe the *Iguanodon* stood upright', and not 'those who believe my wife to be, by the very fact of her birth, a lowly, worthless thing'. I thought again of what Mr Jamsetjee had said to me, years ago: 'One cannot afford principles, if one is trying not to drown.' But it didn't seem to me that Henry was drowning badly enough to forsake such an affordable principle as that.

There was another dream I had, one in particular which had visited me many times since the Crystal Palace and the beginnings of our grand project. It was this: Henry and I behind a lectern at the Royal Society, staring out at a stony-faced audience while the plesiosaur floated between us in a marvellous glass tank. Henry would talk and talk, describing our chemical 'spark' and pointing out each substitution of flesh and bone noted on my lovingly rendered diagram – and then he would make a mistake. Something small. *Plesiosaurus dolidocheirus*, perhaps, instead of *Plesiosaurus dolichodeirus*. But then would come another and another, and each time I opened my mouth to speak, I would find my tongue made of lead. The audience shifted, patience fraying, and when I looked into their scowling faces, I realized that it was all for naught. They did not believe us anyway. They never would.

But that night, the dream was different. When Henry fumbled and I opened my mouth to correct him, I found to my astonishment that I could. The words tumbled out. I looked around in shock – had anyone noticed? Had anyone heard? They had, I think; some of the eyes in the audience met mine, though they looked as full of doubt as always. It did not matter. I turned to the creature then, pressing my hands upon the glass; it was the first time, in all those dreams, that I had truly looked at it. It was a hazy thing, a dreamlike mass of scales and teeth – for the real version was not yet done, of course, and so my imagination must do the work of finishing it – but one thing stood out clearly: a single golden eye, fixed on mine.

I woke with a start. For a long while I simply lay there, staring at the ceiling above. The middle of the night is the ripest time, I have found, for making resolutions. Things which seem troublesome and confusing in the light of day are made plainer by night, all unnecessary complications stripped away. And so I lay there, making bitter promises to myself in the dark. Henry be damned, Clarke be damned, the whole Royal Society be damned – I was so very tired of placing my hopes in other people's hands.

I had failed the first time, bringing new life into the world – and the second, and the third, and at every attempt since. This time, I vowed, would not be the same.

THERE IS A precise moment which everyone who has ever drawn or sewn or sculpted a thing will recognize, and that is the moment at which it becomes the thing it was meant to be. For hours, one's work may look only like lines upon a page; for days, like a pile of fabric; for months, a misshapen rock. And then, one day, when one holds it up to the light and takes a single step back – *there it is!* The myriad pieces come together into a coherent whole.

That morning, I woke early. This was hardly a welcome thing, for all three of us had worked late the night before; we had underestimated the amount of time it would take us to put the whole thing together, and were now running ourselves ragged trying to do so before spring arrived. My hands were still sore from the previous day's stitching, my fingers calloused. No matter how much I scrubbed them, they still smelled of blood and turpentine, salt water and wet leather gloves. But despite everything, I felt a thrill as I rose and looked out of the window into the misty pre-dawn. There was an uncanny sense of significance about the day. Or perhaps that is simply my memory, polishing things in retrospect.

I dressed quickly and went out into the icy morning. It was at times such as this that I was glad I had never had a lady's maid; I loved these small moments, in which no one but myself knew what I was about. The only sounds I heard as I crept over to the boathouse were the cries of birds, the gentle lapping of water against the shore.

Once inside, I lit a match. And there, *there it was* – that moment like the striking of a match itself, the moment it all came together in beautiful and shocking harmony! There was work still to be done, of course; half the teeth to be added, and some of its skin. But the previous day it had been only a pile of flesh, and now ... now, it was a proper creature. A Creature. *The* Creature. *Our* Creature.

I realized with a terrifying sort of finality that this, then, was the day we would do it. The day we would bring it to life.

And so – as you may recall – we did.

. . . my beloved, awake!

— MARY SHELLEY, *Frankenstein*

The all-beholding Sun had ne'er beholden
In his wide voyage o'er continents and seas
So fair a creature . . .

— PERCY BYSSHE SHELLEY,
'The Witch of Atlas'

I LOVED IT. From the moment I first met its strange and terrible eyes, I loved it. Perhaps it was hypocritical of me yet again to love such a thing when I hadn't truly loved any of the others – not even that first, ill-fated mouse – but I could not help it. As I sat and felt the thrum of its frantic heart beneath my fingers, the weight of its life in my hands, I nearly wept with joy. It was a wonder. It was a monster. It was *alive*.

Behind me, Clarke was laughing, clapping Henry on the back; Henry was crowing with delight. Only when he hauled me to my feet and threw an arm around my shoulder, pressing a kiss to my cheek, did I realize I had been counting the Creature's breaths. There was some terrified part of me that felt it would stop if I looked away. I closed my eyes to prove myself wrong – once, twice, three times – and each time I opened them, I felt a rush of relief to see it was still there, still breathing. For just a moment, I let myself bury my face in Henry's shoulder and forget all else in the world – because at last, at last, we had *done it*.

'Come!' Henry cried, clapping his hands together like a child. 'Let's put it in the water, see if it swims!'

'Is it this one here?' Clarke asked, hand on the lever that would lower the table down into the water.

'Yes! Let me through, I'll do it – you can't possibly lift it on your own.'

'Lies and slander! It's only a pulley – get your hands off it, man; I'm perfectly capable.'

Rather jerkily, the table was lowered into the pool until the Creature was mostly submerged, only its head and the curve of its back showing above the water. It seemed so much *larger* now than it ever had when we were building it – and I suppose, at only a few inches longer than Clarke was tall, it was indeed quite a beast. I fell to my hands and knees upon the floor, leaning over to lay my hand on its back once more. It was still breathing, its heart still beating, its lovely golden eye still blinking up at me.

But it did not move.

'Oh dear,' said Henry quietly. 'Is it all right?'

'I don't know.' My voice shook with worry. I felt – quite unreasonably, for we could always bring it back to life again, couldn't we? *Couldn't we?* – a terrible, lurching sense of déjà vu. Its paddles, I noticed, kept twitching and jerking, as if its movements were barely under its own control. And there was something else, too; something even more dire. A jolt of fear ran down my spine.

'Its heart – Henry, its heart is slowing.'

'What?' he cried, aghast, leaning forward to grip the edge of the pool with white-knuckled hands.

'That can't be possible,' said Clarke. 'Its heart was the freshest—'

But he was cut short then, by the softest of sounds: the watery ripple of the Creature lowering its head beneath the water. I thought of the mouse, dead in its water bowl; I thought of the doctor, murmuring, 'She really ought to be crying by now.' I did not dare to breathe.

Slowly, it moved its flippers for the first time in concert. Inch by painful inch, it shuffled itself towards the edge of the table. I recalled suddenly, like a flash of light in the dark, a fact I really ought to have remembered.

'It was conserving its breath!' I cried, filled with a wave of relief so acute I nearly wept. 'It's what they do – sea creatures of all sorts, dolphins and alligators – they slow their heart under-water, to use less oxygen!'

'Oh, what a clever thing,' Henry gasped.

The Creature had stopped moving again, resting halfway off the edge of the table. I tried my best not to worry; it must simply be getting used to its body. After all, its brain had never moved an assortment of limbs quite like these. Out of all our previous tests, this was the one constructed out of the largest number of individual parts. How I wished we had something to compare it to – an account of Victor's creature's first hours, its first stumbling attempts at life – but, of course, he had not stayed long enough to witness them.

The door creaked open behind us, and for a moment I thought hopefully that Clarke was fleeing too, as Victor had.

But when Henry and I turned around, we found him still in the doorway, a rakish grin on his face.

'Whisky or wine?' he said. 'We ought to celebrate.'

'WHO'S A USELESS tinkerer now, eh? A layabout, a miserable sponge, playing at soldiers? Who's not fit to take over the bank now, *eh*?'

At each 'eh', Clarke teetered forward, aiming one pointed finger at the pool. In his other hand was a glass of wine, the contents of which he nearly spilled with each lunge. Beside me, Henry leaned back in the rickety wooden chair he had dragged in from the kitchen and said:

'Clarke, honestly, would you stop talking to the damned thing as if it's your father?'

I had to snicker at that. I had abandoned the wine long ago, after only a glass and a half, but it had been such a generous glass to start with that I could still feel its warm and blurry aftermath. As I lay on my belly by the side of the pool, feeding fish scraps to the Creature, I mused that I should really have another – Clarke's presence was infinitely more bearable under its influence.

'You know you'd say the very same to yours if he weren't so dead,' drawled Clarke, sloshing his glass in Henry's direction. 'What do you say – shall we bring him back? Get one last word in?'

'Oh, no need. I already know exactly what he'd say.' Henry forced his face into an awful, pouting approximation of the portrait that hung above the parlour fireplace. '*You've conquered death, have you? Why, so you can have all the time in the world to lie about?*'

The two of them laughed at that, heartily and bitterly all at once. I had a brief vision of them in their university days, making morbid jokes over a game of poker, commiserating about their ghastly fathers – and, quite suddenly, I was annoyed. Perhaps it was the fact that they had had each other to commiserate with, when I had had no one; or the fact that they had fathers at all to commiserate about.

'You aren't really going to tell him about the Creature, are you? Your father?' I snapped.

Clarke's eyebrows rose. 'Do I look mad? No, of course not. We're not telling anyone – besides Lord Wrottesley, of course. And William Hamilton. Oh, and I suppose we should try the Edinburgh societies, too.' He waved a hand. 'In any case. Until someone respectable agrees to let us present the thing before an audience of our peers, and until we *do* present it, any claims we make will sound like the ramblings of a street magician.'

I knew that, of course. I had merely been concerned that he didn't. I heaved a sigh and went back to gazing at the Creature. It had improved considerably in the past few hours, shuffling its way off the platform and even going so far as to make a few clumsy laps of the pool. It floated before me now in a rather lopsided way, eyeing a bobbing chunk of fish.

'We don't want anyone trying to reproduce it, either, if word gets out,' Henry added. 'Or coming to steal the thing itself.'

'Yes, that is a worry. We may want to invest in some more locks for that door, Henry.' Clarke leaned over the edge of the pool, peering down at the Creature – and oh, I did not like that look upon his face. It was not simply pride in his eyes, not simply satisfaction at a job well done, but rather . . . hunger. A look like the head of a railway company surveying a swathe of perfectly level forest.

'I wonder why Victor never told anyone about his creation,' Henry said. 'Besides Walton, that is. He could have had fame, fortune, everything.'

Clarke snorted. 'It killed half a dozen people, Henry! Admitting to its creation would have been tantamount to confessing to their murder.'

I am not so sure of that, I thought, frowning into the water. Clarke had never read Walton's letters in their entirety, merely the sections that related most closely to Victor's experiments; and Henry had admitted to skimming the more philosophical parts, the tale of loneliness and spite that Victor's creation had delivered atop a barren glacier. There was a certain intelligence, a certain *eloquence*, to the creature's own words that I had found impossible to convey. Whatever destruction Victor's monster had wrought, I was certain that it – or rather, *he* – had done so with a mind of his own.

'Victor was too ashamed in the end, I think,' I murmured. 'And too scared, at the start. He could barely stand to look at his own creation.'

Clarke squatted at the edge of the pool, swilling his wine against the sides of its glass. 'I can see why. It is quite jarring, isn't it? To watch it move, after seeing it for so long as simply— *Gah!*'

Clarke jerked away, for his finger, which he had just placed in the water to wiggle appetizingly in front of the Creature's snout like a worm, had very nearly ended up between its teeth. Henry cackled as Clarke wiped his wet hand on his trouser leg, looking grievously offended; but he had deserved it, I thought. *Jarring!* We had wrought a miracle from sinew and flesh, turned back the wheel of life and death, brought forth a simulacrum of a creature older than humanity itself – and he called it jarring? The ingratitude!

I shall never run from you, I told the Creature in silence, staring into its smooth, jet-black pupils as it finally caught the floating piece of fish, mashing it between its teeth. *Well, as long as you don't commit any murders. Although there are some I wouldn't mind. Clarke is all yours, if you can stomach him.*

IT TOOK NEARLY a week for the Creature to come fully into its own. The three of us took turns feeding it and checking on it – every hour on the hour, and every two hours throughout the night. Even then, I found myself in the off hours yearning to go and see it. Many was the time I sat with it long past my appointed slot, watching it swim in circles and delicate figures of eight. It possessed a peculiar sort of grace, turning and weaving through the water like a flag snapping in the wind. Not once did I ever see it move in a straight line. Everything about it was alternately curved and pointed, delicate and piercing. Calligraphy made flesh.

'Lord, don't you get bored just watching the thing?' Clarke said one afternoon, dropping a bucket of fish scraps noisily to the floor. And then, frowning: 'Are you feeding it from your hand?'

'Don't be ridiculous. It simply eats better when you put in one piece at a time. And wave it in front of its eyes first; I don't think its vision is very good.' I demonstrated with another sliver of fish, trailing it in the water. The Creature, watching closely, snapped it up the moment I let go. 'Why, how do you feed it?'

Clarke wrinkled his nose and made a sweeping gesture, as if scattering seed for birds. At my look of horror, he said: 'Well, I'm hardly going to put my fingers in the water, am I? It nearly *ate* me last time.'

'Good grief – is that why there is so much rotten fish at the bottom of the pool? It cannot eat the pieces once they've reached the bottom, Clarke, it cannot get its jaws around them! Henry, you haven't been doing the same, have you?'

Henry, who was in the corner laboriously cataloguing the amounts and concentrations of the ingredients that went into our life-giving solution, looked up in alarm.

'Erm,' he said.

I threw my gaze heavenward, and dragged the stinking bucket towards me with a screech of metal on stone. 'Useless, the pair of you.'

'Well, then, Mrs Sutherland, you may take care of all its meals from now on, if you so wish. We have a paper to write,' Clarke said coldly, turning to Henry to quip on his way out: 'God forbid we interfere with her infant's diet.'

If he had expected this joke to land, it did not. He exited the boathouse, leaving a ringing silence in his wake. Henry met my eye with a haunted, half-apologetic look, though he said nothing; it was not long before he, too, turned and left, taking his unfinished list with him.

For here, of course, was the elephant in the room. The one I loathed beyond all belief, the one so large I could hardly even blame Clarke for addressing it – for it was what everyone thought, was it not? Whenever a woman without children loved an animal or a cause or anything else – *anything* else besides that which she ought to love most in the world, that which she ought to spend all her days trying and longing for – it was thought to be a substitute for what she did not have. No matter that all three of us had looked upon the Creature with pride and joy; I alone was not its creator, or its artist, or its inventor, but merely a *mother*, most qualified to care for it not due to any intelligence or observation on my part, but due to the perversion of some natural urge. I remembered, vividly, that in the first awful month of my lying-in – though I had nothing but grief to lie in for – Mrs Jamsetjee had come to see me. In her quiet way, she had laid a box of pastels upon the foot of the bed and said: 'Trust me, it will be better if you have something to fill your time.' I'd waited until she left before tossing them to the floor. She meant well, I knew; but somehow that had only made it worse, for how could she not see? It had been she who had given me my very first drawing set, a narrow wooden box I still kept in my bedside drawer, though I'd worn the pencils down to nothing long ago. It was she who had taken me to the banks of the Thames and taught me how to measure the rocks with my thumb at arm's length, how to catch their shadows and pin them to the page. Had all my work since then merely been *filling time*? Was every idea that sprang from my mind, every thing that I had ever fashioned with my own two hands, simply a means of filling the void of my barren, childless life?

No one had ever accused Henry of trying to fill a void, though I knew better than anyone that that was all he did. It had not seemed that way to me at first, when we had met; he had seemed bold and daring, a font of boundless energy. Only in time – after he was let go from his position, after our child was not quite born – did I realize how exhausted he truly was. Any momentum he had, he kept up simply because he was afraid of what would catch him if he stopped. I had seen it the night we celebrated the Creature's creation, after we came back to the house and readied for bed – he was ecstatic, to be sure, but beneath that I could see fear in his eyes. The terror of inaction, of being done. By the next morning he was back at work with Clarke, trying to figure out how soon we could present to the Royal Society, the British Association, the Geological Society, and so on, and so on.

Was it a fault of mine, that I loved the Creature so – that I could not see it in the same way, as a task completed or a tool to be used? Or was it the opposite, a natural inclination of my sex towards love and care? I thought of my grandmother and shuddered; *certainly not*.

And then I thought of Mr and Mrs Jamsetjee. A notion struck me as I knelt by the side of the pool, reaching out to brush the smooth skin of the Creature's back with my fingers – not the entire truth, but approaching it. The notion of a thing that was not one's child, and not a replacement, but something else entirely. Something chosen.

'I suppose I would be upset, too, if you went off with some Henry,' I murmured, as it turned, sated, and swam away.

I SPENT A great deal of time in the Creature's company in the days that followed. As Clarke and Henry wrote letters and went through our journals, condensing years of notes into a single organized lecture, I took up the task of re-drawing and enlarging my diagrams. The thought of presenting them as they were – smudged, covered in stains and crossings-out – was unthinkable. Not to mention that the Creature looked quite different from those initial sketches; not hugely so, but noticeably. And so I kept to the boathouse, with a bucket of fish by my side and a roll of paper across the worktable, attempting to capture its likeness anew.

Maisie noticed the difference, I think. How could she not? I had been too busy for our afternoon walks in those last frantic days of our Creature's construction, so now – especially as the weather was getting better, unseasonably warm for the beginning of April – I made a point of going out with her every day. She must have seen my renewed energy, the way I practically skipped along our seaside paths.

And yet, still, I hesitated to show her. I had made a promise,

I knew. To her, to myself, to Mr Jamsetjee – and I wanted to tell them, truly. But somehow, I could not imagine such a thing without being seized by anxiety, a terror I could not name. Like a coward, I told myself each morning that this would be the day I introduced the Creature to Maisie; and yet each day, some tremulous thing within me whispered, *Not yet, not yet*.

And then, one evening, as I sat by the Creature's pool sharpening my pencils, I heard a splash beside me. I looked up to see its head resting on the wooden surround, neatly atop my pile of sharpened pencils.

'Oh, get off, will you?' I said, though good-naturedly. 'You've already had your dinner. You're not getting any more; I know you'll only spit it out.'

It made a noise, high and keening, and slid back into the water – taking half my pencils with it.

'Oh, damn it all!' I muttered, watching them drift to the bottom of the pool. It had been a very trying day thus far; I had spilled ink on the sleeve of my dress, and Clarke had come in to harass me about some mistake on my diagram of the plesiosaur's skull, and Henry had come in to harass me about a tear in his shirt which Flora had sewn up wrong, and 'Would you just do it, you always do it well', and now this. Worst of all, I had only myself to blame for leaving the pencils so close to the edge in the first place.

As I packed my things to leave, however, I heard another splash behind me. It was the Creature again, and in its mouth – delicate as anything – it held one of my pencils.

'*Oh*,' I breathed. I dropped to my hands and knees at the edge of the pool. The pencil, when I took it from the Creature, was wet and slightly dented by its teeth, but that did not matter. 'You brought it back – for me?'

In answer, it merely blinked, its peculiar sideways eyelids darting across its eyes and back. I laughed and, to my surprise, found my own eyes welling with tears.

'You're . . . real, aren't you?' I whispered. A nonsense thing to say, but it simply tumbled out of me. 'You're really here. You know me.'

It pulled away, vanishing back into the water with nary a ripple. It did not return any more of my pencils, but I did not care. For a long while, I simply sat beside the water, spilling over with pride. What a beautiful, brilliant, *marvellous thing*! All at once, my anxiety of the past few weeks seemed to evaporate, the urge to keep the Creature secret overridden by the urge to tell someone of the miracle that had just occurred – that it had recognized me, thought of me, shown intelligence and care.

And in that moment, I knew precisely who that someone must be.

BEFORE I COULD lose my nerve, I ran back to the house and up the stairs, to where Maisie's room lay. I rapped on her door, a giddy little syncopated sound. When her muffled 'Come in!' sounded through the door, I sprang inside, taking her hands in mine – they fitted so perfectly, how could I not? – and whispered:

'I have something to show you. In the boathouse.'

'Oh!' Her eyes grew wide, her face lighting up in excitement. 'But . . . are you sure? Are you allowed?'

For a moment, I was baffled. 'Allowed? By whom – Henry?'

'No, by . . . well, I don't know! Whoever it is that has had you so bound to secrecy. Parliament? Scotland Yard?'

I held a hand over my mouth to stifle my laughter. 'No, nothing like that! Come, you'll see.'

We slipped out into the evening. Clarke was already in bed, and Henry dozing by the fire, so we would not be noticed as long as we returned before he awoke. A hazy blanket of mist had settled on the garden, and Maisie and I tiptoed across the grass like ponies, lifting our skirts to keep them dry.

'Here it is!' I cried once we were inside, unable to contain myself any longer. I thrust the lamp I had been carrying into her hands and strode forward.

'Here what is? I can't see anything.'

'You will in a minute. Bring the light over here.' I sat by the edge of the water, folding my skirts beneath me. Carefully, I drew my pencil from my pocket and dropped it into the water.

'What am I looking for?'

'*Shh*, just wait.'

Ever so slightly, the surface rippled. I could see the Creature's silhouette down below, though one might easily have mistaken it for a shadow in the lamp's flickering light – until it rose from the water with a mighty splash and set its head upon my lap.

'Oh!' I cried. I was soaked through, though I couldn't bring myself to be cross about it in the slightest – for there it was, with a pencil once again gripped in its teeth and its *head upon my lap*. It might have been an accident, for all I knew, but I was touched regardless. Its skin was knobbly and uneven beneath my fingertips as I ran my hand up its snout, over its head, along the neat lines of stitching around its eyes.

'You clever thing! I know I said earlier there were no more fish for you, but I think you deserve some after that.' I turned to ask Maisie if she would pass me the bucket of fish scraps in the corner but, seeing the look on her face, the words died on my lips.

'What is it?' she said, her voice so quiet that I could barely make out the words.

'Well, that's what I was trying to show you. Come here and—'

'What *is it*?'

The grand explanation I had practised for so long in my head was gone. I faltered. 'It's ... do you remember me telling you about the ancient reptiles? Ichthyosaurs, mosasaurs, plesiosaurs?'

She stared at me as if I were speaking a foreign language. Her eyes darted quickly to the Creature and back, as though she couldn't bear to look at it for too long. I wished suddenly that we had not made its teeth quite so sharp, its eyes quite so shining.

'You said those went extinct thousands of years ago. Why does it have ... God, Mary, why is it covered in stitches?'

'Well, that's precisely it, isn't it! We had to make our own. My uncle – my great-uncle, that is – he was a man of science and ... I had no idea, but I found some of his letters, and he said that he'd gone to ... to cemeteries and the like, and ... It was an experiment. He wanted to see if he could restore life, build a new sort of human, but we didn't use humans, we used—'

'You made this out of *dead things*?' Maisie cried.

'Yes, but ...' I scrambled for something, anything that would stop her looking at me with that awful expression on her face, that mask of shock and horror. 'They're not dead any more!'

'You think that is better?' She was nearly yelling now, her back pressed against the door, and I worried that someone in the house would hear. I rose to my feet, gently sliding the Creature back into the water, and went to take her hands. She snatched them away.

'Maisie, please—'

'This is *wrong*! It's wrong, it's unnatural!' she gasped. 'Good

God, look at it, all those stitches . . . Can't you see? It's a mock-ery of—'

'Of what? The natural order?' My hands were shaking now, as well as my voice. Milling my hurt to anger, as I always did. 'What is the natural order, anyway? The tendency of things to rot and die and . . . and *hurt*? Is medicine unnatural, then? Is this not just the natural progression of medical science, one thing to another?'

'Months,' she carried on. She did not seem to have heard a word I'd said. 'You've been here for months, a year, and all this time . . . I thought that you couldn't tell me, that you were doing something good and important and noble, but this is why you never told me, isn't it? You knew it was awful!'

'No! Maisie, I never meant to keep anything from you, I just . . .' But even I did not know how to finish that sentence. I *had* meant to keep it from her, after all; and this was precisely why, I realized. I had been so afraid of what she might think, too afraid even to admit the possibility that she would not like it, terrified of turning around once more – as I had all those years ago, on the beach by the Needles – and seeing the face of the girl I adored twisted in disgust.

And I had been right to be afraid.

'I ought to . . .' She threw her hands up in the air. I wondered what she was thinking she ought to do. Throw us out? Have the boathouse torn down, and the Creature chased out into the firth?

'Maisie—' I said again, casting her name like a rope out to sea, desperate to catch her again. But the look she shot me then – so awfully, humiliatingly familiar – was enough to stop me in my tracks.

'Don't,' she said quietly. 'Just don't.'

21

*I have no friend, Margaret: when I am glowing with the
enthusiasm of success, there will be none to participate
my joy; if I am assailed by disappointment, no one will
endeavour to sustain me in dejection.*

*

*'Man,' I cried, 'how ignorant art thou in thy pride of
wisdom! Cease; you know not what it is you say.'*

— MARY SHELLEY, *Frankenstein*

THAT WAS THE last I spoke to Maisie for quite some time.

I had never been on this side of the coin. With Henry, I always
knew that it would be he who cracked first; and moreover, it was
nearly always he who had done something wrong. Here, it was . . .
well, I still hesitated to say that it was I who'd done wrong. But I
had upset her, at least. The thought nipped at me, buzzing around
my head like a fly. I wavered back and forth as to whether I was
self-righteous or repentant, angry at her for the way she'd reacted,
or at myself for being foolish enough to show her.

'You and Maisie are quarrelling, then?' Henry asked when I
joined him and Clarke in the parlour with our copy of Liebig's
Animal Chemistry, so that we might extract some quotes on the

vital principle for our lecture. (Maisie had gone to bed with a chill, so for once we were not meeting in the boathouse, which Clarke complained stank of fish.) I stopped in the doorway, hands tight around the book's spine.

'What makes you say that?'

'Because you're usually off this time of evening doing cross-stitch or what-have-you. Is she too ill even for embroidery?'

I allowed myself a sigh. Weekend evenings such as this, it was true, I spent with Maisie – though it was reading we did together. I had not cross-stitched since I was sixteen.

'*Usually* we do, yes. While you and Clarke are secreted in a cupboard playing . . . what likely story is it now? Snip, snap, snorem?'

'Ladies, ladies,' said Clarke. 'If you're quite finished, I have news to report.' He held up a letter. 'You'll be pleased to know I've heard back from Mr Young. He says they have just such a carriage, and assures me there should be no problem with our borrowing it for a spell next month.'

The problem of how we were to move the Creature from its current location in order to present it had been a puzzle from the start. After a great many ridiculous ideas, we settled upon the very simplest: a wheeled tank, drawn by horses. This, we decided, would be far gentler on the Creature than travel by rail, and more private than by steamer (which Henry abhorred anyway, being terribly prone to seasickness). Henry claimed that he had seen just such a vehicle years ago, used to wash away debris from the street after a flood. And so Clarke had written to his 'good friend' Mr Young – was every man in Britain his good friend? – who worked as the Superintendent of Cleansing in Glasgow, to ask if his department possessed such a thing.

'What does he ask in return?' I queried, ever wary of Clarke's innumerable friends.

'Oh, nothing.' He glanced through the letter, then shot Henry a pompous little smile. 'Though I daresay a small donation to the department wouldn't be out of order. What do you say, Henry? What shall I put you down for?' He made a grand show of remembering. 'Ah – that's right. Forgive me, I forgot. No matter. I'll just put something in your name. What's another ten pounds on top of everything else?'

'HERE WE ARE; I have your dinner! Now— Oh, what's the matter? Not your favourite?' I knelt down by the side of the pool, grimacing at the scraps of fish the Creature had just spat back into the water. 'I know. But the cod didn't look too good today; I suspect it's the same batch they had out in the sun all day yesterday.'

Eventually, after much coaxing, it ate some haddock, though it flatly refused to come and rest its head upon the side when I clapped my hands, as I was trying to teach it to do; I supposed it felt it hadn't been given a good enough incentive. Henry kept saying that if I insisted on training it like a dog, I really ought to withhold its food until after it had done its tricks – but I did not want to think of them as tricks. I did not want to wonder, every time it heard my clapping and came to greet me, whether it truly wanted to see me or if it was merely hungry.

'Want to have a look outside, do you?' I asked, seeing it nose against the wooden doors. Reaching through the net, which covered both the water and some feet above it, I undid the latch and pushed the doors open. Clarke and Henry would froth at the mouth if they saw me do this, but the net rose up so high – and the traffic on the firth was so far away – that I did not think there was any real risk in it. I watched as the Creature rested its snout in a square of the net, blinking in the narrow strip of sunlight that shone through the doors. I thought for a moment it might be basking, but when I sat down in the shade at the edge of the pool, it made a keening sound and swam over to put its dripping head in my lap instead.

'There we go. Is the sun too strong for your eyes?' I murmured, chuckling. I looked out across the firth, stroking the thin ridges of scales that ran along its brows. It was a bright and beautiful day, spring as I had not quite seen it in Inverness, the year before having been an unusually rainy one. The seabirds had returned in their clamouring thousands; heather blossomed on the hills, cowslips and dog violets upon the lawn; the sky shone blue through scattered clouds. It was beautiful – and yet, none of it affected me as I thought it should. There had been little to do lately, only waiting for arrangements to be made and replies to arrive, and I found myself listless. I spent long hours with the Creature, telling it my woes like a shepherd gone too long without human company. I took walks along the shore, down the same winding paths I had walked with Maisie once. I plucked buttercups and whitlow grass from the gaps in the rocks, fashioning them into tiny bouquets, only to drop them by the wayside on my return.

Occasionally, I took one to Maisie's door instead. She had been ill for nearly a fortnight now – at first with a fever, which had worried me terribly, and then with a bout of her usual aches and pains. Her new doctor had said it was simply the result of the stress of recovery. She was not going to die, he had assured me on his last visit – and it had embarrassed me that he had felt compelled to say so, that I was so obvious in my worry, standing there wringing my hands like a fishwife awaiting the return of her husband from sea. It embarrassed me further still how relieved I was at his words; I had not been able to stop thinking, those two awful weeks, *The last thing we would have ever done was fight.*

I heaved a sigh, staring out at the distant shapes of boats upon the water. The Creature, perhaps sensing my glum mood, whined again and slid back into the pool.

'Sorry, dear – it isn't you. Here, look.' I stood, squeezing the water from my dress – a pointless effort, really; it had been ruined long ago – and took a handful of pencils from my pocket. I had had to buy a new set in Inverness to replace the ones that had fallen into the pool, and so I thought I might as well let the Creature have the old ones, swollen and dented with tooth-marks as they were. I held one against the water and waved it about, sending ripples racing across the surface. The Creature went absolutely still, its pupils widening.

'Aha, you've spotted it!' I grinned, holding the pencil like a dart. 'Are you ready? There . . . *go!*'

The Creature darted forward and snapped it up with impressive speed. As it swam in circles about the pool, gnashing the pencil between its teeth, I took out my sketchbook. Although the diagrams for the lecture were long since complete, inked and rolled up in the corner of the under-stairs cupboard, I found I could not stop drawing the Creature. There was some subtle aspect of its likeness that I had not yet managed to capture, no matter how many portraits I drew. It inspired a kind of *chill*; the same odd thrill of primal fear that cries, *Run, run!* when the shape of a wolf or a tiger appears through the trees. Perhaps it is strange to say so, but that was one of my favourite things about our Creature. There is something romantic about feeding a predator from the palm of your hand, I think – a creature which might bite you if it chooses, but which chooses not to. But how does one set all that down on paper? How does one turn such awful beauty to lead and ink on a page?

It occurred to me that the very awfulness I loved so much was probably what had disturbed Maisie so deeply. I had thought us alike, she and I. I had thought that she of all people, who plucked worms from the dry ground after the rain and tossed them back into the soil, who read tales of murderers and highway robbers, would understand me. But instead I had found, yet again, that I did not know her at all.

And here, too, was another worry; for if Maisie could not love the Creature, then who would? The Royal Society would appreciate it, surely, for its scientific fascination – but the public? Henry and I had talked before, in that distant way of ideas that are so outlandish they may as well be dreams, of setting up our very own Geological Islands. An array of living, breathing fossils, each with its own enclosure, a zoo of the prehistoric. I had imagined an audience ooh-ing and aah-ing, children clapping in glee as the Creature fetched batons from the lake, our debts paid and our legacy secured. But after witnessing Maisie's reaction, this image had begun to wither in my mind. Now I could only imagine it as a sort of freak show – spectators transfixed with horror, children crying in fright, youths sneaking in after dark to shoot peas at the Creature's head. The very thought made my heart ache. I would never allow such a thing to happen, I thought fiercely; if I had to vet each visitor myself, if I had to keep it trapped in the boathouse for ever, I would.

Something nudged my leg then, and I gasped – but it was only the Creature, of course. I had not heard it creep up on me, it had been so silent. It lifted its head from the water and nudged its snout against my foot again, the wet pencil in its mouth leaving smudges of graphite on the hem of my dress.

'Oh, you frightful thing,' I murmured as I reached forward and took the wet pencil from between its teeth. 'You beautiful, unnatural thing.'

'SO: TO THE Edinburgh Geological Society on the twenty-third of May . . .'

'The twenty-fourth.'

'The twenty-fourth. Then the Geological Society of London on the twenty-first of June—'

'Owen's reading a paper then, too.'

'Oh, good! I cannot wait to see his face! Are we doing the Royal Society of Edinburgh as well?'

'No, they broke for summer at the end of April. And in any case, Sir Thomas Brisbane wrote back to call us "*stark raving mad*", I believe were his exact words. I wonder what he will say when we read at the Royal Society proper.'

'Hold on a moment – we *are* reading at the Royal Society, then?'

'Yes, I heard back from Lord Wrottesley this afternoon.'

'Good Lord, why didn't you say?'

'Because I thought I ought to wait until we were all assembled. Certain parties get rather snippish if they aren't informed of developments at precisely the same time, as you recall.'

From my post in the corner, against one of the slanted walls, I gritted my teeth. The little under-stairs storeroom was too small

for the three of us to be crammed inside, especially in such weather; the unseasonably warm spell of April had bled on into May,
the sort of spring one saw perhaps twice in a lifetime in Inverness, and the little room was so stuffy I felt nearly light-headed.
But with Clarke, as always, complaining that the boathouse
stank, and a mostly recovered Maisie installed in her favourite
armchair in the parlour, our options were limited. So here I was,
trying my best not to catch cobwebs in my hair as Clarke rifled
through the various letters and schedules piled on the small desk.

'What date is the Royal Society reading?' I asked, itching to
leave and finish the missive I was putting together for Mr and
Mrs Jamsetjee before I lost my nerve. It was several pages long,
this letter, with accompanying sketches of the Creature, and I
had felt with every line as if I were spilling my heart's blood
upon the page. But secrecy be damned, I had decided, the debacle with Maisie be damned – I could not let my mentor find
out about our miraculous discovery at the same time as any
other fellow of the Society.

'Patience, patience,' Clarke said, holding the letter up in front
of him. '"Dear Mr Clarke, I have read the abstract you sent me
and, at your recommendation, the full paper as well. I must say,
I found the whole thing only *marginally* more plausible after
reading your detailed explanation, and if it were anyone else
proposing such an outlandish idea, I would not hesitate to dismiss them out of hand. But, as I have known you some years
now, and trust you would not be inclined to lie about such matters . . . I shall give you the benefit of the doubt. And so, against
the better judgement of nearly every one of my peers and council members, I have set aside a spot on the fourteenth of
June" – ah, what a shame.'

'Why is that?'

'That's the week after the annual general meeting, where they elect this year's fellows. I'd hoped we could squeeze in before then, have you nominated. Ah, well; next year, then.'

He turned back to the letter, but I had been watching his eyes before, as he spoke of nominations, and they had been trained on Henry alone. I cleared my throat.

'Have *both* of us nominated, you mean?'

Clarke threw me a look. The sort of look one throws a dog in the corner which is making entirely too much noise. 'The Society does not admit women.'

'It has not admitted any women *yet*. There is nothing in its charters that forbids it expressly.' I should know. During my first summer in London, I had hounded Mr William Whewell, a speaker at one of the Society's public lectures, until he had agreed to check the books for me. *You stand a chance yet, madam*, was his reply when it finally arrived, and I had clung to those words in all the years since as if they were a raft.

'Besides,' I pressed on, 'the Royal Astronomical Society has female members. Mrs Somerville is a fellow, and so was Miss Herschel. And the Zoological—'

'Then by all means, go and join them,' Clarke said drily. 'There are only fifteen new fellows admitted per year, Mrs Sutherland. Admitting you both for the same achievement would seem rather superfluous.'

'*Superfluous?*' I repeated, the word sharp as a knife.

'And in any case, you would need five other fellows to support your nomination, and none of them has the faintest idea who you are.' Untrue; I knew of one man, after all, who would vote for me. 'Even your husband's admittance is hardly a sure thing, after that disastrous affair with Professor Owen. Henry . . .' He threw out an arm towards me in exasperation. *Control your wife.* 'Please.'

Henry looked from me to Clarke and back again, a pained expression on his face. Finally, he said, wheedling: 'It wouldn't hurt to nominate her, would it? Next year?'

I was being tossed a bone. I placed a hand on the desk to steady myself – to prevent myself from screaming.

Clarke let loose a sigh. '*Fine.* I'll put in a word, when the time comes. Now, where was I? Ah, yes – "I have set aside a spot on the fourteenth of June for you and Mr Sutherland to read your paper. I am assuming, Mr Clarke, for the sake of your reputation and of mine, that this is not some practical joke. On your head be it."'

Henry hmm-ed. 'Rather grim.'

'Still, better than the one we got from the Linnean Society.'

They weren't going to mention it. Had they even noticed? I had, of course; the phrase had slid under my skin like a needle. It wasn't as if I hadn't expected something like this, but that did not make it hurt any less.

'When "you and Mr Sutherland" read the paper?' I repeated icily.

Only Clarke looked up at me; Henry would not quite meet my eye. There was a tightness to his face, something like annoyance. It had never been like this before, I thought suddenly and bitterly, when it was only Henry and me; ever since Clarke had arrived, and I had pushed Henry aside in anger, I had found myself set apart. Henry had not needed to beg his way back into my good graces this time – had known, perhaps, that it was not possible – for he had someone else with whom to commiserate now, to hum and agree on how terribly stubborn and unforgiving I was. And now I was third fiddle, in a band that *I* had begun.

Clarke slapped the letter down. 'Good *God*, woman, do you only know one tune?'

'You said before that none of them know who I am.' My voice was shaking with the effort to keep it level. 'How will anyone learn about my part in this, if I am sitting in the audience? Did you even *ask*? Did you mention me at all in the letter?'

'Of course. The illustrations are yours, after all.'

I let out a bark of laughter. 'The illustrations! Is that all I've done? Have you forgotten my research? How many days, *weeks*, I spent stitching the damned thing together? Poring over nerves and blood vessels and bones and yeasts and *my* great-uncle's useless notes – did you happen to mention that the very idea was mine from the start?'

'So it's all yours, is it?' His lips curled. 'You did it all by yourself?'

'That's not what I said.'

'Shall I write back to Lord Wrottesley and tell him it was all a mistake – *Miss Mary* wishes to present her findings herself? I wonder how you'd like it if you really did have to do it all yourself. Who would write your letters then?'

'You think I cannot write? I cannot argue? It's all I've been doing, all my life!' I threw my hands up in the air. 'I would be better off if I had written it myself. If mine were the only name on that letter, at least Wrottesley would have *seen* it before he tossed it aside. Mary Somerville—'

'Lord on high, would you *shut up* about Mary Somerville? Perhaps the reason she's a fellow of the Royal Astronomical Society and you are not is because she, at least, has some common *fucking* decency! Have you tried that, hmm? Imagine what you could achieve, Mrs Sutherland, if you were not such an argumentative cow!'

'*Mr Clarke*—' began Henry, red-faced, but I ignored him and pushed him aside until I was nose to nose with Clarke.

'I should not *have* to be decent,' I hissed. 'I should not have to be *nice* – God knows, you have not one ounce of compassion or propriety in your bones, and yet you've made it this far! I should not have to wait and grovel and *plead* and crush and cut away at myself until I'm small enough to fit at the margins, in the foot-notes! You make all the world a game, where you decide the victor and you decide the rules, then pat yourself on the back for winning every single time! *Yes*, you are clever, Mr Clarke. *Yes*, you are talented. Every man is Shakespeare when he's the only one in London with a pen. You simply cannot bear the notion that, were I to have a turn of it, I would be as good as you!'

He stared down at me, face sour as milk. 'You would not be anywhere without my research.'

I gave an involuntary laugh. 'As we would be nowhere with-out Cuvier, or Conybeare! As Galileo would be nowhere without Copernicus! Shall I go and ask Linnaeus if he would like to be a co-author?'

'*Galileo?* What delusions you have! Oh, forgive me; I ought to say "Galileo and his wife". I'm sure she helped transcribe his notes on occasion.'

'I made a connection you couldn't possibly have imagined—'

'I simply hadn't taken the time to imagine it, my dear; I was too occupied with other work!'

The edges of my vision seemed to blur. 'If you call me "my dear" again, I will put that pen through your eye.'

'For God's sake!' shouted Henry. 'If we could just—'

'And you!' cried Clarke, pointing a quivering finger in Henry's direction.

Henry stood a moment, stunned. 'Me?'

'Yes, *you*! What have you done? Even less than her! You did – what? Some sewing? Not even that! You helped organize some bones? What, in all honesty, have you done?'

A foul look began to gather on Henry's face.

'Careful, Clarke,' he said quietly.

'Or what?' Clarke stepped in close to Henry, his voice low. 'With the amount of money you owe me, I think I would be perfectly within my rights to claim this entire operation as my own. It's based on my research. I funded it—'

'Get out,' said Henry.

'On what grounds?'

'*On the grounds that it's my house, goddamn you!*' he bellowed.

The ensuing silence hung in the room like a presence all its own. One could have plucked it like a string.

Clarke swept his papers from the desk, sweeping everything else to the floor in the process, and slid past me towards the door. On his way out, he bent and muttered in Henry's ear: 'It's not even yours.'

Henry's eye twitched.

Clarke's footsteps clattered down the hall and up the stairs, dislodging dust from the ceiling as he went. There was the slam of a door, one final drift of dust – and all was still.

'How much more would you have let him say to me, then?' I said. 'Or was it only when he implied *your* incompetence that it mattered?'

'You too,' muttered Henry.

For a moment, I was sure I must have misheard him. 'What?'

'You can leave as well. I've never been so ashamed – such childish behaviour, from my own wife.'

I was speechless, though not for long. 'So I'm to be sent to my room like a child?'

He gave no answer. Or, at least, no answer I cared to stay and hear. I spilled out into the hallway, skin buzzing. I longed to hit something, crush something, dash it to the floor and grind it beneath my heel – but I would not, could not. I was an animal declawed; I might yell and spit and scream, but my hands could do no more than tremble uselessly at my sides. There was nothing I could crush but myself.

'Mary?'

As I wrenched open the front door, a voice rang out from the parlour. Maisie was sitting by the fire, her face tight, hand paused in the turning of a page.

'Are you all right?' she asked quietly.

I opened my mouth to speak, but all that came forth was a formless noise, halfway to tears. I pressed my palms to my eyes until my vision spotted black, then turned and ran.

On the banks of the firth, I sank my teeth into my sleeve and screamed. When the ringing left my ears, I stood. Swayed upon the rocks, shut my eyes against the glare of sunlight across the water. There was not even a breeze to relieve me. I envied my great-uncle then, as he was at the end, chasing his misbegotten creature through the Arctic. I could think of nothing I wanted more in that moment than to be cold, to be alone, to have the reason for all my life's miseries laid out before me, a killable thing.

Fleeing the sun, I found my way to the boathouse. It was

dark inside, humid and foul-smelling as the belly of some awful beast. I took comfort there anyway, pushing up my skirts so I could sit and dangle my feet in the water. Shimmering reflections played across the walls. I clapped my hands twice, and up the Creature came to greet me, laying its head in my waiting palms.

'How do you bear it?' I asked, voice a whisper. 'The same little square of water, day after day?'

The Creature made not a sound, but merely gazed at me, its slitted pupils wide in the dark. I stroked my thumb across its cheek, tracing the seams that ran across its skin – and my breath caught.

I ran my thumb over the same place again, to be sure I hadn't imagined it. I had not.

The seam was unravelling.

22

I saw how the fine form of man was degraded and wasted;
I beheld the corruption of death succeed to the blooming
cheek of life; I saw how the worm inherited the wonders
of the eye and brain.

— MARY SHELLEY, *Frankenstein*

THE CREATURE IS *dying.*

Those were the only words that could have brought us together again so soon. My palms still bore crescent marks from when I had stood clenching my fists, and I could almost hear the echoes of our raised voices. And yet here we all were again, hoisting the Creature up from the water on to the raised table, despite its protestations. I held its head, trying to coax it still with scraps of fish while we examined it. The sight made my blood run cold. Out of the water, in clearer light, the situation was worse than I could possibly have imagined. The strange liquid which I had noticed only minutes earlier, sticking to my fingers after I had pulled them, horrified, from the stitches at its head, was leaking from every seam across its body – thick and brown and terrible, smelling of blood and rotten fish.

How could I not have noticed this sooner? Had the Creature really spoiled overnight, like fruit left too long in the sun? Or had I simply not looked closely enough? It hardly ever lifted more than its head from the dark and murky water, after all. I cursed myself a thousand times for not luring it on to the work-table to check up on its health more often — for believing that something so good, so marvellous, could ever last.

I whirled on Clarke. 'You said that it would. Not. *Rot.*'

'It isn't rotting.'

'You mean to tell me that this is perfectly normal?' I shoved my smeared hand towards his face, and he recoiled.

'I did not say that. But I do not think the problem is that it's rotting. I soaked the damned thing in enough turpentine and spirits that it should still be alive centuries from now. The problem is that the stitches are dissolving.' He pulled something off the Creature's back, and I saw that it was a stringy remnant of the catgut we had used. 'As they should. It takes two or three months, usually, for them to be fully absorbed. Except—'

'It isn't healing,' Henry muttered.

Growth/self-reparation. It had been one of the items on our list, tacked up on the wall of the nursery in London — one of the fundamental qualities of life. I cast my mind back, frantically, to the trials we had performed the previous year. Those creatures had healed, hadn't they? But I did not recall ever seeing their stitches absorbed, now that I thought of it; our neat seams had remained. Could it be that, all along, none of our subjects' parts had actually fused? That the catgut — which would last longer above water, but still not for ever — was all that had been keeping them from falling apart?

And if they had never healed . . . had they all been in pain? Was the Creature in pain, even now? For how long would it remain alive, in such a condition?

What have we done?

'We simply have to redo the stitches, then,' said Henry.

'And what if they come out again?' I protested. Its skin had always seemed so delicate, like tissue beneath my fingers. I had a vision of it making a sudden turn or catching upon something sharp, tearing itself in half.

'Then we will double-stitch it. Triple-stitch it. Use tougher thread. We shall quilt the damned thing if we have to.'

'Quilts still need repairing, Henry!'

'What does it matter, in the grand scheme of things?' Clarke cut in. 'It doesn't have to last for ever. We only need it to last as long as it takes for us to gain some credibility, to prove that our methods work. Ultimately – good God, ultimately the stitching doesn't even matter! How many people do you think will come to us saying, "You must help me bring my daughter back to life; she fell on to a factory saw and now she's in twenty-seven pieces"? None! It will be, "You must help me bring my daughter back to life; she died of typhus." What does it matter if she never heals, her rash never goes away? She'll be alive, and we shall have our money.'

I froze, dread snatching the words from my mouth. All these months, I had not thought . . . no, rather, I had not *let* myself think about such questions. About how this science of ours might be applied to humans. From the moment I had read Victor's tale – the moment Henry had asked me, with that wary look in his eyes, 'What, exactly . . . should we bring to life?' – I had cast aside the notion entirely. There were too many un-answered questions. Could such created beings grow and age? Did they have souls? And if so, was it the same soul that had inhabited the body before? Or a patchwork combination, like the body itself? If such beings – as seemed to be the case with Victor's creature – entered the world without memories, then did it even matter? Would memory be preserved in whole bodies, if not patchwork ones?

Such questions had seemed mere curiosities in the Creature's case; as intelligent as it was, I could not imagine it being troubled by existential woes. Which was precisely why I'd suggested an animal, after all. But we were palaeontologists, not philosophers – what did we know, truly? How could we ever ensure that such a science would not be misused? I had thought that once our discovery was revealed to the world, we might pass the matter on to more qualified hands, watching from the sidelines as doctors and lawyers and clergymen had it out in Parliament like baying dogs. Such a thing was not for us to decide – and most certainly not for us to *sell*.

But evidently, Clarke had other plans.

'Come to us?' Henry repeated. From the shock on his face, I suspected that he had followed a similar train of thought.

'You think we will be taking *customers*?' I said, my voice hollow with disbelief. 'We can't even . . . we don't even know what it feels like; it could be agony! This is not at all a complete science, Mr Clarke. To apply this to human beings – to any other being – before we find out how to make them heal properly is pure cruelty.'

'And how do we know that is even possible?' Clarke shrugged. 'I say if it is agony, then we use morphine.'

'What if morphine doesn't work? And even if it does – do you truly think anyone would enjoy traipsing around for ever, in a body that should by all rights be dead?'

'Who said anything about "for ever"? Look at the thing – true, it may not be rotting outright, but even if we do re-stitch it, I'm not confident it will last another season.'

'So we are to make our fortunes by bringing loved ones back

to life, but only *temporarily*? So that they may slowly fall to pieces before their families' eyes?'

'I don't see why not. Is that not already the singular purpose of the medical profession? To delay death? And someone else is bound to improve upon the science soon, I'm sure. But that someone won't be me – I shall be at my new estate in the East Indies, enjoying my knighthood.'

'Christ in Hell, you are *impossible*!' I might have throttled him then, had not Henry stepped in between us and cried:

'None of this will matter if the Creature dies before we can present it!'

I stilled at that. We were expected in Edinburgh by the twenty-fourth; travelling entirely by road, we would be taking a more direct route than the one Henry and I usually took through Aberdeen, going instead south around the Cairngorms. But though this journey was shorter as the crow flies, the roads about the Cairngorms were rough, and with only one team of draught horses (rather than the swifter breeds used by stagecoaches, which were switched every dozen miles), it could take us at least a week. We had planned to leave on the fourteenth, to allow plenty of time for mishaps and delays, but that left barely a week for us to re-stitch the Creature in its entirety.

'We ought to ask for more time,' I said, at the very moment that Clarke said, 'We ought to leave as soon as possible.'

'Are you mad? It's too delicate!' I protested. 'One day rattling about in that carriage and it will fall apart entirely!'

'We can't wait any longer. We are pushing our luck as it is, sliding in at the very end of the season – if we miss these sessions, the Edinburgh Geological and the Royal Society won't meet again until November. There's no chance it will live that long. There's barely a chance it will live until the end of the month. No, we go now, as soon as possible. The carriage should be arriving the day after tomorrow. I'll write ahead to all the fellows in Edinburgh and see who we can gather together at short notice. And then—'

'No,' said Henry.

Clarke laughed – a dry, humourless thing. 'Pardon?'

'It's far too risky to move it now. We ought to wait until the fourteenth as we originally planned, and see what we can do to fix it in the meantime. And if it's still not fit to travel then . . .' Henry gave the crank which raised and lowered the platform a hefty shove, and it slipped beneath the water again. The Creature, clearly relieved, shuffled off and disappeared into the shadowy depths. 'We shall wait until November.'

Despite everything, I felt a flash of gratitude towards Henry then. At long last, we agreed on something. Perhaps the thing upon which we agreed was basic decency and sense, but I was grateful nonetheless. Clarke, meanwhile, looked as though he'd just been slapped.

'Have you finally gone insane, man? After all the fuss I've made, all the strings I've pulled – you expect me simply to write back and say, *I'm terribly sorry, but the creature we brought back from the dead is dying again, so we shall need another six months?* We've already shown our cards – we have to act now! Another six months, and rumours will fly . . . we'll be a laughing stock before we even get on the stage!'

Henry clutched at the bridge of his nose. 'We could still go ahead and read our paper at June's Royal Society meeting, couldn't we?'

'Without the Creature? *Nullius in verba*, Henry – it's their very motto! We can't expect them simply to take our word for it. No, we ought to go now, and that's the last I'll hear of it.'

'Clarke,' said Henry. His voice was quiet, but with a brittle edge. 'Please. Have we not given you enough? We agreed you would take a share of the profits and the credit. Must you take my dignity as well? Might I ask, perhaps, that you stop ordering me about like a trained monkey?'

The water lapped against the edges of the pool as the Creature rose to the surface again. I saw Clarke's eyes dart sideways, his expression turning for a moment even fouler than it already was. I said before that he had looked upon the Creature like a forest ripe for the cutting; now – and I realize this only in retrospect – he looked at it like a man planning to burn it to the ground.

'You're fools, both of you,' he spat.

And he was gone.

ON FRIDAY EVENING, the carriage arrived. It was a huge black-painted thing edged in gold, nearly invisible in the dark apart from the lamps at each corner, and pulled by two enormous pale horses. They looked like ghosts as they were led away to the same draughty stable that housed Maisie's old mare, leaving the unhitched carriage lurking skeletally on the road. We took care to have it parked near the edge of the property, where the road cut through the beginnings of a hill and was flanked by retaining walls on either side; our hope was that, with enough care and patience, we could wrap the Creature thickly in cloth and drag it up the gradual slope from the boathouse to the top of the wall, then coax it down into the tank's upper hatch.

That long, humid evening, Henry and Ramsay (who had been told we needed samples of the water in the firth for some experiment or other) filled the tank with buckets. Afterwards, the two of us trudged back to the house, Henry in his muddy shirtsleeves and I still in my apron. It was late, nearly ten, and my eyes were red and stinging; we had been up since dawn that day, and the day before, re-sewing the Creature's stitches. I had decided from the start that I would not do so without the application of some sort of numbing agent or sedative – something rather more surgical than the chlorodyne in the back of Clarke's little apothecary cabinet – so I'd sent Henry into Inverness for some ingredients. Ether, I had heard, was fairly straightforward to distil with the right equipment, and had been used quite successfully by a number of surgeons in America. But I was so hesitant with the dose, and the Creature so reluctant to breathe through the rag Henry held to its snout, that I could not be sure if it worked at all. Nor could I be sure that my silk stitches would hold any better than the old catgut ones; nor was I certain that the stitching was the only problem. No matter what Clarke had said, there was something about the awful liquid which dripped from the Creature's wounds – something about the way its flesh was puffy and warm beneath my fingers – that spoke of death. Of infection. Of *rot*.

It is a terrible thing to cause pain to something you love, even if it is for its own good – and a more terrible thing still when you cannot be sure you are doing any good at all.

As we entered the house, I jumped at the sensation of something at my back, but it was only Henry, reaching to help untie my apron. Wordlessly, he lifted it over my head and hung it on the coat-stand – which was the last place in the world it ought to have been, really, smeared with gore as it was, but I could not find it in myself to complain. I watched as he carefully unbuttoned my gloves, peeling them away and stuffing them in the apron's front pocket. He did not relinquish my hands then, but rather held them tighter, squeezing them between his own.

'You're shivering,' he said, clearly seeing the bafflement on my face. 'Should I ask Flora to put a warming pan in the bed?'

They were the first true words we'd spoken to each other all day, besides those necessary to arrange the Creature's treatment, and I found I could not return them. I shook my head. I could have told him that it was not the cold that was making me shake – for even now, as the sun set, the evening was warmer than it had any right to be. I could have told him that this offering of his was not an apology – for I could see clearly, in his eyes, that he meant it to be. But I did none of this. Instead, I let him pull me closer, pressing my head against his shoulder. I shut my eyes and let myself remember what it had been like, when I thought his companionship was all I needed to stand against the world. For the barest moment, I wished that I could forget everything that had happened between us since, every foolish or heartless thing he'd said or done, and return to those hopeful days.

But I couldn't, I realized. I wouldn't. Not just for my own sake, but for Maisie's, too; even if she did hate me now, and might do for evermore.

The thought felt like the closing of a book.

'Do you think,' said Henry quietly over my head, 'that we should leave now after all? Try to get it to Edinburgh while it is still breathing, at least?'

Unbidden, my eyes found the door of Clarke's room on the landing above. Earlier, I had seen his curtain twitch, but apart from that I had seen neither hide nor hair of him for nearly two days. He had not left his room at all, as far as I could tell, opening the door only to order Flora to bring him food or post his letters. I had no idea what sort of letters they were; perhaps he was writing to his Society friends, to request a later appointment. Or perhaps he was dragging Henry's name through the mud, to ensure that when – *if* – we presented the Creature, it would be known that the credit ought to go to him alone, and that Henry and I were mere assistants. I found, increasingly, that I did not care.

No, that wasn't right. I did care. I had always cared, so much so that it was like a splinter in my chest. For years I had poked at it, pulled at it, reminded myself over and over of all I did not have. But perhaps, I thought now, if I simply let it be, let the simmering die down, the ache would one day go away. Perhaps if I pretended for long enough that I did not care, it might eventually come true.

'No,' I said to Henry. 'I want to keep going. I want to try to fix it.'

'Even if we miss the meeting? Even if that means it's all been for nothing?'

I looked away. There it was, that ache again – but I had weighed it already, carefully and painstakingly, against the weight of the life in my hands, and it had come out wanting.

I shook my head. *It will not have been for nothing*, I wanted to cry, *no matter what happens – don't you see? Don't you see? Because it is already worth something. It is worth something, even in the dark. Even if no one else ever loves it but me.*

But I could not say it. I could not put it into words that he might understand.

I AM NOT sure what it was that woke me that night. The room was close and unpleasant, those thick-walled Scottish houses not made for such weather, designed to trap all the heat of the day. It was a relief as I threw off the covers and made for the window, bare feet pressing against the cool wood. I had some intention of watching the sun rise, I think. There was a gentle orange quality to the light that filtered through the gap in the curtains, and I thought it must be near to dawn.

What I saw instead through the window made the floor tilt beneath my feet.

The orange glow was not the light of dawn.

'Henry!' I flew across the room, pulling back the bedcovers and shaking him awake. 'Get up, get up!'

'Dear God – what is it, woman?' he muttered, nearly falling to the floor.

'The boathouse!' My breathing was so sharp and short that I struggled to say the words. 'It's on fire!'

'Fire?' The blood drained from his face. 'But—'

The Creature.

'I'll wake your sister.' I pulled him upright and out into the hall. 'You fetch Clarke. *Go!*'

It took only a single knock on Maisie's door before it flew open beneath my raised fist – and there she was, her hair loose about her shoulders, her eyes wide and worried. Despite the fire, despite everything, the breath caught in my throat. These would be the first proper words I had said to her in nearly a month. It struck me as tragically unfair, tragically stupid of me, that it should be so. There were a thousand things I longed to say to her besides this.

'Fire.' I swallowed. 'In the boathouse.'

Her eyes flashed. Was it anger? Alarm?

Would she be pleased, to see the Creature gone?

'I'll wake the staff,' she said, her voice unreadable. 'And the neighbours. You and Henry—'

'Thank you,' I breathed. I would say it again, I vowed, as soon as all of this was over. There was so much I had to thank her for.

And then, tearing myself away – one fire at a time – I turned on my heel and ran.

Perhaps it was not too late. This was the thought that sustained me as I threw on my redingote over my nightgown and my boots on to hastily stockinged feet, the words matching the frantic beat of my heart – *perhaps, perhaps, perhaps.*

As I stepped out into the night, I was struck by three things at once. Firstly: the smoke in the air did not smell as smoke usually did; rather, it was acrid and sweet, strangely familiar. It was only as I took another breath and tasted the air on my tongue that I recognized the scent as turpentine.

Secondly: the grass was wet, as if it had just rained – and damp wood is not known to burn on its own.

Thirdly: the carriage was gone.

There was a sound behind me, the slam of a door. Henry toppled out on to the lawn and met my gaze, eyes wild – and I found I already knew precisely what he was going to say.

'Clarke,' he said, words spilling out between panted breaths. 'He isn't here. I've looked everywhere.'

A strange mixture of relief and fury washed over me. He'd taken the Creature, *he'd taken the Creature*, I would skin him alive – but at least it was safe. At least it had not been in the boathouse.

I watched as Henry came to the same realization. As one, we turned to look. The boathouse was a raging inferno now, flames taller than the building itself reaching up to lick the sky.

'Our notes,' he whispered. 'All our work, our writings . . . our evidence.'

He sank to his knees in the grass, and together we watched as the flames consumed it all.

PART IV

MAY 1856

23

I knelt on the grass and kissed the earth and with quiver-
ing lips exclaimed, 'By the sacred earth on which I kneel,
by the shades that wander near me, by the deep and eter-
nal grief that I feel, I swear; and by thee, O Night, and
the spirits that preside over thee, to pursue the daemon
who caused this misery . . .

— MARY SHELLEY, *Frankenstein*

BY THE TIME the sun rose, everything was ash. I should have
been glad, I supposed, that the fire had not spread to the house;
I am not sure I would ever have forgiven myself, had this
wretched affair robbed Maisie of her home as well. We sifted
through the remains of the boathouse, soaking ourselves to the
knees in sooty mud, but not a single trace remained. Every page
of my leather-bound research journal, every note which Clarke
had snatched from the under-stairs laboratory, even my pains-
taking letter to Mr Jamsetjee – which I had stupidly left in the
boathouse, my sketches not quite complete – had been utterly
destroyed. The stone walls themselves lay in crumbles on the
ground, the mortar having succumbed completely to the heat.

'That alone should show that it was more than a typical fire,
shouldn't it? That it was deliberate? We could call the constable

and have him look at it,' Henry said as we sat slumped around the dining table in the grey morning light, a hasty breakfast laid out before us. I had washed, and dressed, for I knew that I could do nothing while still in my filthy nightgown, but taking the time to *eat* seemed an outright frivolity. My feet tapped beneath the table in my urge to *do something, do something*; every few seconds, I glanced out of the window again, watching the sky brighten bit by bit.

'And then what?' I said. 'Explain to him why we kept so much turpentine there in the first place? All to charge the man with – what? Burning down a shed?'

'Arson, Mary! And theft of a carriage!'

'It wasn't even our carriage. He was the one who borrowed it.'

Henry scrubbed a hand across his face, letting loose a groan of frustration. 'What would you have us do, then? Sit here and let him steal our work?'

It disturbed me still that he referred to the Creature not as our Creature, or our creation, but as our work.

'No, Henry. We go after him and get it *back*.'

Maisie – the silent witness to the morning's events, watching all with a tight look upon her face and the edge of her shawl bunched anxiously in her hands – stood abruptly and left the room. For one frantic moment, it was all I could think about. Why had she left? Was it me? Henry? My insistence on retrieving the Creature? Any mention of the Creature at all? Perhaps she thought it better off gone, out of the house and out of her sight. As was I, perhaps.

'But then what will we do once we find him?' Henry protested, and I tore myself back to the conversation at hand. 'Are we to be vigilantes? Take it from Clarke at gunpoint, and hope that the police and the Royal Society will take our word that it was ours to begin with?'

I was loath to admit it, but he had a point. 'I do not know, Henry. But surely these are things we can work out on the way? We know he's gone to Edinburgh; we know it ought to take a week, though if he runs the horses ragged, he could manage it in less. We can still beat him there if we take the train from Aberdeen.'

'We'll have missed the morning's coaches to Aberdeen already,' Henry said sourly.

'We could get at least part of the way there, though. Or we could spend hours dithering here, speaking to the police, and lose another day.'

'But surely, if we reported him—'

'For *God's* sake, Henry!' I got to my feet. 'Finlay Clarke has friends. He has influence. He has money. There will be no justice with that sort of man. You can stay here if you like, but I'm going!'

'What, on your own?'

'Yes, on my own, apparently!' I turned on my heel to leave. 'It will be a fine holiday, I think. I'll put on my black and my veil once again, and pretend I'm a widow.'

I WAS NOT yet sure what I would say to Maisie, only that I had to say it. It had been too long; I had been too distracted. But I was cut adrift now, my work and my Creature and my marriage – my life – turned to smoke between my fingers, and I clung to the thought of her like a castaway at sea. I had to speak to her before I left, or else I feared I might never work up the courage to do so again.

And besides – though this was definitely towards the end of the list of things I ought to say to her, it was nevertheless an important one – I had to ask her if I might borrow her gig. It wouldn't take me the entire way, not least with her grumpy nag at the reins, but it would be good enough to get me to Inverness, where I might book some sort of passage to Aberdeen.

To my despair, however, I could not find her anywhere in the house. Ramsay, too, was missing; the only people I could find about were Oliver and the old cook, Flora having been sent to lie down after growing light-headed from the smoke. Nerves buzzing, I decided that I would simply have to pack first and find her afterwards. I kept seeing Clarke and that wretched carriage in my mind's eye, slipping further and further away. I kept imagining the Creature battered about in the tank, its feeble cries muffled by the metal. Had Clarke remembered to feed it this morning, I wondered? Had he even remembered to open the vent at the top of the tank, to let in air? But there was no time for weeping now; no time for panic. I would not lose myself to hysterics, as Clarke would undoubtedly expect me to.

I packed only what I must, leaving behind everything that would not fit in a single trunk. My passage I would pay with the pearl bracelet Henry had bought me all those months ago – which I had brought with me to Inverness quite by accident, stashed as it was in my portable desk; at least now it would finally serve some purpose. As I threw the contents of my bedside-table drawer on to the bed in search of my comb, I was surprised to see a stack of papers, neatly wrapped in twine. For a moment, I froze, unable to believe my luck – my great-uncle Victor's letters. Yes, I remembered now, *yes*, I had taken them to bed to read late one sleepless night! Everything else, every scrap of paper, had been burned, but this – these letters – remained. Would it be enough to convince the Society that the Creature was our idea after all? That it was *mine*?

Would anything be enough for that?

I hesitated a moment, torn. In the end, I brought them, wrapped carefully along with the bracelet inside one of my petticoats so that they would not be evident at first glance. Last of all, I packed a pair of waterlogged pencils I had found in the pocket of one of my aprons. With my new sketching kit lost to the fire, they were now the only ones I had left.

'YOU'RE COMING AFTER all, then?' I asked when I found Henry waiting by the top of the stairs, his trunk by his feet.

'Of course,' he said gruffly. He would not look me in the eye. 'I can't let you go halfway across the country after a bastard like Finlay Clarke on your own, can I?'

It was the sort of thing that might once have warmed my heart; now, all I could hear was the note of irritation in his voice, the resignation, that 'let' a cold admonishment. Of course he could not let me do something so foolish; I was his wife. I heaved a sigh, and turned to go downstairs. 'Where's Ramsay? I called for him to help me carry my trunk, but I can't find him.'

Henry frowned. 'I thought he must be with you. The carriage doesn't seem to be ready yet, either. Where on earth—?'

'Shush. Be quiet a second.'

He did, for once without argument, and a moment later he evidently heard it, too – the faint crunch of hooves along the drive.

'For Heaven's sake,' Henry said once we were outside. Slowing to a halt in the driveway was Maisie's little open-air gig,

Ramsay in the driving seat. 'Is everyone stealing carriages this morning and riding off without a word?'

'It's not stealing. It is mine.' Maisie sat with a fat blue carpet bag in her lap and several shawls about her neck, despite the warm day. 'Ramsay, would you go inside and ask Flora to start packing a bag for me? Only if she's feeling better, that is. I've just booked us a spot on the Star coach this afternoon. It will get us as far as Elgin tonight, and continue on to Aberdeen to-morrow morning.'

Beside me, Henry was blinking rapidly, dumbfounded. The sight was almost enough to make me laugh.

'*Pardon?*' he said at last. 'Us? You?'

'Of course. This is the most interesting thing that's ever happened in my life, Henry. Did you think I would miss the end of it?'

Her jaw was set, her cheeks flushed and, *good God*, I loved her. The thought tumbled out of me, too quick for me to catch. I did not care that I should not; I did not care if she was angry at me still; I did not care that she would doubtless never feel the same, that it would surely one day ruin our friendship. In that brief moment, I was content only to love her.

Beside me, Henry snorted. 'It's not in *your* life, Maisie!'

'It's happening in *my* house,' she said – and though she said it softly, there was an edge to her voice I had never heard her use with Henry. 'And in *my* carriage, like I said.'

A complicated expression crossed Henry's face; embarrass-ment, perhaps? Or was it jealousy once again? 'Only as far as the town. From there, we'll make our way to Edinburgh and—'

'And besides,' Maisie carried on, as if he had not said a thing. 'You don't even know where you're going.'

Now, that stumped me as well. 'What do you mean?'

'Flora went in to Inverness yesterday. When she was in the post office, she overheard the clerk complaining about "that damned Englishman who's moved in with the Sutherlands"; he said Mr Clarke asked to borrow their copy of *Bradshaw's*, then ripped a page out of it while the staff were looking the other way. So I went there this morning with my own copy to compare the two.' She opened up her carpet bag and drew out a hefty edition of *Bradshaw's General Railway and Steam Navigation Guide*. It looked nearly pristine, as though it had never been used – except, perhaps, for the purpose of smashing gnats against the wall (its main function in most households of the less-travelled sort).

'Maisie!' I leaped up on to the side of the carriage and hooked my elbows over, straining to get a better look at the book. 'Maisie, you clever thing, that's *brilliant*!'

She did not meet my eye, though the corner of her mouth rose in something like a smile as she handed me the book. *Perhaps*, I thought, *perhaps, perhaps*.

'It was page one hundred and twenty-one that he tore out. Look, I marked it.'

Henry peered over my shoulder as I turned to the page, and together we read, above the many lines of fine print:

EDINBURGH TO NEWCASTLE AND THE SOUTH.

'But these are train timetables,' Henry muttered. 'I thought we'd already discarded the possibility of travelling by rail – too stressful for the animal, too difficult getting it loaded on and off without anyone seeing it.'

'Yes, but he's in a hurry. I doubt he's thinking of the Creature at all,' I said, heart twisting with worry. 'Perhaps ... Oh Lord, perhaps he's not taking the slower route at all, and intends to catch the train to Edinburgh at Aberdeen. But then why is he looking at directions from there to Newcastle?'

'Isn't it the same line, to Newcastle and London both?' Maisie said, turning the book sideways to squint at the cities printed in a narrow column down the left-hand side.

'Well, yes, but there are plenty of other pages that show the times direct to London—' I began, but Henry drowned me out.

'That must be it! He plans to go straight on to London, and skip presenting in Edinburgh at all. Our official slot isn't until the twenty-fourth, after all, and I had always thought it an idiotic plan of his, that we simply try to go early and scramble together an impromptu meeting. He's not even a fellow of the Edinburgh Geological; he'd have no sway . . . Not like with the Royal Society.'

'Well, yes, but . . .' I peered over Maisie's shoulder, flipping pages back and forth. 'As I said, there are plenty of other pages here that show the quicker routes, direct to London. Why would he choose this one?'

'You think he's planning a quick jaunt to the seaside on the way?' Henry said drily.

'No, but . . . well, as you said, he knows we will be looking for him in Edinburgh, and London, too. Would it not make sense to perhaps try to hide the Creature elsewhere?' I groaned, frustrated. 'Or perhaps this whole thing is a ruse. Perhaps he *does* mean to stay in Edinburgh and do a presentation there, and he meant for us to find this missing page . . .'

'It does seem awfully convenient, Flora just happening to overhear him at the post office,' Henry admitted.

'But Flora didn't overhear *him*. Mr Clarke wasn't there at all,' Maisie pointed out. 'The clerk was simply complaining to anyone who would listen.'

'I suppose we will have to change at Edinburgh regardless; we can get off and have a look around Waverley station, can't we?' I reasoned. 'Ask if any of the staff have seen anything unusual? Or if there is any reason someone transporting heavy cargo might choose not to take the express?'

'That would be my vote, yes,' said Maisie.

'You don't get a vote,' Henry retorted.

'Are we *agreed*?' I said, glaring at Henry. He glared back for a moment, then made an exasperated sound – which I took to be agreement – and marched back down the drive. Maisie and I watched him enter the house again, yelling for Ramsay, and then we were left in silence. Maisie stared resolutely at the old mare's backside, its tail swishing as it swatted away flies.

'I'm sorry,' I blurted out. She did not turn to me; instead, she fiddled with the clasp of her carpet bag, clicking it in and out of place.

'Sorry for what?'

Ah. She wanted to make sure I was apologizing for the right thing – for what I had done, not for being found out. I understood so badly it made my heart ache.

'I am sorry for lying to you. For not telling you what we were doing. You were right – some part of me knew, I think, that you wouldn't approve. Most wouldn't. And so ... I kept it all a secret. Well, Henry did, too, but he's Henry. *I* should have told you because it's your house, as you said, and because you had a right to know, and because you are the dearest person to me in all the world, Maisie!'

I saw her startle ever so slightly, eyes darting towards the door. I pressed on, fumbling for words.

'I was just so afraid that you'd hate it! Not even that you'd turn us out, but that you'd see it and think me . . . think me a—'

'A witch?' said Maisie. 'A necromancer?'

It took me a moment to realize she was joking. I laughed, surprising myself. My God, it felt good to laugh again; even here, in the midst of disaster.

'It's science, Maisie! It's simply Nature, put to use. Nature made better. Or . . . well. That was our intention.' I found myself staring at my knuckles, curled around the edge of the door to the carriage. Tired of perching there, I opened the door and climbed in, sitting down tentatively next to her. 'I am not sure, now, whether it was right. But it's done now. And whatever happens to it is entirely my fault.'

There was noise from the doorway, shuffling and swearing. It appeared that Henry had found Ramsay at last. The two of them laid Henry's trunk upon the front steps and then disappeared again, presumably to fetch mine and Maisie's. I felt a hand suddenly in mine, squeezing tightly – desperately, in the manner of those who are not sure when the next chance will be.

'You really do love that wretched thing, don't you? This . . . Creature.'

Hesitantly, I laid my hand over hers. 'I do. It's hideous, I know, but I do.'

She gave a long sigh, face serious once more. 'I . . . have been thinking. About what you said then; about curing death being the "next stage of medicine", or whatever you might call it. I remember reading, once, that many of those who were condemned one hundred years ago for witchcraft or heresy were simply practising what we might today call medicine. And we have not been struck by lightning yet.' She cast a nervous eye towards the sky. 'But even so . . .'

'It was in pain,' I said quietly. 'I didn't know it at first, or maybe I didn't want to admit it, but . . . The mouse, too. We were so caught up in the making of it, the miracle of it – I don't think we cured anything at all.'

'Yes, well.' She hesitated. 'It . . . was only your first try, I suppose.'

I cast her a sideways glance. She was still staring straight ahead, jaw set, the colour high in her cheeks. I felt a smile pluck at my lips.

'What are you saying?'

'I am saying,' she said slowly, 'that if you do plan to commit any more *crimes against God*, you might at least tell me first. That's all I ask.'

'So that you can try to talk me out of it?'

'Oh, I don't suppose anyone's ever managed to talk you out of anything,' she said with a wry smile, and I let loose another laugh.

'I suppose you're right.' I pondered. 'You know, I don't recall there ever being a particular verse saying, *Thou shalt not resurrect antediluvian monsters of the deep—*'

She smacked my hand. 'Stop it, or I shall push you out! I'm still cross with you, you know.'

'I'm sorry, I'm sorry!' I chuckled, my heart singing. 'I'll make it up to you. I promise.'

With a thump, Henry and Ramsay laid Maisie's trunk on the top step, and went back inside one final time. Maisie was watching them, chewing her lip.

'Do you know what I did?' she said quietly. 'Just there, with Henry? Lord, you'll think me such an idiot, but I . . . I pretended I was you. I would never have talked to Henry as I did just then, but you would. I have always thought that if I was simply . . . simply good enough, or nice enough, and I acted as if everything was behind us, then he might be good to me in return, or at least be less of a *tremendous ass*, but—' She swiped a hand across her eyes, her voice tremulous. 'It's as if he doesn't even notice. He doesn't really see me. I'm so tired, Mary, so tired of being his stupid little sister.'

'You are not stupid!' I protested, but before I could continue with a list of her virtues, she cut in:

'I *am*! Do you know what I thought you were doing, all this time? With your experiments? I was trying to guess why you and Henry had to be so secretive about it, you see, and you *did* tell me you were studying rat poisons, so I thought, well, rat poisons are very often used in murders, aren't they? So perhaps you were trying to find a way of determining whether a body had been poisoned by arsenic, and of course you would have to keep that secret, for if criminals ever found out how the test was applied, then they might find a way to counteract it, or even murder *you* so that you would be unable to finish your important work; but then I realized that that would be strange, because the two of you are geologists, not chemists. So then I thought perhaps you were pioneering some geological technique, but one which necessitated testing on live rats and turtles and dolphins, somehow – because I *did* notice the dolphins, by the way – like maybe an acid that can dissolve everything except bones, in order to make the excavation of fossils easier; but it would be incredibly dangerous to let the public know of such a science, because it would provide an excellent method of disposing of a body—'

'Good Lord, Maisie, that's grim!' I burst out at last, stifling my laughter behind the palm of my hand. She almost sounded disappointed that there *hadn't* been murder or poisoning involved in this grand affair.

'Well, I was guessing, wasn't I!' she said hotly. 'And was I really so far off? Were my guesses any more nonsensical than "building an ancient reptile"?'

I could not argue there. I squeezed her hand again, making use of every moment she would allow me still to hold it.

'I am sorry, Maisie. I ought to have told you. I should never have left you in the dark for so long.' A pause. 'And also, I do believe you should start writing penny dreadfuls.'

'I feel as if I have been *in* a penny dreadful!'

Henry and Ramsay emerged from the house once more and began to heft the trunks towards the carriage. I made to pull my hand away, but to my astonishment Maisie only held it tighter, drawing one of her many shawls off her shoulders and spreading it across our laps like a blanket. She shot me a smile, so fleeting I might have missed it had I not been watching.

For the first time in days now – weeks, perhaps – I felt a flicker of hope.

24

During my first experiment, a kind of enthusiastic frenzy
had blinded me to the horror of my employment; my
mind was intently fixed on the consummation of my
labour, and my eyes were shut to the horror of my pro-
ceedings. But now I went to it in cold blood . . .

— MARY SHELLEY, *Frankenstein*

WE REACHED ABERDEEN the following afternoon. By all
rights, we ought to have been there by lunchtime, but just outside Inverurie one of the horses had twisted its leg, and we were
forced to wait for a replacement. Hours we were stuck there in
the blasted heat, in the unpleasant company of a sickly old man
wearing a wig that rightly belonged to the previous century,
and approximately two thousand midges. The unusual weather
had brought them out in full force, and we spent the entire
journey slapping ourselves and scratching like mangy dogs.

It was only four o'clock by the time we arrived, but as it was
a Sunday, the last train had already departed. We even saw it
leaving through the coach window as we drove into the city.
Henry swore under his breath at the sight, cursing everything
from bad weather to bad horses to the Lord's day itself, much to
the horror of the octogenarian. Out of some stubborn sense of

pride, Henry had insisted on paying for our accommodation the previous night, so we had been relegated to one of the tiniest rooms in the inn, adjacent to the stables. In Aberdeen, however, Maisie announced – politely but firmly – that she would be footing the bill, and so we found ourselves in very decent accommodation indeed. It was only after my lengthy and admiring inspection of the room's elegant decor and down-stuffed bedding that it occurred to me that it possessed only one bed; Maisie had booked a room of her own. I was at once filled with envy, wishing that (if it were not for the expense, and the conventions of marriage) I might enjoy the same privacy. Ever since the fight over the Royal Society nomination (and long before that, too, if I were to be honest), I had increasingly felt that I did not know how to talk to Henry. We exchanged simple, necessary questions, of course – *Do you think it will rain later?* or *Have you seen my other shoe?* – but more than that? Anything approaching the casual conversation, the passing remarks and spirited but good-natured debates we used to share, seemed to have evaporated.

Still, that did not mean there were not things I needed to discuss with him, whether I enjoyed the process or not. To spare myself the agony of speaking face to face, I waited until the candles were blown out and the curtains drawn; then, turning to him in the dark, I asked:

'What will we do, once we get the Creature back?'

'If it's still in one piece, you mean?' Henry muttered. 'Well . . . more or less what Clarke is planning to do, I suppose. Show it to the Royal Society, convince them that it's genuine. I'm almost certain we have some bits and pieces lying around in London that would prove the idea was ours in the first place. And then, once we have credibility, the backing of an audience of well-respected men of science, we go to the press.'

I thought of my great-uncle's letters, wrapped in petticoats in my trunk. 'And? What then?'

'What then? Everything we talked about, Mary! Can you imagine the fervour? The excitement? The *money*? We can start work on an *Iguanodon* next, and truly put Professor Owen to shame. That is, if Clarke doesn't throw some sort of fit, and try to claim a piece of all our future projects, too . . .'

Credibility; respect; money. It was all that we had ever wanted. All that we had ever needed. I tried to imagine what I would do, with such a life. Make sure Henry paid off his debts, for a start – find better accommodation for ourselves, and for Maisie, and for Mr and Mrs Jamsetjee. My mentor had brought me into the world of science; now that he had been shut out of it, it was only right that I should bring him back. I would find him an assistant, and a nurse; I would convince the Society to reinstate his grant, or give him a grant myself if they would not.

But – and here was the first point that made me squirm – would he accept it? I thought so; drowning men could not afford principles, and so on. But I was not sure I liked the idea of myself upon the deck, a wealthy patron, tossing out coins to those poor wretches I felt deserved it best. I was not sure Mr Jamsetjee would like that version of me, either.

And here, too, was the second point.

'Do you really think it is . . . alive?'

Henry shifted. 'What do you mean?'

'Do you not remember the state it was in the last time we saw it? And that list we made at the very beginning? Growth, self-reparation – the defining qualities of life. Our Creature cannot *heal*, Henry.'

'Well . . .' He heaved a sigh. 'We can always make another, if it doesn't survive. Or replace some of the rotten parts, and see if we can bring it back to life again.'

I sat up at once, outraged. 'We cannot just— When Clarke wanted to rush the Creature down to Edinburgh, and you disagreed, I thought that . . . Do you not think we should find out what went wrong, how to make flesh repair itself, before we go about creating another?'

'But such a thing might take years, decades – it might not even be possible!'

'So that's it? We create more and more creatures, bring them into this world only to suffer, then kill them quietly when they're of no more use to us?'

'That's the way of all animals, is it not?'

I could think of no fitting response, beyond the inarticulate cry of disbelief that escaped my lips. He was right – that was the thing. Old horses went to glue, unwanted calves to slaughter. But this . . .

This was different. This was ours. This was *mine*.

'Mary,' he said, his voice grown soft, and somehow that was worse than if he had shouted at me. A tingle of dread ran down my spine, and I wished suddenly that he would – that he would fight back, and make this a proper argument, instead of saying the awful thing that I suspected he meant to say next. 'Mary . . . I know what this is about.'

'You do, do you?'

'You cannot think of it that way.' He swallowed, the pale shape of his throat bobbing in the dark. 'It is only an experiment. It is only natural, that you should have formed a special fondness for it, but it was never actually our—'

'Oh, for goodness' sake; I do not care for it because I think it is our *child*, Henry!' I cried. Here it was again, the notion I loathed with an intensity even I could not fully comprehend. What I understood was this: I cared for the Creature, yes. I loved it, as one might very well love a child – or a symphony, or a master-piece, or a beloved pet raised from infancy, or anything else perfect and beautiful that one has helped shepherd into the world. What I despised was the notion that it was a replacement – some inferior substitute to that which I *ought* to have brought forth by natural means, through agony and blood. The hollow that our poor daughter had left inside my heart was one that might never be filled. But – and here was a thought I had kept buried for a very long time, too afraid even to think it – I was still not sure how much of that grief belonged to her, and how much belonged to the version of myself I had hoped to find alongside her. The bliss of motherhood. The completeness I would finally feel, holding her in my arms. The knowledge that I had at last completed the task for which God, or Nature, had made me.

But was I ever truly made for motherhood, with thoughts as selfish as these? With a body that had borne me through it, but barely – like a boat thrown upon the shore, too damaged to stand the journey home? Nature was the realm of woman, so it was said, reason and science the realm of man; yet never had I felt so made for anything as when I had stood in my gloves and apron, lightning sparking between my fingers, striking life into inanimate matter. And which realm was that, precisely?

'Well, why *are* you so damned attached to it, then?' Henry said, and here at last was the argument I had wished for.

'Because! Because even in the glue factory, they have the mercy to shoot the horses quickly! And because this thing is so much larger than us, don't you understand? To simply toss such knowledge into the world without taking the time to understand its faults, to make it safe—'

'And what if we never understand its faults? What if it is beyond us – beyond our entire generation? Do we still not deserve some reward for what we have achieved?'

'"We"?' I cut in, unable to stop myself. 'Why, I thought you and Clarke were the only ones who deserved any recognition.'

He gave a groan of frustration, dragging his hands down his face as if he meant to claw off his skin. He seemed to be gathering every scrap of self-control, trying his level best not to argue. Finally he said, in a clipped voice:

'I *had* hoped we could present the Creature together, Mary, I did, but – if the Society will not allow it, then the Society will not allow it. There is no use fighting tooth and claw when we are already in a precarious position.' He rolled on to his side, battering his pillow into better shape. 'The first thing we must do is retrieve the Creature, and then we can speak about your troubled conscience as much as you like. Though I must say, it's a little late for regrets.'

And with that, he fell silent, feigning sleep in such an obvious manner that he must have known I would see through it, yet clearly did not care. There was nothing for me to do but try to settle down as well, though I was certain it would be a long time yet before I succumbed to sleep. Had I truly come so far, only to end up in precisely the same spot Victor had, mired in regret? *Did* I truly regret everything?

One thing was certain: we had done it now, snatched fire

from the gods, stolen it down to Earth – and it was only a matter of time before we began to burn.

WE ROSE EARLY the next morning, traipsing our way through the mist to the station to catch the first train. As Maisie and I sat on a little bench just inside the foyer with our trunks, watching an infuriatingly slow queue shuffle Henry towards the ticket booth, the smell of fish and fried foods drifting down from Shiprow market was enough to make me ill. Every time I shut my eyes, I could not help but picture the barrels of writhing eels we had passed on the way, the blood that pooled between the cobblestones, that terrible fishy substance that had seeped from the Creature's stitches on to my hands—

'Are you all right?' Maisie asked me quietly, as I pressed my sleeve to my face.

'Yes . . . I'm fine.' I tried my utmost to clear my mind; it would do no good at all if we missed the train because I was too sick to board. 'Shouldn't I be the one asking such a thing, in any case? You looked quite exhausted yesterday evening.'

She waved a hand dismissively. 'Oh, I'm fine now. A good night's sleep was just the ticket, I think. I've been quite well, really, considering that being bumped about in a carriage usually gives me a headache. It almost makes me wonder if . . .' She paused. 'It always makes me wonder if . . . perhaps I would be better, if only I made myself go out and about more.'

I turned, ready to argue that that was pure nonsense – that surely if exerting herself would cure her of her various ailments, it would have done so long ago – but she raised a hand to stop me.

'Oh, I know. It never lasts. I'll prove myself wrong soon

enough. But – still, I can't stop thinking it. Perhaps if I *this*, perhaps if I *that* . . .'

She looked so tired and sorrowful again, violet circles dark beneath her eyes. Her hands were twisting in her lap. I reached across and untangled them, pressing them between my own.

'It is not your fault,' I said quietly.

She did not reply, but tilted her head back and leaned against the wall of the station, watching the pigeons squabbling in the rafters. A moment later, a train rattled in and the billowing smoke drove them off in an indignant swarm. At the ticket booth, it seemed that Henry had finally reached the front of the queue and was now engaged in a hearty argument with the ticket seller. Perhaps the train was full, I thought, heavy with dread; it was May, early for the holiday season, but the weather had been so beautiful of late that many seemed to be travelling early. If Clarke had indeed taken this same route, travelling at a reasonable speed with such a cumbersome load, then he ought to have arrived in Aberdeen around the same time we had the previous afternoon; the very fact that he was not here in this station with us, negotiating the loading of the Creature's tank on to the back of a freight train, meant that he must have driven his horses half to death, or else switched them for a fresh team along the way. If we had to miss this train and take a later one, we would fall even further behind.

'Surely your Creature's distress isn't your fault either, then?'

I startled, shaken from my thoughts. 'Pardon?'

'Earlier, before we left Inverness, you said that it was in pain. That you weren't sure whether it was right to have made such a thing at all. And I've been thinking about it for days now, about why it bothered me so, and I . . .' She trailed off. When she spoke again, her words were rushed, as if she meant to get them out of the way.

'I watched you, you know. You and the Creature together.'

'What?' I said, feeling a tad self-conscious. 'When was this?'

'It was only once or twice, after I had that horrid fever last month. I was out on one of my walks the first time, just passing the boathouse on the way up the lawn, when I heard this splashing. And a laugh. Yours, of course. The door was cracked a bit, so I stopped to look in, and you were sitting there by the water, reading a book aloud – as if it were a bedtime story!' She gave a laugh, soft and incredulous, like she could hardly believe she was laughing at all. 'Its head was on your dress, and it was just as . . . *uncanny* as the last time I'd seen it, still as strange and fearsome, but even so, I couldn't help but think that it looked . . . happy. You both did.'

My throat felt tight. I did not know which day in particular she was referring to – I had passed many afternoons in a similar fashion, reading it my notes or lecture drafts (or sometimes even passages from natural history books on the 'might of antediluvian reptiles'). I could see the scene in my mind's eye nevertheless, a patchwork collage of happier days.

'It loved you very much, I think. *Loves* you, that is,' Maisie carried on. 'And if it is miserable on occasion, or if it is in pain – well, so am *I*. And yet, I don't believe my making was a mistake. You couldn't have known that life would be so unkind to it. You care for it, and that is what matters most.'

She looked at me, eyes wide and earnest, and *oh*, I thought, if she did not stop that soon, I would start sobbing upon this station bench. I remembered the awful look upon her face the first time she had seen the Creature; I had been so sure, then, that I had spoiled everything yet again, that the only reason she, too, had not run off to France to be rid of me was that she could not travel on her own. But somehow, miraculously, she had proved me wrong. She could learn to care for a monstrous thing.

I nodded, my throat aching too much to speak. With a smile, she relinquished my hand – too soon, I thought, seized by the shameless urge to reach across and take it back again – but Henry was striding towards us, three tickets held triumphantly aloft. Hurriedly, Maisie and I stood to gather our luggage; a shaky breath, a surreptitious wipe of the eyes, and (I hoped) he would not notice a thing.

'I managed to get two for the ladies' carriage and one for the smokers',' Henry said, breathless, thrusting the tickets into our hands just as the whistle blew. 'We shall be in Waverley by three o'clock.'

'SIR,' SAID THE watchman sharply, 'even if I were permitted to share with you the private details of our passengers, I could not help you. A hundred trains pass through this station every day, and countless passengers – I can't be expected to notice every one.'

'But I'm not talking about a passenger, I'm talking about a *tank*. A large black one, filled with liquid. Have you seen anything of that sort?' Henry pressed. 'Or heard anyone talking about it, heard the stationmaster complaining about some last-minute piece of cargo, anything strange at all . . .?'

Beside me, Maisie give an inaudible sigh and pressed closer to my side. It had been a long day, and I could tell she was struggling. We had not, in the end, arrived in Waverley for three o'clock, due to stoppages further down the track; instead, we had crawled into Edinburgh an hour late, and had spent another hour since being shuffled from one side of the station to another, speaking to various authorities. First it was a ticket agent, who directed us to the day watchman, who directed us to the station-master, who was not in, whereupon the stationmaster's assistant sent us down to the freight section of the tracks to speak to the day watchman there. We were the only members of the public present, and had been receiving some odd looks from the group of rather raucous railway workers who sat smoking nearby.

There was a hearty *slam* as the watchman shut the window of his little booth, cutting off Henry mid-tirade. He stalked over, fuming, to where Maisie and I leaned against an adjacent wall.

'Well, that was utterly pointless. He maintains he has not seen a thing, and that even if he had, he would be unable to do anything without some attestation from the police that the tank contains stolen goods,' he muttered. 'I knew we should have gone to the police.'

'And if we had, they would have told us that we have no proof!' I said, exasperated. 'None that they would believe, in any case. They would have laughed us out of the building.'

Henry scrubbed a hand across his face. 'It isn't too late. We could still go to them, say that the tank contains . . . valuable chemicals, or some sort of zoological specimen, or—'

'Hey!'

The voice was deep and loud, and came from the direction of the smoking railway workers. Their break was clearly over, for most of them had now returned to loading crates into a nearby railway car, but one in particular – tall, with a flat cap and an expression that was either peeved or else etched into a perpetual scowl by wind and coal smoke – was walking towards us.

'Yes, yes, we're going!' Henry called out, flapping an irritated hand, but the man called out again as we turned to go.

"Scuse me, sir! Misses! You were asking about a tank?'

At that, we stopped. I stepped closer, hardly daring to hope.

'We were,' I called out, doing my utmost to keep my voice level. 'Why?'

The man came to a halt some ten paces away, the squat end of his cigarette still burning.

'Was a man here yesterday,' he said slowly. 'Came in with one of the freight trains, up in front with the engineers and the like. Now, there's no supposed to be passengers on any of the freight, but they says he's got "special permission", just ask the station-master . . .' He gesticulated with the cigarette, waving it in small circles. 'So I go and get the stationmaster, the two of them have a wee chat – a long wee chat, mind – and all of a sudden, it's, "A'right, lads! Let's get this car changed over, come on, quick now." Right strange thing it was, too; a great big tank strapped to the top of a coal car. No explaining where it came from, why we was only loading it on ten minutes before the train left, nothing.'

'And the man?' Henry asked. 'What did he look like?'

He said, after a long, contemplative drag of his cigarette: 'Posh bugger.'

'Sounds like our man,' I said drily.

'There was a moaning, too,' the man continued, and we all fell still. I felt my heart twinge, sudden and sharp, like someone had cut the strings.

'What?'

'I heard it, when we started rolling the car.' There was some-thing in the man's face now, something slightly . . . afraid.

'Sounded like a wounded animal. That man of yours said something about it being the tank, old metal groaning, but ...' Slowly, he shook his head. 'I know what old metal sounds like.'

For a moment, I was so full of worry and pain and the pure, unadulterated urge to wrap my hands around Finlay Clarke's neck that I could not take it; I swayed upon my feet, eyes screwed tightly shut. It was only when I felt Maisie pressed up beside me, taking my hand in hers, that I dared open them again.

'Which train was it?' Henry was saying.

The man took another deliberate drag of his cigarette. 'Well ... my job's very important to me, y'ken. If it ever got back to the stationmaster that I'd been talking to youse, spreading rumours about strange dealings at the yard ...'

Ah, there it was. Henry heaved a sigh and fished a few shillings from his coin purse, tossing them over. The man held them up and snorted.

'Three bob?'

'Oh, fine,' Henry grumbled, and handed over some more. Seemingly satisfied, the man tucked the payment into his jacket pocket.

'Six-forty to Newcastle,' he said at last.

'*Newcastle?*' Henry repeated.

'It stops at Newcastle, you mean? On the way to London?' Maisie asked quietly.

'No, miss. That one stops at Newcastle Central, then comes back up in the morning. I should know.'

I felt some small stab of triumph at that, that I had been right – that Clarke had taken the timetable to Newcastle for a reason. But *which* reason?

'Why the devil is he . . . ? Oh, Christ in Heaven, never mind,' Henry muttered, clearly thinking the same. 'We'll work it out later. Thank you for your help, sir. Now, come on – let's get to Newcastle, I suppose.'

He marched off in the direction of the passenger platforms. Maisie tugged me gently along, her fingers laced through mine, and I was just about to follow when the man called out again behind us.

'What was it? Inside that tank?'

I looked back to see that troubled expression on his face again – the face of a man who's seen a ghost, or a miracle, or a monster.

'Check the papers in a few weeks and you'll see!' Henry called back, with an uncharacteristic bark of laughter. But the man kept looking at me, the question still in his eyes.

'It's ours, that's what it is,' I said, with as much confidence as I could muster. 'And we're going to get it back.'

25

There is an expression of despair, and sometimes of revenge, in your countenance that makes me tremble.

— MARY SHELLEY, *Frankenstein*

WE RUSHED TO book the next evening train to Newcastle, due to arrive at a quarter to eleven. Maisie, who was looking wearier by the minute, closed her eyes the moment we took our seats, and while I did not begrudge her the rest, I also did not relish the opportunities for conversation it left me. Fortunately, after a terse few hours arguing over Clarke's potential plans and a dinner of unpleasantly squashed ham sandwiches we had bought at Waverley, Henry, too, began to snore and I was left to stare out of the window in peace. I had spent so long now gazing at the passing countryside that it seemed unreal to my eyes, one long smear of greyish-green beneath the darkening sky.

'Where are we?'

I turned, startled, to see Maisie awake.

'A little past Berwick,' I said. 'Near Lindisfarne, I would guess. I saved you some sandwiches – would you like some?'

She nodded and took one, eating it in excruciatingly small bites. I studied her as she stared out of the window, much as I had been doing only moments before – the flyaway hairs at her temple, the sharp curve of her jaw, the prim way she returned the sandwich to her lap in between bites.

She turned, too quickly for me to pretend I had not been watching her, and smiled. 'What are you thinking about?'

'All the books I should have brought with me,' I said, and she laughed.

'Lindisfarne . . .' She looked out towards the horizon. 'That's the monastery, isn't it? The one that was attacked by the Vikings?'

'Yes, in their dragon boats.' There had been an illustration of them in one of my grandfather's history books. It had been a terrible book overall, full of far too many Roman wars for my liking, but that particular woodcut still stuck in my mind.

'I wonder what they would have made of your Creature.'

'Oh, they'd have tried to get it on their side, I think; it would have come in very handy for scaring monks.'

'What is that you've got there?' Maisie asked, and I startled. I had been clutching the Creature's pencils in my coat pocket, I realized, rolling them back and forth between my fingers. I lifted them out for Maisie to see, and watched her face as she put the pieces together – the cracks, the toothmarks, the way I held them as if they were made of glass.

'Oh,' she said quietly. She turned back sharply to the window, and for a moment she seemed to be lost in thought again, chewing her lip anxiously between her teeth. But then she leaned forward with a curious sort of urgency and said: 'Mary, you do . . . forgive me, don't you?'

I blinked, taken aback. 'What?'

'For everything. For what I said about your Creature that

first night, and for not talking to you for so very long. All I could think of was the cruelty of it, all those lizards or what-have-you sliced into bits, playing with living things as if they were just toys to be put together in different forms, but then—' Hesitant, she looked me in the eye. 'Then I saw you that afternoon and I realized that wasn't it at all. But still, I didn't talk to you. I simply didn't know what to say.' She gave a bitter laugh, staring down at her lap. 'I know you once said that you had never forgiven anyone. So that's why I thought to ask if . . . Well, I would understand, if . . . That is to say, I hope it's not too late for me to—'

I reached over and grasped her hand. I thought of all she had done so far – securing us a coach from Inverness, putting us up in Aberdeen, holding me steady at the station as the world tipped beneath my feet.

'Maisie,' I said softly, a smile in my eyes, 'you might just be the first.'

UNFORTUNATELY, DUE TO the lateness of the hour and a lack of easily bribed witnesses, we had far less success at Newcastle station than we had had in Edinburgh. We spent a fruitless half an hour wandering about and questioning staff, but when the stationmaster caught Henry in the yard waving shillings at a pair of unimpressed railway workers, we were promptly escorted from the premises. And so we found ourselves outside the station as the streets slowly emptied for the night, the trail grown cold.

'It's not that big a town, is it?' I said, more a plea than a statement of any known fact. 'There can't possibly be that many places to hide. And he wouldn't have taken another train out, would he? If he had wanted to go straight to London, he would simply have taken a direct train in the first place.'

'Probably. Perhaps.' Henry shrugged, looking at his wits' end. 'I don't know, Mary. I won't pretend to understand the man's motives. *Maisie* ' – he barked over his shoulder – 'let's go. We should find somewhere to stay and start again tomorrow.'

Maisie, who had spent the past hour sitting beside the ticket office, gazing at a wall of maps and posters for bathing machines at Cullercoats Bay, jumped and hurried over. It worried me how pale she was, how tightly drawn the line of her mouth. The sooner we all got some rest, the better.

With that thought, however, it seemed I had cursed us, for it took an age to find somewhere to stay. Half of the inns were shut up for the night, and the rest were already full to bursting, what with the glorious weather of late. At last, as the church bells tolled midnight, a cab driver on his way home took pity on us and found us an inn so far outside the city that it was practically in the next town – if one could truly count Wallsend a town, being as it was slowly eaten by the growing sprawl of Newcastle. The inn in question was the King's Head, a ramshackle place that both looked and smelled as though it had once been a barn. After a considerable amount of begging, the proprietor brought some food to the one room we'd been able to procure. And so we sat – atop the beds, as there were no chairs – eating a modest supper of cold meat and potatoes, in decidedly low spirits indeed.

After the meal, as Henry and I unpacked our night things, Maisie sat silently upon the narrow window seat. Her brow was furrowed; with pain or with thought, I could not tell.

'Are you feeling all right?' I asked, the question we passed between us like a shuttlecock, forever batting it into the other's court.

'Yes,' she replied. 'It's only . . . I think I'm just tired. It is good to be sitting down.'

I sat beside her, still concerned. 'I wish we could have a proper holiday here. I liked the look of all the bathing machines and such at Cullercoats. Salt water is supposed to be curative, isn't it?'

Maisie made a face. 'I've had quite my fill of salt-water baths, thank you. They used to make us take them all the time, at one of the convalescent homes I stayed in, even in the *worst* weather. Until my mother intervened.'

'That sounds rather the opposite of curative.'

'Ah, but everyone knows the more unpleasant a thing is, the better it is for you!' She leaned back to rest her head against the cool glass of the window. 'Could you possibly read to me? Just until . . .' she cast a wary glance at Henry, who was poring over a map of Newcastle and the Tyne '. . . until my medicine begins to work.'

'Of course. Is this one yours?' I picked up a book that lay on the windowsill, and saw with surprise – and some guilt, for it hadn't even crossed my mind to bring such a thing – that it was a small leather-bound Bible.

Maisie cracked open one eye. 'Oh, no, that was here already. I suppose someone must have left it. Or perhaps it's the owner's.'

Idly, I began to flick through the Bible until I found a peaceful-sounding verse: a garden, and a valley, and pomegranate trees in bloom. The well-thumbed pages spoke to its being read far more often than my father's had been, though it was notably free of the annotations which had covered nearly every page of his. I had spent many hours scrutinizing those notes, trying to glean something of his character from the passages he liked best. In the end, the most informative discovery had not been any verse, but the paper I had found tucked between the pages – the one upon which he had been teaching my mother to write.

Elizabeth Frankenstein, I thought, the name holding a new weight for me now that I knew of the Frankensteins' chequered past. I had never liked the name Brown; I had felt (in a guilty sort of fashion, as if the thought alone were akin to spitting on my mother's grave) that it was common, uninteresting. But she had not wanted it either, evidently. She had wanted to be married. In her short, dreary, drowning life, it was one of the last things she had wished for. And she had never been granted it, even in death.

'Found any more cardinal sins to commit?' Maisie quipped when I stopped reading, and I could not help but chuckle.

'Why, yes; I think I've covered pride and wrath well enough. Which one shall I choose next?'

Eventually, we retired for the night; or, at the very least, I lay down and closed my eyes, begging sleep to come. I felt as if I had not rested, not *truly*, since the night of the fire. It was more of a fitful half-sleep I suffered that night, a wakeful dream, full of flames and flesh and shifting silhouettes beneath dark waters. I thought I was dreaming still when Maisie shook me awake – her face seemed to float before me, a pale phantasm in the dark. But then the vision fell away and there she was before me, grinning, her eyes glittering.

'The Baths,' she said, breathlessly. '*I think it's at the Baths!*'

IT WAS A warm night, warmer than it ought to have been. I was glad of this, at first – a two-hour walk in the freezing cold would undoubtedly have been much worse. But as the tracks stretched on ahead of us, and the day's humidity turned to mist that wreathed the trees in an otherworldly sea, I began to feel as though we had crossed some fateful boundary. We were adrift, lost in a world which belonged only to the ghostly forms of stopped trains that rose occasionally like slumbering giants from the fog.

The Salt Water Baths was a pool that sat directly upon the sands of Cullercoats Bay, just north of the mouth of the Tyne, its waters refreshed each day by the incoming tide. It was a tremendously popular attraction, and I recalled seeing posters advertising its prices and opening hours tacked all over the station – which was odd, considering that just the day before it had been suddenly and indefinitely closed.

'I heard a woman complaining about it when we came in earlier,' Maisie had said, once she'd shaken me and Henry awake. 'She'd bought a three-day ticket this weekend, but when she came back this morning it was completely shut, with a sign on the door saying "Closed for Cleaning". And then I thought, well, wouldn't that be a good place to keep the Creature? An enclosed pool of salt water – just like your boathouse, but larger.'

'Well, technically, the boathouse was situated on an estuary, so who can be entirely sure how the Creature would react to pure salt water, but . . .' I could see the cogs of Henry's mind clicking. 'Why on earth would he even bring the Creature there?'

'To give it a larger enclosure, perhaps? Allow it a chance to exercise, after so long shut up in the tank? Or . . .' My stomach flipped at the thought. 'To repair it, if it was becoming too damaged to carry on?'

That threw rather a pall over the three of us. Maisie looked to the floor; Henry, grimacing, turned back to the map he'd spread out at the foot of the bed.

'But even supposing that is the case, how would he have got it there? It's miles away from Newcastle station.'

'No, no, you see—' Maisie leaned over Henry's shoulder to point. 'When I was waiting for you two, I kept seeing freight trains pass by, going towards the coast. They must be taking this line here, which goes right to the quays at Tynemouth. And that isn't too far at all from the Salt Water Baths; Clarke could have had the tank transferred on to a barge like any other cargo, then practically floated it straight into the Baths when the tide was high. And it would be quite easy to continue by sea to London from this point, anyway; no more bribing stationmasters, or having to shuffle the tank from train to train. He could simply sail down the coast and up the Thames.' She looked up at me then, as if suddenly coming back to herself. 'Or am I writing penny dreadfuls again?'

'No, Maisie, good heavens – no, I think this may just be it!' I threw my arms around her neck, so grateful I thought I might cry. 'How on earth did you put this all together?'

She turned a little pink. 'Oh, no, it's nothing. I had a very long time to look at those maps in the station, you know.'

'Yes, well,' said Henry. He was already rifling through his trunk, picking out new clothes. 'Let's see if we're right before we sing and dance about it. Maisie, you know how to get there?'

At that, she looked suddenly anxious. 'Well, yes, it should be easy enough – you only need to follow the railway. But . . . are we really going now? It's the middle of the night.'

'Clarke's already had far too much of a head start. No reason to give him any more.'

'But there won't be any carriages at this time of night,' I protested.

'We'd better get started, then, hadn't we?' he replied sharply. 'We can take a coach back in the morning, if we come back at all. If these baths really are where Clarke is keeping the Creature, we'll have to make alternative plans.'

As he bustled about the room searching for his shoes and his pocket watch, I leaned close to Maisie and whispered, 'You can stay, if you like. You've already done so much, and you look as though you need the rest.'

She considered this for one long moment, then sighed and took up her shawl. 'No, I can do it. I want to be useful.'

And so, here we were. My heels were beginning to smart, my shoes not meant for walking such distances. To my relief, the countryside was gradually giving way to the lifeless streets of Tynemouth, the cloying mist of earlier snatched away by a sharp sea breeze. As we finally came in view of the coast, a cry sounded out from behind us, and I turned to see Maisie clutching a hand to her bare head. Further down the beach, and rapidly winging its way out to sea, was her bonnet, its ribbons trailing behind it like the plumage of some great bird of paradise.

'Leave it. We don't have time,' said Henry, marching on regardless. Maisie simply stood, her eyes closed, hand still pressed to her head. I did not like the way her shoulders were heaving, silently pulling in breath after shallow breath.

'Are you all right?' I asked for what seemed the hundredth time.

She gave a nod – a barely perceptible jerk of the chin – and we continued on.

At long last, another mile or so down the beach, we came to a bluff overlooking what was unmistakably Cullercoats Bay. It looked as though a bite had been taken out of the coast, lined above with a row of cottages and below by several dozen sailboats, tethered in groups to the shore as if they were huddling together for warmth. Only two buildings stood on the beach proper, one small and steep-roofed with a little clock tower at its side, the other much squatter and closer to the water. My eyes settled upon the larger one, my heart stuttering suddenly with nerves.

'There it is.'

'How do you know?' said Henry. It seemed that the closer we came to potentially finding Clarke, the more agitated he grew, like a hound scenting blood.

'Because it says "Salt Water Baths" on the front,' I replied curtly. Truthfully, if it had not been for the writing, I may not have recognized the building for what it was. I had been expecting it to look something like the baths at Lymington I had once visited as a girl – an open-air affair quite separate from the sea itself, fed by water pumped in from the ocean. But these baths were enclosed, of course, and would not even need pumps. When the tide was high, as it was now, seawater flowed through a number of arched openings in the wall and straight over the lip of the pool. How wonderful the view must be from inside, I thought, looking out through those windows on to the open ocean.

And how easy it could have been for Clarke to sail right up to the building and transfer the Creature inside. This theory of Maisie's was seeming more and more likely by the minute.

We set off down the slope, picking out a winding path to the beach. The incline was a steep one, and tiny pebbles skittered beneath our feet with every step. Just as we neared the bottom – as I began to wish we had taken a less perilous path, the rocks seeming to grow larger and sharper as we descended – I saw Maisie stumble and slump to the ground.

'Maisie?' I cried. She looked as if her legs had simply given out beneath her. She began to cough, her breath coming in wheezing gasps.

'Oh, dear Lord,' said Henry. 'Is this really the time?'

''M fine,' she gasped out between coughs, drawing a tiny bottle from her skirt pocket with shaking hands. Henry's eyes narrowed in suspicion as she unscrewed the lid and took a sip.

'What is that?' he asked sharply. He bent to peer at the label, then reeled back like he'd been shot. 'Good God, is that – *laudanum*? Maisie, what in Heaven's name! Who gave you that? Which crackpot was it this time?'

'Henry,' I said, my voice a warning.

'Father would be rolling in his grave! Don't you remember what he said about that friend of his, Mr Greengrove? Within the year, he said, slinking around opium dens. I can't believe—'

'Dear God, would you shut up! Just *shut up*!'

There was a moment's stunned silence. Without meaning to, I had shot to my feet, my hands balled into fists. Henry's face was thunderous.

'I will not be spoken to in such a manner.'

'I won't have you speak to her in such a manner!'

'She's my sister!'

'Then act like it!' I stepped closer, my teeth bared. 'Would it kill you, Henry, to display just one ounce of fraternal love and care, the barest sliver of human compassion? No – no, that's beyond you, isn't it? Have you ever stopped to consider what it might be like in her shoes? In anyone's, for that matter?'

'Do you really think this is the time to—?'

'The time, the time!' I threw my hands up in the air. 'It's never the time, is it? Never the time for me to air my grievances, never the time for you to listen, never the time for you to make up for anything you do—'

'What is *wrong* with you?' he cried, face growing red. 'Why do you always insist on being such an . . . an argumentative *hag*, day in, day out? Why did you even marry me, if you despise me so?'

'Henry,' gasped Maisie.

'I wonder the same myself,' I hissed.

'*Mary*,' Maisie said. 'Both of you, be quiet! Listen.'

And that's when we all heard it clearly – a low, baying sound, like the howl of wind through narrow streets. But it was not coming from the streets above.

It was coming from the Baths.

'That's it,' I whispered. The sound was like an ache, stirring in my heart and in my bones. We were so very close.

Beside me, Maisie was still wheezing, although her cough had subsided. She began to rise shakily to her feet, and I offered her my hand.

'Maisie, dear – there's an upturned boat over there, against the wall. Would that suit you? To rest there, while we go inside?'

She nodded, and took my proffered hand. When we straightened up, I was shocked to find Henry close beside me.

'This,' he murmured in my ear, every word sharpened to a point, 'is not finished.'

Oh, no, I thought as I watched him stalk down the sand ahead of us. *No, I rather think it is.*

THE BATHS WERE locked for the night, of course, but salt and seawater are hard on wood, and one of the side windows was so weakened that a few quick bashes with a rock was enough to render the latch useless. Inside, down a narrow corridor and past a handful of dressing rooms, we came through an arch and found ourselves on a sort of railed balcony running about the building's edge, overlooking the pool on the floor below. It was a beautiful place, if clearly a little past its prime – so much so that I would have thought it quite reasonable for it to be closed for cleaning after all. The pool was lined with cracked tiles of a vivid sea green, and a row of grimy windows in the ceiling let in shafts of moonlight. A rusted network of beams and struts supported the roof above, looking in the dim light like the skeleton of some gigantic beast.

And there, at the end of the pool, gazing out to sea through one of the arched inlets, was the Creature.

My heart sang at the sight of it – its mottled scaly head, the graceful line of its neck, its tail swiping fitfully to and fro beneath the surface. At first, I wondered why it hadn't simply swum away as the tide came in, but as we clattered down the rickety metal stairs, I saw why. There was a rope around its middle, tied to a nearby pipe.

'Oh, my dear!' I cried out, and immediately it turned, recognizing my voice. I ran to untie the rope from the pipe, then fell to my knees by the side of the pool. It made that noise again, that awful keening, as it lifted its head from the water and laid it gently in my palms.

'Oh, my dear,' I said again, softly, tears pricking at my eyes. Almost all of its stitches had been redone with thick silk thread, leaving ropy scars across its body like the seams of a quilt, but apart from that its condition did not seem to have improved one bit. My hands came away sticky and brown from its head.

'I'm sorry,' I whispered. It merely blinked at me, filmy horizontal eyelids sliding across its yellow eyes.

'Where on earth is the tank?' Henry was saying. 'I suppose it must still be on the barge, or whatever damned thing Clarke sailed it up here with . . . Perhaps it's further up the beach? I'll go and have a look around. If we can't find it, we may have to ask around in Cullercoats—'

'Yes, of course.' I waved him away, busy inspecting the Creature for new splits or tears. 'You go. I'll keep watch over it and try to get this rope off.'

I heard him run back the way we'd come, footsteps clanging up the stairs. If the fish bones on the bottom of the pool were anything to go by, then the Creature was still eating, at least. I slipped my hand into the water to try to free it from its tether – and it was then that I realized something vitally important.

'This water's warm,' I murmured. Warmth was relative, of course; it was an English beach, in the middle of the night. I wouldn't have wanted to swim in it. But it wasn't *cold*, not like the waters of the firth – and not like it would have been normally, if not for the unusually hot afternoon.

Finally, the pieces clicked into piece.

The heat. It had been right at the start of that spell of warm weather that the Creature had begun to fall apart. Again, heat was relative, but for a thing born in an icebox, a thing made of *meat* – that small change in temperature was evidently just enough to let it spoil.

Were we too late, I wondered? Was it already too far gone?

'That bloody fool,' I whispered. 'We need to get you north again, don't we? Don't worry. I'll make sure of it.'

'You'll do no such thing.'

Slowly, I turned.

There, standing in a shadowed corner beneath the walkway, was Clarke. There was a bleary, dishevelled look about him, as though he'd slept in his clothes – and, judging by the dark woollen blanket I spotted balled up in the corner, he probably had. I might have laughed, might have asked him how on earth he planned to stop me when it looked as though he could barely stand – were it not for the neat little pocket revolver gleaming in his hand.

I cursed myself for my stupidity. Clarke had been willing to travel night and day to get the Creature south as fast as possible – of course he would be willing to forsake a comfortable night's sleep to keep watch over it. I weighed my options, eyes darting to the stairs, but he must have seen me do it, for he raised the gun and aimed it squarely at my head.

'Don't move.'

'You wouldn't,' I said, without truly meaning to. There is always that part of us, I think, that supposes ourselves immortal – *not me, not today, not like this.* And besides, it was Clarke; he was a bastard, to be sure, but a bastard who thought himself civilized. The sort of man who got his way through blackmail and manipulation, who would never dream of dirtying his own hands with something so callous as murder.

Or, at least, that was what I had thought until now. I watched as something flashed across his face, something sharp and cruel.

'Oh, Mrs Sutherland,' he said, his voice almost unctuous. 'Little Miss Frankenstein. I very much would.'

I had forgotten one crucial thing, I realized. He had known war. And war was the most civilized form of murder there was.

My blood ran cold.

He walked slowly towards me, drawing something out of his left pocket. It was a spool of thick thread, I realized, the same sort he'd used for the Creature's new stitches. I heard it give a quiet hiss, and slide smoothly back into the pool.

'You're going to tie me up as well?' I said, struggling to keep my voice steady. If I managed nothing else that day, I would do this: I would not let him know how much he scared me. 'What will all the beachgoers think, hmm? When they come in to see the marvellous creature and spot me tied up as well?'

'I'm not starting some kind of circus sideshow, you imbecile. Hands, out. Now.'

I did so, hating myself for it. 'Why here, then? Why not go straight to London?'

'Because there were bits falling off it – why else? I knew it might not last the whole way to London, and I was right. I'll take it there soon enough, once it's rested. Provided those stitches hold.' Clenching one end of the thread between his teeth, he wound the spool around my outstretched wrists, his other hand still holding the gun steady. I flinched as his fingers brushed my skin, so violently it was like I'd been burned. 'Besides, I knew a man here. The owner of the Baths.'

I laughed. It sounded more than a tad hysterical. 'That's always it, isn't it? *You knew a man.* Do you ever wonder how little you might have made of your life if you didn't have all your connections? If you didn't have money to make up for your mediocrity?'

He glared at me, hand tight around my bound wrists. I could see the sweat on his brow, my own ghostly reflection shining in his eyes.

'Shut up.'

'But money cannot buy you talent, can it?' I could not fathom why I was still talking; I was trembling with fear, my heart beating so fast it ached, but now that I had started, I could not stop. 'You cannot buy ideas, or discoveries. Hence why you have to steal them.'

'*Shut your mouth.*'

If I had any sense, I knew, I would. But I have never been a sensible soul. I have only, ever, always, been angry.

And so I spat in his face.

He pushed me back then, right against the edge of the pool, pressing the cold barrel of the gun to my forehead. I closed my eyes. It was only then that the thought truly sank in: *I will die here*. And the oddest thing was that, although I had done nothing, really – the Creature was not saved, Clarke would go on to take all the credit – I felt as though I had won some small victory. For just this once, I'd driven *him* to rashness; just this once, I'd incited in him but a fraction of the rage he always stoked in me. I had finally seen his composure crack, his face twist with fury, at the realization that I would never be silent. Not here, not ever.

Which is not to say I had no regrets as I tottered there on the edge, ready for the bang. They flashed before my eyes, a stream of images almost too quick to parse: the Creature's rotting head on my lap, Mr Jamsetjee's shaking hands, the faded wallpaper of the nursery, Catherine's lips against my own, Maisie . . .

Maisie, who would hear the gunshot from that little over-turned boat outside. Who would go back to that lonely house in Inverness, to her books and her bedroom and the gloomy memory of her father lingering in the halls; who would live the rest of her life with the knowledge that she had heard me die and done nothing to stop it. A fact I would not begrudge, of course. But I knew she would.

And then, as if the very thought had summoned her from thin air, I heard her voice.

'Mary!'

My eyes flew open. Clarke, momentarily distracted, turned to look. There on the walkway, with her hands over her mouth, stood Maisie.

'Oh, for Heaven's sake,' Clarke muttered as he aimed the gun her way and pulled the trigger.

At that very same moment, I seized him by the collar and stepped backwards, dragging him down, down, into the dark and rippling waters.

26

Back to the infernal pit I drag thee chain'd,
And Seale thee so ...

— JOHN MILTON, *Paradise Lost*

I, too, can create desolation.

— MARY SHELLEY, *Frankenstein*

WE HIT THE water hard. Even if I had thought to take a breath before I fell, it would have been driven out of me by the impact, by the weight of Clarke on top of me. The echo of the shot still rang in my ears, a dull whine against the silence of the water.

And we sank.

It was hard to see through the darkness, and harder still to move, every action made heavy and dreamlike. As I blinked against the sting of the salt, I realized that I'd lost my grip on Clarke's shirt. He had twisted around to face the surface – one well-placed kick and he would be up again, ready to clamber out. I saw, in my mind's eye, the gun which must have landed on the edge of the pool as we fell; I saw him snatch it up, turn it again on Maisie and me. There was no chance he would let us go after this, I thought.

And so I hooked my half-bound hands around his head and squeezed, trapping his neck in the crook of my elbow.

A stream of bubbles left his mouth. He struggled and bucked, raking the skin of my arm with his nails, but I did not let go. Even as my own chest ached for air and the edges of my vision began to darken, I held on.

There was a curious sort of tug then. Not another movement from Clarke, though there was plenty of that a moment later as we both looked down and saw what it was. The Creature had wrapped its jaws around his shoe. I could tell what was going to happen a moment before it did; I saw the instant the Creature realized that this part of his hide was far too tough to bite. Clarke jerked his foot away, but with surprising speed – the sort of speed that made you remember that it was a predator, after all – the Creature darted upwards and sank its teeth into the meat of his calf instead.

Clarke screamed. It was a voiceless thing – he had no air left even to make bubbles, I think – but I could tell he was trying to scream by the way he tensed in my arms, his face contorting. He twisted and flailed, but that seemed only to make the Creature bite down harder, blood blossoming from the wound in diaphanous clouds of red. I let go. The Creature tugged again, dragging him deeper, and I pushed up towards the surface.

I did not look back.

I took in half a lungful of water as I broke the surface, so desperate was I to breathe. I almost went under again, and I think I would have, had I been alone. I had not one single ounce of energy left. But I was not alone, of course – and just before I sank, a hand reached out to reel me in.

It was not the most graceful rescue, by any means. She caught me by the sleeve of my dress and dragged me to the edge, where she heaved and hoisted and pulled until I flopped on to the side like a wet fish in my thirty pounds of soaking petticoats. I felt a dizzy wave of relief at the sight of Maisie unhurt; Maisie, apparently, not even grazed by the shot I had interrupted. For what seemed like an age, we simply sat there, clutching each other and breathing raggedly. I coughed a fair deal of water into Maisie's lap; she did not seem to mind.

Abruptly, the surface of the water broke again. A hand slapped the edge of the pool, then an arm, and finally a face. Trembling upon the tiles, hair plastered across his forehead, Clarke looked at me and *roared*. It was a raw, animal sound, part water and part spittle and part blood.

I think we both realized at the same time that the gun was lying an arm's length away.

We both dived for it. Fortunately, as I was slightly less drowned and significantly less mauled, I reached it first. I could have thrown it away, I suppose. I could have kicked Clarke back into the pool and let him go, as I had already done once before – my arms loosening from about his neck; leaving him, in a questionable act of mercy, to the Creature, for it to do with as it wished. But as I looked back and met his eyes . . .

Part of me wishes I regretted it. It says something about me, I think, that I do not. Perhaps it says that I am a monster. Or perhaps it says that I am simply committed to a sense of justice in the world – the sort of justice which I knew would never be served in a court, or in the public eye, or upon a Society stage.

Or perhaps I only did it because the look he gave me then as I pointed the gun at him was – of all things, the *cheek* – a look of doubt.

It does not matter, in any case. The result is the same.

I shot him right between the eyes.

27

'Oh! Peace, peace, my love,' replied I; 'this night, and all
will be safe; but this night is dreadful, very dreadful.'
— MARY SHELLEY, *Frankenstein*

THE SHOT FELT like a blow to the chest. It split the world in
two: the moment before, and the moment after. I barely even
noticed as he slid limply back into the pool. My left eye was
stinging. At first I thought it was the salt water, but when I
reached up to wipe my face, my fingers came away smeared
with blood.

Behind me, Maisie staggered to her feet and retched against
the wall.

Slowly, I placed the gun back on the floor. I shuffled to the
edge of the pool on my hands and knees, and through the horrible red stain of the water the Creature rose up to greet me. It
laid its head upon the tile, and I swallowed hard.

There was a scrap of cloth between its teeth.

'Good Creature.' I reached out to stroke its head, and in
doing so noticed that my hand, too, was speckled with red. It
should have turned my stomach, perhaps. But I had made far
worse messes while building the Creature; I had had far worse
than blood on my hands.

'Good Creature,' I whispered again. 'Thank you. Clever wee thing.'

Over at the corner of the pool, where the ocean flowed in to replenish it, the water was still clear – and so it was there that I knelt and splashed my face, my hair, my hands. The spatters on my dress would not be got rid of so easily, however. As I surveyed the ruined sleeves, I realized that the scratches on the outside of my arm where Clarke had clawed me were welling blood. There was an idea to be had there, floating through the dim and dreamlike haze in which I found myself. I reached out and snatched it up, examining it from every angle.

And then I bent towards the lip of the pool, where a few tiles had broken sharply in half, and cut my palms to ribbons on their edges.

AS WE MADE our way down the beach, hugging the side of the Baths, I saw that the tide was turning. Inch by inch, it was carrying all the flotsam and jetsam left by the day's visitors out to sea; and inch by inch, it shrank away from those great arched inlets on the Baths' seaward side. Soon the pool would be cut off entirely until the next morning's high tide – and the Creature cut off with it.

Yet another reason to hurry, hurry, *hurry*.

'How are you?' I asked Maisie. How absurdly normal a question that was, I thought, for a time like this – but then, perhaps that was why I asked it. She had nearly screamed earlier when I had pressed my palms to the front of her dress, covering up the spatters of Clarke's blood with smears of my own, as I had done to myself a moment before. 'It's all right,' I had whispered, 'it's all right – I fell on the beach, do you hear me? I cut myself on the rocks. You helped me up and, silly me, I didn't realize how much I was bleeding until I'd ruined both our dresses. Now come, we don't have much time.'

'Better,' she said now, though her voice was still thin. She was clutching my arm with a vice-like grip, as if afraid I might float away if she let go. Or perhaps, as we waded out into the shin-deep tide, she was more afraid *she* was going to float away.

'Are you sure? Earlier, you were—'

'I'm fine.' She bit her lip. 'I took . . . quite a bit more than I usually take.'

'Maisie!'

'I'll be fine! I just couldn't stand sitting there, being so *useless*. And then, after all that, I wasn't any use at all. I just stood there and stared while he . . . *he*—'

She shook her head vehemently. The rest of her was shaking, too, I noticed. I was about to stop her, tell her that she had been *far* from useless, ask again if she needed to stay back and rest – but before I could, there was a shout from behind us. There on top of the bluff, waving his arms about and yelling something inaudible, stood Henry. Why on earth had he not come to *help*, I wondered briefly, bitterly – had he already walked so far up the coast that he had not heard the shot? But it did not matter now. I watched him take a tentative step down the bluff, then frown as a shower of pebbles tumbled down the slope. He turned and made for the longer path down instead.

'Quickly, quickly,' I murmured, pulling Maisie around the corner of the Baths so we were both out of Henry's sight. I knelt down beside one of the inlets and clapped twice. Nothing. I clapped again and again, wincing as the cuts on my hands stung – until finally the Creature poked its long neck out.

'There you are!' I stepped backward, towards the open ocean, nearly falling as a wave hit the backs of my knees. 'Come on, come here. I'll get the rest of that rope off.'

But it would not come. Another overeager wave surged forward, hitting the wall of the Baths with a *slap*, and the Creature shrank away. From the shore there came another yell, much closer than before.

'*Mary!*'

'Mary,' said Maisie, in an entirely different tone. She looked at me – her eyes wide, her dress smeared with blood, strands of her hair coming undone and whipping about her in the salted breeze – and my heart lurched for a dozen reasons at once.

I'm sorry, I love you, I—

'I know,' I said, and reached down into the water to grab the rope that still ran around the Creature's middle. 'I know.'

The noises it made as I dragged it out to sea nearly broke my will entirely. I could hear Henry, too, splashing into the water and cursing my name, every other word lost to the wind. With one hand, I clung to the rope; with the other, I clung to Maisie. Again, again, I looked back at her, a question in my eyes – *is this too far, do you need to let go?* And again, again, she shook her head.

Finally, as the water reached my armpits, every other wave lifting me gently from my feet, the Creature seemed to grow calm. It was the cresting of the waves that had scared it, I think, the froth and the noise. Now, it drifted to the end of its tether and back, testing its weight in the water. Once, I thought I caught it looking off towards the northern horizon, which gave me some sliver of hope. It had to know which direction north was, didn't it, in its reptile brain? Or had that part been a dolphin's? Perhaps it would feel the touch of some soothing, cooling ocean current and follow it up the coast; perhaps it would reach Scotland, the Shetlands, the Arctic sea. Perhaps it would be all right.

Or perhaps not. That was the worst of it – not knowing.

Henry was only twenty feet away and getting closer. Our eyes met. I saw him form the words – *Don't you dare!* – but I was not listening. Instead, I threw my arms around the Creature's neck for the very last time.

'My darling, my glorious little monster!' I whispered, fumbling at the knot on its back. 'Go on, then. At least, if you are to die – if this was all for nothing – then you shall die free.'

And with that, the rope fell away. The current took the Creature, and it was borne away by the waves, lost in darkness and distance.

PART V

THE END

28

And do you also believe that I am so very, very wicked?

*

Make me happy, and I shall again be virtuous.
— MARY SHELLEY, *Frankenstein*

'I HAVE TO say, that is . . . highly unusual,' the inspector said.

He was speaking, of course, of my surname, not my story — for I would never have been so foolish as to tell the man the truth.

'Might I ask why you wish to go by your maiden name?' he said, his tone carefully free of any accusation or suspicion. I watched as a drop of ink fell from the nib of his pen, obscuring the very last letter of *Frankenstein*.

Once I said it, it would no longer be just a thought, a notion, a spiteful little dream that kept me awake in the small hours of the morning whenever Henry and I fought. Once I said it, it would be real.

Though, in all honesty, my mind was already made up. It had been made up the moment the Creature slipped from my fingers and Henry crashed into me, turning me around and shaking me by the shoulders until my head throbbed and the stars blurred. For a moment, I had thought that he would drown me. I think he might have thought so, too. But no; instead, he had screamed. He had screamed and shouted and cursed my name and cried a dozen hateful things, none of which I now remembered – for all I remembered was looking into his eyes, screwed up with rage and despair, and thinking, *I am so very tired of pretending to forgive you.*

The men who found us on the beach, I later learned, were named Mr McLean and Mr Wilkinson. They were fishermen, residents of the small row of houses at the top of the bluff, who had been woken in the early hours of the morning by the sound of gunshots and had come down to investigate. There, of course, they discovered a man in the surf screaming at two sodden, blood-soaked women, one of whom appeared on the verge of collapsing. It was not long before Henry was dragged from the beach by his armpits and locked in a room in the Baths, awaiting the arrival of the village constable. It was not long, either, before Maisie and I were installed by the fire in Mrs Wilkinson's living room, awaiting the arrival of a jug of cider she had insisted on heating up for us. It was a kind gesture, made only slightly less kind by the fact that Mrs Wilkinson clearly expected repayment in the form of a full account of the night's events. After an hour or two of my reluctant, non-committal answers, however, she gave up, and I was left to sit by the fire in peace. Clutching Maisie's hand in mine, staring into the flames, calculating and calculating.

It was not as though the police (or anyone else, for that matter) would ever believe the truth. It was unlikely that they would believe even a part of the truth – that I had shot and killed someone, shot and killed a former military consultant with his own gun, which I had taken from him by force – all while my husband, who owed this same man money, stood by outside. No, even if I begged for the hangman's noose, my confession would only be seen as a desperate ploy to draw attention away from Henry. The best I could do, then, was concoct some sort of story that exonerated all three of us, as unlikely as that seemed. That, and hope that the evidence was too circumstantial to convict Henry outright.

But afterwards, once all this mess was over . . .

'I am planning to live apart from my husband.' There; it was said. It was made real.

The inspector stilled, his eyebrows flying up towards his hairline.

'Has he been unfaithful?'

I resisted the urge to scowl, because of course that was all anybody truly cared about – the only case in which, rarely, one might be granted a divorce.

'Only to those ideals he promised me he would uphold, sir. So, I am going to stay with a friend.' Then, slowly, deliberately, lending it an air of truth: 'For the time being, that is. Until we resolve our differences. And while I am away, I do not want the newspapers hounding me.'

'Ah, yes – what is it they're calling it now? "The Bathhouse Murder"?' he said wearily, adjusting his spectacles. 'Well, all right. I'll make a note of it. I appreciate your letting us know, rather than simply running off under a false name. Happens with far too many witnesses, you know. Now, do you think I might have your statement?'

For a moment, I considered pointing out that it was by no means a false name – but it was not my legal one, either, I supposed. And besides, it did not seem the time. Gathering together the details of my story – the story I had softly told Maisie by Mrs Wilkinson's fire, the story I had muttered in Henry's ear during my brief visit with him in the gaol, the story whose strength I hoped was in its closeness to the truth – I began.

'We came to Newcastle on holiday, at the recommendation of Mr Clarke himself. My sister-in-law – Miss Sutherland, as I'm sure you know – has suffered all her life from disorders of the lung, and Mr Clarke, who has some medical knowledge, suggested that a spell at the seaside might do her good. He recommended Cullercoats, as he knows . . . knew . . . the man who owns the Salt Water Baths. He was travelling down to Newcastle anyway, and he suggested that he go down a day or two ahead of us to make arrangements. Oh, I should say, he'd been staying with us at my husband's family home in Inverness for some time before this, too. We—'

'He was staying with you? For how long?'

'Since . . . last May, I believe. Yes, late May.'

'That's quite some time. What was his business there?'

'He and my husband were good friends, ever since university. They were conducting some sort of scientific research together – something to do with soil, and how it affects the transformation of bones into fossils . . .?' I smiled guilelessly. (This, we hoped, would explain both Clarke's involvement and the profusion of rats, if anyone thought to interrogate the staff.) 'I do apologize. You shall have to ask my husband for the details.'

He nodded, underlining something on the page. 'And you arrived in Newcastle . . .?'

'On Monday night. It was far too late to bother Mr Clarke, so we found a room for the night – a difficult thing this time of year, as you likely know; it was nearly one in the morning before we finally got to bed. But then Miss Sutherland began to get one of her awful headaches, and asked if we might go out – on occasions such as these, she has found that so long as she's moving and taking in the fresh air, it keeps the headache at bay, so we often end up on very long walks at the oddest of hours . . . And she's had such a hard time of it lately, we would have happily walked with her until dawn if it would have helped.'

'What time was this?'

'Oh – about two, I think, when we left? Two thirty? Maisie wanted to go and see the sea, so that was the direction we headed. We were just walking past Cullercoats Bay when we heard a loud noise from the Baths – I thought at the time that it sounded as if something had fallen inside the building, a metal beam of some sort. Just as we were discussing whether we ought to go and investigate, Miss Sutherland's bonnet blew off into the sea. She chased after it, and I chased after her, for she faints sometimes when the spells come on, and . . .' I gave a wry laugh, holding up my bandaged hands. 'Silly, isn't it? I tripped over the hem of my own dress. It must have been a buried scrap of metal, I think, or else a very sharp shell or rock. Whatever it was, I didn't even notice how badly I was cut until I was out in the waves, trying to coax Maisie back. I'm afraid I spoiled her dress completely. Then Henry caught up with us, and he was not pleased at all – he scolded Maisie for running off into the sea for something as trivial as a bonnet, and scolded me for running after her, and for managing to hurt myself in such a ridiculous manner . . . and that's when the men from the village found us.'

'You didn't hear the second shot?'

I frowned. 'No . . . I think that must have been when Maisie and I were out in the water. Miss Sutherland, that is to say. We were quite distracted.'

He wrote for a very long time, pen scratching across the page in row after neat little row. After a minute or two, restless, I started to speak:

'Sir, if that is all—'

'Were you aware, Mrs Sutherland,' the inspector said slowly, peering at me through his pince-nez, 'that your husband, according to Mr Clarke's accountant, owed him a sum of . . .' He checked his notes. 'Four hundred and eighty-four pounds?'

For a moment, I was too stunned to speak.

Four hundred and eighty-four pounds.

'No,' I said hoarsely, and for once I did not have to lie. 'No, I did not.'

'Hmm,' said the inspector. There was a great deal contained in that small 'hmm'.

'Very well,' he said at last. 'You may go. Ask Miss Margaret Sutherland to come in, if you would.'

THE SILENCE THAT hung between Henry and me as we sat together on the bench outside the inspector's office was – like the velvet drapery in the Sutherland family drawing room – long, heavy, and entirely unpleasant. At the end of the hall, next to the constable who was supposedly watching Henry, a great grandfather clock sliced the quiet into seconds. Henry kept rubbing at his wrists, making the cuffs that bound him to the bench jingle and clank.

Finally, when another officer came to ask the constable a

question and the pair became absorbed in conversation, Henry turned to me and broke the silence.

'I can barely stand to look at you,' he said, quiet and sharp.

'Then don't.'

'I simply . . .' His fists clenched and unclenched in his lap. 'I don't understand why.'

'He was going to kill me! And your sister!'

'Yes, *that* I understand – well, no, in fact, I really don't; I'm sure there were a thousand ways you could have resolved the situation without shooting him in the head, but—'

'And how would you know?' I cut in. 'You weren't there.'

'I told you, I hardly even heard the first shot! I was in the village, trying to ask that wretched boatman whether he'd seen any . . .' He waved a hand. 'Never mind. It doesn't matter. What I don't understand is this: why *release it*? Years of work, gone just like that! This was our chance to finally make something of ourselves, Mary, and you threw it all away.'

I looked straight ahead, examining the cracks in the opposite wall. 'For you and Clarke to make something of yourselves, perhaps.'

'Why, *you selfish—*'

'Oi!' The constable glowered at us, and Henry leaned back in his seat again.

'So, is that it?' he whispered once the constable's attention had strayed once more. 'If you can't have all the fame and the glory, if you can't be a shining example of the talents of your sex, then I can't have anything, either? You sabotaged us both for the sake of your pride?'

Pride – what a tricky word that was. It was pride that had turned the angels into demons, pride that had doomed Babel, pride that had tempted Eve; it was the sin of believing oneself capable of great things, worthy of better. It was the worst sin a woman could commit. Had I pride? Of course; for what else was I to have, when hard work and humility and civility yielded naught? I had resigned myself, now, to the fact that I would never have money – never enough of it, at least, to change the workings of the world. I had longed for so many years to be recognized, remembered; surely, this quiet and self-sufficient dignity, the knowledge that I *could* and I *had*, no matter what anyone else believed, was less prideful than standing behind a lectern awaiting applause?

And, of course, it had not all been about pride. Above all, I had done what I did for the Creature's sake. That, I suspect, is what needled Henry the most; the fact that I had chosen the Creature over my own husband.

'And now,' he muttered, seemingly having given up on my response, 'they suspect me of murder. Will you be happy then, when they hang me?'

My stomach twisted. 'They will not hang you, Henry.'

'Oh, won't they?' He gave a rather hysterical laugh. 'What do you think, then? Will they transport me? Ten years' hard labour?'

'They have no evidence.'

'They have a gun and a body, and the only man at the scene when the shots went off!'

'They also have two witnesses who will swear upon your innocence! And . . . Henry, listen to me. If it comes to the worst, we *will* tell them the truth. I'll admit to it. We can find some way to convince them that—'

There was that laugh again, sharp and bitter. 'That my *wife*

368

shot a man in cold blood? The man to whom *I* owe hundreds of pounds, whom *I* had every motive to kill? I barely avoided assault charges on the two of you, and you think—'

'Perhaps you'll die, then, Henry,' I hissed, a lump in my throat. 'Is that what you want me to say?'

Behind him, the door to the inspector's office swung open, but Henry did not turn around. Rather, he stared at me, head tilted slightly to one side, an odd look in his eyes, as if he had finally solved a long and difficult puzzle and found the answer lacking.

'Do you have any heart at all?' he said quietly.

My throat grew tighter still, tears welling in my eyes. In the doorway, Maisie froze like a rabbit, looking mortified.

'Of course I do, Henry,' I said, gathering my shawl about me and rising to leave. Despite my best efforts, there was a peculiar sadness to the words which I could not shake. 'It simply isn't yours.'

IT WAS TWO weeks before Henry was released. There would be a full trial in time, we were told, for which we would be duly notified; but the lawyer with whom we spoke seemed quite confident that since there was not enough hard evidence to keep him in gaol, there would not be enough evidence to have him convicted, either. The boatman whom Henry had rudely woken from sleep to ask if he had recently hired out any unusual barges could attest to his whereabouts at the time of Clarke's death; Mrs Wilkinson swore (due to, I could only assume, a combination of poor eyesight and an active imagination) that when she had been woken by the first shot, she had looked out of the window and seen Maisie and myself standing on the opposite bluff.

Then there was Clarke's accountant, whose books had been thoroughly examined for evidence of Henry's debts, the process of which had turned up several strange inconsistencies that threw into doubt even the fact that Henry had been in debt at all. (Though I, for one, was certain these inconsistencies had far more to do with Clarke's dubious history of bribery and black-mail than Henry's innocence in that regard.)

We were free to leave Newcastle, then, at least until a trial was scheduled, which could very well be months. Maisie and I did not wait for Henry to return to the King's Head and retrieve his things; out of some unspoken agreement, we merely col-lected our own luggage and went to the station. At the counter, Maisie asked for two tickets to Aberdeen – and then, suddenly anxious, turned to me with a question in her eyes. I blew out a long breath, thinking of the townhouse in London, where most of my belongings still lay: my books, my father's Bible, the less-favoured dresses that I had chosen not to bring with me to Inverness. I would have to go back for them eventually, I knew. There were ties to sever still, loose ends to be tidied up. But I could not stand to think of such practical matters now; the very idea made me exhausted, a tiredness that surpassed the mere physical need to sleep and slipped into a sort of bone-deep longing – the aching desire to go *home*. Wherever that truly was, now.

'Two tickets,' I said quietly, and her face glowed with relief.

'AM I A monster, Maisie?'

I watched her reflection in the train window cast me a com-plicated look. Outside, the coast sped by; dark clouds, heavy with rain, hung like a hazy watercolour above the anxious waves. Every crest looked to me now like a wake, every ripple the result of some dark shape slipping beneath the water. *Is that it, is that it? Did it make it north again? Is it safe?*

'He wasn't a good man,' Maisie said at last.

'That wasn't my question.'

She pondered awhile, staring at her folded hands for so long that I thought she must have decided not to answer. But finally, she said:

'Does it matter? The Creature was a monster, and yet you loved it just the same. A monster is simply something . . . irregular, isn't it? Something strange?' I could hear the smile in her voice, even though I couldn't see it. 'And I've always thought you a little strange.'

'Yes, but the Creature never shot anyone, did it?'

'It did nearly bite someone's leg off.'

'It did, but that's . . .' *What it was meant to do,* I tried to say, but the words struck me oddly, sent me spiralling down another well of thought entirely.

I didn't have the slightest clue any more what *I* was meant to do.

'Do you regret it?'

I looked out towards the distant clouds and bit my lip so hard it stung. Slowly, slowly, I shook my head. 'No.'

Then: 'Do you think I should?'

'I think that's entirely up to you,' she replied.

At last, I met her eyes. She looked tired, as I'm sure I did; her dress was a bland beige tartan thing, bought to replace the one we had ruined with blood and salt water. But despite all that, she seemed to me sharper than ever – a knife with the rust scraped away, revealing the metal true beneath. I thought of that girl I'd first met, clutching her brother's lapels, weeping at her father's funeral. I had not seen her cry since. She had kept herself dull for so long.

'How can you be so . . . so *good* to me?' I whispered, finding it hard to speak. 'So calm, after everything that's happened?'

For a moment, she seemed lost for words. Her hand shot out to take mine, pressing her cold fingers against my knuckles.

'Well,' she said at last, 'I did take a fair bit of laudanum before we got on the train . . .'

My head shot up. '*Maisie!*'

'I'm only joking!'

'Lord, Maisie, that's terrible!' She was giggling; and now, to my mortification, so was I. We bubbled over like pots left too long to boil. I gave her foot a kick. 'Stop it, people are staring!'

'You stop it!'

'It was you who started it!' I managed, one hand pressed over my mouth to stifle my laughter.

Once we had regained our composure, wiping our streaming eyes as the couple in the opposing booth shot us stern looks, I said:

'We're terrible, Maisie. We're terrible women.'

She grinned. 'We are.'

29

It is true, we shall be monsters, cut off from all the world; but on that account we shall be more attached to one another.

— MARY SHELLEY, *Frankenstein*

IT ENDED, I suppose, much as it began: with another black-edged letter.

Normality, I had found, was a surprisingly easy thing to feign, and a harder thing to make real. Occasionally, on my early-morning walks, my feet would still carry me to the site of the old boathouse, now nothing more than a black smear upon the lawn. More than occasionally, I would wake in the night with a jolt like gunfire, heaving breaths that tasted of blood and salt, like drowning anew each time. Or, no; it was like having been drowned already, remembering only in fits and starts that I ought to be dead.

Despite all my worries, despite all the hours I spent staring at the wallpaper in the dark, trying to forget the feeling of thread cutting into my wrists and cold metal against my forehead — despite everything, the sun still rose. The tide came in. We ate and slept. The slashes across my palms scabbed and began to heal, leaving pale scars in their place. When Maisie was laid low for a week with another fever, I lay beside her and read to her in whispers.

On her first day out of bed, as we sat by the fire – I reading, and she swathed in blankets, sorting that day's post – there came a sound from Maisie, an 'Oh!' as if she'd been stabbed with a pin. I looked up and saw in her hands, of course, the black-edged envelope. Slowly, she turned it over and read the address, then held it out to me.

'It's my grandmother,' I told her once I'd opened it, with no great surprise. What did surprise me, perhaps, was the hollow pang I felt at the news; though it was not for my grandmother precisely, but rather for what she might have been. That old, familiar ache of the mother-shaped hole in my heart.

'Oh dear,' said Maisie quietly, reaching out to place a comforting hand on my arm. I was more thankful than I could say. After all, I knew that if anyone else understood that ache, it was she.

'When is the funeral?'

'Tuesday.'

'Ah, no chance of making that.'

'No.' And I was rather grateful for it. I looked back at the letter, turning the page . . . and froze. I backtracked, reading the line I had just spotted a second time, for I was sure I must be mistaken, but no. I read on, eyes moving with frantic speed, taking in the news one disjointed phrase at a time.

Typically, in cases of intestacy . . . investigate all possible . . . but could not find your certificate of birth; so I contacted . . . in a small town, near Southampton . . . name, on the local register of births, was not Mary Brown, madam, but Mary Frankenstein.

And the same register confirmed that, two days before your birth, your parents did in fact—

Abruptly, I stood. Maisie looked up at me with wide and worried eyes.

'I . . .' I swallowed hard. 'Excuse me for a moment.'

Clutching the letter to my side, I made for the front door.

Outside, in the fresh air, I leaned against the warm stone wall of the house and took a long breath. My hands shook with rage, or shock, or perhaps even relief – a strange mixture of the three, most likely. I felt as though the world had shifted below my feet; that everything I had ever known about my childhood had been cast in a different light, every pointless jibe and obstacle I had encountered made even more pointless by the fact that I need not have suffered any of it. My life, it appeared, had been founded on a lie.

And yet . . .

And yet, I mused as I stared at the seagulls wheeling distantly over the firth, had anything truly changed? Besides my opinion of my grandmother, which was now lower than ever – unless, of course, she herself had not known. Was it she who had orchestrated this, or was it simply an unfortunate accident of fate?

Carefully, as my racing heart began to slow, I conjured in my mind an alternative reality, one in which I had known the truth from birth, and tentatively mapped its borders. Would my life have been all that different, had I known that I was not a bastard after all? Perhaps I might have had a happier childhood, or suffered less at the hands of men like Finlay Clarke. Perhaps I might have married a different man than Henry. But then again, perhaps not; I was still the daughter of a housemaid, conceived out of the respectable bounds of wedlock. I could imagine that in my grandmother's mind, that was equally shameful, another blot on the family name. And perhaps it no longer mattered. If I was entirely honest in my estimations, I suspected that my path in life would have been much the same.

. . . And that path, I thought now as I glanced at the parlour window and caught the curtain twitch as Maisie darted out of sight, was not such a terrible one, in the end. A smile plucked at my lips; slowly, I let my hand unclench around the letter, and smoothed out the creases I had made.

At least some good might come of this sorry affair.

Inside once more, I handed the letter to Maisie and waited while she read it, her eyebrows rising with every word.

'You—?'

'Yes.'

'And your grandmother, she simply . . . lied about it?' She looked up, and it made me terribly happy to see how furious she was on my behalf.

'Well . . . I do not know. My father was already very ill when he brought me to Wight; it's possible he wasn't able to tell her the full tale before he died. Or he couldn't bear to. And if she did know about the marriage, then . . . perhaps she couldn't bear the thought that her precious son had run off with a house-maid? She wanted to paint my mother as the villain, the vile seductress.'

'Yes, from what you've told me, that does sound like something she might do . . .' Maisie muttered. And then, with sudden glee: 'If that were the case, she must have been *seething* when she heard that you and Henry had eloped, too.'

I gave a bark of laughter, and dropped into the chair beside her. 'You're right. And she'd be seething still, to know that I shall now have the house.'

'What are you going to do with it?' Maisie asked, and I did

not think I was imagining the anxiety in her voice. I hurried to assure her:

'Oh, sell it! At once! I'm never setting foot in it again.' A dismaying thought occurred, and I winced. 'Ah . . . Well, I suppose that will be up to Henry, really, seeing as all of it is *his* by law.'

Maisie chewed her lip. 'Surely he will be reasonable, though, won't he? Perhaps you might split the money; he could set up an allowance for you, like I have with my inheritance. It would make sense, if you are to continue living apart.'

'Perhaps.' It would be the honest thing to do – on both our parts, I begrudgingly admitted, considering I had dashed all our dreams of riches when I set the Creature free. I could only hope that despite the animosity between us, Henry would choose the honest thing, too, rather than simply use the lot to pay off his debts. Although now that Clarke was dead, perhaps he had fewer worries on that front.

'Probably best to wait a bit, though, before you ask him,' Maisie said, grimacing.

'Yes! Yes, let the situation cool down. I'll bring it up after the trial, perhaps. And after I've gone down to Wight myself, to sort out the rest of her affairs.'

She gave a hum of agreement, and turned to stare into the fire. There was something poised in that moment, some unspoken thing I longed to ask, until I could bear it no more. I got up and knelt by her chair, clasping her hands in mine, and the words spilled out.

'Come with me.'

It sounded more like a plea, a reckless longing thing, than any sort of question. She blinked.

'I . . . yes, all right. I wasn't sure if you—'

'There are some stops I need to make along the way. London, I suppose, to gather the rest of my things, and Canterbury.' I had written to the Jamsetjees, of course, a nonsense letter full of vagaries and cryptic messages that I had penned in a daze the day after we returned to Inverness – for as much as I felt they deserved the truth, now that I had no proof, I could not think of a way to tell them without seeming like a raving madwoman. Still, they deserved *something*; at the very least for me to give them back their Leyden jar. 'You must meet Mr Jamsetjee – you remember, my mentor – and I think you would get along splendidly with Mrs Jamsetjee, too. But after that, on Wight . . . oh, the cliffs, Maisie! White as snow, taller than anything, and simply bursting with fossils! I must get you an ammonite; even if we can't find one on the beach, there are plenty sold in town—'

'I already said yes!' she laughed. 'You don't have to convince me. It sounds quite delightful. It will be warmer there, too, won't it?'

'Absolutely. We could winter there, spare you some of the cold and rain – or in Canterbury.' I had a plan brewing in my mind now; a plan involving my newfound inheritance, my newfound lack of anything to do with my life, my long-standing promise to myself that I would get Maisie out of this dark and dreary house. And perhaps, too, there was a way to get my mentor his money and his assistant after all.

'And then later, after the trial is over and everything is sorted out, then perhaps . . .' I tried to suggest it casually, as though I had not been thinking it for days, even before the news of my grandmother arrived. 'We could go somewhere else. Visit the continent.'

She gave me a long, appraising look. Anxious, I babbled on.

'You did say you wanted to visit Paris, didn't you? We could go on from Canterbury to Dover, and Calais – I have an old friend there who might be willing to put us up while we arrange travel south . . .' For, after all, what was the use of having your closest companion abandon you for the crime of caring for her too fiercely, if you could not later exploit her guilty heart for free accommodations? 'From there, maybe up through Belgium – or we could simply keep going south if you like, where it's warm. Though it'll be harder to get back that way. What do you think? I'm sure that—'

'All right.'

'Really? Are you sure?'

'You're the one who suggested it!' she cried, exasperated, and I grinned.

'I know; I just thought I'd have to work harder to convince you, that's all.'

'I am . . . willing to try.' She bit her lip. 'But Mary, I need to ask . . . I need you to *promise* . . .'

She met my eyes, as if she was steeling herself for some awful revelation, and my heart broke at the sight.

'Promise me you will not tire of me. Because I've seen how you and Henry go about everything, always rushing hither and thither, doing five things at once – and I cannot *do* that, Mary. I can't stomach another trip like that awful dash down to Newcastle.'

'Ah, but I was so looking forward to visiting the Baths again,' I said wryly, and she swatted the back of my arm.

'Be serious!'

'I am!' I leaned forward, chuckling, and squeezed her hand. 'I promise, Maisie. I don't want to go with Henry – I want to go with you. And I don't care if we don't get far, and have to turn back at Calais. I don't care if you're trapped abed three weeks out of every month and it takes us a year to get to Paris! Well, that is to say, I'd care, of course – but I wouldn't *care*.'

There was a smile tugging at her mouth. 'A year? I'd have to ask my solicitor for quite the advance on my allowance for that.'

'Tell him it's for your health, then. Get Dr Harris to write you a note; I'm sure he would. Or perhaps there's some Parisian specialist you simply *must* see. I may well have an allowance too by then, don't forget.'

'And if that doesn't work, if Dr Harris refuses? Or Henry doesn't let you have anything? If we run out of money entirely?'

'I'll get a job. I'll do illustrations for magazines, take in mending, sell jellied eels.'

She laughed. 'Do you even know the French word for "eel"?'

'It'll be *éel* or something, won't it?' I threw an arm out, as if to catch imaginary passers-by. '*Vous, madame! Voulez-vous un éel frais?*'

'All right, all right!' she laughed. 'We'll go! Just bring plenty of books, for the days when I'm of no use entertaining you. Oh – you should bring the one you're writing, too.'

Now, that gave me pause. I frowned, puzzled.

'What do you mean?'

'Don't be shy! That notebook you scribble in every evening. I thought it must be a book, but . . . Is it a journal, then?'

'Ah,' I said. Yes, that. How to describe such a thing, the thing which had started simply as a way to keep my hands moving the night after I gave my statement to the inspector – for if they weren't occupied, I thought I might tear my hair out instead. But it had become something more since then. Whenever my heart raced, when my thoughts buzzed about inside my head, I would crack open the spine of my little notebook and pin them to the page. Once they were there, set out in neat little rows, I could begin to see them as a pattern. A story.

'Yes,' I said, searching for the best way to describe it to her. 'I suppose you could call it that. But also . . . well, all of our notes were destroyed, as you know. A few scraps remain in the study in London, all very early musings, theories we've since disproved. The most complete record' – I tapped my head – 'is what I can remember.'

Her eyes grew wide. 'You're writing *instructions?*'

'No,' I said hurriedly. 'No, nothing as detailed as that. I had so many vials, Maisie, so many trials fermenting at once; I can't remember exactly how it all went together. The recipe's gone. I could reproduce it, perhaps, with a few months' experimentation, but . . . I am not sure I would want to. The book is only an exercise.'

A confession, a voice in my mind supplied. I thought of Victor, his deathbed memoir. He had intended his account to be a cautionary tale, a warning against the inevitable disaster that awaited anyone foolish enough to follow in his footsteps; was that what I intended mine to be as well? And was it inevitable, this disaster? Could such a grisly science ever be used for good? It had done harm enough in my and Henry's hands; Lord only knew how much worse it would have done in Clarke's. It was out of his reach for ever now, of course, but . . .

How could one ever be sure that another Clarke would not come along?

Sometimes, when one reaches a conclusion one does not fancy in the least, one does not jump on it straight away; rather, one circles it, like a starving cat around a rat that is past its best, weighing one undesirable option against the other. I did so, uneasily, while Maisie rose from her seat and announced that she was going to find an atlas, and the rest of the afternoon was spent tracing line after line on a map of Europe, only half of which ever ended back at Inverness.

AND SO IT all came to this.

It was a beautiful day in Dover, the water shining like a jewel beneath the sun. A gentle wind blew scudding clouds across the sky. The air was full of the chatter of passengers, the smell of the sea, the cries of seagulls and of squalling infants woken by the scream of the whistle – and the whisper of a young boy asking what I was doing, before his mother shushed him and pulled him along.

Even I was not entirely sure what I was doing, as I held my leather journal at arm's length over the railing of the ferry. The cord that was meant to keep it closed now dangled limp, swaying in the breeze; an overeager wave hit the side of the docked boat, coating my arm and the notebook in a fine smattering of spray. But still, I did not move.

I had left Maisie at the other end of the ferry, nearest to the dock, still chattering with Mr and Mrs Jamsetjee through the railings. I had already said my goodbyes; I had said them, in fact, on the train over, as the pair had accompanied us to Dover to see us off. The past few weeks with them in Canterbury had been strange – Mr Jamsetjee watching me like a hawk, Mrs Jamsetjee forging a quiet friendship with Maisie. I had told them almost nothing of what had transpired, besides that Henry and I would be living separately from now on. This they had accepted with grim-faced nods, likely thinking of the trial in the papers, 'The Bathhouse Murder'. In the end, just as his lawyer had anticipated, Henry had indeed been acquitted, the verdict like a weight lifted from my chest as soon as it was announced. Now, it was done. I owed him nothing.

But for all that the Jamsetjees tactfully refrained from asking about my past, they were clearly very curious regarding my future. Mr Jamsetjee, I think, had begun to guess what I was plotting from the moment I told him I was selling my grandmother's house. He never said it outright, but circled it with ever more pointed questions, eyes sparkling with amusement:

Wherever do you plan to live after your Grand Tour, then, if not in London or Wight?

You have sorted this bookshelf quite beautifully, Mrs ... Well. Mary, rather. Why was my assistant never as good as you?

Miss Sutherland seems to have truly fallen in love with Canterbury, has she not?

She had indeed. Every day, it seemed, there was something else about the town that delighted her – the canals, the cathedral, the quaint Tudor houses ... It was only the distant dream of Paris, I think, that had convinced her to leave at all. But I would not ask her this, not yet. It was one thing to agree to a tour of Europe, another thing entirely to abandon the home one's family had owned for generations and set up anew in an unfamiliar city (and with a woman one knew fine well was a murderer, a madwoman, a witch). I would not rush her.

But one thing remained.

I gazed into the shifting waters and thought again – as I was always thinking – of the Creature. It was no great mystery to me why many of the cities Maisie had picked out for our journey contained old and venerable universities: Luxembourg, Strasbourg, Ingolstadt. She could tell, I think, that it ate at me; the question of *what had gone wrong*. The last of these locations I had nearly struck from the list entirely, flinching at the thought of the city which had borne my great-uncle's own monstrous creation – though I supposed if I ever wished to find the answer, I ought to start at the very beginning.

But *did* I wish to find the answer? Was it worth it? Even if I happened to find the Creature again one day – as unlikely as that seemed – could it ever be repaired, or would it have to be entirely remade? And even supposing there was a way to make resurrected flesh heal and grow, to ensure that whatever beings I conjured forth would be free from rot and pain – what would such a science do, when unleashed upon the world? Would it bring forth a utopia free from suffering and sickness, as my great-uncle had hoped? Or a living nightmare of patchwork flesh, wherein a body is merely a means of conveying oneself from one place to another, replaced with a fresh vessel every time it grows too old?

How dangerous is the acquirement of knowledge – such had been my great-uncle's warning. Yet I had not heeded it.

I held the journal between forefinger and thumb, watching as the hungry waves lapped at the side of the boat like frothing tongues. I saw, in my mind's eye, the book floating downward, bleeding ink, its pages spread like a fallen blossom.

And then I snatched it back, heart racing, and strode back towards the boarding ramp.

'Mary! Did you see it?' Maisie called out when she saw me, for that had been my excuse – that I had wanted to see if I could spot France from the other side of the boat. Her smile wavered as I drew closer; she had clearly noticed the wild look in my eyes. She let out only a small 'Oh!' of surprise as I swept past her, leaped across the startled ticket collector's rope, and hurtled down the ramp. Ignoring the cries of protest behind me, I ran to Mr and Mrs Jamsetjee – who were only a dozen paces away, having just finished conversing with Maisie – and thrust the journal into my mentor's hands.

'Keep this!' I cried. 'Please? Keep it for me!'

'I . . . well, yes, all right, but Mary, why?' he began.

'When a carriage crushes someone in the street, is it the wheel we call dangerous, or the reckless driver? When one man stabs another, do we blame the assailant or the knife? The fault is not in the steel, but in what one *makes* with it – a bridge or a war-ship, a scalpel or a sword! And even then, cannot a sword, in the hands of one abused and made weak, be used to defend? Cannot a scalpel, in the hands of one ignorant or uncaring, maim and torture?'

'Swords, scalpels – my dear, what on earth do you mean?' Mr Jamsetjee said, sounding quite lost. I could see the ticket collector out of the corner of my eye, glowering fiercely, but I pressed on.

'I shall not throw away my scalpel, sir. It does more harm than good now, but I have worked too hard and too long to abandon it entirely.' I realized that I was still clinging to either side of the journal, and released it now fully into Mr Jamsetjee's hands. 'Keep it for me, but I beg of you, do not open it. Not until I return. Or unless I am dead, of course.'

'*Dead?*' cried Mr and Mrs Jamsetjee in chorus.

'Madam, we depart in under a minute,' the ticket collector urged, and I finally allowed him to usher me back towards the ramp, still calling out behind me:

'But when I return, you have my word, sir; when I return, we shall make something of it! Even if it never sees the light of day – if it *shouldn't* see the light of day – even if those fools at the Society never care to look—'

I was drowned out then by the screech of the whistle. Having at last herded me back on board, the ticket collector fastened his rope and took up the ramp, glaring at me all the while. There was a lurch beneath my feet as the ferry began to move, and I might have fallen over had Maisie not put out an arm to steady me.

'Good Lord! Come and sit down, would you?' she said, bemused. I cast one last look back at the dock, where Mr and Mrs Jamsetjee were waving, clearly puzzled by the whole affair.

It will be ours, I thought to myself, and sat at last.

The breeze picked up as the ferry drew further from the shore. Maisie sat so close to me on the bench that I could feel the warmth of her pressed against my side, the hem of her skirt fluttering against my ankles. I met her gaze, and was struck once again by how delightful it was to see her face in the sun. The Creature, in all its eerie glory, had been made for the cold; Maisie, I thought, had been made for warmth.

'You are such a peculiar creature,' she said fondly, and I could not help but laugh. I twined her fingers in mine and turned once again towards the open sea.

'That I am.'

Author's Note

I HAVE A confession to make: the first time I read *Frankenstein*, I didn't like it one bit.

I was fifteen, and hated on principle any book that wasn't about outer space or wizards. Like all the other classics I'd read for English that year, I thought it was too slow, too flowery, too *old*; I thought the prologue was pointless, and the backstory boring, and that Victor was a bit of a wimp. Now, after having read the book countless more times in the intervening years . . .

Well, all right. I stand by my last point. Victor *is* a wimp.

But I've come to appreciate the book in so many other ways as well. Not just as a piece of literature, but as a piece of history. Like all good science fiction, *Frankenstein* is a time capsule, a window into the worries of an era — a time in which science was advancing at (what was to some) an alarming rate, in which bodies were regularly snatched from graves and sold to medical schools for dissection, in which medicine itself was at once miraculous and horrifying. I love *Frankenstein* in the same way I love the ENIAC, or the Wrights' aeroplane — sure, its descendants today might run smoother and faster, but isn't it a *marvel* to look upon the very first?! And, even more marvellous, to know that the entire genre of science fiction — a genre whose creators and fans have, in subsequent centuries, often tried to pretend as though women don't exist — was born from the nightmares of an eighteen-year-old girl, one dark and rainy summer?

The idea for this book came to me in my last year of university. 'Came to me' sounds very dramatic; I was eating pasta, I think. I was looking at photographs of the Crystal Palace dinosaurs for an essay I was writing on nineteenth-century palaeoart, trying my best not to get tomato sauce on the pages, having only just narrowly missed spilling some on the copy of *Frankenstein* I was reading for a different essay entirely . . . when the two subjects came together suddenly in my mind. *What if?* What if some wildly experimental Victorian palaeontologist, some descendant of Frankenstein, decided to try a fossil reconstruction of a far more literal sort?

And then I laughed and finished my pasta, because that was the stupidest idea I'd ever had.

Weeks later, my family asked me if I had come up with an idea yet for my final-year research/creative writing project. I said, shamefacedly, that I had not. *Well* . . . I had one, but it was ridiculous. They demanded to hear it, and loved it, of course — and the next day, I went sheepishly to my adviser to try to pitch 'Frankenstein, but, like, with dinosaurs?' for academic credit.

The original project was meant to be a seven-thousand-word short story (*ha*), but by the time I submitted it to my ever-gracious advisers, it was well over thirty thousand and still straining at the seams, so as soon as I graduated, I set about turning it into a full-length novel. Despite the surreality of its premise, I've done my best to make the world of *Our Hideous Progeny* as real as possible; Richard Owen was real, as are the Crystal Palace dinosaurs, the life-sized statues that sculptor Benjamin Waterhouse Hawkins created to illustrate his palaeontological models. (You can still see them at Crystal Palace Park today.) The books Mary and Henry read, the theories they discuss, and the people they meet are all true to life – including the women who regularly attended scientific society meetings, all of whom were talented scientists in their own right. And Jehangir Jamsetjee, while fictional, is heavily inspired by Ardaseer Cursetjee Wadia, eminent Parsi naval engineer and the first Indian to be elected to the Royal Society.

Mary herself is named for three real-life Marys: Mary Shelley, of course; Mary Anning, expert fossil-hunter and self-taught palaeontologist; and the celebrated mathematician and astronomer Mary Somerville, so-called 'Queen of Science' of the nineteenth century. It was Somerville who served as the biggest inspiration for my own Mary's personality – though perhaps not in the way that you might think. Although Somerville expressed plenty of frustration in her own writings about her place in society, I couldn't help but notice that in all her contemporary biographies, her friends and peers constantly stressed how *nice* she was – how humble, how pleasant and soft-spoken, how devoted she was to her children and husband. In other words, she was (apart from her interest in science) the ideal Victorian woman. It occurred to me that perhaps one of the reasons why she attained the recognition she did in her own time was that she managed to walk that perilous tightrope, to be both brilliant and, crucially, *non-threatening*; or, at least, as non-threatening as a woman with her talents could be.

I say all this, of course, not to make light of the obstacles Mary Somerville overcame, or to detract from her work – she was a brilliant scientist, even before the word 'scientist' was invented, the default term at the time being 'man of science'! – but rather to point out how she may be an example of survivorship bias. If it was difficult for Mary Somerville to make a name for herself, how impossible would it have been for all the women who couldn't bring themselves to grin and bear it? Who weren't well connected and financially secure? A woman, perhaps, with a hot temper and a prideful streak, who was seen to be shirking her duties as a mother and a wife – a woman who posed a *threat*?

It was from this that Mary Elizabeth Frankenstein was born.

So if you like her, if she strikes a chord, this one goes out to you: the angry women, the threatening women, the solitary and the abhorred; women with cold hearts and sharp tongues, who play with fire and fall in love with monsters; women who love women, women who didn't know they were women at first but know better now, those who thought they were women at first but know better now. *We shall be monsters*, you and I.

Acknowledgements

I OWE ABOUT a thousand thanks to a thousand different people who helped me in any number of small (or enormous!) ways in the writing of this book. To name just a few:

Thank you so much to my agent, Sue Armstrong, my editor, Kirsty Dunseath, and all the other fantastic people at C&W and Transworld – and, on the other side of the pond, to Tamara Kawar, Wendy Wong, Tina Dubois, Millicent Bennett, and the wonderful folks at ICM and Harper. Without all of your love and support for this novel (not to mention your hard work, expertise and spot-on feedback), *Our Hideous Progeny* would quite literally not be the book it is today. Woo #TeamHideous!

Thank you to my parents: to my mother, for reading countless drafts, for being the most fun teacher I've ever had, and for enduring all my fifteen-year-old griping that first time I read *Frankenstein*; and to my father, for instilling in me a love of sci-fi and storytelling, and for being my first-ever NaNoWriMo buddy. (I don't care if he's 'wildly unsuitable for middle-grade audiences', Mortimer Creed the ten-year-old crime boss still holds a special place in my heart.) Thank you to all my family, for your endless support and enthusiasm. And Trishy, I promise I'll have another chapter for you soon . . .

Thank you to Dr William Kimler, my adviser on the project

that would eventually become this book; it was your class which made me fall in love with this era of scientific history, and it was your expert knowledge and feedback on the early drafts which helped me bring Mary's world to life. Thank you, too, to Dr Sharon Setzer, for working with me to craft a degree that allowed me to pursue such a delightfully odd idea as my final project.

Thank you to Kat, critique partner extraordinaire (who must have read this book ten times over and deserves a medal), and to the whole of the trusty Shade Brigade, Sam and Kit, for always cheering me on, helping me patch my plot-holes, and enduring my never-ending collection of Fun Victorian Science Facts.

Thank you to librarians, archivists and historians the world over, and a special shout-out to Martin J. S. Rudwick, whose *Scenes from Deep Time: Early Pictorial Images of the Prehistoric World* I must have filled with about three hundred Post-it notes.

Thank you to every teacher who has offered me encouragement and advice on my writing, and to every reader and friend who has ever said nice things about my work – you've convinced me to abandon a respectable future in engineering and pursue the vain and frivolous life of an artist instead. I hope you're happy! (No, really, I do.)

Thank you to Xena, the best cat/lap-warmer/writing partner the world has ever known.

And thank you, of course – where would I be without her! – to Mary Shelley.

ABOUT THE AUTHOR

C. E. McGill is a writer of speculative and historical fiction, born in Scotland and raised in North Carolina. Their short fiction has appeared in *Fantasy Magazine* and *Strange Constellations*, and they are a two-time finalist for the Dell Award for Undergraduate Excellence in SF/F Writing. They live in Scotland with their family, two cats, and a growing number of fake succulents. (The real ones keep dying.)